PHYSICIAN
Extraordinary

David Weiss

PHYSICIAN
Extraordinary

A Novel of
the Life and Times of
WILLIAM HARVEY

DELACORTE PRESS / ELEANOR FRIEDE

Manufactured in the United States of America

First printing

Designed by MaryJane DiMassi

LIBRARY OF CONGRESS CATALOGING IN PUBLICATION DATA

Weiss, David.
Physician extraordinary.

I. Harvey, William, 1578–1657—Fiction.   I. Title.
PZ4.W429Ph [PS3573.E415]   813'.5'4   75-6912
ISBN 0-440-05916-X

*For Peter Giddy
Remembering
the road to Piccadilly*

AUTHOR'S NOTE

All the chapter-head poems and chapter-head excerpts from poems are by Stymean Karlen.

All the words in italics are the actual historical words of the character using them.

PHYSICIAN
Extraordinary

Blood needed a body to flow in
And bodies were created
The centuries that expired
before the bodies knew
they needed the blood
to be a body
Were the bodies grateful

The world's pre-space was
an ocean of blood
before blood was put
into the bodies
bloodmarks are still on the sun
since pre body times
The sun floated in blood

Now the bodies are so obsessed
with the mystery of blood
Its life giving powers
Is it instinctive resentment
that makes the bodies spill blood
with so great a necessity
Blood needs a body to flow in

Stymean Karlen

lood needed a body to flow in
And bodies were created . . .

Her Majesty grants Caius College the privilege of collecting annually the bodies of two criminals executed in Cambridge, or in the castle, or within four miles of the University, but only for the purpose of performing a medical dissection, according to the ancient custom.

William Harvey read the pronouncement posted on the entrance to Caius with a mixture of fear and fascination, and wondered how his fellow student, Matthew Ross, felt about the dissection. They stood in front of the Gate of Honour, the heart of the College, and he shivered, for the sun was vanishing quickly this January afternoon, and it was becoming very cold. Yet he had to pause, for this was a vital moment. Ever since he had arrived at Cambridge almost three years ago, he had waited for this occasion, and yet, he thought, he was not certain he could endure this practice. William turned to Matthew to find out how he felt, and hoped that his fellow student was a little afraid too.

They were coming from a tavern on the High Street, where they had been welcomed for the money they could spend, although visiting taverns was forbidden by the university. Like all the students of Caius, they had walked first through the founder's simple, small Gate of Humility, then under the more elaborate Gate of Virtue, and to the crown of Dr. John

Caius's achievement, the large, ornate Gate of Honour. This was a ritual observed by everyone, even the tutors and Dons. William felt the founder's presence most vividly here. John Caius, dead recently enough to be recalled personally, was reputed to have been the most eminent physician of his time, but William thought that the Gate of Honour expressed the founder's imagination at its most lively. This entrance suggested Italy, and was unlike any other structure in Cambridge.

Matthew said critically, "These dissections are a waste of time, but they will be celebrated with all the pomp that is possible."

"That is no reason why you should be disdainful."

"There are many reasons, but one will suffice. Dissection of the human body is a profanation of God's design, and civilised men do not favour it."

"Caius did. He struggled hard to achieve this privilege."

"It is a barbarous custom. It destroys the soul."

"Caius was a pious physician, and he was respected by our Queen," William reminded Matthew.

"Many say because he practised magic on her person. Otherwise, why would she grant him what so few people believe in, or approve?"

"Because he was skilled in anatomy and cured her when no one else did."

"You question too much. You poke about where you shouldn't." The twenty-year-old Matthew spoke without any doubts, and regarded his eighteen-year-old friend as foolish. The air was icy with the sun gone. There wasn't any heat at the Gate of Honour, and he was freezing. At least in the tavern where they had played dice the excitement had kept them warm. "Will, dissection is atheistical, the business of surgeons who work only with their hands. Not of scholars. It is natural that our bodies are governed by the four humours— blood, choler, bile, and phlegm—and you should accept this learning instead of being choleric."

William didn't reply, although it was difficult to restrain himself. He had no wish to upset anybody, but his loyalties

4

were becoming divided. He wanted to accept Galen as his fellow students did, yet he had observed that the human body didn't always perform as that doctor had written.

Matthew said, "If we are any later for supper we will have to sit far away from the fire. It will be so chilly I will never digest the meat."

"In a moment." William had to study the announcement again. For so long as he could remember, he had wondered about the structure of the human body. Yet there were so many prohibitions against dissection; the Queen's permission was essential, and even then many feared that God's vengeance would fall upon those who wielded the knife. But he was curious, too.

Matthew reflected irritably, Harvey was intoxicated by his interest in the human body. Matthew knew better than to allow anatomy to lure him into foolishness. He was older, and he came from a better family. His father was a physician, while Harvey's was merely a merchant. His friend wore a plain doublet, hose, and cloak, but Matthew's fashionable grey doublet, silk hose, and hip-length cloak possessed the grace of Her Majesty's favourite courtiers, Essex and Raleigh. He knew he was favoured with noticeable good looks, a tall, big-boned young man whose blond hair and blue eyes conveyed a sense of health and quality, while Harvey's complexion was dark—and, worse, Harvey was short, with black hair, a lean, pointed face, and a restless manner. It was remarkable that he possessed the coveted Matthew Parker scholarship; he was so stubborn in his views.

Matthew decided to settle this argument beyond question. He stated, "Everyone who knows anything about medicine knows that Galen did not practice dissection or approve of it, and neither did Aristotle."

"Is that why they teach us so little about anatomy or medicine?"

"You shouldn't be dissatisfied, you have the Parker scholarship."

"To study medicine, not logic and rhetoric and theology."

5

"We have also studied astronomy and astrology, and they have taught us much about our condition. Even about the French disease."

William was silent.

"You look flushed. Do you have the French disease?"

"I'm fine. But I wish we learned more about medicine."

"We learn what is necessary. Cambridge has great influence at Court. Elizabeth's tutor, Roger Ascham, was a Cambridge man, and so is Burghley, his son, Cecil, and Walsingham. If you cultivate the right people, you could go far. That is why my father sent me to Cambridge." However, before the hall where they ate, Matthew hid his cloak behind the back stairs and donned his surplice, and William followed his example. "Now they will not know I won at dice," chuckled Matthew. "Two shillings. I showed the townsfolk, the rabble, that we learn many things at Caius."

By the time they had reached the dining hall, all the places at the common table that were close to the fire were gone. They had only one remedy: to sit in their surplices to keep from freezing. No one discussed the impending dissection or speculated about medical matters, or asked them where they had been. Everybody was occupied with obtaining the best boiled beef, bread, and beer, for there were no second servings. They sat at the second table; the first was the Fellows' table, to which were admitted only noblemen, gentlemen, and a few Masters of Arts.

William knew he should be grateful that he was at the second table, for the third was for those of low condition, and the food was most sparse there. But his neighbor, Robert Darcey, dozed off from exhaustion, and he was sickened by Ralph Wilkins's gluttony. The slumbering Darcey had left most of his meat, and Wilkins gulped it down before anyone could halt him.

Then their tutor, George Estey, a clergyman who taught Latin, gave them a moral lecture from the Epistles of St.

6

Paul. William thought unhappily, Nothing could be done without a demonstration of piety.

He was relieved when Estey was interrupted by the entry of Thomas Grimston, an M.D., a learned anatomist, and the only teacher who discussed medicine. Estey halted his admonitions, for Grimston wanted the attention of the students. The stout, middle-aged Grimston wore an elaborate ruff, and William realized that the physician was dressed especially for this moment.

Grimston said, "Tomorrow it is advisable that all students who are interested in the study of medicine take part in the annual dissection. And you will be wise to warm your garments before putting them on, for you must attend the hanging, which will occur on the village green. You must observe carefully how criminals die so you will understand the symptoms of death. It will be done with the sunrise." When he saw that some of the students were pale and several looked faint, he reassured them. "Your fear is only in your mind. Once you witness a few hangings, you will become used to them."

No one asked any questions—they were discouraged—but William's mind was full of them. Why were the two criminals being hanged? Did they know that their bodies were going to be cut up? That their souls might be destroyed? And thus all hope of resurrection and eternal life gone? After Grimston left he turned to Matthew to obtain his views, but his friend was engaged in an animated discussion with Henry Scrope.

This medical student was burly, blunt-faced, black-haired, with thick hands and a clumsy body. William was surprised that they were talking, not about the hanging or the dissection, but about Scrope's stable; Scrope had an independent income, and was studying medicine only because his father believed that the Queen favoured doctors.

But weren't they afraid? Suddenly he blurted that out.

Scrope was amused. He said, "They are not hanging us."

"Have you ever done an anatomy?"

7

"Yes. But you will never become a good physician if you ask so many questions."

Matthew said, "That is what I keep telling him."

They were so arrogant William felt inadequate. But such an admission would give them an advantage that could harm him, so he said, "I have never seen a hanging or a dissection. I hope I will learn from them."

The next day the students were awakened before dawn, and after a hasty breakfast and an extra helping of beer they were marched out to the nearby village green. The sun hadn't risen yet, and a grey mist hung over the gallows, and there was the smell of rain in the air. The gowned figures of his companions looked as if they were in shrouds. He felt suspended in a grotesque world, for the students were shapeless in the mist. Rain began to fall, and it increased his gloom.

Grimston ordered the students close to the gallows, and as the two criminals were taken out of the cart William was shocked. One of the victims was just a boy, and he was so terrified he couldn't walk but had to be carried up to the gallows. And as the elderly executioner, who was drunk, propped up the stricken victim, so that his head could be put in the noose, William noted that he had a child's body.

William whispered this to Matthew, who retorted, "He is old enough to be hanged. Maybe he refused to work."

Scrope added, "The legal age is fourteen. He must be that old."

"But what could he have done? Doesn't anybody know, Scrope?"

"He probably stole something. It doesn't matter. Once he is condemned, he is done. Ssh. The hanging is about to begin."

Students laughed nervously, yet most of them crowded about the gallows, but William couldn't move. Even so, he had to observe, although he didn't want to look and he could scarcely breathe. He saw that the other victim was about thirty and stood with hopeless resignation and mumbled,

8

"Please, dear Jesus, forgive me, merciful and gracious," but the boy cried out, "I'm too young, my father is dead and my mother is ill and . . ."

The hangman's noose choked off any further words, and Grimston stated, "This is being done so virtue may prevail. May God rest their souls."

It was starting to rain heavily, and Grimston ordered the bodies cut down before they became soaked and unable to be used that morning.

Scrope disagreed. "It is too soon. We ought to let them hang there."

William was glad when the bodies came down.

"A small thing"—Scrope shrugged—"their lives." His pleasure evaporated with the ending of the hanging, and he complained that the executioner was an incompetent drunk. And as they were led to the hall, which had been converted into an anatomy theater, he grumbled, "Now, after we profane God's work, the body, we can return to being fools, as we are."

He vanished then, ignoring the dissection, while Matthew told William, "Scrope loves a good hanging, but he can't stand the sight of blood."

Grimston, wearing his best clothes, conducted the dissection as if it were a theatrical event. He sat proudly in a high-backed oak chair, where he was elevated above everyone else like royalty, and ordered the surgeon, Joe Ent, to start. The doctor had no intention of soiling his hands; dissection was beneath him, was for surgeons, who lacked learning and didn't know any Latin. The cutting instruments were on the table, a bucket alongside for the used parts, and Grimston told the students to circle the bodies and to observe closely. The physician doubted that the boy was a good subject—he was so small, frail, and young, not yet developed into manhood. Then the body was in an awkward position, the head hanging over the end of the anatomy table. Grimston commanded Harvey to move the body into a better position, and

9

when the student hesitated, afraid of touching it, the doctor shouted, "Harvey, you will never be a physician if you are afraid of death! Adjust the corpse! At once!"

William realized there was only one way to obey sensibly. He lifted the limp body in his arms, and suddenly he thought himself bewitched. The body, although wet from the rain, was warm. He could have sworn a muscle moved. And as he deposited the boy carefully on the table, he was sure he felt a pulse in the legs he was holding. He raised the body and turned it over onto the left side, so that the weight of the chest where the heart was rested on his hand. When he felt the quiver of the flesh, he shivered.

He wasn't sure what to do next. Matthew motioned frantically to him to desist, other students glared at him as if he were mad, and Grimston's displeasure was obvious. Yet he was almost sure now there was life still in this body, and that if he acted swiftly it might be maintained. But if he succeeded he might be accused of witchcraft or other evil practices. Grimston would be furious, for bodies were difficult to obtain and they would have to wait another year for a full dissection. And he knew the royal edict. All medical students at Caius had to learn it.

If the hanged criminal comes alive on the table the person who does this is held responsible for reimprisonment and a second hanging.

Even as these fears assailed William, there was an overwhelming need to go on. Ignoring the rebuke in Grimston's eyes, the surgeon's ire, the amazement of the students, he sought to continue life in the body with a single-minded concentration. He massaged the chest, the lungs, the heart. Nothing seemed to happen, and when the body didn't stir he recalled what he had done when he had felt faint—he had put his head between his legs, and that had brought blood to his head and revived him.

He did this with the body of the boy, pushing his head down between his legs, rashly, he felt, into another world

perhaps, perhaps limbo, and he might be forever cursed; only
Jesus had brought anyone back from the dead. But something
in him said the boy wasn't dead yet. And as he went on there
was a change in the body, and William was frightened, as if
he were on the threshold of a forbidden mystery. Yet he was
too involved to halt. The body seemed to shake, and he hurriedly wrapped it in his surplice to warm it, and he longed to
shout: *Boy, can you hear me?*

Instead, it was Grimston who yelled, "Harvey, this is sacrilegious!"

"Sir, that is not my intention." Why did he have to explain?

"You are bringing a criminal back from the dead."

"Sir, he was never dead. We are merely encouraging what
life is still in him." He thought, He was simply keeping a door
open, but he didn't explain. If this body would just speak,
show some sign of life! He wanted to hit it, but he restrained
his impatience and caressed the face.

The eyes opened as if the boy were emerging from a nightmare, and he whimpered, "Please, Jesus, save me from further
torment."

William looked for guidance to Grimston, who replied,
"You have set a dangerous example. You have contravened
the punishment of the Crown."

Wilkins stated: "Sir, it is witchcraft. The soul has gone out
of the body and the devil has returned. Only Jesus can save."

"Yes," said Grimston. "I will not pay for his reimprisonment and hanging. Harvey, are you prepared to do so?"

Most certainly not, William intended to retort—he had
barely enough money for his schooling—yet something in him
resisted saying so.

Wilkins sneered, "Harvey costs us money and wastes our
time. And simply to save a thief who stole a sheep."

The boy murmured, "Sir, it was only a piece of bread."

"One of you stole a sheep."

"It must have been the man. I took only bread. We were
starving."

"What is the difference! Knave, you stole something!"

"Sir, my name is Silas. I was willing to work, but there was no work. Don't break my neck again. Please, sir?"

William said, "It wasn't broken. You wouldn't be alive if it had been."

"But they want to kill me again, sir!" cried the boy, staring up at the faces circling him and not seeing a trace of mercy anywhere. "Please, sir, I've paid for my sins. Just to face death is awful enough."

Wilkins stated, "You still did wrong. Doctor, he must be executed again. We have paid for two corpses. And Harvey is blasphemous."

The students shouted their approval of Wilkins's words, while the surgeon grumbled that he needed two bodies for a proper anatomy and moved closer to Silas to end this dispute by cutting the boy's throat, holding a gleaming knife in his dirty, bloody hand.

The boy moaned to William, "I gave up praying, sir. My name is Silas, but I gave up praying. I knew I shouldn't, that it was a sin."

"As I said," Wilkins insisted, "he is possessed of the devil. That is the only reason he returned to life, not anything Harvey did."

While the boy trembled with fear, he made no effort to resist the impending death or to flee, but lay cowering like a stricken animal as the surgeon regarded him with satisfaction and said, "The body is too young for a good dissection, but it is sufficient for a start."

His knife was at the boy's throat when William knocked it away. He did this instinctively, and he had no idea what to do next, but the boy had clung to life with tenacity, and that was worth something. He asked Grimston, "Doctor, how much will it cost?"

"What, Harvey?"

"The boy's life, sir."

"That is not our concern. It is worthless."

"But, sir, if I could pay something?"

"It is the expense of a new hanging that is our difficulty."

The grizzled, aging surgeon grumbled, "Two shillings, Doctor. One for me and one for the hangman. Sir, dissection is not a trick. Not everyone can be a ripper. It is a great inconvenience to reach the heart under the ribs. It takes strength in the arms and the chest. I was specially bred."

"Two shillings?" William repeated.

Grimston nodded.

That is impossible, William thought, this is as much as my father allows me for a month. Then he saw Matthew standing in the rear, as if his friend wished to avoid him. Yet Matthew didn't look angry, but puzzled. William asked him, "Can you lend me two shillings?"

Matthew didn't reply, and Grimston asked angrily, "Ross, where did you obtain such a sum of money?"

"What money, sir?" mumbled Matthew.

William implored, "I will pay it back somehow. Please lend it to me!"

Grimston asked, "Ross, did you win the shillings at dice?"

"Doctor, I wouldn't think of such impiety!" Matthew was outraged.

William repeated, "Matthew, you will get it back. I promise."

His friend shook his head, disgusted with William's softness, and said, "It is a waste of money." Then he sighed, unable to resist William's entreaty, and handed him the two shillings, looking very sad.

As Grimston took the money he said, "Remember, Harvey, you are responsible for this criminal's life. If he cannot support himself, you will have to do so. We must not question or oppose the authorities."

William assented even as he wondered anxiously what he was getting into. He tenderly raised the boy off the table, thinking this was his first patient. The surgeon was preparing to begin the delayed anatomy on the other victim, and Silas was on the verge of fainting again.

Grimston said apologetically, "The hangman was incompetent, in drink. Unfortunately, the college could not afford a trained executioner."

Silas could hardly stand, and William noticed that the boy was in rags and that his feet were bare and bleeding. Yet his pleasant, round face had become ruddy, and his red hair gleamed.

"Remember, Harvey," Grimston reminded him firmly, "if this criminal commits any more crimes, you will be held responsible for them too."

Silas whimpered, "I won't sir. I will pray every day."

William shrugged. He didn't believe the boy. But he had gone too far to turn back, and he said, "Doctor Grimston, his feet are in such a deplorable state, I think it wise to take him to his home. May I, sir?"

"As you wish. I doubt you have suitable judgement to be a physician."

"May I borrow your horse, sir? I doubt he can walk."

"Your zeal exceeds your common sense. The horse will cost a shilling."

It was an outrageous price, as much as a labourer earned in a month, but William, feeling he had no choice, said, "Thank you, sir."

"I will extract it from your scholarship if that should be necessary."

"But, sir, the money hardly provides for my needs as it is."

"All the more reason you should not risk it."

"You will take away my scholarship, sir?" William was stricken.

"That will be considered. You can go. Before you spoil this anatomy." As William hesitated, with Silas at his side now like a shadow, Grimston gave the outstretched corpse a wallop with his fist to verify that it was dead, and added with gratification, "The lesson won't be completely wasted after all. Joe Ent, you can commence."

The surgeon flourished his knife triumphantly, and began at the throat as if it were a treasure. William had heard that dissections started with the heart, but today Ent first cut the throat from ear to ear and stated gloatingly, "No one will bring this corpse back to life!"

William's excitement faded as he saw the mutilated flesh, and he felt weak. The table was splashed with blood; then the brains, a grey messy blob, were thrown contemptuously into the bucket. It was painful to think of this corpse as a person. He pulled Silas out of the room before the boy became a patient again.

William wanted Silas to ride on the front of Grimston's horse, to point the way, but the boy said that wasn't fitting, and insisted on sitting behind him. And when the heavy grey mare galloped, Silas, who had never been on a horse before, clutched William so tightly it hurt. Then William's spirits improved. The rain ended, the sun started to shine, and the cold air in his face was invigorating.

Silas confided, "Sir, I'm not a thief. My father was killed fighting the Armada, and my mother is hungry and ill. It was only a bit of bread. We had no money, no food, not even a root or a scrap of barley."

"How old are you?"

"I'm not sure. I can't read or write, and there is no record, sir, but when they caught me—I shouldn't have taken it from the gentry's table—they said I was fourteen. They wanted to be sure I was old enough to hang."

"Did your mother know that you stole the bread?"

"No. And my sister didn't want me to do it. She said she would earn the money somehow, but I couldn't let her do that. Could I, sir?"

William didn't reply. He was growing uneasy again. The country was becoming unpleasant as they entered the swampy outskirts of Cambridge.

Silas said, "Sir, I didn't mean to cause you all this trouble."

"You mustn't apologise for being alive. How do you feel now?"

"My back hurts, and there are pains in my neck and head."

"I will examine you when you are home. I may be able to help you."

"Sir, you have done too much already. I must not burden you any more. Besides, my home is a godforsaken place, not fit for a gentleman."

"Let me decide that."

"As you wish, sir. But we must get off here. The rest of the way is swampy, and the path is not safe for a horse. You are a magician, sir."

"It was common sense, nothing more." William dismounted, helped Silas off, and after he made the horse secure he followed the boy.

As Silas led him through the swamp, he proudly pulled a wool cap out of his doublet and declared, "You see, sir, I didn't mean to commit a sin." He put his cap on his head. "I'm no vagabond."

"You must rest when you get home."

"There is no rest for the poor. When the Lord closes the door on you, you do not expect it to open. My life, great sir, is yours."

William was embarrassed; he felt barely more than a boy himself. His heart sank. Silas grabbed his hand as if he would never let go.

"What is wrong? Are you ill?" Was the boy having a relapse?

"My family will think I am possessed of the devil. We were not blessed by the Church before we were hung, and now the other one will rot in hell and maybe I will also. Maybe I should have died."

"No, you have suffered enough!" Of this, at least, he was certain.

"Sir, will you protect me from the evil spirits? You have learning."

"Silas, you are not possessed of the devil." But William hesitated. He was afraid even more now of what he was getting into.

Silas's home was a sad little ruin on the verge of collapse, and it was impossible for William to believe it was a healthy dwelling. All of the timbered hut was one room where the family lived, ate, and slept. The damp clay floor was covered with wet rushes, except for the wooden pallet next to the fireplace on which the mother lay. Her head rested on a sack of chaff, while Silas and his sister had rough mats for sleeping and a round log for a pillow.

William felt awkward. Silas's mother and sister stared at him as if he were an intruder, and when they saw his clean, neat garb they shrank from him as if they had done something wrong, even though they didn't know what it was. Silas hurriedly assured them that this gentleman was from Caius College and was not hostile, but they were still apprehensive, and his mother sobbed, "Child, did you get any food?"

"No. But he saved my life."

"Not my life," she grumbled. "Rachel, what will we do?"

Rachel, William noticed, looked exactly like her brother, with the same fair complexion, red hair, and gentle, round features. He wondered if they were twins, and he was surprised at how well she spoke as she asked Silas, "Did you try what you told me you were going to do?"

"Yes. But I failed. I will tell you about it later."

His mother cried, "What are you hiding from me?" She turned to William. "Sir, my children always keep things from me. Did he sin?"

"No," William replied, even though he wasn't sure, but Silas had such an imploring look in his eyes William couldn't reveal what had happened. "Your son wants me to examine you. I am a student of medicine."

17

"I'm not bewitched, sir, I'm not bewitched."

She recoiled from him as he approached her. Poor thing, he thought; her emaciated condition was clearly from lack of food—he didn't have to be a doctor to know this. He felt her pulse and noted that it was still regular, although slow.

"Sir, my horoscope is poor. Everything has gone wrong."

Rachel added, "Since my father was lost at sea. Is she very ill?"

William liked the quality of her voice, and that she was pretty in spite of her rags. He sighed and said, "I don't know."

"But you are a student of medicine? Aren't you?"

"Just a beginner." But when he felt Rachel's contempt, he ransacked his pockets until he found a sixpence, then another penny, a halfpenny, a second halfpenny, and put all of the money into Silas's hand.

The boy exclaimed, "Eightpence? Sir, this is a fortune!"

"What do you want for it?" Rachel asked suspiciously.

"Nothing."

"No one gives the poor anything. You must want something in return."

"It is what your mother needs most of all. Money for good food."

"Where did you get it if you are just a student?"

"I won it at dice." This wasn't true—it was part of his father's allowance—but dice was easier to say. And it is silly to want her good opinion, he told himself, but somehow he did. "If you get some good nourishment for your mother, she should improve, and this money will provide that. It is what she needs most. Meat especially."

"That is impossible. Two years ago we could buy a pig or a goose for fourpence, but now they cost eightpence. We can't spend it all on flesh."

Silas said, "Sir, Rachel worries too much. We can buy great raisins for a penny, or prunes for a halfpenny. We can live on them for a long time. And I can get cheap bread made of beans and peas and oats. We don't have to have meat."

"It would help your mother," said William. He examined

18

Silas, who seemed all right now, and told him to eat properly, rest, and keep the air in the hut as fresh as possible. Then, as he turned to leave, he couldn't resist saying, for Rachel still regarded him suspiciously, "Why do you fear me?"

"I'm not a fool, an ignorant, dull-witted country girl."

Silas said proudly, "Rachel has taught herself to read and write, sir."

"I have no expectation that any man alive will treat us kindly."

Rachel was frail and slight, but her glowing blue eyes were beautiful, and William replied, "I'm sorry if I've been clumsy, but I'm just a learner. However, I do think good food is the best medicine."

Silas said, "God bless you, sir. Rachel, he did save my life."

Rachel took twopence from her brother and said, "I will get some meat at once. Silas, what is the name of your saviour?"

"I don't know."

"William Harvey. Silas, if you need any help, I'm at Caius College."

"Thank you, great sir. But don't fear, I will not trouble you again. Yet if you ever need a service, it will be an honour to provide it." And as he escorted William to the horse, he added, "My sister has a sharp tongue, sir, but when I tell her what you did . . ."

William halted him and mounted the horse. "That isn't necessary. She is right to be suspicious. Everyone wants to be rewarded for what he does."

"You don't, sir."

"Yes, I do. I want you, as my patient, to recover. Get as good food as you can. As I told you, food should be the best medicine." He rode back to Caius even more uncertain whether to pursue the career of a physician. He didn't want to feel disloyal to Cambridge, but he felt he had learned so little, and yet there was so much to know.

never doubt my certainty
I never doubt my doubt
The Judge in me
is my instinct
Hang the Judge if you must

William Harvey, son of Thomas Harvey yeoman, from the town of Folkestone in the county of Kent, born April 1st, 1578, educated at Canterbury School, in his sixteenth year has been admitted as a Pensionarius Minor to the Scholar's Mess on the last day of May, 1593, and pays for this entrance into the college, 3 shillings and 4 pence.

But this was just his introduction to the university, William thought, yet Grimston was intently reviewing this entry in the College Books.

It was the day after the hanging, and the physician had summoned him to his rooms. And as Grimston read these words for the edification of the student, William felt that while the physician professed to be a judge, actually he was the prosecutor, and he enjoyed this role. William was tired, hungry; he had slept very little the previous night—his mind had refused to rest, turning over and over the various reasons why Silas could have survived the rope—and he had been called away in the middle of dinner, the big meal of the day.

He noticed that the physician spared nothing in the service of his own comfort. Grimston possessed the best rooms in Caius; his study was spacious, high-roofed, and a fine fire in the hearth warmed him. The doctor sat behind a splendid solid oak table, and he said, "What do you have to say for yourself?"

William sensed that Grimston expected him to fall at his feet, but he couldn't cringe, although he was afraid. "Sir, I don't understand."

"Apparently not. Yet you have been a student at Caius almost three years, and you are the present holder of the Matthew Parker Scholarship."

"Yes, sir." William wondered unhappily: Is that threatened also?

"You could be sent down from Cambridge for what you have done."

William couldn't nod in agreement, although he knew that it was expected. Instead, he stood stiffly and felt feverish.

"You ruined our dissection. The surgeon, clumsy blunderer, made several mistakes, and we had no second body upon which to rectify them."

"I'm sorry, sir, that was not my intention."

"There is no hope of another anatomy until next year."

William couldn't feel shame, although he knew he was supposed to.

"We can only have a dissection in winter, since we have no means of preserving the cadavers. You should know that."

"But, sir, the boy was still alive. His heart was still beating."

"You didn't help him. He will come to a bad end. Why don't you play catch ball? Like the other boys."

"I don't like catch ball, sir." William was confused. Silas was a patient to him, but evidently dying was not always a medical complaint.

"You cannot bring back the dead. I am a strong upholder of learning, but such tricks as you performed yesterday could discourage our growth. We could get the reputation of being miracle workers, which we are not."

William longed to ask Grimston why he thought Silas had survived the hanging—it was a great and vexing problem—but the physician cut his question short. "You will be well advised to be more careful in the future. You will be on probation the next few months. Then it will be decided if you will be allowed to pursue a Master of Arts degree."

"Sir, if I don't obtain that degree I can't study medicine."

"That may be just as well. None of the previous holders of the Matthew Parker Scholarship have gone on to study the healing arts."

William's inquiring mind prevailed over his fears, and he

blurted out, "Sir, why do you think he revived when I put his head between his legs?"

"Study Galen. He has been our mentor for fifteen hundred years. I expect you to memorise his precepts. Then I will decide whether you are fit to become a physician."

Matthew told William, "You were lucky to get off so easy. You could have been sent down for what you did. When will you return my loan?"

"When I see my father."

"Make it soon. I need the money."

William, who had returned too late to the dinner table to obtain any food, didn't answer. The other students were hurrying off to study theology with Estey, and if he didn't join them he would be in worse trouble.

Estey declared that since the human body was God's design, any tampering with it was the work of the devil. Most of the students nodded, then fell asleep, and William's attention drifted away. He asked himself: How much had the movement of the blood sustained the flicker of life in Silas? He thought back to the moment he had discovered the thing that beat in his chest. He had been five or six; he didn't remember exactly. But the thump thump thump had kept him up all night. He wondered: Is the blood sovereign? It seemed to him that when the blood was affected, so was everything else. If he could only chart its course.

The gaunt, elderly Estey stood over him and snapped, "Harvey, your gown is not on correctly. You can be fined for such disrespect."

William sat submissively, as Estey desired, and the latter returned to his sermon while the student continued to reflect about why Silas had survived.

A week later, when that question continued to puzzle William, he decided to investigate it for himself. Their morning studies had been postponed, owing to the absence of Estey, and he didn't want to use his free time to play catch ball or to go into town, as was favoured by the other students. Instead, he climbed the stairs of the hall to the attic.

He chose a low rafter that he could reach without strain, and threw two nooses over it. One was a simple rope such as was used in a hanging, but the second was a silken halter that was soft and sleek.

Then he tied the first noose around his neck. The thing under his ribs began to go thump thump thump, although he was careful how he placed the rope. And as he tightened it slowly, the thought of the noose closing around his neck, even the soft silken halter, which he was trying now, caused him to ache with fear. He felt a hammering in his head, the thump thump thump was a menace now, and he could hardly breathe.

William was standing under the low beam with both nooses around his neck, afraid to tighten them any further and yet curious to know what would happen next, when Matthew ran in and hurried to his side to halt him. Matthew was afraid that William was considering suicide; some students did when they couldn't endure the hardships and punishment.

William said, "I wanted to find out why Silas survived the hanging."

"Your flights of fancy could drive you out of your wits."

"What is wrong now?" William was relieved to be free of the nooses, and that the thump thump thump was less and he could breathe normally again.

"Grimston is inspecting our quarters. If you are not there when he comes, you could be sent down. Hurry!"

As they left, William asked, "How did you guess that I was in the attic?"

Matthew didn't want to say he feared suicide—it would offend William—so he said, "I thought you might want to try an experiment."

They arrived at their room before Grimston appeared, and it gave them a moment to tidy it. Their roommates, Ralph

Wilkins and Robert Darcey, had returned also, alerted by other students. The four of them stood by their beds now. Their room was divided into four sleeping parts, which was the general practice. The majority of students slept four in a room, except for noblemen and rich men's sons, usually in monastic severity, to express their homage to God.

They had a chest for linen and clothing because they had paid for it, a trestle table to study on, and four simple stools to sit on. Each of them had a pewter candlestick to read by, and a Bible given by the school.

Even so, when Grimston entered and stood by the bay window, where he obtained heat from the sun—there was no fireplace, that was only for privileged persons—William felt their lodging was more like a cell than a chamber.

Grimston surveyed each student critically, and Harvey most of all. Their appearance was satisfactory; they wore their gowns to the ankle; the beds were made, and there was no dirt except crumbs under Wilkins's bed. He overlooked this sin, for Wilkins kept him informed on the surreptitious activities of the other students. He declared, "This is the most important period of your life."

They nodded, as was expected.

"Do any of you know the new statutes that have been promulgated?"

"Yes, sir," Wilkins volunteered quickly, "we mustn't indulge in any excess of apparel, or leave Caius after dark, and we have sworn to subscribe to the Queen's supremacy and to our blessed Protestant faith."

"Good. Your fathers do not send you here to be troubled by new ideas, but to have your minds settled."

Wilkins assured the doctor that he was dedicated to learning; Ross stated that he was determined to uphold the antiquity of Cambridge over Oxford; Darcey mumbled that they were both right; and Harvey said nothing as he wondered if the ignoring of medicine was an oversight or deliberate.

Grimston asked, "Harvey, have you anything further to say?"

"I've been studying Galen, sir, as you requested."

"You could spend the rest of your life doing that with profit."

"But his views on the blood are confusing, sir."

"You mean you are confused." Grimston was pleased that Wilkins laughed at Harvey's stupidity. "I strive to bring you up as learned men, but you make it difficult, Harvey. You lack character."

Matthew felt compelled to say, "Sir, he didn't intend to do wrong."

"You test my patience. On what authority do you speak?"

Matthew bit his lip but was silent, flushing and looking embarrassed.

Satisfied that he had put him in his place, Grimston felt happy now. He had made it clear that conduct was the most vital thing to be learned, that he knew how to limit their natural inclination to sin. He surveyed the room, and he was gratified that they were living in the proper austere manner, except for a few private amenities. He was proud that his chambers were worthy of a nobleman.

After Wilkins was sure that Grimston had retired to his rooms for the rest of the day, he suggested they venture into town. He did it at least once a month, he bragged, to a house where the girls were very imaginative. He grew more enthusiastic than William had ever heard him before.

"What about Grimston?" asked Matthew.

"We can slip out at dark, when he will be sleeping."

"But the gates are locked when the sun goes down."

"Matthew, there are other means."

"Do you know the way?" asked Darcey, who looked interested for a change.

"Every foot of it. I told you, I go every month."

"What about the watch?"

"Good luck to them. They are seldom around after dark. They are more afraid of robbers, rogues, and vagabonds than any of us." But as Harvey wavered, he snapped, "Are you afraid? You must be a virgin."

"It isn't that. But—"

Wilkins interrupted knowingly, "The girls will assist you if you are inexperienced."

William said, "I have no money."

Matthew was surprised. "You had eightpence the other day."

"I lost it."

Matthew regarded him sceptically, but Wilkins stated, "Harvey, you mustn't mortify your flesh. Let us make a collection for our scholar. Unless he prefers the saltpeter in our soup, and the cold baths."

William wasn't sure what to do. Most of the students treated chastity as a contrivance created to humiliate them, yet the university assumed that their flesh was a thing to mortify and subdue. Yet he was tired of continence. Often he dreamt of possessing voluptuous girls, but he disliked the thought of sharing, of being one of many.

Wilkins, however, was not to be dissuaded by his doubts. He found sixpence he could spare, extracted another sixpence from a reluctant Darcey and threepence from a protesting Ross, handed the total to Harvey, and said, "You can't refuse now unless you are afraid."

William sensed that Wilkins was using this generosity to test him, determined to lead this expedition to show his own superiority. Yet part of him didn't want to be left out. He joined the others.

Wilkins waited until it was dark. Then, after he was certain that the courtyard was empty, he led Harvey, Ross, and Darcey across it to the chapel. To their surprise, he descended into the cellar, which was used as a crypt. He whispered, "No one ever goes here. They are afraid. Most people think it is haunted. Even the college authorities."

A moment later they were on the street, and he turned off on a back lane which was more like a cow trail than a footpath.

"Do we have to go much farther?" Darcey whimpered. He had just scratched his face on a low, overhanging branch.

"Not much. I have taken this route many times," boasted Wilkins. "No one ever uses it at night. Darkness comes early in winter."

He stopped before an old wooden house, and William stared at it with misgiving. He could smell the stench of the fens; it was in a poor quarter of Cambridge. But as Wilkins took them around to the rear, he noticed that it had several wings and was larger than he had expected.

Wilkins knocked on the back door, and smiled as an old woman opened it. She must be eighty at least, thought William, a toothless hag with shrunken jaws, and bent over from the damp and cold. But she recognized Wilkins, who asked, "May we come in?"

"We don't take students generally," she replied in a harsh cackle.

"You remember me."

"Do you have money? No credit, boy. Not any more."

"We are willing to spend sixpence a girl. Call the madam."

The old crone hobbled out, and William observed that this room was furnished like a parlour. There were chairs for sitting, a fireplace, a broken flagged floor, a raftered ceiling, and dingy, dirty hangings.

It was Madam Flora who returned. Her frizzled red hair was dyed in imitation of Queen Elizabeth; she was overdressed, overpainted, and her tightly corseted waist exaggerated her enormous bosom. But she knew Wilkins. She took sixpence from each of the students and said, "I want no complaints. We are not pigs." She put them into cubicles separated from one another only by a flimsy curtain.

William lit his candle, as the middle-aged madam instructed, and saw a pallet with a straw mattress and a girl sitting on it. She was young, but she stared at him impersonally. His impulse was to flee, but he was afraid of what the others would say. He noted that her auburn hair was attractive, her complexion fair, and she reminded him of Silas's sister, for there was a resemblance and she was pretty. But achieving his manhood, which he had looked forward to for a long time, suddenly seemed ugly as he heard Wilkins grunting in the next cubicle.

Before he could retreat, the girl said, "I'm Julia. Be quick. Or we will freeze. It's cold outside, but the madam doesn't allow us any heat. She says it will only make us lazy." She pulled William down on the pallet, and he realized that under her shift she was naked. And as her small but firm breasts pressed against him, he didn't need any fire.

He whispered, "We'll manage."

Suddenly she was naked, and he was lying on top of her soft body.

"Come in! Come in!" she kept crying, and guided him until he was.

His passion was over before he expected, almost as quickly as it had begun. He felt he had lost his virginity without truly enjoying it.

"You're not a little boy," she said. "You can have it again."

"I have no more sixpence," he said, although he still had one.

"It doesn't matter. As long as you don't sit in the parlour, Madam Flora won't know. Some take longer than others, although the young ones come fast. This is just my ordinary working day. We'll go slower now."

He knew how to enter her this time, and he did so slowly, carefully.

"You're a good sort," she whispered. "I'll show you a few tricks."

When this encounter was over he felt better. It hadn't been too quick or disappointing, and he had less doubt about himself.

She said, "You're not inspired, but you're considerate. When the weather is warm I will really please you."

He gave her his other sixpence to express his appreciation, and she regarded him wonderingly and said, "The rich are never so generous. Would you like another? Nothing fancy, but it could be pleasing."

He wasn't certain he could, but before he could reply Madam Flora swished open the curtain and said, "Time's up. Somebody is waiting."

William was ashamed that he lay naked, but the madam ignored that and added, "Julia, I think this boy wants to become a regular."

"I'm a student," he explained, "a medical student." He wished his heart wasn't beating so wildly at the sight of Julia's naked body.

Julia said, "He is willing." She put on her shift. "I'll give you something special next time. Do you read books about medicine?"

"Occasionally."

"Could your medical books protect me from the French disease?"

"I don't know. I'm just a beginner."

"None of them knows," declared Madam Flora, glaring at him.

Julia said hurriedly, "You had better go. Before I get dismissed."

The others were in the parlour already, but he refused to discuss what had happened, even with Wilkins, who was jealous of the amount of time William had spent with his girl. It is enough, he thought, that I have not failed myself.

The return to Caius was without incident, and they got back in time to attend the nightly prayers in the room which had been used for the anatomy.

And, as they went to bed, Wilkins grandly told his fellow roommates, "As I predicted, all turned out for the best."

William, however, was remembering Julia's parting words: "You did very well, boy. You were considerate, a gentleman."

29

or a perfect man
criticism is sculpture
on a garbage can

The next few months William realised more than ever: If he didn't get his bachelor of arts degree, he couldn't get any other. And that he needed perseverance and endurance. Each day he rose at four and ran in place to put heat in his body; then he went to chapel. Lectures began at six—after a breakfast of bread and beer—and lasted for four hours. Dinner followed, and was the big meal of the day: beef and broth with salt and oatmeal. Then he studied until supper at five, except for an occasional hour for catch ball or a walk. The nights were devoted to more study, and William often fell asleep over his books. But these hardships were supposed to make the students worthy. Free time was bad for morals. He knew these views by heart.

He also devoted himself to his studies. Rhetoric, the high, medium, and low styles, grew familiar to him. Next he studied logic, which was second in importance only to theology.

William resented that there was no study of mathematics or history, that in astronomy he was taught Ptolemy, while geography was devoted to the works of Pliny. Sometimes his misery at the thought of all the unnecessary subjects that were being stuffed into his head gave him the feeling that he would be driven out of his wits.

One night he was hoping desperately for a change, for a subject which would absorb him, when Matthew invited him to see a play at the Black Bear Inn. "*A Midsummer-Night's Dream*. By a Will Shakespeare."

He liked plays, but he found himself answering, "It is unseemly."

"You sound like Grimston. What is happening to you?"

"We are not supposed to leave the college without permission."

"You always obey? Is that why you brought the thief back to life?"

"Matthew, I didn't bring him back. You know better than that."

"I know that you are studying too hard. You are losing your wits."

"I don't want to risk my degree."

"Wilkins and Scrope give Grimston and Estey handsome presents. Why don't you try that? Then you could get out more."

William sighed. He was tired of studying, yet he felt it was wrong to be distracted, with the final judgement just a few weeks away. He said, "I must wait. Has Wilkins gone off to the house lately?"

"I don't know. He hasn't told me. Are you interested in going again?"

"I might be. But I don't know the way. Do you, Matthew?"

"No. Now, however, that the climate is growing warm, it could be a useful place to visit. Only you have become a model of discretion."

Yet several nights later, when Matthew told him that Silas was waiting outside Caius and wanted to see him, William started out at once.

Matthew was surprised, considering William's previous caution, and he asked, "Do you want to hazard your degree for a vagabond?"

"That is not the point. Why did you tell me that he is waiting?"

Matthew shrugged, "I felt sorry for him. He looked so imploring."

"That is the way I feel. Did he say what he wanted?"

"I think he desires you to go with him. But I wouldn't. Grimston will think that you are flaunting his mistake in his face."

"Silas is my first patient. Matthew, I can't desert him now."

"You're a fool. Most physicians never visit their patients but prescribe from a distance and let the apothecary take the risk of catching whatever contagion may prevail. That is what you should do."

"But I won't know what is wrong if I don't see the patient."

William was glad that it was raining, for the bad weather discouraged being outside, and no one was about. Silas stood under the Gate of Humility, shivering and soaking wet, but he looked in good health; yet he was so upset that William asked him, "What is wrong?"

"Nothing with me, thank you, sir, and my mother is better. She is able to walk again. It is my sister who is feeling poorly these days."

"I'm not a physician. You know that."

"You saved my life, sir, and cured my mother. If you could aid Rachel, I would be eternally grateful."

"At the moment that is impossible." Silas was so disconsolate that William added, "It is too late. I would never find my way back."

"What about tomorrow, sir? It is Sunday, and students go out then. If you could just examine her, with your eye I'm sure you will cure her."

"You expect too much."

"Sir, you mustn't be pessimistic. When should I meet you?"

William knew he should say no, it was foolish to become involved again, however Silas was enamoured of his views, yet it would give him another chance to find out how Silas had felt at the moment of hanging. That was the best evidence. So, even though William sounded reluctant, he said, "I will meet you here tomorrow at noon. And let us hope that the rain stops."

"It will, great sir. The stars were favourable the day I met you."

* * *

32

On Sunday the rain had ceased, and the journey to Silas's home was without difficulty. The hut was unchanged, but this time it was Rachel who lay on the rude pallet and her mother who sat beside her on a rough log. They were surprised when William entered, as if they hadn't expected him to come.

William wasted no time, but examined the girl as the mother cried, "Her body has grown to excess in two months' time. It is strange."

"But I'm not with child," Rachel sobbed, "I've not been incontinent."

"Perhaps she is bewitched," said Silas.

William was puzzled. Her stomach was swollen, and her white, set face was frightened, and her symptoms were of pregnancy, yet the expression in her eyes gave him the feeling that she hadn't been incontinent. But he realized that he mustn't take anything on faith; he must observe as carefully as he could. He asked, "Have you eaten regularly lately?"

"We had meat last week, and I wasn't used to it. I got sick."

The mother said, "But her stomach was large already."

Silas explained. "I followed a great hunting party last week, sir, and picked up some of the game they left."

"And before that what did you eat?"

"Raisins mostly, sir, and prunes. It had a strong action on my bowels, but no lasting ill effects. Rachel ate lots of them."

William asked her, "Is that when your stomach started to swell?"

"I'm not sure. But when I grew large I took several purgatives."

Silas added, "I got them from an apothecary in Cambridge."

"Do you remember what they were?"

"Very well, sir. The apothecary gave me a cordial which contained oil of ants, the fat of dried vipers, and turpentine. But he also considered the planet that governed her affected parts, and gave me the herbs of Venus. They contain senna and prunes. He said it was a powerful purgative, and that if the first didn't work this would cleanse her blood."

33

William shuddered. He knew both remedies. His mother had used them when he had a stomachache, but they had made him feel worse and given him much wind. And in Rachel's case prunes had been added to prunes.

Rachel cried, "I took them all, but my stomach only grew larger. I must be bewitched. I have been born under the wrong star. Our fate has sickened ever since our father was killed fighting the Spanish Armada."

She looked so ashamed William couldn't believe that God, whatever His servants on earth preached, could be so cruel. He asked, "May I touch your stomach?" He prayed that his hand would be firm.

Rachel was tragic, as if her purity were about to be violated, but Silas said, "Mother, he helped you. You recovered. We must trust him."

Although their mother nodded, Rachel shrank from William's touch, but she didn't flee. He couldn't tell whether she hurt from the pressure of his hand or from fear. There was a sensual bulge to her breasts, and she had gained weight, and he could understand a man fancying her. With the increase of flesh on her face, she had become pretty. Then there was an odor like that of the sewer and she looked ashamed. Prunes upon prunes, his mind repeated, and great raisins.

Rachel implored, "Sir, what shall I do to save my life?"

"Stop eating so many raisins and prunes."

"But they are all that we can afford!"

Your stomach is distended with the wind. And your digestion has been upset by melancholy."

"No," she said, "there is nothing wrong with my mind. I may be bewitched, but I have not sinned."

Silas said, "You have had much wind and melancholy, but you are impatient of them, as you are of so many things."

William said, "You probably ate too much after starving, then took food which brought the wind, and that could be why you are so swollen."

The mother asked, "Sir, what remedy do you suggest?"

"I would eat simply but with more variety."

34

"How can I?" Rachel cried. "We are so poor and starving."

"No longer starving," Silas said proudly. "I've been promised service with the rich Squire Foster. We will have enough to eat, at least."

William said, "Then dine moderately. And perhaps nature will affect the cure. But do not take any more purgatives."

Rachel reminded him, "You said you weren't sure what is wrong."

"Of course I'm not sure. I'm not even sure I'll be a doctor. But I do feel that nature is the best physician. I would, as I suggested, eat simple foods, try not to be melancholy, and then, if it is as you say, you are not with child, your swelling should subside and eventually go away."

Rachel was so angry William expected her to jump out of bed to attack him, but she didn't have the strength. Her mother was shocked, and mumbled that just because they were poor was no reason to question Rachel's virtue. Silas, however, nodded, and said, "We won't be able to eat as well as our betters, but I can get some eggs and milk."

Rachel repeated, "No man has done his will on me!"

Her mother said, "Her belly is the work of the devil."

William said, "A good diet should rid you of the vapours. You have a comely face, warm blood, and I don't think you were incontinent."

She blushed so violently her delicate skin was alive with colour.

William liked her feeling, but he said, "You mustn't be hasty. I can understand why you don't trust men, but you must get over your melancholy."

"Sir, our life has not been happy."

"It will be better now," said Silas. "Squire Foster has a great manor and uses many servants. We will get food for my service."

"And you do look improved," said William. She was watching him intently as he examined her completely; her anger had given way to curiosity. He found nothing wrong, and he thought, If she could give herself some attention, brush her long, auburn hair, bathe her face, give her body a fresh start, her high-boned fairness could be appealing.

As he turned to leave, Rachel mumbled, "I'm grateful for what you did." She liked that he didn't look down on her, or eye her lasciviously, as did the other students. "But I'm sorry that Silas had to trouble you again."

"I believe your swelling will vanish, although it may happen slowly."

"Then you agree. I'm not with child?"

"You said you weren't."

"But the devil could have bewitched me and put sin within me."

"No!" shouted the mother. "We have been punished enough!"

William was halfway to Caius before he remembered what he had wanted to ask Silas. The boy was at his side, so he would not get lost in the fens, and suddenly William blurted out, "What did you feel when you recovered consciousness after the hanging? Anything unusual?"

"I was numb. I didn't think I had any legs. I will never steal again no matter how hungry I get."

"Do you recall a loss of breath, a quickening of the blood?"

"I was surprised that I could see my feet. Great sir, may I serve you when you become a bachelor of the arts? I could rouse you for breakfast, clean your boots, dress your hair, and carry your messages and letters."

"I can't afford it."

"All I need is a place to sleep."

"Besides, I'm not sure I will have a satisfactory disputation."

"You will," Silas said confidently. "Sir, you could be right about Rachel. Our hut has been full of wind ever since her stomach swelled."

The disputation for the bachelor of arts degree was held in May in the University Church of Great St. Mary, the heart of

Cambridge. William learned that he was to be examined there
with Darcey, Wilkins, Scrope, and Matthew, and that there
were to be two other doctors in addition to Grimston: Lancelot Browne from London, who was one of the Queen's physicians, and Ian Andrews, a Scot, who attended James IV of
Scotland, the possible heir to Elizabeth's throne. He was apprehensive at the thought of appearing before such worthies;
even Wilkins was afraid.

Wilkins took special care with his gown, and said, "Grimston will fail us if it doesn't hang perfectly. I wish they would
allow us to grow a beard. It would give us more dignity.
Matthew, did Scrope cut his?"

"He is not coming," said Matthew as they paused at the
Gate of Honour for a last look at each other to be certain
they were properly garbed.

"Why not?"

"He's been excused. His family are helping to entertain the
Queen, and Her Majesty likes young, attractive men about her
who ride and dance skillfully. Scrope is a splendid horseman
and a dexterous dancer."

Darcey asked wonderingly, "Will this excuse be accepted?"

Matthew stared at him as if he were stupid. "Of course it
will be!"

Everyone was silent as they approached Great St. Mary.
Then they became part of the gowned procession marching up
the nave, and the four medical students sat at the foot of the
rostrum, in the first row. Other students crowded in behind
them to listen to their disputation, and all eyes were on the
rostrum where sat the three physicians.

William stared eagerly at them, hoping he would find in
one of them a friend rather than an adversary. Grimston had
been placed in the center, as a courtesy to his post at Cambridge, although the two other physicians were of greater
reputation. William sensed that the one on the right, the elderly Ian Andrews, was not a dove but a falcon, with knife-
sharp features drawn tautly over a bony skull.

He wasn't sure what to expect of Lancelot Browne, who was tall, lean, middle-aged, and looked more the courtier than the doctor. His face was long, well-shaped, and his brown hair, mustache, and pointed beard were meticulously trimmed.

Grimston began the disputation. He tested their pronunciation of Latin. Matthew's replies were uncertain; Darcey mumbled that he was from Norfolk, as if this excused his accent—Norfolk was favoured at Caius; Wilkins said that whatever he had learned, he had learned from the great Dr. Grimston, and that he had memorised the statutes of Elizabeth; and William spoke accurately. He knew that his Latin was better than the others, but he was the one whom Grimston criticised most severely.

Neither of the other physicians said a word during this examination, but when it was finished Andrews stated, "Dr. Grimston, I hear there is much impiety among the students. Instead of Cambridge being a holy and learned university, the students indulge in such forbidden pastimes as cards, dice, bathing, playgoing, and other immoral exercises."

"Agreed!" cried Grimston. "But I have put an end to their more sinful behaviour, although they still betray God occasionally."

Wilkins said, "Sir, I hope to become worthy by following your teachings."

"Splendid! You are on the path to true learning."

But still, William noticed, Browne had not said a word.

Darcey repeated Wilkins's words in fumbling Latin, and while Grimston winced at his bad pronunciation and Andrews was critical, Grimston said, "I will wait and see how you conduct yourself the next three years."

William was silent, however, and Matthew followed his example.

Grimston asked, "Have you two nothing else to say for yourselves?"

William said, "Sir, will there be any instruction in medicine in the study for a master of arts degree?"

"Why do you ask?" said Grimston, as if that were an impertinence.

"Sir, I would like to learn about the human body, but . . ." He halted.

Browne cut in abruptly. "Young man, you haven't so far?"

"Not much, sir."

Grimston said angrily, "Harvey, as I warned you earlier, you could be deprived of your scholarship. You lack humility."

"Yet," said Browne, "you do have the Matthew Parker Scholarship now?"

"Yes, sir." William couldn't resist adding, "At the moment."

"Do you know it is the first medical scholarship given in England?"

"I am honoured, sir." William felt this was a crucial moment.

"But he is ungrateful," said Grimston. "Poor in faith and piety."

Browne said, "Dr. Grimston, we mustn't be so low in knowledge that we beg for it only at the church door." Yet before William could feel he was being supported, he was told, "Harvey, you mustn't be arrogant because you saved a poor thief's life. That doesn't make you a Jesus."

Matthew said, "Sir, it was God who showed him the way."

"Perhaps," Browne said dryly, "and that he detected breath in the body."

"Blood, sir," said William. "Begging your pardon. That is what led me to believe there was life still in him. It wasn't a miracle but a simple act of healing. As if, sir, the blood called me and said he was alive."

Andrews grumbled, "You were atheistical," but Browne asked him, "Have you seen your patient since?" William hesitated as Grimston scowled and Andrews regarded him indignantly, but when Browne repeated, "I would have," William nodded, and Browne went on. "Was he recovered?"

"I believe so, sir."

"Why do you think he survived the hanging?"

"Sir, it seems most likely that he fainted and became limp."

"Or perhaps the hangman didn't tie the knot strongly enough."

"I didn't think of that, sir." William was excited. "It is possible."

"Healing should be the art of the possible," Browne said, "yet it rarely is. Too often the doctor only looks for what he wants to see."

Grimston and Andrews had grown deferential, and William had a sudden hope that Browne called the tune and all was not yet lost.

"However, Harvey, in the pursuit of a master of arts degree there will be medical readings. Of Hippocrates, Aristotle, and Galen."

"Sir, I have memorised Galen and Aristotle. It was Dr. Grimston's wish, and I have obeyed him faithfully."

"It shouldn't harm you," Browne said cryptically.

Matthew suggested, "Sir, William is an excellent scholar."

"Are you, Ross?"

"I want to know what is inside the human body, sir, but it is so hard to find out. We have just one dissection a year, and I am not certain we should have any. Some say it is barbarous, others a profanation of God's work. It is confusing, and much of the time I don't know what to think."

Browne said, "There is much that we do not understand. But anyone who makes the effort is worth encouraging."

"As long as he has the true Christian faith," declared Andrews.

"Sir," said William. "I'm grateful that I'm a student at Caius."

"Gonville and Caius," corrected Andrews. "Your college was really founded in the fourteenth century by Edmund Gonville, a Norfolk rector."

"I know, sir. But everyone refers to our college as Caius."

Grimston said, "You question too much. Dr. Browne, it worries me, and is why he has been put on probation."

Browne reflected ruefully, Grimston found questions troublesome and believed that parents sent their sons to Cambridge to have their minds settled, not changed. But young Harvey should be encouraged. And at the moment that was still reasonably simple. He said, "Dr. Grimston, probation was wise, no doubt, at the time, but he does seem fit now to continue his studies for a master of arts degree."

Grimston replied, "Sir, I appreciate your views, but first he must subscribe to the Thirty-nine Articles, the Queen's supremacy, the Queen's statutes, and the Prayer Book."

"I do, sir," said William, and the other students joined him.

Grimston added, "Remember, now that you are eligible to pursue a master of arts degree, no one advances to any degree in this university who goes forth from his college except clad in a gown reaching down to his ankles."

There was a loud chorus of "Amen!"

The four students were accepted for their bachelor of arts degrees, but William felt he had achieved very little. Grimston and Andrews still sat on the rostrum, keeping their distance from the students, but Browne stood beside him and encouraged him to speak. William was excited, yet flustered. Browne's attention was a potent lure, but he didn't know whether to trust it.

Browne asked him, as he drew William apart from the other students, "Harvey, what do you plan to do after you finish Caius?"

"I'm not sure, sir. I came here to learn how to be a doctor, but . . .?"

"Now you are discouraged by the absence of medical subjects?"

"Yes, sir. And so little is known."

The Queen's physician stared intently at him. Browne had discarded his scarlet robe, and William saw that he was dressed like a courtier. His doublet was close-fitting and accentuated his slim waist and his tallness. His ruff was perfectly cut and framed his attractive features, and there was a dagger on his hip, which had been hidden by the ceremonial robe. But face to face there were also shadows and lines on his countenance, William observed, and while his eyes were penetrating, they were also sad.

"Harvey, what makes you think you are qualified to be a physician?"

"I'm not certain, sir, but I've been interested since I was ten."

"And now you think too much time is spent studying Latin and theology?"

"It is possible. What do you think, sir?"

Browne's tone grew scornful. "There are two kinds of medical students. The first and more common is the memoriser, who seeks to do everything as it is in the books, although no book is infallible. They usually end up at Court, because they know how to dress, how to ride, and, most of all, to be agreeable. Their medical training should have been stifled at birth. The second kind, and they are rare, seek to view the human body through their own experience. To use nature whenever they can. But, most of all, to see."

William felt despair. I will never be a good doctor, he thought; I see so much less than I want to.

Browne, annoyed at how easily the boy was discouraged, said sharply, "But you expect me to radiate goodness and charity. There is none of that in illness, but an enemy that is often implacable and deadly."

"But what can I do, sir?" William sounded helpless.

"Perform miracles, no doubt, as you did on the hanged thief."

"Sir, that was no miracle!" William was furious. "I know that the circumstances were not normal, but I had to help him. I cannot say why, but I had to. And I did not subvert God."

Browne felt better; at least this young man could get

aroused. He said, "When you make up your mind—if it favours medicine—call on me in London. After you acquire your master of arts degree. You cannot study medicine in England, there is no school here worthy of the name."

"Sir, what would you recommend?"

"Padua, Bologna, Basle. Any of them are superior to what you will learn here. I can advise you when you are ready."

"Sir, I will work hard for my master of arts degree."

"All good medical students work hard. It is the least they can do." Lancelot Browne wrote out his London address and gave it to William, who put it inside his doublet as if it were a treasure.

Before he could ask this physician any further questions, Grimston called him and the other three students to receive a final admonition. He had to prove that he hadn't lost any of his authority, and he was envious of Harvey's interest in Browne's words. He stated, "Remember that as bachelor of the arts, you have taken the first vital step toward becoming gentlemen."

 have tried to know the fast
flow of water
I have tried to know the slow
I have tried to know the
stagnant condition
I have tried to understand why
As though in the end I would
understand all

Thomas Harvey was proud of his son's achievement. He sat in his oak-panelled living room, which was the centre of his large timber and brick house in Folkestone, and, to increase his satisfaction, reread the statement that William had received his master of arts degree. Then he turned to his eldest son, who stood silently before him, but he hid his praise. He felt it was a great honour that one of his family had graduated from Cambridge, but he didn't want his son to be proud; vanity could lead him to desire more than William could accomplish. He regarded him sternly, so that the boy would remember who made the decisions for the family.

Three years had passed since William had earned his bachelor of arts degree, and he was relieved that his days at Caius were over. It was 1599, and on this mild June morning he recalled Grimston's criticism, Browne's advice, Scrope's ignorance, Darcey's fumblings, Wilkins's scorn, Matthew's friendship, trips to the brothel, and visits from Silas to assure him that Rachel had recovered and if he ever needed a servant Silas would serve him faithfully. But although he was moved by the boy's devotion, he had declined his offer. He felt no nostalgia for the days he had spent at Caius. While he had retained the scholarship, the subjects he had studied for his master's degree had disappointed him. After six years at the university, he still felt remote from medicine. The stress had remained on Latin, theology, logic, rhetoric, with a smattering of astrology and biology, and more readings of Galen and Aristotle. There had not been any dissections since Silas. That incident had caused the anatomies to be considered wasteful, and this privilege had been revoked. And now his father was suggesting that he join the family business.

"Son, aren't you listening?" Thomas asked impatiently. The boy hadn't replied, as was his duty. Thomas was annoyed.

"Of course I am, sir. But I thought I went to Caius for other reasons."

"It was to contribute to the respect I have earned."

William shifted uneasily. He was supposed to stand motionless when his father addressed him and to obey without question, but he was twenty-one, and he no longer felt like a child. Yet his father was accustomed to exerting authority. He wondered if this could ever change. He stared at his father in an effort to find the best way to approach him.

Thomas's long, pointed face, firm, determined jaw, strong, prominent nose, short grey beard were all an expression of his self-assurance. William knew that his father could be hard, that it would be difficult to change the merchant's mind, and yet he could not hesitate any longer, for he was resolved that there must be no more confusion about his future.

"Son, I expect you to answer when I address you."

"Yes, sir. But I would like you to understand how I feel."

"Cambridge was supposed to make you a gentleman!"

"I'm sorry. I didn't intend to cause you any offence."

"But you have with your indifference to my wishes. You don't seem interested in the prosperous business I've worked so hard to establish."

"It's not that, sir, but what about medicine? You were pleased when I won the Matthew Parker Scholarship. And that was for the study of medicine."

"It was a great honour. When you received it, I felt you could become a gentleman."

William blushed. His father was showing an emotion unusual for him.

"Yet it is not necessary to use it to study medicine. None of the students who preceded you in the Matthew Parker Scholarship have gone on to study medicine, but used it to ease their way through Cambridge."

"Sir, I thought you supported my desire to be a physician."

"That could be a foolish desire. You should be more practical."

Thomas Harvey is determined to be, William reflected; in the years he had been away, there had been a great improvement in his circumstances. His father was Mayor of Folkestone again, as he had been in 1586, and his fine furniture revealed how fortunate he had been in business. In the few days that William had been home, he had learned that his father's shipping venture now reached as far as Venice and

Constantinople. However, he said, "I didn't know you had a poor opinion of physicians."

"Poor opinion? That is hardly the way to put it!" Thomas snapped that with an obvious air of grievance and stood up abruptly and walked stiffly to the window, limping. "I have good reason to feel the way I do. No physician has been able to cure my leg or hip."

Yet my middle-aged, middle-sized father possesses a fine carriage and a commanding presence, William told himself; but he didn't want to imitate him, he didn't want to imitate anyone, but how could he tell him?

"Son, five years ago, when I was alighting from my horse I slipped and felt a pain in my ankle. When I had trouble walking I summoned Dr. Lowe, who examined me with much Latin and then said that I had sprained it. He called the apothecary, who dressed it with an ointment, and then we drank a bottle of wine which Lowe insisted would aid the cure. Instead, the pain removed into my knee and settled in my hip. I sent for another doctor, Mr. Griffith, a Welshman who lives in Hythe, and he bled me."

"I wouldn't have done that. Your body needed rest."

"That is what I thought. I went to bed and sought to sleep soundly."

"Sir, perhaps you saw the wrong doctors."

"No! They understand nothing and cannot see! My pain lingered."

"I intend to see better. And you needed a better doctor."

"There are none!" His father rushed on, his indignation growing, "Six months ago, when I alighted again from my horse, I felt a pain in my hip. I feared the old disease had come again, and I went to bed, but I could not sleep, no matter how I prayed and sought to set my mind at rest."

"Father, you could have caught a chill."

"I thought I was bewitched," grumbled Thomas. "No matter how I lay, the pain swept through every joint of my body. Your mother was alarmed, and called Dr. Lowe and Dr. Griffith, but even though they bled, purged, and sweated me,

46

my joints were so numb and feeble I could not walk for a long time. Your mother was afraid that I would be a cripple. But when spring came and the weather grew warm and dry, my body seemed to mend, and I was able to walk, although still with this ache in my hip and this lame leg.

"Sir, it sounds like the gout."

"That is what several other physicians said. When I felt better, I hired a coach and went to London. Dr. Ames said I should go to Bath, that it was a fine place and the company was good. Dr. Pyke was against it, he advised me that it would harden the humours in my joints, and make them more brittle. Dr. Horton was certain I must neither drink wine nor any strong drink and eat only once a day, but Dr. Rutson stated this was foolish, that the blood must be kept warm with much eating and drinking. In the last year I have consulted nine physicians, and I have obtained a different opinion from each."

"Didn't any of them help you?"

Thomas growled, "I told you, none! At the best, all they do is but guess, and then they dissemble their opinions and comply with the patient's wishes, and for their own profit and without any wisdom of their own."

"Father, if I became a doctor, perhaps I could help you."

"Do you think I'm a dog to be cured of the distemper with one look?"

"You could have caught a chill from the dampness of the sea."

"Nonsense, I love this location. Harveys have lived in this part of Kent since the fourteenth century. Look!" In his enthusiasm, Thomas grabbed his son by the arm and pulled him over to a large bay window whose view was both east and south. For the moment, forgetting his pain, he burst with pride as he pointed to the world outside. "When I moved here, I chose the most fitting soil to build my mansion. Here the prospect is fair and pleasant to the eye. We can see the hills, the woods, and, always, the sea."

"I like the view too. It is one of the best in Folkestone."

"That is why I remain in this coastal area. The harbour below is fine, and if we have many showery days, it is fitting, it is part of the sea, and the sea has gratified my wishes."

William listened attentively, for his father spoke with passion.

"My grandfather, Thomas, whom I was named after, left my father four oxen, five horses, eight hogs, poultry, carts, ploughs, and forty sheep. I was expected to be a farmer like my father, a sheep farmer," he said contemptuously, "but I had more sense. I may have been born a yeoman, but my seven sons will have the opportunity to become gentlemen. I have built my business into a fine coastal and cross-Channel fleet, and with the aid of my family I expect the Harveys to become merchant adventurers. My ships already trade with the Levant, but I need persons I can trust."

His father's intense grip hurt William's arm, and he winced. Yet the view from this window gave him pleasure too. On a clear day he could see water for many miles. However, he knew, despite his affection for the country, he couldn't stay in Folkestone as Thomas wished. Only it was not simple or easy to say.

"What I'm trying to explain is . . ." William halted. His father was regarding him as if he were faithless. "You see, I . . ."

"Stop mumbling, Will. I'm sure you didn't at Cambridge."

But Thomas's irritation spurred him to say, "I want to be a doctor."

"You know my views. I sent you to Cambridge to become a gentleman."

"Dr. Browne is a gentleman. And a renowned doctor. He thinks I could become a good physician."

"I would rather have you serve God. Who is this Browne?"

"He is a physician from London who examined us at Caius."

"I had enough of London doctors. They are no better than the rest."

As Thomas's eyes wandered about the harbour below them, to count how many of his ships were in port today, William used this moment of distraction to recall his last meeting with Dr. Browne.

It had been several weeks ago, just before graduation, and the London physician had come to Cambridge to attend the ceremony at Caius.

He invited William to attend him in his rooms, which was considered an honour, and Wilkins and Darcey regarded William enviously, but he was nervous. He had had brief conversations with Dr. Browne each of the previous years, but others had been present, and little had been said.

Browne looked even more the courtier in his fashionable garb, yet the lines and shadows on his long face had deepened, and William sensed some unhappiness in the physician.

And Browne greeted him curtly and said sharply, "Harvey, there isn't much time left for you to make up your mind."

"About what, sir?" he answered, although he suspected what was meant.

"The pursuit of medicine. There is no school of consequence in England. Here the soil is barren, but at Padua there is fertility."

"Sir, is that why you wanted to see me?"

"Some useful things seem to have seeped into your mind. You have a natural soil for cultivation, but it will not be tilled here. The holder of the medical Fellowships are permitted to repair for the continuation of their studies to the Continent. It is rare to find a student who is not set in his ways."

"Sir, why do you encourage me?"

"In a few years I may need a young man to assist me. If you prove worthy, although that is still dubious, such a post might be available when you return from Padua. Assuming Caius hasn't damaged you too much."

"Doctor, how can I thank you?"

49

"You have nothing to be grateful for. Advice costs nothing, and flatters the giver."

"Sir, Dr. Grimston won't approve of your recommendation."

"That will be amusing. Do you still possess my London address?"

"Yes, sir. I have treasured it."

"Most young men would. But you still have much to learn."

"Doctor, do you think I will like Padua?"

"I don't know. That is your problem."

His father interrupted his reverie with a sarcastic "William, you are always daydreaming. You will never be a practical man of affairs unless you are more forthright. But fit only to be a doctor."

Challenged, William blurted out, "That's exactly what I'm going to be!"

"After what I said?" Thomas was outraged. "Don't you feel any allegiance to your home? To your family? To me?"

Father, have mercy on me, William prayed, even if you haven't changed, I have. I have been away from home for eleven years, since 1588, and it doesn't mean the same thing to me any more, and hasn't for a long time.

"Son, have you no respect for my opinion?"

"Great respect, sir. But Dr. Browne thinks I could be a good doctor."

"Another quack, no doubt. Will, you were born the year Drake sailed around the world, and I swore then that you would follow the sea, as he did. It is the noblest calling of man, and it has kept us free from invasion."

But William had to go headlong now, before he lost his courage and gave in to his father's insistence. He turned away from the view of the sea so that it wouldn't bewitch him as it had Thomas and said, "I must study medicine. I have treated sick people and healed them." He added proudly, "I have even witnessed a dissection." He hoped that his father wouldn't ask him for details, for he had seen little of it.

Horrified, Thomas asked, "Are you proud of such blasphemous behaviour?"

"It is necessary if I am to learn how to treat the human body."

"Didn't the authorities object?"

"No. Caius was allowed to take the bodies without interference on the part of Queen Elizabeth's officials. Father, there is so much to learn about the human body!"

Thomas yearned to retort, "Better to leave that to God," but as he stared at William—short, with black hair, dark, piercing eyes, and a restless manner and a rapid speech when excited, as now—it was difficult to discourage him, much as he wanted to. He paused to collect his thoughts. Yet when his eldest son added that he desired to continue his education at the University of Padua, he was startled, and he asked why.

"John Caius, who founded my college, studied at Padua."

Thomas looked unimpressed.

"And he was Queen Mary's physician, and later Queen Elizabeth's."

"A useful situation. It is an honour to serve the Queen."

"John Caius was the most honoured physician of his time."

"Is that the real reason you want to study at Padua?" Thomas wondered if his son possessed Catholic leanings, like John Caius, and he was afraid of this possibility. "Are you being truthful?"

"Padua is renowned for its anatomical school and the doctors who have taught there. It is the best school in Europe. I must go!"

"But it is a Catholic university."

"That doesn't matter. The students come from all over Europe, and some are from England. Even the Queen approves of a good Italian education. And Lancelot Browne, who recommended Padua, is her physician, and he has promised to introduce me to her if I get my medical education there."

This was an inducement difficult for Thomas to resist. His idea of a good post was with the sovereign, and he sensed that

William would not listen if he tried to stop him. But he had to say, "Are you sure, son?"

"I'm positive. Dr. Browne assures me that if I do well at Padua, I will become his assistant in London and be introduced at Court." He didn't like exaggerating, but he was driven by a force that was overwhelming.

When Thomas assented and promised to help him, William hugged his father with a passion which left both of them shaken.

His father asked, "When did you become attracted to medicine?"

"At the time of the Spanish Armada, sir." His mind went back to it.

The ten-year-old William felt that something was wrong when his father's steward summoned him to see his father at once. Joshua's tone was urgent, and the boy had to obey. There were rumours that the Spanish Armada was approaching the English coast and was going to strike at any moment. It was the summer of 1588, and he knew that his father was worried about his fishing fleet and coastal service, an easy prey for a victorious enemy. Yet he followed the burly, middle-aged Joshua reluctantly. He was proud of what he had been doing when he had been interrupted. He and a dozen other boys were drilling on the village green with homemade St. George staves as part of the army of Englishmen preparing to repel the invasion.

"You look smart," his father said, pleased that his son was dressed better than the other boys, but William was unhappy when his father added, "You must go to the safety of London. As my eldest child, you mustn't risk the Harvey name and inheritance by staying in Folkestone. It could be dangerous. The Spaniards could invade us right here."

"Up our steep cliffs, sir? They are very difficult to climb."

"The land is flat by the Leas. And they possess a great store of armour, and the largest fleet ever assembled."

Joshua was packing his mother and the five younger children off to London, forty-one miles away, but William felt grown-up, for his father was speaking to him alone, and he cried out, "Father, I can't run away! My duty is to be by your side! As you taught me!"

Thomas was moved by his son's resolution, and he allowed him to stay.

The next few days there were many tales about where the Spanish intended their invasion. Then, on an evening William never forgot, he heard the drums sound. He ran out of their large house on the corner of Rendezvous and Church Streets and joined his father, who hurried to the top of the hill that overlooked the harbour.

Beacons flared from headland to headland.

"Our warning system," his father told him, pleased that William wasn't afraid. "Smoke by day and flame by night. These beacons on hill and church tower are passing the message along the coast to Dover and inland to London that the Spanish have been sighted. Near our shores, probably."

The following morning it was reported that enemy galleons were off Plymouth and threatening this vital port, and Thomas and the men of Folkestone prepared their contribution to the defending English fleet. Thirteen frigates had been freshly painted, tarred, and caulked, and supplies were being stored, but William felt they were too small to oppose the enormous Spanish galleons.

Thomas grumbled, "They are not fit to fight, although they cost us forty-three thousand pounds, and they will be used for decoys after they supply our fleet."

"Sir, are our affairs so desperate?"

"They could be soon. We drill with staves because there is no ammunition available, all has gone to the fleet, and I hear it is insufficient there. Howard and Drake have powder only for a few days."

"Then why do we train on the village green?"

"To keep occupied, and because every county should be

responsible for its own defense, but we are too wanting in strength to oppose a landing."

"You expect it here, sir?"

"We are the gateway into England. Hastings, where William the Conqueror landed, isn't far away."

Nonetheless, when the thirteen sails put out of Folkestone to join the English fleet and William stood with Thomas to watch them, he was glad he was old enough to be by his father's side.

That week there was news that the Spanish Armada had been sighted off Weymouth, then Portsmouth. From its easterly course up the Channel, William realized the enemy was sailing in the direction of Folkestone and that the invasion could occur there. He noticed that the wind had swung to the west, driving the Spaniards in their direction, and he heard the roar of guns, although he saw no ships. Most of the village waited and watched from the West Leas, where the navies should be sighted first. But since his father was occupied, William chose his own place of vantage to view what everyone expected would be a battle before their eyes. The rest of the family were in London, and in the confusion his absence wasn't noticed. Each morning now he climbed the east cliffs, which were the highest land along the coast.

Then there were shouts as huge, lumbering Spanish galleons came into view. William was shaken: The towering hulls and lofty masts were so much larger and more impressive than the smaller English ships that trailed them. He couldn't believe that the enemy could lose. But he observed that the English ships were swifter and moved more easily. The armada didn't turn in at Folkestone or make any effort to land, but sailed in an easterly direction towards Calais.

He went to bed, wondering whether Drake was afraid. He wished the thing in his chest didn't thump so violently. He got up, unable to fall asleep, and went into the living room and found his father sitting by the window.

"Something is burning," Thomas said suddenly, "I can smell the smoke."

"Sir, is it from the harbour?"

"No, it is much farther away. But I must investigate."

"May I come along?"

"If you don't bother me with questions."

"I think you might see better from the east cliffs."

Thomas regarded him suspiciously, but he heeded his suggestion, and as they reached the cliffs they saw that the French side of the Channel was aflame.

Thomas exclaimed, "Drake must have filled fire-ships with straw, pitch, and gunpowder and driven them at the Spaniards! There go my ships!"

"Father, do you think he will defeat the enemy?"

"They will be terrified. They will not expect devil ships, it is not a thing noblemen do. But what can you expect of Drake, he is no gentleman."

"I thought you said he was our greatest sailor."

"Too reckless for my taste. We could still lose."

The next twenty-four hours there was constant smoke by day, and at night fires lit up the sky with a lurid ferocity, but William couldn't tell whether it was English or Spanish ships that were burning. A great sea battle was taking place in his presence, and he couldn't see it.

Then the sky darkened ominously, the wind veered abruptly to the west, and a fierce squall swept up the Channel with sudden, vicious force.

His father said mournfully, "Typical Channel weather. It could disperse our fleet just when they have the advantage and wreck all my frigates."

William was stunned by the quickness and violence of the squall. One moment it was clear, with a light wind and an easy swell; the next, without warning, there was a gale and a driving rain. Nothing could be seen.

When the storm subsided many hours later, the waiting began. There was no word about the outcome of the battle.

William stood on the dock with his father, and as the day passed without any news, the anxiety became physical pain. He thought that waiting was one of the hardest and cruelest things to bear. He lost track of the time, and he was full of doubt. Then, just before nightfall, a ship was seen approaching from the battle. Those on the dock saw that it bore an English flag and greeted it joyously, but Thomas was apprehensive.

"William, the rigging is burnt from cannon shot, there are gaping holes in the hull, and many of the wounded are lying on the deck."

As the frigate docked, the crowd waited anxiously and impatiently to hear the result of the battle.

The seamen replied that nobody knew, not even Drake, who was at sea with the body of the fleet. William was shaken by the large number of wounded, and that some of the dead had been brought back. The boy noticed that most of them were Spanish, that there were only a few English wounded and dead.

His father grumbled, "They have transformed one of my supply ships into a hospital. I will never be able to clean the blood from it."

William grew ill at the sight of the wounded men. Many moaned as they were helped ashore, and there was so much blood he shuddered. No one seemed able to quench the bleeding, as if the blood ran without reason.

William noticed that the sword made clean wounds, but the gunshot wounds were deep and narrow and bits of cloth had been carried into many of them, and most of these were infected. Interested in seeing what could be done, he trailed the wounded men to the tents where the surgeons tended them. No one questioned his presence, assuming he was a cabin boy. Then he couldn't go in. The surgeons applied burning oil to the wounds, and the screams of pain were more than he could bear. Yet all the surgeons were doing this.

He asked one of the seamen who was bringing in the bodies

why this was done if it hurt so much, and the tanned, smallish sailor snapped, "All gunshot wounds have a poison, and the boiling oil drives it out. What are you doing here, boy? You should be back at the ship, getting us rum."

William fled until he came upon a soldier lying on the ground, his flesh charred and swollen, and crying out in his pain. The wounded man was speaking Spanish and motioning to his mouth to indicate that he wanted to drink.

William got him a pint of water, and the wounded soldier drank it without a pause. Next to him the bodies of two dead Spanish officers had been left sprawled on the ground and were giving off an odious stench.

He asked a passing English sailor, "Is this healthy?"

The sailor, who kept a considerable distance away from the corpses, replied, "It is a common practice. They are noblemen. We can obtain a ransom for their bodies. Although one of them lost a leg. Boy, you wasted that water. The Spaniard you gave it to is beginning to die. It is dangerous to touch the body when the moon is in motion."

The wounded man died soon after. But how can I stop feeling, William wondered, even if I am ignorant and foolish? He possessed such a wanting to stop the bleeding, but nobody seemed to know how.

A week later there was the news that the Armada—the part that had survived the English attacks and the foul weather— had dispersed northwards and the peril of invasion had ceased.

And now he desired to be a physician, and to do something about what he had seen as a boy. He said to his father, who had waited impatiently during his reverie, "I remember the wounded from the Spanish Armada, and how most of those who were brought ashore died."

"You couldn't do anything about it. You still can't. That was God's will. And they were mostly Papists. They had fallen into error."

"Father, I believe I can do better. I don't hold that boiling

57

oil is the best way to cure gunshot wounds. It burns rather than heals."

"That is not a doctor's province. The surgeons do this. Will, I thought after you saw how the Armada was defeated you would prefer to follow the sea."

This was the point at which their views diverged, and William said, "Thank you for promising to help me at Padua. You won't regret it."

"Would you go if I withheld my permission?"

"Sir, you have your ships and I have my reasons."

The following Sunday Thomas gathered his family around him to say prayers for William's soul. They sat in the foremost pew of their church, St. Mary and St. Eanswythe, one of the oldest churches in England, and Thomas was proud of his brood. All of his breed had survived childbirth and infancy— even the daughter by his first wife, Juliana, who had died young—and he didn't know any other man in Folkestone who could say that; at least half of the children born perished at birth or soon after. But it was no wonder, he thought; he was sure he knew more about the care of the body than most physicians, and this gave him much solace. He bowed his head in prayer and made certain that his children did so also.

William couldn't concentrate on the services. Now that he was going to leave his family, he was becoming intensely aware of them. He stared at them so he would remember them clearly when he was in Italy, as if that would help him in moments of loneliness. Next to him was the sixteen-year-old John, then the fourteen-year-old Thomas, the eleven-year-old Daniel, the nine-year-old Eliab, and the five-year-old twins, Michael and Matthew; his sister, Amy, who was two, was in his mother's arms.

She sat by his father, and he felt it would be inhuman not to miss her. He liked his mother's shape and texture. Her dark colouring was good—the blood ran well in Joan Harvey, his

father said—and her features were pleasant and gentle, and she was still slender although she had borne nine children. And while she had given her life in obedience to his father, William knew she had her own views. He longed to know what she thought about his journey to Padua; he doubted it would be an imitation of his father's opinions. But she must behave as if Thomas were infallible; that was the custom.

His father was saying quietly, "Let us thank God that He has brought us peace."

When it came time for William to leave, he sensed that his father was still upset by his departure. He was going to Venice on one of his father's ships; it was September, 1599, and there was no danger from the Spanish, yet he saw a sign of his father's agitation. Everyone was assembled in the living room to say farewell, and William noted that Thomas was unconsciously kicking the table with his ankle, which he did when he was worried. No wonder Thomas had a pain in his leg; this could be the cause of his trouble. But to say this might make him lose his temper.

William saw an anxious expression on his mother's face, and he realized that she was concerned about his journey. His brother John was envious, Eliab was curious, Thomas and Daniel were arguing while the twins, Michael and Matthew, were too young to know what was happening. He saw his mother adjust her hair, which she did when she was troubled; yet she waited for her husband to speak.

Thomas rose and strode about with a quick, emotional gait, although he still limped from the ache in his leg, and declared, "Will, I mustn't reproach you on your last day in England, but I'm disappointed that you still want to go. I shouldn't have allowed you to stay in Folkestone when we were threatened by the Spaniards." He stated that with genuine grief.

"Father, it goes beyond that. It isn't enough to make a face at the devil and think that will cure the patient."

"You are blasphemous. The devil plays a vital part in sickness."

"And sometimes so does poor sanitation."

"So many English sailors died of the epidemic after we lost less than a hundred men, it would discourage any reasonable person from pursuing the study of physic. None of the physicians knew how to cure the plague."

His father went on to complain about the fourteen shillings a month it had taken to feed and pay a single seaman to oppose the Armada, but William recalled that more men had died from flying splinters than from cannon and musket shot, and far more from disease, hunger, thirst, and dysentery. He wondered what his mother was thinking; she sat so silently. He didn't expect his brothers to voice an opinion—that wasn't considered fitting—but surely she must care about his being away for several years.

Thomas stated, "Remember, Will, you must remain an Englishman wherever you are, and never lose control of the situation," and Joan Harvey longed to add, *"May God love and keep you,"* and to embrace her first-born.

Instead, she sat submissively, as her husband expected her to. He prefers, she reflected, that I know many home remedies, that I use the kitchen leavings as a stew for the servants, and save the drippings of the candles so they can be formed into more candles. But the high point of her life was her climb up the stairs to her children's bedrooms to see that they were securely tucked in and to kiss them good night. There wasn't any moment in her existence when she wasn't longing to see her children, but she doubted that their father felt this way.

And as William said good-bye and she saw tears in his eyes, she couldn't restrain herself. She cried and couldn't stop, in spite of Thomas's annoyance, until her eldest child assured her that he would be careful.

Even so, she had to warn him, "Not even doctors are immune from the plague. God is quick to punish us for our sins."

He wanted to reply, "The plague is not the result of God's

wrath," but he knew she wouldn't agree. He promised her that
he would be pious while he thought, Medicine needs more
than piety. He must observe and learn from nature.

His father said, "Joan, you mustn't worry. Will is of very
good courage. He has my blood in him. As long as he doesn't
allow the corrupt and contagious air of Papist Italy to infect
him, he will remain a Harvey."

She said, "But now that he is to undergo the looseness of
those southern parts, how can we be sure?"

"He is my son. And a graduate of Cambridge."

"Yes, Thomas." Joan adjusted the collar of William's great-
coat so that it would protect him from the wind and the chill
of the sea, and added, "Son, that should help you. You do
have the look of a gentleman."

Then he was kissing his mother, embracing his brothers and
baby sister, and kneeling before his father to receive the family blessing. But as William saw Thomas wince with pain as
he leaned on his walking stick, his son blurted out impulsively, "I think I know how to cure your leg and hip!"

"No one can! Nine physicians couldn't help me! How could
you?"

"If you stopped kicking the table when you are upset, the
pain should vanish. Try that. If one fibre in your calf muscle
is hurt, pain and limping are apt to follow. A nerve may be
damaged and cause your distress."

"But you are not sure?"

"Not yet. However, if I could examine you, I think I could
help you."

"No, no! Get up! You will be late for the ship, and it will
not wait. And you had better hurry before I change my mind
and forbid you to go."

William rose, fixed his ruff so that it fitted loosely—he
didn't like tight clothes—and hurried out of the house before
he cried. He was resolved that when he returned he would be
able to say to his father, "*I will be able to cure you.*" Then he
would be a physician.

61

he new new new
is losing its newness . . .
The old old old
is gaining an oldness . . .

*The University of Padua in the Republic of Venice
decrees that the degree of bachelor of medicine requires a
minimum of three years, attendance at all the regular lecture
series, practice with a famous physician for a year, and proof
that the candidate has visited the sick.*

William stood before the entrance to the medical school,
this edict firmly planted in his mind, and studied the newly
constructed fabric. It was on the western islet of Padua, the
ancient heart of the city, and it was called the Piazza della
Sapientza, but he heard many students around him refer to it
as *"il Bo."* The Ox, he translated to himself, pleased with his
knowledge of Italian. The anatomy of this world delighted
him. He admired the symmetry of the three-storied yellow
block, and felt that it was a temple built to commemorate the
glory of medicine. The entrance gate, framed by delicate col-
umns and a semicircular arch, was dominated by an impressive bas relief that stressed that the university was the territory
of the Most Serene Republic of Venice.

Now he understood why John Caius, who had studied here
sixty years ago with Andreas Vesalius, had designed Caius in
the Italian fashion.

William had travelled on one of his father's ships to nearby
Venice, and the sights and sounds of the great maritime city
had excited him, but the medical school was the heart of the
Republic for him. And as he waited for Matthew at *il Bo* this
October afternoon in 1599—his Caius schoolmate had come
several weeks earlier by land—he eagerly observed the stir
about him, as if that would give him a clue to the future.

Despite the threat of rain, the unseasonable chill, the

Piazza del Bo was crowded with promenaders. At Caius, he thought, no one would be about. Here many students paraded so they could be seen in their glittering finery, ostentatious swords and daggers, and elegant capes and silk doublets. He heard Italian, French, German, and many other languages, reminding him that Padua was reputed to be the most civilised centre of learning in Europe. Then soldiers on horseback rode through the Piazza del Bo and forced everyone aside so they could pass. They wore the insignia of the Republic, and William saw that Padua, with all of its learning, was also a garrison town.

The next moment, as the soldiers vanished, Matthew embraced him and declared excitedly, "I'm not living in the university, as we did at Cambridge, but with a professor who resides nearby. He teaches mathematics. Galileo Galilei. He takes in boarders to earn more money."

"But you say he is a professor?"

"They don't earn much. It is not an elevated profession. You can board with him. His woman is an excellent housekeeper."

"You are certain that living there is permitted?"

"It is encouraged." Matthew was disgusted with Will's ignorance. "Most of the quarters of the students are in the homes of the professors. They do it to have enough to live on. The professor is inclined to melancholy and can be rude, but he has the best lodgings in Padua. Will, you must get settled before school starts tomorrow."

Galileo's house was a solid fabric on the Via Vignali, a narrow, winding street near an open square, and William liked its splendid garden.

He was surprised that Galileo's housekeeper, Marina Gamba, was scarcely older than himself, a handsome girl, dark-haired and dark-eyed, and with a soft, voluptuous face and figure.

She greeted William warmly, and thanked Matthew for bringing her another attractive boarder. For a moment Wil-

liam was flattered; then he told himself this was an illusion,
she was interested only in what he could pay.

Marina led him into the study for the professor's approval,
where he saw a strong-jawed man with a square beard sitting
behind a huge desk, studying a Latin scroll. As he was ordered to approach by Galileo, he realized that the professor
was also younger than he had expected, in his thirties, yet
formal and preoccupied. Galileo complained about being interrupted even as he stared at the student with expressive,
impatient eyes. He fondled a large celestial globe by his side,
and wore his boots as a protection from the chill, although the
stove was lit.

"So!" he snapped in Italian. "Another fool who wants to be
a physician!"

William was glad that his Italian was as good as his Latin,
and he replied in the same language, "Sir, I would be honoured to live here."

"You will learn nothing here. This is merely a boarding-
house, nothing more. Young man, where do you come from?"

"Cambridge. England."

"I know where it is! Marina, what do you want of me? The
English are little better than savages, without any ability at
private meditation."

"Galileo, I want to introduce you to our new boarder."

"Then do! Can't you see that I'm at my devotions?"

But when she did, he didn't catch William's name. I have
more serious problems than another boarder, he thought
sadly, ignoring their departure; I have so much else to endure.
I am in desperate need of money, my sister Livia desires to
marry but cannot without a dowry, and, worse, she wants
things I cannot afford, as if I were a Venetian patrician instead of a struggling astronomer. Yet he knew that Livia felt
she had a just claim, for he had provided another sister,
Virginia, with a dowry so Virginia could wed—only to be on
the verge of being arrested for debt until he could supply the
money. He rose abruptly and strode over to the window
which looked out on his beloved garden. There the world was

64

infinite and was his. He fingered his lute, but while he was skillful, no melody came. If he wished Livia settled, he would have to earn more money. It was not enough to give private lessons, to take in students as boarders, to cast horoscopes for the Grand Duke. He must find more income. Until then, he couldn't satisfy Livia's needs, no matter how pressing they were.

He thought out what he must answer to his mother:

"Dearest Giula, persuade Livia that she will lose nothing by waiting. Tell her that there have been queens and great ladies who have not married until they were old enough to be her mother. Thus pray see her as soon as possible and convey to her that she must remain in the convent and I will continue to pay her board there. While I live she will not starve."

When he began to write, he wished he had a fitter subject for his wits. He had been contemplating the views of Copernicus. None of his colleagues put him above Aristotle and Ptolemy, yet he believed in what the Polish scholar had suggested. If he could only see for himself! But the spyglass he was labouring on in the hope of viewing the heavens and verifying Copernicus's assumptions showed him nothing. This new boarder had good eyes; they had regarded him without reverence, yet with respect. Yet how could he be a physician, with all the indecent dependence on Galen and Aristotle? The Englishman must have a want of intelligence, Galileo decided, and as he began to play the lute a melody came to him, and he felt less harassed and overburdened.

William was delighted that Marina gave him a room to himself and that it looked out on the beautiful garden. He heard someone singing in the next chamber, and he thought the voice was appealing and assumed it was another student's. When it stopped he was disappointed. He sat on the balcony of his room that evening and wished he could sing like that.

Then a quarrel broke out in the garden below him. The professor was shouting that he couldn't afford to give a student an entire room and his housekeeper was answering that

William Harvey was a grown man and shouldn't have to share his quarters.

"I can't afford the space," Galileo grumbled, "I need more boarders."

"Put the blame where it belongs, then," she retorted. "You beggar yourself to support your mother, brother, and sisters, and neglect your great natural gifts. These days you are so busy trying to earn extra scudi, you haven't time to perform any experiments."

"It is an inconvenience. As is your concern for this student."

"He is observant, quick-witted, brighter than the others. I can tell."

"He is not worth your consideration. The English are not good at medicine, they prefer the sea, like the Venetians, as you will find out when he faces the temptations of the Republic. Now leave me alone. It is an ill-favoured night, dark and cloudy, but I may be able to see a little."

Galileo was seeking to look through his spyglass when William descended into the garden to defend himself.

However, before he could say a word in the growing darkness, the professor snapped peevishly, "Do you know anything about astronomy?"

"A little sir. Aristotle says—"

"I know what Aristotle says!" shouted Galileo. "But that was two thousand years ago. Although the physicians still swear by him. Do you?"

"I'm not sure. Much that he wrote seems wise and yet . . .?"

"That is one of the difficulties of medicine, nothing is sure. I started out to be a physician, but it was too uncertain a world for me. At least, when I perfect my spyglass I will be able to understand the heavens." Galileo left abruptly, as if that reminded him of work he must do immediately.

Matthew, who had heard their raised voices, entered, and William asked him, "Is Marina Gamba his housekeeper or mistress?"

"Both."

lthough I speak to you
your ears are turned the other way
Although you say not one word
My ears are always turned to you
The sentence lost both ways
would make eloquent speakers
of stones

Girolamo Fabrizi d'Acquapendente, Doctor of Philosophy and Medicine and Professor of Surgery and Anatomy, celebrated and most skillful.

This inscription was above the anatomy theatre, and William and four fellow students hurried eagerly towards it. They had been told that the first dissection of the term was to occur there this morning, and they had been ordered to attend. It was two weeks later, and it was cold enough finally for a cadaver to be in sound condition. Matthew, who was one of the four students, had informed William that Fabricius—as everyone called him—gave the best anatomy lessons, and that the first one was considered the opening of the term. His companions' enthusiasm had convinced William that Matthew was right. And he could hardly control his own excitement as they reached the entrance to the medical school.

Matthew halted before the archway and declared, "Fabricius's anatomy theatre in Padua is regarded as one of the wonders of the world."

William hoped so. The lectures he had attended had repeated the words of Galen and Aristotle, and they had bored him. There had not been any classes with Galileo or any further discussions. The professor of mathematics had been involved in other matters, and had treated him as just another boarder, curtly.

But now, he repeated to himself so he would believe it, Fabricius is to hold the first dissection of the term, and that could be exciting.

Baruch Mendoza, who was Dutch, although his name was Portuguese, stated, "This is why I came to Padua. Fabricius is the best anatomist in Europe. Second in skill only to Vesalius, who taught here."

The other students paused too, as if each needed a moment to control his emotions, and William sought to understand them better.

Matthew's tall, fair good looks attract favourable attention, William reflected, but he wished his friend were not so eager to please. Matthew continued to quote Galen and Aristotle to support all his medical views.

He found Baruch Mendoza more inquiring and reserved. Mendoza was slight, with an olive skin, long features, very dark eyes, and it was difficult to think of him as Dutch, although he came from Amsterdam.

The Parisian Jean Riolan was slender, long-legged, with sharp features, and a prominent nose, and he fancied himself a ladies' man. But William, while he felt that Riolan made a fashion of mocking everything, liked the Frenchman's passion for observation.

The most assertive of the students was Caspar Hofmann, who was from Nuremberg. This stout, red-haired man with his short beard and mustache was the model of the young physician. William sensed that he was older than the others, but that he refused to admit it, and guessed that he was about twenty-seven, and ashamed that he was still studying medicine at that age. Yet he was proud of his learning and his ability to memorise. Hofmann boasted he could remember anything if he set his mind to it.

Now, however, William noticed that each of them was pale. He wondered if they were as afraid as he was. Was that the real reason they had paused?

As no one made the first effort to enter the anatomy theatre, their hesitation was observed by Emilio Parisano. He was late, yet as protégé and assistant to Fabricius it was essential that he arrive ahead of his master and have everything prepared. The swarthy, excitable physician, ten years older than most of the students, yet close enough in age to feel threatened, yelled, "The Maestro is on his way! You must get to your places before he arrives, or he won't start!"

"We are honoured by your interest, sir," Hofmann said automatically.

"It is not amusing. I could have you dismissed myself. Go in."

They did, humbly, as Parisano demanded.

Once they were inside and out of his hearing, Hofmann muttered, "He is a poor anatomist. He attacks a body like a barber. Son of a bitch."

William, to give himself courage to face the corpse, repeated to himself as he climbed up the spiral staircase to the top landing where the new students had to stand: "The anatomy theatre of Padua is considered one of the wonders of the world." And now he knew why. Built recently, in 1594, after Vesalius had legitimatised dissections, it had been constructed to give the observers the best possible view.

At the bottom of the anatomy theatre was an oval space twenty by twenty-four feet, just large enough to contain the table for the cadaver and the anatomist and his aides. William was intrigued by the continuation of the oval floor into five concentric galleries, which were for the observers. Small landings led to each one, and the top gallery, where he stood as befitted a new student—there were no seats—was hardly wider than the lowest level. Now he realised what made this anatomy theatre unique. It rose so steeply and the vision was so concentrated that he was gazing down through a funnel to where the dissection was to take place.

Matthew was on one side of him and Riolan was on the other, and as the other students crowded in around them, he felt dreadfully cramped—there were only eighteen inches of space between the front and the back of the gallery. Yet while he stood just three feet above those in the gallery beneath him, because of the structure he could see over their heads no matter how tall and bulky they were.

Everyone's eyes focussed on the entrance. Fabricius was arriving.

Four candelabra and eight candles lit the anatomy theatre, so that the flickering shafts of light gave illumination to the centre and left everything else in darkness. William was very nervous. The anatomy theatre was chilly, for it was November, and he was shivering—but he knew it was not from the cold. He was not sure he could look at the dissection, especially after what had happened with Silas. Then, to his surprise, for no one had told him about this, part of the floor rose, and he realized that there was a stone chamber underneath.

Matthew whispered knowingly, "The stone chamber is the dissecting pit. Until Vesalius, all the anatomies occurred there. But now they use it to prepare the body, then they raise it through the hole in the table."

"Look!" exclaimed William. The body was rising on the marble slab, as if from the dead, and it reminded him of Silas.

"What's wrong? You sound terrified."

"He is so young." The boy who lay there was almost as small and youthful as Silas, but not quite. He wondered if he would have to relive the anguish of Silas. Then the knife went in, and nothing stirred.

"Fabricius is a clever anatomist. He makes sure that his anatomies are dead. Before Vesalius, when dissections were forbidden here, they had a trap door through which they could drop the bodies into the canal when they were raided. Clever, wasn't it?"

"Matthew, are you afraid?"

"What for, Will?"

"The sight of the flesh, the scalpel. Aren't you nauseous?"

"Of course not!"

Yet as Fabricius continued to open the stomach and referred to the various parts which Parisano lifted up at his command, Matthew became white and sick while Mendoza whispered, "Harvey, I feel faint. Don't you?"

70

"Yes." William clutched the rail to keep from falling.

"You mustn't faint," murmured Riolan. "They say that if Fabricius sees a student faint, he forbids him to attend any more classes."

"What a waste," grumbled Hofmann. "Fabricius is making us a circle of idiots. We should study Latin and Greek so we could know Galen and Aristotle in their original tongue."

William fought to control his nausea, for Fabricius was approaching the heart, the part of the body he was interested in most, and he had never seen this organ exposed. It was still difficult to watch—he was only a short distance away from the bloody knife, and directly over it, which gave the dissection a gory reality—and he saw Matthew turn away, and Hofmann vomited, and Riolan and Mendoza stood unsteadily, but he stared on even as he grew dizzy and his nausea increased. One thing did help him. He hammered at himself to gain courage and resolution.

"I must look. For how else will I know? Now I don't even know the simple things. I must see as I look. I must study the body accurately. This is the time. I don't even know how the blood flows. Or where. Galen says, *'The venous blood is produced by the liver and then perfected by mixing with three spirits, the natural arising from the liver, the vital from the heart, and the animal from the brain.'* But I'm not sure that is true. I must read Vesalius. And ask Fabricius in class tomorrow what he thinks. This blood seems to move incessantly."

At this point he forgot his nausea as Fabricius held up the heart. It was smaller than he had expected, and yet, his mind rushed on, unique. He wondered: Can it be a muscle after all?

Then Fabricius held up his other hand for silence, the heart still in his right hand, and a hush fell on the audience, and William listened intently. The professor of medicine declared like an orator:

"*I have found valves in the veins, and a discussion of them must be preceded by an expression of wonder at the way in which these valves have hitherto escaped the notice of anato-*

*mists, both of our own and of earlier generations, so much so
that not only have they never been mentioned, but no one
even set eyes on them till 1574, when to my great delight I
saw them in the course of my dissection."*

Fabricius, with a tone of triumph, ended the anatomy. He
threw the heart down the drain.

William was upset; Fabricius didn't appear to have any idea
what these valves signified, but was concerned only with being
first. He could have stayed here all day. After what Fabricius
had said and this first view of the heart, there was so much to
learn. He knew that even though dissections would still be
difficult to endure he could now experience them without
cringing. He strode out of the anatomy theatre, determined to
find out more about the heart, while Matthew staggered out;
Riolan and Mendoza looked shaken, and Hofmann had vanished. William felt like another man. It was the first time he
was seeing the heart as it was.

That night he studied what Vesalius had written in *The
Fabric of the Human Body,* but although he read for many
hours and several candles burnt out, he found little that fur-
thered his speculations. He agreed with the Vesalius who
wrote: *"We are forced to wonder at the art of the Creator, by
which the blood passes from right to left ventricle through
pores which elude the sight."* But he was unhappy when the
anatomist appeared to contradict himself, adding in a second
edition of the *Fabrica: "In considering the structure of the
heart and its parts, I bring my words for the most part in
agreement with the teachings of Galen; not because I think
these on every point in harmony with the truth, but because,
in referring at times to new uses and purposes for the parts, I
still mistrust myself."* William stopped in disgust. Didn't Vesalius have any respect for himself? He slammed shut the *Fabrica.*

* * *

He was more optimistic as he entered Fabricius's lecture the next day. The students were told that the professor was going to speak about the valves in the veins, and William sat where he would hear best, near the podium of the great hall of the university, where the lecturer stood. It was nine in the morning, a more reasonable hour than many classes began, he reflected; most of them were between six and eight, when the students were still sleepy. Even so, he noticed that while the Aula Magna was crowded and he heard numerous languages again—although everyone was supposed to understand the teacher's Latin—many of the students were dozing as they waited for the class to start. But he felt wide awake as he admired the lavishly decorated walls with their mixture of sacred and profane art. He liked that they reflected the Venice of Titian and Tintoretto. Yet more prominent than the rich colours flooding the great hall were the banners proclaiming the glory and the sovereignty of the Venetian Republic. So with all of its reputation for freedom of conscience, he thought wryly, the students would be aware of its supremacy.

Matthew was beside him; Mendoza and Riolan, who had come later, were in the row behind; Hofmann was conspicuous in the first row, directly before the podium where Fabricius was expected to speak.

However, the professor didn't stand there, as was the custom, but stayed in his seat while his assistant conducted the class as Fabricius watched. And Parisano didn't discuss the valves in the veins of the heart. Instead, the youthful physician held up plaster models of various parts of the body and ordered the students to identify them.

Fabricius knew he no longer had to stand to express his stature as a teacher; he felt he had become a lasting monument, that his reputation would outlive the other professors. From the moment he had arrived at Padua, he had entry into the great houses of the Venetian nobility; he had studied with the best physician of his time, Fallopius; and now, like da Vinci, he bore the name of his birthplace, Acquapendente.

73

Besides, it hurt him to stand. His gouty legs no longer were fit to support his overweight body; it took a harsh effort these days to perform his anatomies; he wondered if anyone had noticed how his hands had trembled yesterday. It is work for a young, sprightly man, he thought angrily, and I am sixty-six and my hands are wrinkled, tired, and shaky. Seated, however, he could still feel like an eagle, and then he was less conscious of his shortness and fatness, and his body became impressive.

Fabricius was wishing the German students' accent wasn't so barbaric—he longed to be spared their miserable Latin—when he heard a good tone. It bore an English inflection, but the grammar was flawless. Then he heard what the student was asking. Fabricius was shocked.

The English student addressed Dr. Parisano without permission. "Sir, could we discuss the heart? The valves of the veins and their purpose?"

Fabricius rapped sharply for order, then said harshly, "Are you above the others, young man?"

"No, Your Honour, but—"

Fabricius cut him short. "What is your name?"

"Harvey, sir. From Cambridge. In England."

"You are not the first from there. But the most insolent."

"I'm sorry, Doctor, I didn't mean to offend. Sir, your discovery of the valves in the veins was such a great invention, worthy of Vesalius himself, I had to speak."

"I've done more than Vesalius," he grumbled, but he looked pleased.

"Sir, it must rank with any of the discoveries of the past. Thus, it was impossible for me to suppress my question. I'm sorry if I took a liberty, but it aroused me to the expectation of even greater things."

Fabricius beamed even as he sought to remain stern. This student, even though he was English, was intelligent. He asked the class, "Do any of you realize the value of this discovery?"

"Oh, yes, great sir!" Hofmann hurried to be first. "It is amazing!"

74

Others joined this chorus of assent, but William heard Riolan whisper contemptuously, "Now the lying begins."

William did believe it was a vital discovery, and he said, "Sir, it is the most illustrious thing I've learned so far. What does it mean?"

There was so much respect in the young man's voice that Fabricius was moved. He ordered Parisano to sit down, which irritated his assistant and added to the young doctor's anger against the student who had interrupted him, and Fabricius stood up. It was quite an effort, but as he elaborated on his discovery that the valves in the veins of the heart were like little doors, he felt younger and very remarkable.

When he finished, Harvey said, "Thank you, sir. But why?"

"Why what?"

"Doctor, I don't understand what function the little doors perform."

"They delay the passage of the blood downwards. Into the lower limbs."

"But sir, you said they opened upwards."

"Yes. They do. Does that distress you, young man?"

"No, sir. But it does confuse me."

"It should. You are a student."

As Fabricius expected, the others laughed—Hofmann loudest of all—yet William felt compelled to ask, "Sir, if the valves open upwards, is it possible that the blood is moving in the opposite direction?"

Fabricius glared at him as if he were suggesting a heresy, yet William had to pursue this inquiry one more step.

"Is the blood moving towards the heart itself, sir?"

"It is not possible."

"How can we be sure, Doctor?"

"I am sure. You are deluded."

"Sir, I didn't say it was so. But I wondered."

"It is theologically impossible. When Servetus dared to differ with divine authority, he was burnt at the stake."

"Nonetheless, sir, Servetus is honoured as a learned physician."

75

"But dishonoured by the manner of his death. Harvey, you may think yourself above the other students but your vanity can be a dangerous thing."

Yet, William thought impatiently, it is not enough to know that the valves in the veins of the heart open and close. They have another purpose, he now believed. So, in spite of Fabricius's intimidating stare, he had to venture one more question. "Sir, if the valves do open upwards, as you said, how could the blood move downwards?"

The students were horrified at Harvey's impiety, and Fabricius snapped furiously, "If you pursue this matter any further, you will be dismissed!"

William recoiled in shocked silence. As he sat down, feeling ill, he thought angrily, No one wants to take any risks.

Harvey looked in such torment Fabricius was sorry he had been so severe. He liked the respect with which Harvey had addressed him. The Englishman had better manners than the Germans. And now that his authority was reestablished, he could say, "If you pursue these matters because some day you hope to become an anatomist, there is a possible excuse."

"Thank you, sir."

"You may have natural gifts. But do not dissect humans."

"Vesalius is reputed to have done so before he became a professor."

"He stole corpses from the cemetery in the dead of night, but any student who does so will suffer the same fate as the bodies they despoil. Two students were conveyed to the Council of Ten a few years ago for stealing the corpses of criminals, and they were hanged and quartered."

A shudder went through the class, and everyone was silent, even William. He thought bitterly, Before they performed a dissection here they should seal off the heart so no one could see it or touch it.

William was startled when, after the class ended, Fabricius called him to his side. That was unusual. Then he said, "You were too insistent."

"As I said, sir, I am sorry."

"I know what you said. Did you mean it?"

"I tried, sir."

"You might be as good a student as any in the Aula Magna. But you must be more temperate. Perform dissections."

"Sir, you stated they were forbidden!"

"You are an innocent. Of course dissections on humans by the students are forbidden. But there are other ways to pursue your fantasy if you intend to risk your life and future."

"Sir, I'm not sure it is fantasy."

But now Fabricius was weary, anxious to be rid of this student whose emotion was becoming too much of a burden. He was sorry he had felt a moment of mercy; that could be a mistake. Yet when he saw the tears in the young man's eyes, he said slowly, "You may perform dissections on animals. You have a lively mind and much passion. But you must control your curiosity. Or it could lead you to the stake."

Yet William knew that now he had to explore the action of the heart.

He bought a fish at the market and studied the still-beating heart. As it pulsated before it died, it pushed out the blood. Here is something different from the teachings of Galen, he thought. Had Galen observed accurately? Or did the blood return to the heart, and through the veins?

At supper he mentioned this to his fellow students. Hofmann ignored him; Riolan said that no one was interested; Matthew was bored; Mendoza thought an experiment, if allowed, might teach them something.

"It is allowed. Fabricius gave me permission to dissect animals."

Giovanni Cattaro, a fellow student and a native of Venice, said, "Harvey, tonight is the time to rid yourself of virginity and comprehend the world."

"I know the world! I am not a virgin!"

"I can testify to that," laughed Matthew. "He lost it in Cambridge."

"It is different in Venice," said Giovanni. "Better." He bragged about the girls he had had, should have had, and could have had.

He went into such detail that William shouted, "You have no heart!"

"You are offended, friend? I didn't mean to offend, but to please, to teach you the devices of this world. And it will do you good."

"Later." There was an experiment he wanted to try, but he needed help.

When he asked the students to aid him, Hofmann stated, "It is all known. Galen wrote the heart is a churn and a furnace that heats the blood."

Matthew added, "And the lungs are the fans that cool the blood."

"Galen could be wrong," retorted William. "Galen is not a god."

"Not to believe him is heresy," said Hofmann, and he reminded William that Servetus had been burnt at the stake for stating that the blood passed from the right side of the heart to the left side.

Giovanni said, "And I know the most accommodating ladies in Venice."

Tonight, William thought, Giovanni has dressed to look particularly dashing. His dark, curly hair was unusually well combed under his broad-brimmed hat, and he wore a blue cape that heightened his good looks and prepared him for this great occasion. And William, who had not known any woman since he had arrived in Padua, had a sudden desire to join him. Yet he must pursue his experiment while it was still in his mind. Otherwise it would be lost. As Riolan, Matthew, even Mendoza joined Giovanni, William caught Matthew by the arm. Matthew was annoyed, but the firmness of William's grasp made him realize that words were superfluous. If he valued Will's friendship, he must heed him.

After the others were gone and they were alone, William tied a cord around Matthew's forearm. He made sure that the cord pressed hard enough to shut off the flow of the blood in the veins.

But he was unable to tell whether the venous valves were controlling the passage of the blood downwards to the extremities of the body, as Fabricius taught, or—as he believed—their purpose was to encourage the movement of the blood in the opposite direction. He loosened the cord so that the blood flowed naturally again in Matthew's veins, and from what he saw he was inclined to the view that it was moving towards the heart. But if this was so, Fabricius was wrong. To say this was dangerous. And he had no proof. Yet, half convinced that his suppositions could be right, he told Matthew what he was thinking.

Matthew was shocked, and he cried out, "It is inconceivable!"

"That the valves in the veins direct the blood towards the heart?"

"Fabricius taught us otherwise." Matthew wished William were not so curious. He thought fearfully, this could get them both in trouble. Now that the experiment was over, he felt sick, although it hadn't hurt. He should have gone with Giovanni; that would have been safer. And William wanted to start another experiment. Matthew retreated from his friend's clutch and said, "You must not allow the devil to take possession of you."

"That is nonsense. There is nothing sacred in the blood."

"It is a gift from God. It should not be tampered with."

"We are studying to be physicians, not priests."

"Be content with what we know already. Will, you must not go against our cherished beliefs. The liver is the central blood organ. And while Padua is freer than Cambridge, it is not that free. Your views could intensify the difficulties the

79

university is having already with the Venetian authorities, and could close us down. Pursue other business."

"Is it too late to join the others?"

"I don't think so."

Yet outside the house William felt confused. He knew he should be thinking of the women they desired to have, but he was relieved that Matthew could not find horses or coaches to convey them to Venice and they had to turn back. Now he could draw a diagram of the heart as he remembered it. That was a fit subject for his wit. He was glad that Marina had given him a room to himself. He heard the lute in the next room, and a sweet Italian song, and Matthew left him disconsolately, as if the love lyrics stirred his frustrated yearnings, but for him it was the conversation of contentment.

Then he heard someone crying out in pain. He ran to the door and he realized that it came from the next room and that it was a plea for help.

f you like my work
I will be the first
to believe you
If you don't like my work
I will be the first
to believe you . . .

Galileo, in his nightdress, stood barefoot in the hall. He looked distraught.

William, the cry still echoing in his ears, wondered what was wrong. Galileo was nervous and upset. Then the professor glared at him. "Sorry," William said. But as he started to return to his own room, Galileo halted him.

"I have never heard Marina cry before. Harvey, do you know any medicine? But, no, you cannot, you are here only a short time and prefer Aristotle."

"Sir, is she very sick?"

Galileo paused, frowned, then growled, "If I knew, would I seek aid?" He turned abruptly and started back towards the room next door.

William hesitated, thinking, Galileo had acted out ₊of fear but now his pride had become more important. Yet he heard sobs in addition to the cries, he couldn't ignore the anguish in the professor's eyes, and Marina called out, "Galileo, please do not desert me now!" William resolved to be firm, and asked, "Sir, may I view her?"

"With your book learning?" Galileo's tone was contemptuous.

"With whatever I have learned, sir."

This time it was Galileo who hesitated; then, suddenly, he shrugged, as if he had no other choice, and said angrily, "I don't know what to do! None of the physicians will come, and Marina is in great pain."

William followed Galileo into the room. Marina lay in a huge bed, in her nightdress. There were velvet draperies over the bed, curtains on the windows, wooden stools and a large oak chair, a fireplace to keep the large room warm, and candles to give light.

"I have many afflictions!" cried Galileo. "But I never expected this! She is without energy and in genuine pain."

She had thrown back her covers, she was sweating so profusely, and she was frightened.

"Harvey, do you know anything at all about medicine?"

"A little, sir."

"Nonsense! Either you do or you don't!"

He heard Marina groan, and he edged closer. Although she looked pale and wan, her body was fuller than usual.

Marina whispered, her eyes closed, "Galileo, who is it?"

"William Harvey, the English student from next door."

"Keep close to me." She opened her eyes to reassure herself.

Galileo muttered, "I had no suspicion she was ill when we went to bed."

"Sir, when did the symptoms start?"

"She complained about pains in her stomach and that they moved to her abdomen. Do you know what is wrong?" The professor was surprised.

"It is possible, sir."

"I thought it was something she had eaten, but she insists not, yet she will not tell me, not on pain of death or of excommunication."

She sobbed, "I will be excommunicated anyhow."

"Nonsense! You are but a poor peasant girl!"

"I am not poor or a peasant. I was born in Venice, and my father was well-born. I am a lady." Colour came into her cheeks with this emotion.

"All Venetians think they are well-born," Galileo muttered. "It is a curse. Young man, what are you waiting for?"

"Sir, I cannot be sure unless I examine her, and it is not allowed."

"I allow it. That is enough. Do what is necessary. I am not the Pope, to send your soul to hell. Come, hurry, before she starts weeping again. I will heed your judgement."

William studied her body, whose naked outline he could see through her nightdress. When every detail was fixed in his mind—her wide hips, her full breasts, ripe and large, her swelling abdomen—he was sure. And yet? He wavered, unable to take the final step for proof.

Galileo, who was hovering about him nervously, cried, "Go on!"

"Sir, it will require touching her."

"Then do so. She is not a sacred object. A Madonna!"

He felt her stomach to be certain he had the precise curve—and realised, with a start of joy, his hands were an instrument in themselves—and pressed softly. She winced, but did not

cry this time, although she instinctively covered her face and
breasts with a gesture of shame. He was not annoyed. She
had told him what he wanted to know.

"I'm terribly cold, Galileo," she whimpered.

"Yes, yes," said William. "You may cover yourself now."

Galileo, fidgeting, grumbled, "This is one of the longest
nights I have spent. It is the only reason I allowed you in, but
this is folly. You simply desired an excuse to fondle her. All
the students do. I see them view her with lewd eyes."

William had no intention of being dismissed now. As Galileo sought to push him out of the chamber, regretting his
previous impulsiveness, he evaded his grasp and cried out,
"Sir, don't you want to hear the truth?"

Galileo paused as if struck. "Of course I do. But you abuse
it."

"No, sir. She has been impregnated. That is what hurts
her."

Galileo was amazed. "It is impossible. I did not ask for
children."

"Her stomach and abdomen have swelled, yet there are no
signs of gas."

"Marina, am I to not enjoy any ease or quiet? Tell me he is
wrong."

She lay motionless and didn't reply.

"He must be wrong. I cannot afford more mouths to feed."
Good God, he thought, fate cannot be so malicious. Thanks
to the increase in the number of his boarders, he had been
about to buy his sister Livia bed curtains for her dowry, but
now he couldn't afford it. Is no enterprise of mine ever going
to succeed? he wondered desperately. "Harvey, I will have you
punished for making a false and slanderous diagnosis."

"No," said Marina, "it is not false, Galileo."

"He is not a physician or a midwife."

"The moon has passed without my blood running. It is a
sure sign, I have been told."

Galileo sat down as if crushed.

"It is your child. No one else has ever known me."

"Perhaps."

"Aren't you happy?" This time it was Galileo who was silent. "I haven't even thought about anybody but you."

Galileo, with a gesture of despair, stood up. "It will never be settled."

Marina added, "I am only his housekeeper. He never takes me anywhere. But I am not a courtesan."

"That is a change," Galileo said wryly. "It is estimated that there are over eleven thousand courtesans in Venice. For a population of one hundred thousand, it is an amazing number."

"You will not marry me. You sing of love on your lute, but your heart is elsewhere. In the stars."

Galileo blinked.

"I'm his disgrace. If I were a patrician woman it would be different, only he wouldn't be comfortable with her."

"Marina, now you are being theatrical. Venetian. I did not seduce you. You came to me willingly."

"You prefer the stars," she whimpered. "They are your harem."

"You do not understand. Harvey, are these the signs of labour?"

"No, just the early pangs of birth. She is months away."

"Many months?"

"Probably. It is hard to tell."

"You do not know? The doctors who consult the astrologers claim they do, that when they calculate the stars they can choose the month."

"I would not depend on such uncertain calculations."

"Neither would I. Especially since they see the stars incorrectly. Or not at all. What do you recommend as treatment?"

William remembered that his father had brought many children into the world without the loss of one, and recalled what Thomas Harvey had done and advised the anxious patient and the sceptical Galileo. "She must live in a state of felicity. Without agitation. Keep away the screamers, and then both the mother and the child should survive."

"That is sensible," Galileo agreed, while Marina relaxed somewhat.

"And keep everything clean. Use a sensible but not too large a diet. Nourish the mother and the child, but not to excess. Warm wine and good fowl that is easy on the digestion, as long as it is applied temperately."

"And logically."

"You will also need a new housekeeper. She must not work."

Galileo grew indignant. "My mother worked when she carried me."

"It is not advisable. You must hire someone to do the housework."

"I can't afford it."

"Then raise your charges."

"That means you too, Harvey."

"If she does heavy work, she risks her life and the child's."

"Don't listen to him, Galileo," she pleaded, afraid he would learn to live without her. "I have to go to the bread shop and the fish stall, and we are out of fruit and vegetables. Only I know where to get fresh anchovies, which you love."

Galileo felt betrayed by his passion for Marina, but he said, "The doctor must be obeyed."

"He is not a doctor!"

"He makes sense enough to be one. Harvey, does she need a midwife?"

"Please, not yet!" she implored. "They are a stupid lot!"

"I agree," said Galileo. "Most of the midwives are sluts who cannot earn money elsewhere. They should be trained, but they are not."

William, gaining confidence, for her pain had vanished as her anxiety lessened, said, "She doesn't need a midwife. Natural care is enough."

Galileo took Marina's hand comfortingly and sang to her sweetly, and she sank back contentedly and gradually fell asleep. Then he whispered, "Young man, you have a high regard for nature, don't you?"

"I'm convinced that it contains the cure for most ills and the chief purpose of the physician is to aid it as much as possible."

"It is my view of the heavens. Do your studies progress?"

"When I differ with Signor Fabricius's view of the venous valves, he scolds me and threatens me with dismissal. Although I may be right."

"It is dangerous to disagree. I have been waiting for reappointment for more than a year, but it continues to be deferred."

"Is it because . . . ?" William paused, not sure how to express it.

"Say it, Harvey, because of Marina. It will not affect my good name. That is gone because I dispute their blind faith in Ptolemy, although I teach his doctrines. They call me *The Wrangler* and say I am ridden with canker. And they do not like my amorous situation with Marina, although it is common in the Venetian Republic, but they call it an *irregular arrangement* and look the other way when they see her. Come, if you are interested in the course of the blood I have something to show you." He pulled William towards the door.

"But, sir, you must be very tired."

"She sleeps soundly now and will not miss us. Moreover, I have forgotten the uses of sleep. If she stirs, I will hear her."

Galileo led William upstairs to the attic, which was directly above his bedroom, and which was fitted up as a laboratory. There was an aperture in the roof and an odd instrument, which he had never seen before. It was long and narrow and pointed upwards through the aperture, and the professor strode about as if this were his Presence Chamber, and as important as any belonging to an emperor.

"This is my spyglass. There is a combination of two glasses

in this hollow tube, and its purpose is to magnify objects so they will look nearer and larger. When I improve it, I hope to verify the conclusions of Copernicus. You know who he was, I trust."

"Yes, sir. He was a Polish doctor."

"God rest his soul. Do you know he studied medicine at Padua?"

"No, sir. Most of the talk is about Vesalius and Fabricius."

"Worthy men, no doubt, but Copernicus saw beyond them. He was extraordinary." Galileo's voice became eloquent. "While he became a medical attendant to his uncle, he was also military governor, judge, physician, tax collector, vicar-general, and he reformed the coinage. But none of these gifts would interest me if he hadn't written *The Revolution of the Celestial Orbs*, in which he says the sun, not the earth, is the centre of the universe. It is of enormous consequence."

"Sir, do you agree with his findings?"

"Essentially, yes. But until I can prove it, I am laughed at." He patted his spyglass affectionately and added, "My day will come, however, when I perfect this instrument. I am not many years away. What are your conclusions about the blood, Harvey?"

"None yet, sir. I am just starting. As I am in medicine itself."

"You are observant. And have a nose for the truth. That is why I brought you here. I have no sympathy for those who *inquire not what the truth is, but what others say it is.* You do have your own mind."

"I don't think Signor Fabricius approves."

"It is the climate of the time. Aristotle stated that the universe was perfect and unchangeable, and that is what Fabricius prefers, although Copernicus contended otherwise and I am inclined to agree with him."

"Have you any proof, sir?"

"As I told you, not quite. But nature cannot refuse me her secrets forever. Then I will laugh at the extraordinary stupidity of the multitude. If you are so interested in the blood, come over here and I will show you one of my experiments with it." He took William away from the spyglass, encased in leather and on a marble stand, which fascinated the student. It was such a harmless, insignificant-looking thing, and yet the professor regarded it as if it were remarkable indeed. Galileo showed William a lamp which hung on a chain from the ceiling and swung it back and forth. Then, as the student watched intently, not certain what the professor intended, he said, "See, it moves back and forth like a pendulum, one, two, three, four."

William saw that Galileo's fingers strayed to the pulse in his wrist as he added, "I can count the pulse and the pendulum together. So many swings, so many beats, even though the distance of the swing grows less and less. The pendulum swings, the heart pumps . . ."

"*The heart pumps!*" William repeated excitedly. "Do you think so, sir?"

"That is a mystery, that is my way of speaking, and yet if I had the time I would devote myself to studying the functions of the heart." Galileo shook his head regretfully. "But I prefer mathematics. Things can be measured exactly, facts can be proven, but medicine, the treating of disease, is a blundering, uncertain sort of business."

"Signor Fabricius says it is better to leave such matters to God."

Galileo shrugged.

"Should I suppress even within myself what I have learned?"

"I cannot make you less than yourself. Only you can."

"Yet I am threatened with hellfire if I continue to question the use of the valves. Or even dare to investigate them on a human body."

Suddenly the tension, anxiety, and discomfort of the last few hours overwhelmed Galileo, and he had no energy left. I have enough of my own difficulties, he told himself wearily, without assuming any others. He grew blunt. "Young man,

you were useful in the bedchamber, but you must not lose
your piety. Good day."

However, at the door of the laboratory William couldn't
resist asking, "Sir, aren't you tired, too?"

Galileo drew himself up proudly, as if that were an inferior
emotion, and declared, "I cannot permit myself to succumb.
Now that I have another mouth to feed, I must prepare my
papers on Dante's *Inferno*. My skill in mechanics requires me
to report on its dimensions."

"Sir, should I look in on the patient?"

"It is not necessary. Now that she is no longer afraid of
dying, or of me, she will sleep soundly."

"I hope the Council of Ten will not punish you for . . ." He
halted.

"Because of the *irregular nature* of my household. Say it, it
is no secret. If they do not renew my appointment, I will
teach elsewhere. Who knows if the best men are recognized?"
He dismissed Harvey. But when he saw the student's unhappiness, he added, "As I said, the pendulum swings, the heart
beats, the blood may lead you somewhere."

"Thank you, sir. I will pursue the matter with devotion."

Galileo threw on a dark cape and a skullcap to protect
himself from the cold and the drafts, of which he had a
special horror, and said, "It is better to keep warm. But pursue your investigations, and when I begin my lectures I will
review the blood and its motion."

"Thank you again, sir." Galileo looked like an owl now,
peering into the sky, and he kept shivering, although William
didn't think it was that cold. "But suppose the authorities
don't like what you say?"

Galileo laughed contemptuously. "Intelligence is not a
common gift. If they do not like my work, let them do me the
great favor of not reading it." He shut the door to preserve his
privacy.

When William returned to his room, there was no sound
next door.

ince birth
and all through life
you try
to teach yourself how to sleep
in order to learn how to die
but then at the end
you plead for more rehearsal time

School settled into a pattern the following year: Mornings were spent at lectures; afternoons William performed dissections on animals; and evenings were devoted to the study of the texts of Aristotle and Galen, the *Fabrica* of Vesalius, and the writings of Fabricius.

William applied himself to these activities, but as the session ended in the summer of 1600, he wondered if he hadn't been too emotional with Fabricius and Galileo. There hadn't been any intimacy with them, either.

He heard that Galileo was reappointed to the chair of mathematics and that his salary was doubled, to 320 florins. Marina gave birth to a girl, whom the professor named Virginia, after his oldest sister. But there were no discussions of the motion of the blood. Instead, Galileo explained the dimensions of Dante's *Inferno*, as if to hold it up as a warning to impious students, and taught them the universe of Ptolemy. The professor acted as if the informality between them had never existed. Fabricius continued his lectures on the structure of the body and conducted one more dissection, but the heart was avoided as if it were a dangerous subject.

William felt that a curtain of silence had dropped around Padua to shut out certain subjects. He mentioned that to his friends, and the only one who responded was Mendoza. They were sitting at the dinner table, planning how to celebrate the end of the session. They were also welcoming back Marina, who was serving them after a long absence. He noticed that she approached him with averted eyes, as she had done ever since he had examined her, as if that had been shameful. Tonight, to commemorate the successful completion of the

session, she gave them fried liver, which was considered
a delicacy in the Venetian Republic, but William was more
interested in Mendoza's reply to his inquiry.

Mendoza drew him into the garden, where they would be
alone, and whispered secretively, "It is because of Bruno, who
taught here and was arrested by the Inquisition. Recently he
was burnt at the stake."

"I heard," said William. "Mendoza, many talk about
Bruno. How should his burning affect us? We are Protestants."

Mendoza gave him a strange look but said, "To the pious
an heretic is an heretic. Officially, it is said, that is why Bruno
was punished."

"Do you think there were other reasons?" Mendoza looked
so serious.

"He was burnt because he was a follower of Copernicus. It
is why Galileo is so cautious these days."

At that moment Galileo strode into the garden with his
short, vigorous walk, looking squat in his monkish robes.
When he saw the students his pleasure vanished and he looked
annoyed. He retreated to the large arbour in the rear of the
garden and sat under the trellis so that it was a sanctuary,
making it plain that he did not wish to be approached.

William, who had a strong sense of privacy, took that as a
signal to leave the garden. Nonetheless, he was upset by his
friend's opinion. On their way back to the dining room he
said, "I don't see why the burning of Bruno should affect the
professors in Padua."

"Bruno taught here. They are afraid that they will be asso-
ciated with him, especially if they criticise Aristotle."

"I criticise him. He is not infallible."

"Some think so. The Republic uses him to justify their
politics. Are you going to the Grand Carnival this evening?"

William shrugged. He yearned to go; he was tired of studying. But he resisted admitting this, and so he said nothing.

Giovanni halted him at the entrance to the dining room and
said, "Of course our studious friend is going to Venice with
us. No one with sense misses the Grand Carnival. I know

every good house on the Grand Canal." He was excited, and he wore the garb of a dashing gallant.

Riolan said, "Giovanni never does anything without a woman in mind."

"It is better than wetting one's breeches in one's dreams."

"Harvey, don't expect any nymphs. Giovanni is no scholar."

"I've had six women this year. Riolan, can you do better?"

For an instant William thought they would come to blows. Then he realized that they preferred words to blows—that was safer.

Matthew added knowingly, "Women are the best cure for our ills. Venice will be full of pleasure."

It was many months since William had visited the city, and he went eagerly. The students, led by Giovanni, approached the great square before San Marco, and he thought: Here atmosphere is all. There were lights and colours and gaiety everywhere. He saw many men and women in masks, and he wished he had worn one.

Giovanni exclaimed, "I know that young lady as well as I know my own name. Yet she is avoiding me."

He indicated a slender, tall lady in a black mask with a hood of velvet over her shoulders and a three-cornered hat on her head. What William noticed most was the grace with which she moved, and that Giovanni blushed when he saw her and looked more like a schoolboy than a courtier.

"Introduce us," whispered Matthew, "if she is so desirable."

Giovanni hurried after her, and as she was about to enter the theatre with her two linkboys, he halted her. She said she didn't know him, but when he heard her speak he was positive she did. "Nina Robusti!" he shouted. "Your father studied with mine! In the studio of Tintoretto. Are you going to deny me your beauty, too?"

"You have very little wit," she replied, "and less grace."

"You do me wrong. You do know me."

She turned away, and William, although he was attracted

by her elegant movements and her lovely voice, said, "Giovanni, our condition does not suit the lady. You must not act foolishly."

"I am not doubtful. I lodged in her father's house when I was a child. Her father and mine were colleagues. They painted together."

"Then you must have offended her."

"If I did, I pray for her forgiveness." Giovanni turned towards the masked lady, who had paused, amused by the unexpected protection of the English student. "Nina, I would know your voice anywhere."

William prodded, "Do you ask for her forgiveness?"

"Most willingly. If she will forgive me." He knelt at her feet.

She started to dismiss him and brushed her mask, and it fell off.

Giovanni cried, "I knew it was you! Nina, why did you tease me?"

She didn't reply, and William felt she wanted to avoid Giovanni. But he understood his friend's impetuosity. Nina was beautiful. Her blue eyes, fair skin, light-brown hair and full features were finely wrought. Then he felt short, for in her high heels she was taller than he was.

Giovanni wanted to join her, and she said, "I am engaged." When he insisted that she needed protection, she added abruptly, "Perhaps I do. If this English gentleman is free, possibly he will do me this service."

William felt this was intended as much to refuse Giovanni as for any other reason, but he bowed politely and said, "I will be honoured."

"Nina Robusti," she added.

Giovanni, suddenly pretending it didn't matter, muttered, "William Harvey, he is so studious you will be safe, no doubt." He strode off, affronted, the others trailing him, except for William.

Nina told the linkboys to light and to lead the way, and waited for William to join her. As they entered the theatre, she said, "The play is of little consequence, by the Roman Plautus, but my father painted the scenery, and I am eager to see whether they are using it properly."

An attendant seated them in a box over the stage.

"I have no confidence in the play, but my father's hand is firm."

The story irritated William. The lover in the comedy was swearing fidelity to his mistress while his hands strayed over her maidservants.

She asked, "Do you like the scenery?" He thought, Her father had sought to represent virtue and devoutness, but the women he had painted were sensual and pagan. "Or do you find the figures improper?"

"Not at all. They are lovely."

"My father adores the female form."

"That is evident."

"My father was called before the Inquisition for painting such figures in a religious work. They said this was heresy, and freed him only on the condition that he use these figures only in the theatre."

"They seem suitable for that purpose."

"I came to judge that. I knew Giovanni. He cannot keep his hands off a woman. He always pestered me with his attentions. It was tedious."

There was a pause while they both watched the comedy. Then it grew loud and vulgar, and she blushed and looked away.

"Come," she said suddenly, "I have seen enough." She hurried out of the theatre, assuming he would follow.

He wasn't sure he should be agreeable, yet he enjoyed her vivacity and beauty. He thought it was remarkable how much at ease he felt with her. Venetian women were reputed to possess highly developed amourous instincts. He wondered whether she did. He followed her, slowly.

Outside, she said, "My father was forbidden to go in. He had a quarrel with the management. But now they will have to pay him."

"Was that the only reason you wanted to see his painting?"

"My father wanted me to verify whether they used his work as he painted it. He was afraid that the Inquisition might prevent that. I'm going to his studio to tell him what I saw. Would you like to meet him?"

He didn't want to relinquish her company, so he nodded yes.

Escorted by the linkboys, who were in the service of her father, they reached the studio after a few minutes of walking. It was near the piazza of San Marco and off the Grand Canal, a house of ancient origin, with a red tile roof and an entrance decorated with vivid lion heads. The studio was on the top floor, the third, and they climbed a winding stone staircase and entered a sumptuously fitted chamber. The light was from the north; there were spacious windows, and a handsome balcony which looked out on much of Venice.

Her father, who was waiting anxiously for her, ignored William and asked nervously, "Did they use my Venus and Adonis?"

"They used the Venus. The male figures were left off."

Her father, who was slight, spry, grey-haired, with a long beard, sharp features, and a manner even more impulsive than Nina's, exclaimed, "At least no one is going to stop me from painting as I wish." He regarded William suspiciously and asked, "Who is this young man?"

"A medical student. A friend of Giovanni Cattaro's."

Robusti frowned. "Giovanni is untrustworthy. His mouth is loud."

"I am not a close friend, sir," said William. "Just an acquaintance."

"Do you know anything about the body? Have you done dissections?"

"I have witnessed several, and have learned a few things."

"And, of course, know what Latin will cure?"

"That is no way to treat a malady, sir. What is troubling you?"

"An excess of envy and spleen. Can you cure that, young man?"

William was puzzled, and Nina explained, "Tintoretto expelled my father from his studio as Titian expelled him. We are cousins. Robusti was Tintoretto's family name. He altered it to establish himself."

"Young man, we know you want to see her again. All students want to."

Nina cried out, "Antonio, I do not pass judgement on your acts!"

"I will go! I know your mood. But remember, he is English!"

William blurted out, "Is that a sin?"

"No. But you will want to return to your homeland. The English do." He walked out abruptly, fondling the dagger at his side.

"Your father is right about my wanting to see you again."

"Do you like him?"

"His hands are unusually long and slender, and his face is sensitive and delicate, almost too much so, almost fragile."

"You didn't answer my question."

"You are not one of my professors."

For an instant she was angry, and then she burst into laughter.

"May I see you tomorrow night? Please? I would be honoured."

"I am engaged."

"The following night?"

"It is too soon."

"A week from tonight?"

"Can you wait that long?"

"I can wait as long as is necessary."

"I could be an embarrassment to a medical student. My father is in disfavour because of the sensuality of his painting."

"Even in pleasure-loving Venice?"

Nina nodded.

"Then why don't we meet in Padua?"

That amused her, and she asked, "Are you always so persistent?"

"Only when it is what I desire. I will return tomorrow evening."

"I do have another engagement."

"Perhaps you can spare me a moment." He kissed her hand and hurried out. He also made sure that he knew her address and how to reach it.

Nonetheless, the next day was an anxious one. Giovanni wanted to know what had happened, and when he refused to tell him, although it was evident that he was interested in Nina, Giovanni said, "I doubt you will listen to me, but be careful. She is being courted by Carlo Labia, whose father is influential. They are patricians, and he is a suitor to be feared."

William recalled Giovanni's words as he approached Nina's rooms the following evening, although he assured himself that this warning was just an expression of his friend's jealousy. He was afraid that she would not be home, yet he had to keep his word. Night had fallen and the winding stone staircase to the third floor was dark, and he had to feel his way.

At the door to the studio William heard an unfamiliar masculine voice. He paused, and his anticipated enjoyment ebbed. He listened intently.

This man said passionately, "Nina, I am tired of your flirtatious ways."

She replied, "I do not flirt. I never have."

"When your sweet voice is music, when you are gowned in sensual silk! And you tell me that you do not solicit my senses and my heart!"

"Carlo, please, I have another engagement tonight, and you delay me."

William felt better now, but Carlo retorted, "You make an

appointment with me first, then inform me that you cannot see me."

"Carlo, I do not need any man's approval for what I do."

He said mournfully, "I have forgotten all my other pleasures because of you. But you will not put me off any longer."

"Do not touch me!" she cried.

"Who would you invoke? God or the devil?"

"Please?"

"My hands are as strong as your father's, even if I'm not a painter."

William couldn't endure the satisfaction in his voice, or her gasp of pain, and he ran in. Nina was seeking to pull free of a tall, dark, sharp-faced young man, whose arms were around her. When she saw William she murmured with relief, "I didn't lie. My appointment has arrived."

Carlo released her unwillingly as William approached, and his hand went to his sword, as if to use it on the intruder. Then, deciding this was not the moment for such an attack, he stood motionless. But when William bowed to acknowledge his presence and to give himself a chance to determine what to do next, Carlo, not to be outdone, bowed too, and said, "Nina, I can compose the most elegant verses to honour you."

"Which you borrow from Ovid. Signor William Harvey comes from the famous University of Padua. He studies with Fabricius."

But William realized that they were in love with the same girl.

Nina added, "Actually, Carlo, you take nothing seriously."

"I regard you with devotion."

She said sceptically, "When you prefer a little Mass in the morning, a little gamble in the afternoon, and a little lady in the evening."

"Not since I have met you, Nina. You have become my only extravagance."

However, this time, when he went to grasp her, William stepped between them and said, "Pardon me, but the lady is engaged."

Carlo scowled and said, "Signor, you come at a most inconvenient time."

"I come at the time it most suits the lady."

For an instant William thought Carlo would lose his self-control. His hand returned to his sword instinctively but when the medical student didn't cower or retreat, he hesitated.

Antonio Robusti stood in the doorway and said softly, "Carlo Labia, would you attack a gentleman without a sword?"

There was no answer.

"It is hardly the act of a Venetian patrician."

"Do not mock me, Robusti. You are in enough difficulties as it is."

"William Harvey has come to attend me, as well as my daughter."

"Since when have you glorified a student of physic?"

"Since when have you glorified constancy?"

Carlo turned to William unexpectedly and stated, "Do not trust her fair fragility, her feminine helplessness. None of it is true. She is not weak and soft, but domineering, capricious, and bad-tempered."

"Only with you," she retorted.

"You like to make me suffer. To mock me to my face."

"I am glad that one woman has learned how."

His face hardened. Then he addressed William: "You will be better off if you leave this lady alone and attend to your physic. Nina, I must go, but I will return."

After Carlo was gone Robusti said, "You must be careful, Englishman, he is mad enough with passion to venture an evil deed, and since he is one of a family that rules the Republic, he will assume it is his right."

"Giovanni Cattaro warned me about Carlo Labia."

Nina asked, "What did you tell him?"

"Nothing. He has a loud mouth and a vulgar view of women."

Robusti said, "This student is right."

"Sir, I try to be observant."

"Even in matters of the heart?"

"In all things. It is one of the things I am learning here."

This time Nina smiled as if she didn't believe him.

Angered, William pointed to a newly painted Apollo on an easel and said, "That male figure is the most accurate I have seen in a painting."

Robusti replied passionately, "Where can I find more truth! I love the human body! When my cousin, Tintoretto, was young, he dissected corpses so he could see the motion of their muscles, and he taught me to do so in the same way. Harvey, have you seen the anatomical drawings of da Vinci?"

"No, sir. I didn't know that he made any."

"He did many drawings of the heart. Are you interested in anatomy?"

"Very much. Do you think the blood is governed by the heart?"

"It is a mystery. But what I have learned is that when one is young, ardour overcomes whatever maladies that afflict us, but when we age chronic ills begin. Then the grand amour turns to dyspepsia and vertigo."

"Father?"

"I know, Nina, I talk too much. Especially when a young man attends you. At least Signor Harvey seems to possess some wit. It is a trait which eludes Carlo. He expects his wealth to command." He hurried out.

The rest of the evening was a joy for William. They sat on Nina's balcony, and she wanted to know everything about him. But much as he enjoyed her mind, which was alert and expansive, it was her beauty that fascinated him. Yet, despite his desire for her, he didn't touch her. He wanted to trust her emotion, and he sensed that Nina had the same attitude. When he left, insisting that he would return tomorrow, she didn't argue but kissed him warmly.

The next night William reached the studio just as darkness was falling. Carlo stood in the doorway with a soldier in attendance. William started to greet him, then was stupefied;

at Carlo's signal, the soldier attacked him. He backed against the wall as the assailant came at him with his hand on his sword. Yet William couldn't flee. Then, as the soldier neared him and tried to unsheath his sword, in his impatience he broke it off at the hilt. Nina dashed into the street, having witnessed the ambush from her balcony, where she had been waiting for William, and threw herself between William and the would-be assassin. Then she shouted, "Labia, you are a flea! You suck the blood without risk. You hire a bravo to fight for you, and you expect me to share your bed?"

The bravo was disgusted—his sword had cost money, and he wasn't paid for failure—and he fled before she could summon the street constables.

"Don't you ever fight for yourself?" she sneered.

Carlo strode away as if he had been violated.

Robusti arrived a moment later and told a furious William, "I should have warned you about the bravi, the hired assassins who frequent Venice. Carlo Labia is rich and powerful enough to afford the hire of a bravo to kill for him. Signor Harvey, you must be more careful."

William had no intention of giving up Nina. The passion with which she embraced him when she saw that he was safe sent his blood surging through him. "I will wear a sword," he announced. "And a dagger."

Nina trusted his feelings now, and arranged to see him in the chambers of a friend who was living in Rome at the moment. The address, near the Ponte del Vecchio, was unknown to Carlo. As she led William there, she whispered to him, "It is the Jewish quarter. The ghetto. No one will think of looking for us there. Least of all one of the Labia family."

It was a safe quarter, cut off from the rest of Venice by wide canals. The house was old, but the studio, which her father had used as a refuge when he had been threatened by the Inquisition, was large, warm, and cheerfully comfortable.

The night they came together he couldn't think of anything else. He was unable to tell whether he was the first; then she gave him such delight it didn't matter. He was glad that she took the kind of precautions that led him to believe that they would not need a midwife.

When it came time to part, she said, "Now that you love me—do you think it madness, not worth the risk?"

"Nina dear, you have given me the greatest happiness I have known."

"And am I well wrought?"

"Apollo would have approved and done you reverence."

"I was the Venus for my father."

"Your own father?" He was shocked.

"There was no incest. It was my outward self he used."

William consoled himself. If he was not the only one to view the splendours of her body, he was the only one to enjoy its loving. Of that he was almost sure. He wondered if he had all of her love. She had not responded with sighs or tears, but as if they had made a bargain.

Nina asked, "Will I see you tomorrow evening?"

"Tomorrow and every night I can travel here until my studies start."

he greatest and the smallest
Are of a like kind
And they have that in common
The greatest being only one
And the smallest being only one
of the greatest number there are

By the time school resumed, William and Nina were passionately in love. She felt he had risked his life for her, and he didn't question this view. He felt safer now that he wore a sword and dagger and took fencing lessons with Giovanni, who was pleased with William's natural quickness and skill.

Nina was upset that when classes began he saw her only occasionally, but he refused to relinquish any of his studies for her, although that was her wish. Finally, not liking that she was excluded from this part of his life, she suggested that they visit her father at the studio.

She told William, "He is interested in anatomy, and he is eager to discuss it with you, since it is an interest of yours too."

But William, although he liked Antonio Robusti and longed to ask him where he could view Leonardo da Vinci's drawings of the heart, approached the studio near the piazza of San Marco hesitantly. He feared that Carlo still intended to ambush him, and he didn't trust Nina's motives. And he was surprised by Robusti's first question. He had just greeted the painter, and he wanted a minute to look at Robusti's newest canvas, a female nude, to see if it was Nina, when the painter blurted out, "Harvey, can you obtain a female cadaver?"

"Sir, I'm not sure I understand you."

"Your Italian is excellent. Don't you want to understand?"

"It is against the regulations. No dissection is allowed unless the professor of anatomy is in attendance."

"Vesalius stole cadavers so he could perform his anatomies."

"He was the professor of anatomy."

"It is still being done, but you are afraid." Robusti turned away from William in disgust.

Nina looked disgusted too, and William said hurriedly, "Sir, I love the human body as you do, but if I am caught I will be expelled or worse."

Robusti sneered. "The authorities' threat of punishment is a joke. They know Leonardo and Michelangelo stole bodies so they could learn anatomy. It is a common practice among the better painters. Look!" He pulled William over to his canvas to view his opulent Venus. "The muscles of the pubic regions are wrong. Unless I can examine carefully, I will never get them right. Yet this must be a virtuoso expression of anatomy, my masterpiece, not another copy of the idealized female. Don't you want to see the drawings of Leonardo?"

"Very much, sir."

"Some are in the university and are based on his direct observation. But for me to obtain them is a risk."

Nina added, "As great as you would take, William."

He was tempted, yet he still wavered. The idea of stealing a corpse repelled him, although he knew it was done.

Robusti said, "Vesalius spent long hours in the cemetery turning over bones. It is a common quest in Padua. This is one of the few medical universities where it is done. Isn't that why you came here, Harvey?"

"I came . . ." He halted. I do not owe anyone an explanation, he thought angrily, not even Nina. "Sir, that is my concern, not yours!"

"He is a coward, daughter," Robusti said sadly. "He is like most of the doctors. They quote Galen and Aristotle and keep a safe distance from the dissections and know nothing of anatomy. You are a fool to flatter him with your affection. He is not even interested in the greatest draughtsman of all, Leonardo. Harvey, do you think da Vinci begged permission from the Pope when he dissected thirty cadavers?"

"I think he did what he had to do." William turned to go.

Nina cried out, "Then you don't intend to help my father?"

"What will you do if I don't?"

"Please! Please!" Robusti said impatiently. "I have no intention of interfering in your business. I will find my cadavers elsewhere."

Nina was not conciliatory as she stood before the canvas, and now William was sure she hadn't posed for this Venus. The nude was heavier than Nina, and resembled Titian's work, although he realized it would be fatal to say so. He replied, "I will return tomorrow evening with my answer." By then, he thought, I might find out whether any cadavers can be obtained, and whether such an endeavor would be risky.

At dinner the next afternoon—on Sunday the big meal was in the middle of the day—the students assembled to learn from one another's experiences. There was no sign of Galileo, who usually ate alone, and Marina had a maid to help her serve now. When William brought up the subject of anatomies and wondered where bodies could be obtained, for the first one of the term was due soon, Giovanni announced, "I have been assigned that duty by Fabricius." He took a scroll from his doublet and read: *"Let the professor of anatomy choose a student to assist him who has studied for at least two years and, if possible, who has seen other anatomies. And let it be his duty to see that the instruments and other things are provided and to collect the bodies for those wishing to watch the anatomy."*

Giovanni paused, waiting for their congratulations, but Hofmann was envious, Riolan was sceptical, Mendoza looked disappointed, as if he had expected to get this post, and Matthew whispered to William, "I didn't want it. It's a dirty business. Cadavers can be hard to find."

William told Giovanni, "You should be pleased. It is an honour."

"I know." His friend beamed proudly.

"But isn't it very difficult to obtain cadavers?"

"That depends. At the moment the Council of Ten is in a merciful mood, so hangings are scarce and there are no bodies available, but let there be a threat to the state, or have such a crisis created, even if it is imagined, and there will be subjects for our anatomy table. And there are other ways of obtaining cadavers. Have you seen Nina Robusti lately?"

William shrugged noncommittally.

"What is worrying you? You look distracted."

William drew Giovanni into the garden so they could talk

privately. He saw Galileo sitting nearby, deep in thought, and he said softly, not wanting to disturb him, "I've been wondering about cadavers."

"You want one for yourself?" Giovanni was surprised.

"Not for myself, but a friend is interested. Would that be possible?"

"Anything is possible in Venice. See me after our first official dissection, which is in several weeks, and I will know better."

This increased William's haste as he returned to Robusti's studio that evening. My effort should please Nina, he reflected, and prove that I am not a coward. It was dark when he reached the entrance, and he didn't see Carlo lurking in the doorway. The patrician, who was alone, as if to prove his bravery, attacked him with his sword. William recoiled and Carlo, in his eagerness and nervousness, missed his aim and ran his sword into the wall of the house. This blunted the point of his weapon and bent his blade, but he was too excited to notice that. William, his own sword drawn now, easily thrust aside Carlo's clumsy lunge. But this only aroused the patrician more. In his rage, as he hurled himself at William, he slipped and fell on the wet stone, and as he did he cut himself with his own sword, and fainted at the sight of his own blood. William was surprised that Carlo regarded the blood as an enemy; to him it was a friend, the sustainer of life, and he hurried to Carlo's side to revive him.

"Water in the face will help," Nina said coldly, standing nearby.

She appeared from upstairs with her father; they had witnessed the attack without saying a word. "Antonio, should we duck Carlo in the canal?"

"His father would mind. And Pietro Labia is one of the Council of Ten. Harvey, did you find out anything about the cadavers?"

"Yes. But first I must tend Carlo before he loses too much blood."

"It is just a slight wound," Nina said contemptuously. "Yet you must act the physician, William, whatever the circumstances."

When William revived Carlo, the patient was sure he intended to kill him. William reassured him, "It is just a flesh wound, it will heal quickly."

Carlo whimpered, "It is a terrible thing, a family failing, the sight of blood, especially my own, makes me faint. My father and grandfather suffer from this affliction, too. I saw this happen to both of them. Harvey, can you cure me? I have tried the most learned astrologers, but they say that I have been born under the wrong star."

William said, "It is in your mind. It is your fear."

"I am not afraid!" Carlo struggled to his feet, looking for his sword.

Robusti said, "One word about this and the disgrace will be shameful."

Carlo cried out, "Tell no one, please, it will be unbearable!"

"If you leave us alone from now on."

"I promise, Robusti. And you too, Harvey."

Nina added, "You could enter the church, which would please God."

Carlo muttered, "I am trained to be a patrician." He limped away.

William asked, "Signor Robusti, do you think Carlo will keep his word?"

"It is hard to say, but he may. Will you be able to get any cadavers?"

"It is hard to say," William couldn't resist replying, "but I may."

"That is no answer."

"When will I see the drawings of Leonardo?"

"When you fulfill your part of the bargain."

After Robusti was gone, Nina was not her usual passionate

self. When William tried to make love, she was so distracted he had to ask her what was wrong. This annoyed her, and she retorted, "I suffer because of *your* precious heart and blood. You put them ahead of everything. Even us."

Yet he couldn't halt his investigations. At the next anatomy, he asked Fabricius for a moment alone. The professor granted the favour hesitantly; it was against his principles, but he liked Harvey's wit and thoroughness.

Fabricius didn't move from his chair, from which he had conducted this anatomy while Parisano had performed the dissection. As William sought to formulate his words properly, he thought, This was unsatisfactory: Parisano was crude, more the butcher than the skilled anatomist, and Fabricius was becoming old and feeble, and his lesson stressed Galen's *On the Bones*, with only a few references to Vesalius's *Fabrica*. The professor was careful not to find any errors in Galen, although the *Fabrica* revealed many errors, and so there was little to learn.

Giovanni puttered about the anatomy table, curious as to what Harvey desired to ask, and Fabricius shouted at him, "You can dispose of the remains later! You are a student still, not a physician!"

Giovanni strode out, muttering to himself, while the mutilated corpse lay between Fabricius and William. But William couldn't allow this to deter him, for it could also lead him to the truth, and it gave him the courage to say: "Sir, I hear that da Vinci has done drawings of the human body which are remarkable for their knowledge of the anatomy."

"You are young, restless," grumbled Fabricius, "with too much energy."

"I have been told that Leonardo's drawings are quite precise and that some of them are in the university. Is that true, sir?"

"You are too curious. It could cause you much trouble."

"I hear Da Vinci made discoveries about the structure of the heart."

Fabricius replied sternly and reprovingly, "Young man, the heart is meant to be understood by God alone."

"Sir, could I see da Vinci's drawings?"

"No. It is against the rules."

"But, sir, I could learn from them."

Fabricius said curtly, "You exhaust me. I've no more time to spare. The rector is ill and needs my services."

Fabricius left to examine the rector. At the bedside—which was a great concession, for he rarely visited his patients; he believed an eminent doctor lowered himself by such a practice —he told his anxious patient not to worry, he had all the remedies he required. He gave the elderly, nervous rector a profusion of herbs, drugs, and ointments in large doses to improve his appetite, to moisten his digestion, and to clear his blood. When the rector became worse, Fabricius resorted to his favourite remedy, bleeding. By the thirteenth bleeding the patient had succumbed.

William's disappointment in Fabricius grew when the professor told the students there would be no more dissections now; because of the tranquillity of the Republic, there were no cadavers. Thus, William was receptive to Giovanni's suggestion that the students perform a dissection themselves.

"But how?" he asked, remembering how difficult it was to get cadavers. He was part of a group of students standing on the Piazza del Bo. It was winter now, and William shivered from the cold. Yet no one moved as they waited for Giovanni's reply. He noticed that all the students were intent: Riolan, Mendoza, Hofmann, Matthew, and some new ones, including several from Cambridge. "It is said no cadavers are available."

Giovanni retorted knowingly, "There are ways."

"Do not ask," Riolan added, "but assemble here two nights hence."

Giovanni concluded, "As Fabricius's assistant, I possess the keys to the anatomy theatre and to the instruments, and I will perform the anatomy."

"Maybe I will obtain a cadaver after all!" Robusti exclaimed after William told him about Giovanni's plan. "I will attend. Masked, as is the custom, and as all the students should be so they cannot be exposed. If I cannot get a body, at least I can view one." He refused to allow Nina to join them in spite of her insistence until she agreed to disguise herself in male attire and to wear a mask, and William assured him that Giovanni had said the cadavers would be female.

Giovanni had implied to William that he had a special reason for this, but he hadn't told him why. Then William was angry at himself, for only when he was about to leave did he remember to ask Robusti, "In return for this favour, will I see Leonardo's drawings?"

"Of course," said the painter, "if I see the right cadavers."

At the Piazza del Bo everyone wore masks. There were no guards about, and William was told that they had been bribed. The immediate concern was the cadavers. Giovanni, who had arranged everything, asked for volunteers to aid him in this task. No one responded, but then, as William sensed Nina's contempt, although she stood in the shadows with her father, looking like his young male companion in her doublet, breeches, and mask, he joined Giovanni. This caused Matthew, Riolan, Mendoza, and several of the new students who were eager to be accepted to follow him.

Giovanni ordered Matthew and Mendoza to go to the cemetery of San Pisano and, handing them the keys to a burial monument, said, "You will fetch the body of a pretty twenty-year-old girl of noble birth, who is thought to have been poisoned. But my dissection will show that she died for other reasons."

"Isn't this dangerous?" Matthew asked apprehensively.

"No. They will never expect us to take a body from a locked grave. Now hurry, I will expect you back soon."

After they were gone he assigned Riolan to lead the others into the anatomy theatre, except for William, Hofmann, and two of the new students. He took this group to the Church of San Antonio and went to the chapel with the painting of St. Luke surrounded by kneeling students. Giovanni said with satisfaction, "This is dedicated to our patron saint, St. Luke, and fits our purpose." He commanded William to lift up the lid of the coffin which had been put there just a day ago. William obeyed reluctantly, and he felt worse when he saw a middle-aged nun inside.

"Take her out," Giovanni ordered. "Hofmann, help him. You brag about how strong you are. Come on, she won't hurt you. She's dead."

"What about her soul?" murmured Hofmann.

"It is already with God," said Giovanni. "Hurry, we have much to do."

He told the two new students to watch the nun, who was placed on top of her coffin, and he hurried into the vault below. As he lit the way with his candles, he directed William and Hofmann to extricate another newly buried body from a tomb and said, "This is a young prostitute who also died suddenly. These cadavers will give us an excellent opportunity to study the uterus and the hymen."

When they returned to the anatomy theatre with their cadavers, Riolan put everything in order. The body of the young noblewoman was placed on the slab, as if even in death she had precedence, and Riolan, on Giovanni's instructions, arranged a ring of candelabra around the pit. The other two corpses were laid on the floor, which left little room for anyone but Giovanni and Riolan, who was acting as his assistant.

Giovanni was proud he was well prepared. Texts of Vesalius's *Fabrica* and Galen's *On the Bones* were on the table, where he could use them if necessary; there were knives, saws, razors, needles, and a pair of scissors.

William saw Robusti standing in the first row with the

students; he didn't recognize Nina at first, she looked so much like a student, and then he realized it was she by her long white hands, which gripped the wooden rail to keep from fainting. This wasn't unusual and didn't attract any attention; many students fainted when they saw a dissection.

Giovanni, who was proud that he never sickened at the sight of flesh, announced, "Fabricius will not cheat us. He says there are no cadavers, but the real reason is the cost. Riolan, is someone on guard outside?"

"The two new students from Cambridge who brought the nun."

"Good. Now, Riolan, I will prove I was right." He cleaned the young noblewoman of her pubic hair and then dissected her uterus as he said, "Solely for the sake of her hymen. If Fabricius will not show us these parts, we shall see them for ourselves. Riolan, it is as I thought. This girl was not poisoned. Her hymen is not entirely whole."

Riolan remarked caustically, "So she was not a virgin. As was assumed. That is not unusual. Even among noblewomen. Especially in Venice."

"You don't understand! This girl ripped her hymen without the intervention of a man."

"Giovanni, are you certain that this killed her?"

"I will prove that with my dissection of the other cadavers. Hofmann, release the trap door. We will drop her into the canal. Many have been buried there, and the body will not be recognized now."

He continued the same procedure on the nun while everybody waited for what he would find. William squirmed uneasily, yet he couldn't leave; he felt that would shame him in the eyes of the others, particularly Nina, and he was curious about what Giovanni would discover.

Giovanni dissected the uterus until he reached the hymen, and then he exclaimed, "She is as I expected. Her ovaries are shrunken, as happens in organs that are not used. I have dissected a virgin."

After this body had been disposed of in the same way as that of the noblewoman, he turned to the prostitute. He dissected with even more care and industry, and when he came to the uterus and the hymen he proclaimed triumphantly, "She is as I thought. Her ovaries are swollen from constant use. She is the only one who is not malformed. Riolan, I won our wager."

"What wager?" cried William, shocked.

"Harvey, I am not an ignorant surgeon. I had a wager with Riolan that the ovaries in these three females would be different, and he disagreed. Hofmann, release the trap door. She belongs in the canal with the others."

"No!" declared William. "There is more to be done on this anatomy!"

"You wish to fondle it?" Giovanni asked contemptuously.

"More can be learned. You dissected only the pubic regions."

"It was all that was necessary. Riolan, pay me."

The loser reluctantly handed the victor the scudi and strode out angrily. For a moment Giovanni stood by the cadaver of the prostitute, as if to deny William's request, and then he shrugged and said, "If you want to take the risk, it is on your own head. But be sure to clean up when you finish, so no one knows that we have been here. Otherwise, the scandal might cause us all to be expelled. You also, despite your learning and wit."

A minute later William was alone with the partly dissected cadaver, except for Nina and Robusti, whose excuse to the departing students was that they were Harvey's guests and thus were obligated to remain. But as he ignored them in his passion to explore the anatomy of the heart, Robusti shouted in vexation, "I thought you wanted this cadaver for me!"

"Examine it if you wish. I have work to do."

Robusti joined William at the side of the prostitute—Nina, stricken with horror, couldn't look—and said disgustedly, "That friend of yours, Giovanni, destroyed the parts I desired to see. You haven't kept your part of the bargain. There is nothing left here for me to paint."

"What about your promise to show me Leonardo's drawings?"

Robusti muttered, "Nothing good comes from too much trust. I have learned little here. I cannot risk stealing the drawings. Come, Nina."

She waited for William to join them. When William, fascinated by the cadaver, remained beside it, she snapped sarcastically, "Go in! Go in! I can always find a new favourite if I wish to." She left with her father.

He couldn't follow Nina. Here was a full-grown human, only recently dead, vitally worth looking at. He might not obtain such a grand chance again. The cadaver called urgently, "Come closer, familiar young man."

Robusti had grumbled on his way out, "These idiot students would dig up the sacred bones of Livy and Petrarch, who are buried in Padua, for a few scudi," but the painter didn't realise how important this anatomy could be.

The prostitute's features were still young and beautiful, and William thought she might have been poisoned, as was rumoured. His attention turned to her pubic region, where men had enjoyed sensual pleasures and had treated her as if the final good of her body lay therein, and none of it was intact. These parts, which had enriched her with gold and with a tomb of marble, were mutilated. He heard the bell in the bishop's tower toll the hour of four, and he realized it would be morning soon and there was no time to mourn her fate. The guards would be back with the dawn, and he had to hurry. Yet with all of his desire to explore her heart, he hesitated.

Nina had needed a last word, too, and had sneered on her departure, "You will be alone with her and her ghost could haunt you, and you have no power to exorcise it. Only the Church has prayers for exorcism."

She assumed he shared the common beliefs about the spirits

of the dead. He wasn't sure he did, although from childhood he had been taught that when the dead were torn from their graves, demons, servants of the devil, followed. Yet no one else could tell him what he should or should not do. As William stood there he asked himself, Is this mysterious part of man's universe the seat of sensation, the guiding force behind all of human behaviour, as Aristotle had maintained? Or is the heart just a pump?

He picked up a clean knife to cut open the cadaver at the point where the heart was located, and he felt as if he were embarking on a voyage of discovery. He covered her face so that it wouldn't distract him, and as he came to her heart he prayed that she would forgive him. Then he extracted her heart tenderly.

He stared intently at what he held. It was the first time he had handled a human heart and seen it so close. Nowhere else in the world, he thought, could I find such an opportunity. In this instant he was glad he had come to Padua. But he was confused. Aristotle had stated that the number of ventricles in the heart varied with the size of the person, but that most people possessed three, yet this heart had two, as had all the hearts he had seen. He noticed that the septum of the heart was denser and more compact than any other portion of the body except the bones and the sinews. How could the blood pass through such a thick substance as this? Yet this was what Galen had taught, and what everyone seemed to believe. The septum was so solid William couldn't see how even the smallest particle could be transferred through it from the right to the left ventricle. He shook his head with doubt, then despair. Perhaps the motion of the heart was to be comprehended only by God. Yet as his hands fondled the heart, he thought it felt like a muscle; it could be a pump.

At that moment the candles flickered and burned blue. A cold wind blew through the room, and he wondered if a demon was present. He regretfully but quickly dropped the cadaver into the canal. He made sure that the anatomy theatre was precisely as they had found it. As he eased the heart through the trap door, he prayed for her. And that God would be good to her. Better than man had been. He prayed with reverence.

The next time William saw Nina was at their refuge near the Ponte del Vecchio. It was the Sunday after the midnight dissections, and when he asked whether her father had been able to obtain Leonardo's drawings of the heart, she replied that she had more important matters to discuss.

She led him to the high Venetian windows that opened on the canals. She felt it was an appropriate moment to say what was on her mind, for Venice had transformed William. He was no longer as beardless as a boy, or short-haired. Now he wore a trim, neat beard which fitted his pointed chin, a thick, carefully groomed mustache, and his hair was long and cut below his ears. His dagger was sharp enough to slice meat, and his sword was easy to handle, yet strongly constructed. He looks the gentleman, she observed approvingly, with his padded doublet, puffed sleeves, short hose, bright garters, and fine cape. He was dressed to please her, and yet some things, she knew, had to be clarified.

Before William could say a word, she started the speech she had prepared: "Carlo has offered me jewels from Alexandria, furs from Scandinavia, cloth from Flanders, and what do you offer, William?" She halted his protestations of love and added, "Carlo's father is able to use the dockyards of the Arsenal, which has made Venice a city of ships. Wouldn't your father want you to establish a trading post here?"

"He has written me about such a possibility."

"If he did, you could remain here in Venice."

"What about your father's promise to show me Leonardo's drawings?"

"He meant it, but only selected members of the faculty can view them. Why don't you ask Fabricius to show them to you?"

"I did. He refused."

"If you stayed here, I'm sure you would get to see them eventually."

"Stay in what capacity, Nina?"

"You could practice medicine in Venice, teach in Padua, and represent your father's interests here and earn handsome profits for both of you."

He said, "It is possible. But I will need more time to decide."

Pleased, Nina strove to speed his decision with all of the skill at lovemaking that she possessed, and it was considerable.

Yet he was not content. Nina made him feel vital, but he no longer believed there were three ventricles in some hearts, as Aristotle said.

In Galileo's class—as Bruno's burning faded into the past —he heard the professor question Aristotle again. This gave William the courage to ask Galileo to obtain the anatomical drawings of Leonardo da Vinci.

Galileo replied sharply, "So you can flout the authorities?"

"So I can question Aristotle accurately, sir, as you do."

"And what will you learn then?" Galileo asked critically.

"Whatever I can, sir."

William's downhearted look reminded Galileo of the trials he had endured searching for the truth, and he said, "You think I have no heart?"

"Sir, I think you may be afraid to offend the authorities."

"I know what you did at the anatomy theatre."

"Sir, that is not quite as it sounds."

"Did you learn anything from the cadaver? Anything worth the risk?"

"I learned that Aristotle could be wrong about the heart."

"Your scepticism may be useful. I will see what I can do."

Galileo obtained the drawings, which were in the university library, saying, "They won't be missed for a few days, there

117

are thousands of volumes in it, the glory of our world. You can view them in my laboratory, where you will not be disturbed." He led William to the attic, where there was a new spyglass. "I hope you find what you are looking for."

Leonardo's drawings fascinated William. The artist's view of the heart was the most accurate and comprehensive he had seen. Leonardo had been especially concerned with the valves of the heart. His valves turned upwards, as if the blood moved back to the heart. Yet in Leonardo's notes, although he drew the septum as solid enough to be a barrier, he wrote in support of the belief that the blood passed from the right ventricle through the septum into the left ventricle. This added to William's confusion, and to his determination to follow his own conclusions.

He said this to Galileo when he returned the drawings, and the professor replied, "I hope this teaches you to trust your own eyes."

"It has made me more sceptical of some of the things we are taught."

When William was ordered to appear in Fabricius's office a few days later, he was afraid that the midnight dissections had been discovered and that he was about to be punished, perhaps expelled. Instead, Fabricius asked him what he was studying.

"The heart, sir. I have proof it has two ventricles, not three."

"Your persistence could cause you difficulties."

"They are the findings of Vesalius, sir."

"And of Leonardo. Why don't you study generation? Your dissection of animals is skillful. Who showed you Leonardo's work? *The Wrangler?*"

"Why should he do such a thing, sir?"

"I esteem him as a mathematician, but I find his lack of caution distasteful, and he ridicules those who don't agree with him."

"Sir, do you agree with him?"

"He has not proven that Copernicus is correct. He should leave such assumptions to the Church. The heavens are God's domain."

"Sir, Leonardo's suppositions are my own, too."

"You mustn't suppose, you must know." Fabricius looked at the university papers on Harvey to confirm that he was a native of Folkestone and a graduate of Cambridge. Then he added, "However, I congratulate you. You have been appointed Councillor for the English Nation."

"I am honoured, sir. What are my duties?"

"You will speak for the medical school and my anatomy theatre."

"Is that all, sir?"

"This could lead to becoming a professor here. As Vesalius did. But first you must practise with a famous physician for a year."

"With you perhaps, sir?"

"An excellent idea. We must make sure that you visit the sick in our hospitals. It is one of the most useful instructions we have created."

"An instruction I'm looking forward to, sir."

"Was it *The Wrangler* who showed you the drawings of Leonardo? I will not harm you if you tell the truth, and it will help you become a professor."

"Sir, will I be able to speak for the other students now?"

"Within reason. Harvey, you are a stubborn man. It could cause you many difficulties."

William told Galileo how Fabricius had questioned him, and Galileo was pleased that the student had held his tongue. He confided, "I dispute many of their cherished beliefs. I doubt that the earth is the centre of the universe, but when I suggest that I am reviled. But as my studies progress, I should be able to settle that issue. I improve my spyglass constantly, and one day I should see the heavens as they truly are."

Galileo took William into his attic and asked him to gaze through his newest spyglass. But while William could see the moon more clearly, and the stars were distinct, they looked only a little larger than before.

Galileo cried out, "Do you see?"

"Not very much, sir."

"I'm close but not close enough."

"Sir, when do you estimate that will be?"

"God's wonders aren't revealed in a day. But think what it will be like to see the marvellous things in the heavens, to be the first to reveal His wonders. To know them accurately. To see them as they truly are!"

Galileo's voice took on a note of exaltation, and his eyes glowed.

Then he said, sadly now, "If they don't order me to desist."

"Why should they, sir?"

"Do the authorities encourage you to pursue your independent inquiries about the nature of the heart and the motion of the blood?"

"No, sir."

"They prefer Aristotle's views. They are more comfortable with them."

"So much is mysterious. Sir, it is unfortunate."

"Not mysterious, but unknown."

"That is the way I feel about the blood. You say the earth moves; I believe the blood does, too. Perhaps in the same way, around and around."

"It is possible."

"But I have no proof, sir."

"Neither have I. Yet. That is why I must improve my spyglass."

William sighed. "I wish I had that kind of an instrument to examine the body. As you desire something that makes distant objects larger, I need something that will make objects closer. In the body itself, that would show the structure of the very drops of the blood."

"It would be wonderful."

"Sir, it won't work."

"Harvey, what gives you that mournful idea?"

"Whichever way I turn, I feel my path is blocked."

"If you feel that way, you are not in love."

"Is that necessary, sir?"

"With whatever you pursue to an irrevocable end. Did Fabricius offer you the bribe of a professorship?"

"It was suggested, sir."

"Are you accepting it?"

"It has advantages. And you are a professor, sir."

"Only because I have to support a family. Think carefully before you accept. I wish I didn't have to teach. Have you learned much of value?"

"I have learned there are many errors in the search for truth."

"Even in my teachings?"

"Sir, I don't know enough about the heavens to question you."

"You will criticise me when it suits your advancement. Yet I have proven Aristotle wrong. As Leonardo proved that Aristotle was wrong about the heart."

"Leonardo was wrong too, sir. He didn't go far enough."

"Did anybody, in your opinion?"

"No, sir," William said sadly. "Not even Vesalius, who went further than anybody else. He stopped on the verge, like the rest."

"And gave up his professorship finally. As I should if I were wise."

"Sir, then you think that I should return to England?"

"That depends on what direction you wish to travel."

This wasn't the reply that William desired, and he turned to depart.

"Besides, Harvey, all men of sense are of the same religion."

"What is that, sir?"

"No man of sense tells."

By 1602 and the end of William's studies at Padua, he was certain that he had learned some things about the heart and the motion of the blood that were not being taught at the university. This gave him the courage to bring his conclusions to the attention of his fellow students. He told them that Fabricius was wrong, that the valves of the veins indicated they aided the blood to return to the heart.

Fabricius had finished the last dissection of the term, and all that was left was approval for their medical degree, and William and his friends had remained in the anatomy theatre to discuss their prospects.

Riolan mocked, "Harvey, your idea is preposterous!"

Hofmann shouted, "You mustn't say such things, or even think them!"

Matthew warned, "Will, you could lose your degree for what you said."

"No one dares to heed you," Mendoza added. "The risk is too great."

"It is indeed," said Giovanni. "Are you applying for a teaching post?"

William was silent. He had promised Nina that he would speak to Fabricius about this, but now he couldn't. He strode out angrily.

He had an appointment to take her for a gondola ride while he told her what had happened with Fabricius. But when he arrived at her rooms he didn't go in, but paced outside, trying to decide what to do. The more he pondered, the more he realized that Venice was not the place he wanted to make his future. Yet he had to face her.

Nina was upset that William was late, but she waited until they were in a gondola to ask, "What did Fabricius say?"

"I wasn't able to talk to him."

"Why not?" She regarded him suspiciously.

"He was busy, and so was I."

"I don't believe you. You didn't even try. That is why you are late."

He thought, They were in the sumptuous, floating world of Venice, and he had spent more money for this gondola than he could afford, yet his father would help him if he stayed, provided he was part of his father's business. And Nina had become as gilded and opulent as this pleasure-loving city.

She sensed what he was thinking, and she said, "I dress as befits my position. It is sensible to attract attention to one's virtues. It is Venetian."

He liked the way she adorned her lovely breasts, her voluptuous body, her long legs. But Venice didn't have the answers he sought.

"Will, you've fooled me. You promise but you never keep your word."

"I tried, I swear I did. But I can't. Venice can be beautiful, and it is different from anything I have known. Here the freedom and the way of life often is admirable, perhaps unique, but I can't stay."

"I could make you stay!" she flared furiously.

He stared at her uncomprehendingly, then looked incredulous.

"I could be pregnant by you."

"But we took precautions. You said you knew how."

"What will you do if I am?"

He shrugged but he grew pale.

"Would you submit?"

"Nina, I would not desert you."

"Would you marry me?"

"If it was necessary."

"As a Catholic?"

"No." He was positive now. "I cannot wed in a faith that is not my own." His voice hardened, and he sat stiffly, unable to touch her.

For an instant she seemed to laugh; then she was sobbing,

and she couldn't stop as she cried out, "My father warned me that you would want to return to England, but I didn't believe him. I thought I could keep you here."

He was homesick for his family, even as he knew he would miss her very much, and he had to move on—his imagination was fired by Leonardo and Galileo and his own discoveries—and he was eager to continue his explorations. Yet he said, "I will return," but as he embraced her, she wrenched free and shouted, "You are not staying, no matter what I say!"

"I would if you were pregnant."

"But you know that I am not!"

"Are you, Nina, dear?"

The yearning to say yes was almost more than she could endure, yet she sought to sound cold as she said, "You mean you would give me preference even over your medical speculations?"

"When you need it."

"Do you think I am more important than they are?"

"Each thing I love has its own value."

"I am not a thing!" she exclaimed passionately, unable to remain cold. "William, do you wish to separate from me?"

"Would you come to England with me?"

"Never!" When she saw his hurt look, she added hastily, "I couldn't endure the bad weather, being Catholic in a Protestant country. Don't worry, I'm not a crafty woman who feigns pregnancy to hold you. Yet if you loved me, you wouldn't think of leaving me."

"Nina, I do love you. But I must return to my native land."

A week later William, as Councillor for the English Nation, was part of the brilliantly clothed procession which was the centre of the ceremony that was installing a new rector for the university. It was an affair of great magnificence, but he felt like a bird in a cage.

The moment that mattered was the day he received his degree as a doctor of medicine. It was April 25, 1602, and as he was handed his elaborately illuminated diploma, he sighed with relief.

Dr. Johannes Thomas Minadous, Professor of Medicine, declared: *"We will now solemnly decorate and adorn the noble William Harvey, with the accustomed Insignia and ornaments belonging to a Doctor."* He gave him a book of philosophy and medicine, put a golden ring on his finger, and placed on his head the cap of a doctor. The professor announced: *"As an emblem of the Crown of Virtue."* Then he bestowed on William Harvey the Kiss of Peace with the Magistral Benediction.

Nina watched the graduation ceremony, hidden so that William couldn't see her. He is clever, she thought, but too restless, too inquiring for his own good. And now our affair is over. He is returning to his roots. Then he seemed to be coming in her direction, and she fled. William wanted to speak to Giovanni, who had accepted the post he had considered.

When he found his friend, who was joyful at having been honoured, he said, "Congratulations, you will make an excellent anatomist, probably better than I would. You are good with a knife, and you will be impersonal, you will regard the body simply as an object to be examined."

"You could have had this position if you wished. You were the best student in our class."

"But you are the best anatomist. The appointment is fitting."

"Yet even *The Wrangler* thinks you have wit. And he rarely praises anyone."

"I will miss him."

"Are you going back directly to England?"

"As quickly as I can."

"Be careful, Will."

"You too, Giovanni."

He walked away to make his final travelling arrangements.

will be as humble as a chair
to be sat on by man or mare
then pushed aside
and even by death denied
while I will be called—Pride

William Harvey, M.D., The University of Padua.
"Father, this makes my degree official." William said this with gratification, and he hoped that Thomas shared his sense of accomplishment.

"Will this permit you to practise in England?" His son had arrived home just a few minutes ago, and Thomas was still feeling very emotional.

"The diploma says so." William read it for confirmation. *"This document authorizes the recipient to enjoy all the privileges enjoyed by the Doctors at the Schools of Paris, Cambridge, Oxford, Bologna, Perugia, Basle and Vienna.* Father, how is everybody? Are they well?"

"Everyone is fine. You are not the only one who knows physic." It was a sunny May day, and Thomas blessed God that he lived in Folkestone, where the air was good. But he was amazed at the change in William. While his oldest son hadn't grown any, as he had hoped, there were vital differences. William dressed with style now, his posture was straight, without a trace of deference, his beard and mustache were appropriate for one of the Queen's courtiers, and he wore a sword and dagger in the Venetian fashion. This troubled Thomas; this could be a disadvantage in England.

William noticed that the swelling on his father's foot had vanished since Thomas had taken his advice. Then Joshua brought in his mother.

She thought gratefully, William still possessed a facial likeness to his father and looked in good health. But when she saw his Venetian garb she was worried that he had been infected with Italian license.

He greeted her with an affectionate embrace, but he was

troubled that she seemed pale and ill. He wanted to examine
her at once, and he suggested this to his father, who frowned
and said, "It isn't fitting."

Joan Harvey, eager to see what her son had learned, replied, "Thomas, you have told the neighbours how proud you
are of his medical degree."

Thomas grumbled, "Your mother exaggerates, but you
probably won't do her any harm. Question her if you wish.
But modestly, remember."

William examined his mother, and he couldn't find anything wrong. He said, "Mother, perhaps you have been overworking."

"No," Thomas stated firmly, "she has two maids these days.
My business has expanded." He was surprised by his son's
thoroughness. The doctors he knew stood at a distance, mumbled some Latin, and depended on the apothecary's remedies.
William wanted to know how was her appetite, did she sleep
soundly, was the house properly aired? The last question annoyed Thomas, for he felt it questioned his judgement, and
he snapped, "We have the best air in Kent. It is why we have
thrived while others have sickened and died!"

"You have always known how to conserve the health of the
body."

"It is no wonder you have become a physician. You inherited that talent from me."

"I'm grateful, Father. And for all the help you gave me."

"You wrote that Venice was a fine port to improve my
trade with Turkey and that you could aid me there. What
made you change your mind?"

"I missed my family. Where are the others?"

Joan replied, "John wants to be at court, but Thomas and
Daniel are apprenticed to a merchant, and the others are in
school and they will be home soon. Eliab, with his love of
learning, resembles you. What are your plans? I trust you will
settle here."

"Mother, I am qualified to practise in London."

"That will depend on who supports you. Otherwise, you could starve."

"I hear that the fees in London are the best in the realm."

"You could practise in Folkestone. We need physicians."

Thomas declared, "Your mother is right. None of our doctors has helped me. But you did. My foot is better since you prescribed for it."

William didn't answer; he was thinking of the College of Physicians in London, where, if he got a Fellowship, he might be able to pursue his explorations—the one place in England where that might be possible. He announced, "I must consult Dr. Browne in London. The Queen's Physician Extraordinary told me to see him when I returned from Padua."

Thomas said, "He will have forgotten you by now. The Queen has been ill. There is much distress in the country about her poor health."

"The Holy Spirit is about to take her. William, you must not interfere."

"Mother, the Queen would ignore anything I say. But I must make an effort to see Dr. Browne." When he saw the tears in her eyes, he added, "My family does matter to me. I will be here often."

His brothers were home, and he showed he was glad to see them by embracing them as ardently as he had his mother. Eliab wanted to know about Padua, and had William actually dissected human beings? William nodded, and saw that his mother looked shocked and his father uneasy. He pointed out, "We did dissections to understand anatomy," but he doubted they realized how vital that was.

His mother mumbled, "This is sacrilegious, it profanes God's work," while his father cried out, "You free the devil in man!"

But when he didn't respond as they wished, Thomas ordered Joan to take William to his old room, which they had kept for him just as he had left it. He was touched, but he knew he had to go to London. Long after midnight he lay on his old trestle bed listening to the thump of his heart. It beat so regularly, he reflected, it could be a muscle that did pump the blood. This stirred his resolve to investigate further.

A week later William presented himself to Dr. Browne, who resided in a large timber house on Ave Maria Lane. He was surprised by Harvey's interest in Galileo. He said, "It is Fabricius's instructions that carry weight in England. You have learned much from him, but you must get a license to practise medicine from Cambridge."

"A degree from Padua permits me to practise medicine anywhere in Europe."

"In theory, yes. Yet for a doctor to qualify to practise medicine in London, he must be admitted into the College of Physicians. And no one is accepted unless he has an English degree. It is the custom."

"Sir, I went to Padua because you said Cambridge was insufficient."

"It is. But some of the proprieties have to be observed."

"You said that Padua was the best medical school in Europe."

"Possibly it is. But all our doctors must be licensed in England. It is the only way to keep out the quacks. And this power has been given to the College of Physicians. An M.D. from Cambridge is essential."

"Great men—Vesalius, Galileo, Caius, Fabricius—are my license to practise here. I cannot plead at Cambridge when I know their studies are inferior."

"Your obstinacy creates difficulties. Perhaps you should return to Padua and practise there."

"If I cannot be an English physician, I do not want to practise."

Dr. Browne sighed and looked away from him.

"Sir, you were the one who said *there is no school of consequence in England,* who suggested that I go to Padua for my medical degree."

"It was still your decision."

"Sir, you gave me your address and said a post might be

available when I returned from Padua, that you might need a young man to assist you."

"I don't remember."

William repeated what Browne had said word for word.

The physician's impulse was to dismiss this impudent young man. Yet he had made inquiries at Padua about Harvey's progress, and had been informed that this student was outstanding, the best in his class. He could use such diligence in preparing instruments, chemical cordials, herbs, and to carry out the many other duties that wearied him.

"Sir, may I serve you? I will follow your instructions faithfully."

"Apply to the College of Physicians and we will see what happens."

"Thank you, sir. How should I apply?"

"To me, directly. I am a Censor of the College, one of the four examiners who judge the qualifications for admission and a Fellowship. I have been a Fellow for a long time, and I was elected a Censor in 1599."

"May I apply now, sir?"

"No. It must be through official channels. Prepare your credentials and present them in writing and you will be called for an examination."

William said animatedly, "Sir, I will do this at once!"

"There is no need for haste. It could take several years."

William's joy turned to despair, but he couldn't give in to this, and he blurted out, "What about my services to you, sir?"

"You can assist me. If you are diligent. The pay will be low."

"I will manage, sir. I am honoured to labour at your side."

"So much for your manners. Rent quarters where you can be reached quickly. If you are free for dinner Sunday, you will be welcome."

William rented a room in an ordinary on Ludgate Hill. The Queen's Arms was near St. Paul's and a short walk from Dr.

Browne's house, and he liked that it contained men of all classes. Their variety excited his imagination, and he saw why they preferred The Queen's Arms, for, unlike most inns, the food was good, as were the wine and beer, the linen was scrupulously clean, which was unusual, and the large dining chamber was a good meeting place.

He observed the titled men who lived here cheaply so they could spend more at Court; the stingy men, who desired to save the cost of housekeeping; the Templars, who came to pray at St. Paul's; the adventurers who had no home. They were, he felt, concealed Papists, prodigal sons, and country folk on their first visit to the world of London. He was fascinated even more by the excitement on the streets.

Paternoster Row overflowed with booksellers, and he was delighted when he found an English edition of Vesalius's *Fabrica*. He bought also *Venus and Adonis*, by Will Shakespeare, and John Stow's *Survey of London*.

He walked the busy streets daily. He wondered how the City could contain any more people, it was so crowded. Bread was offered free on Cornhill if he purchased a pint of beer for a penny, and he loved the Thames, which seemed to be everybody's thoroughfare.

He wished he knew what Browne intended. He felt that the physician had a special reason for inviting him to dinner. Perhaps Browne planned to introduce him to other doctors. London was filthy, cramped, and reeked with evil smells and dank, oppressive air, and was mean and murderous at night, yet he felt it was the only place in England where he could hope to use the best resources of his craft.

Dr. Browne didn't want to discuss medicine. He said, "I have enough of that during the week. Sunday is for other satisfactions."

He introduced him to his daughter. Elizabeth was tall, slim, with sharp, pretty features, brown-eyed and brown-haired. She reminded William of Nina—she was the same age and height—and he was attentive to her at once. Without realizing it, he was eager to be in love; it had been such a pleasurable experience in the Venetian Republic.

Elizabeth thought, Her father's interest in this young doctor was sensible: Harvey was intelligent, and his experiences in Italy were intriguing. She wished he were taller—he was too short to suit her vision of a husband, and now she understood why her tall father referred to him as "little Harvey"—but otherwise he was attractive. Most of the doctors she met were elderly, dull, pompous, and even the younger ones were inclined to be solemn, but this one seemed free of such traits.

There was a halt in the conversation while they ate the fowl and fish; then she asked, "Dr. Harvey, do you intend to remain in London?"

"If it is possible. It is certainly my hope and intention."

Dr. Browne asked, "Even if I don't encourage you to practise here?"

"Sir, I'm accustomed to discouragement. I find it everywhere I go. I will simply have to find another way."

She stated, "I am sure that my father can find a place for you."

"Elizabeth, that is presumptuous!"

"Father, you know that is true."

He didn't contradict her, and William felt he would do much to please her. "Miss Browne, I trust I will have the pleasure of seeing you again."

"It is possible." Then her tone hardened. "But it is not inevitable."

He wondered if she was fickle, and his impulse was to drop the matter. Yet he liked her fine, high-boned features and her milk-white complexion.

Dr. Browne asked, "Harvey, could you attend me tomorrow morning?"

"Yes, sir. If it is essential."

"I doubt the Queen will think so, but it might be useful for you if I took you to meet Her Majesty." He thought, A young, attractive doctor fresh from Venice could be just the medicine she needed.

"Thank you, sir. I will be honoured." The dinner was over, and Browne, looking tired and aged, indicated that he should leave, but William had to add, "Miss Browne, may I attend you next Sunday?"

"What do you propose, Doctor?"

"The grounds about Westminster are lovely at this time of the year."

To suggest indifference, she appeared languid as he rose to go, but she brightened as her father—out of William's vision for the moment—nodded approvingly, and she replied, "If you would like to, Doctor."

"I would like to very much. When should I call for you, Miss Browne?"

"Next Sunday. After dinner."

Dr. Browne wore his most fashionable dress and, as William helped him into the coach, muttered, "The Queen likes well-turned-out men about her, but now I suffer from the gout and require a stick to get about. I am worn out from attending her. She insists that I keep her young, yet she does nothing to preserve her energy. Harvey, if you are ever called upon to serve a monarch, although that is unlikely—the probable successor to the throne, James of Scotland, prefers Scottish physicians—learn to flatter, that is far more important than a knowledge of physic."

"Then why are you visiting Queen Elizabeth today, sir?"

"She wants me to assure her that she is in good health. I and a dozen others. Her entourage is composed of many physicians. Even though she seldom listens to any of us, she likes to have all of us about her."

This was William's first visit to the Palace of Whitehall, and he was dismayed by the lack of order. The many buildings lay in an indiscriminate sprawl from Charing Cross to Westminster. But the Presence Chamber was handsome, and he liked it, although the Venetian-marble floor was slippery.

Browne discarded his cane, which he had used until now, in spite of William's admonishing "Sir, it is unwise."

"It would be more unwise not to," retorted Browne. "The Queen dislikes the sight of any infirmity. It reminds her of her own."

Thus, William expected to see an old lady. The Queen was sixty-eight; she had been deprived of her mother at a very early age; she had endured an excess of strain. Instead, he saw a figure adorned like a young woman's, who sat regally on her chair, which was elevated above all the other chairs, as was the custom. She held her head high, her body straight, as if infirmities were for those less strong. Her black velvet gown was embroidered with gold brocade, and her string of diamonds shone like the sun. Then his keen eyes saw that the skin beneath the heavy layer of cosmetics was wrinkled with old age, and only her hands were youthful.

Browne whispered to William, "I suffer so from the gout, I should have a chair when I attend her, but it is forbidden to sit in her presence."

She heard his voice and asked angrily, "What must you keep from my ears?"

"Your Majesty, I was simply telling my young friend, Dr. Harvey, that you understand physic better than all the physicians."

"That is no great compliment. Who is this young doctor?"

"Your Majesty, he just graduated from Padua in the Venetian Republic."

"I know where it is," she said testily. "Why does he attend you?"

"He hopes to assist me, Your Highness, and I desire your approval."

Elizabeth ordered Browne to present Harvey, and he knelt and kissed the royal hand. As she motioned imperiously for him to rise, he couldn't tell whether she was responding to his presence. He thought, She was a genius at not committing herself. But she did indicate that she wanted a word with him. She said, "Young man, I hear that the University of Padua has explored the issue of longevity. Do you recall any of their conclusions?"

"Your Majesty, that question is not answered easily."

She said caustically, "You are as evasive as all the others."

William felt he was on trial. He didn't answer.

"And your silence indicates ignorance. Browne, if this is the best this young man can do, he is not fit to serve us."

William blurted out, "Your Majesty, I want to serve you very much!"

"But speaking plainly?"

"Madam, I doubt speculation about longevity is a fruitful exercise."

"What makes you assert this?" She scowled and was angry again.

"Your Majesty, longevity is the quality of your reign. Your influence extends far beyond the limits of earthly life."

"Is this why you seek preferment?"

"Your Majesty, it is because you have encouraged wit and learning."

She observed William more intently, not certain whether this was wisdom or flattery. Then she asked, "Have you any more conclusions?"

"Madam, the longevity of your reign is a blessing to your realm."

She smiled and said, "Dr. Browne, this young man appears to possess a good head in addition to good legs. You may bring him again."

Yet, instead of consulting Browne, as William expected now, she turned to her favourite, Dr. John Dee, who shuffled to her side, bent from age. He was the only person in the Presence Chamber to whom she offered a chair, and she ignored the other doctors as she asked him what he thought.

Browne whispered irately to William, "Dee has never qualified as a physician, yet she prefers him to anyone else, and has for forty years."

William had heard about Dee, one of the most renowned philosophers of her reign: astrologer, alchemist, historian, astronomer, geographer. His hands shook with a nervous tremor as he held the arms of the chair to seat himself properly. And, next to Dee, William observed, Elizabeth looked younger. He leaned closer to hear what wisdom Dee uttered.

"Madam, I note that you have been dispirited lately."

"Not in all details, gentle Dee, but I am pained with a wind in my stomach and a looseness of my bowels, and I fear to venture forth."

"It may be the flux. Your Majesty, I will consult my horoscope."

"Quickly, please. The discomfort grows daily."

"Madam, I will inform you tomorrow of my findings. Meanwhile, I have some herbs which will ease your difficulties until my angels speak."

"Your comfort makes me feel better already." She turned back to William and said, "We are to see a comedy, *The Taming of the Shrew*. Would you like to view it? It is reputed to contain a touch of Padua."

William followed the Queen and her entourage to the hall where the comedy was to be performed. She ordered a stick to help her walk without assistance, and her velvet train was borne by four gentlewomen.

The Lord Chamberlain's Men were the best actors that William had seen, and *The Taming of the Shrew* amused him, although he thought the tone of the play was English rather than Italian. Yet when Elizabeth asked him, "Is this comedy accurate?" he replied, "Reasonably so, Your Majesty."

He was more interested in the play given the next day, *Hamlet*. He was fascinated by the poet's constant references to the blood and his dramatic use of it. When the tragedy ended there was the customary prayer for the Queen, but the audience didn't leave, as they usually did, for Elizabeth still sat, as if many deaths were still being acted out in her memory.

So many I have experienced, she thought sadly; this work reminded her poignantly that they were still with her. At the end she could hardly remember all the bodies strewn about the stage, yet this was her time, she knew; the stage became the scaffold upon which stood Essex and Mary and many others. She told herself, The scribblings of poets were slight against the slayings that reddened the pages of her days, and yet his *Hamlet* was a reflection of her realm. Will I be remembered most, she wondered, by the deaths that have bloodied my reign? Yet, by comparison with her father and her half-sister, she had been compassionate. Elizabeth saw the youthful bearded face of Essex, her father gross and greatly swollen: then the Queen of Scots protruded between them—not beautiful, as so many proclaimed, but old, as old as herself. And now Mary's son was the probable heir and the protector of the Protestant succession. This brought a smile to the Queen's lips, although she was not in a mood to smile. Did the waiting Court know that they were play actors, and she the best of them? But no, she told herself; she was alone in this, as she was in so many things, so many things that had developed strangely and not to her satisfaction. Today she dressed in virginal white silk to signify that she was the wife who was wedded to England, and to show her red hair and vivid complexion at their brightest. Yet death was knocking on her door. It was in this play, in the tone, the pessimism, the suicidal meditations. She had kept death in exile for many years, but all that remained now was to lead her body, blindly and stumbling, to the final resting place. Yet she had sought with every beat of her heart to make her rule, her country, and those about her, even this poet, Will Shakespeare, consequential.

The Lord Chamberlain, whose men had acted so skillfully, was saying, "Your Majesty, here is Dr. Dee come to consult with you."

Elizabeth dismissed the Court except for the physicians in attendance, and ordered them to join her and Dee, but only she and Dee sat.

William longed to ask the Lord Chamberlain's Men their view of *Hamlet,* but the Queen had summoned Browne and he was by Browne's side, and so he followed him. This time he saw the Queen with different eyes. Yesterday's black velvet had been a wise choice, he thought, for today's white silk etched Elizabeth's age and her long, lined features, and the red hair, which was obviously a wig hiding sparse grey hair, and her decayed teeth. The Queen had been stately when, at the start of *Hamlet,* she had entered without a cane to display her vigour, but now it was evening, the final scenes had been played with lights, and she looked very tired. Whatever is wrong with her, William thought, it is serious. If I could only examine her. Ask questions. Judge her blood. But I am only a spectator, he realized, as are the other physicians except for Dee. Anything else will jeopardise the attention I have won.

Dr. Dee wore a black cap and gown, as befitted his position but they didn't hide his age or feebleness. His white ruff was spotted with his own spittle, and his long, white beard was straggly and unkempt.

"I cast your horoscope, Your Majesty," he said, "and unfortunately—"

She interrupted, "The heavenly bodies are not in the best conjunction."

"You are wise, Madam. That is exactly so. I spent, as a doctor, many hours last night in *judicial* astronomy, to determine the course of your ailment. Purging and bleeding must be applied only at the propitious time. It is the position of the planet Jupiter that decides the correct moment, but it is not in the proper orbit at the moment."

Her heart sank. She cried out, "Then I am in danger!"

"Not totally, Your Majesty. The moon exercises vital effects upon herbs according to the time when they are picked and prepared and given, and this astral influence is favourable. That is why I administered my medicinal herbs yesterday. Madam, you do look better."

William thought Elizabeth looked much worse, but she forced a smile and said, "Dr. Dee, you are reassuring. As you always are."

"But if you wish to live longer," he mumbled, "you must remove yourself from this damp palace. My horoscope says, *'Beware of Whitehall!'* "

Elizabeth shivered despite her reputation for resolution and courage.

"Madam, Richmond is the warmest of your palaces and the best for your constitution. And for your residence there the stars are favourable."

She nodded, but as she and Dee hobbled out, the Queen ahead of him, as was the custom, William could not tell who was the more feeble.

Browne said, "I am glad you restrained your impulse to contradict Dee. He has never obtained a degree in medicine, but he won her confidence when she was young. And she likes his astral forecasts. Now especially, since his horoscopes justify her claim to America."

"But she is ill, sir. Gravely perhaps. It is evident."

"I know. If she lives another year, it will be a miracle."

"Sir, I would have paid almost any price to attend her."

"There is a little white worm gnawing inside of her, and it is too late."

"It shouldn't be, sir."

"It is."

William offered Browne his arm, and the older physician waved that aside.

"The Queen must not see me in poor health. Harvey, should we expect you this Sunday?"

"I am looking forward to it, sir. Your daughter is charming."

"And young. It is a great virtue."

lie is used
to avoid the truth
The truth is used
to avoid a lie
When is either used
for its own sake
Eternally yours

Mr. Harvey, a doctor of medicine in the University of Padua, must present himself for examination to the College of Physicians.

With this necessity in mind, William visited Elizabeth each Sunday and assisted Dr. Browne the rest of the week. He sensed that her father was interested in him as a son-in-law, and that she was responsive to him.

The more she knew him, the more she enjoyed his company. William is clever, Elizabeth thought, for my father gives him opportunities that he does not give to anyone else. Clearly William is a physician with a future. She was pleased that he regarded her as tender and beautiful, and that he respected her intelligence. He listened to whatever she said, whether they took a drive or spent the afternoon in her parlour.

William liked Elizabeth, but he was upset by Browne's attitude. He asked again if he could apply for admission to the College, and he was told by Browne, "You must wait, Harvey. You must not hurry matters."

Months had passed and much time had been wasted, and he was worried.

"The moment is not propitious. If I ask you to wait, I have reasons."

A bookseller was at the door, pleading with Browne to attend his wife. "Sir, whoever examines her differs on the nature of her ailment, but you will know," and Browne replied, "I cannot. My noble patients occupy all my time. Harvey, tell this man to call an apothecary."

Browne returned to preparing his new statute for admission

to the College of Physicians and read it to William: *"Every Fellow is required to be learned in physic, to be able to lecture on Anatomy, and to know Galen."*

"Sir, I thought you didn't favour the ancient devotion to Galen."

"I don't, but it is still a requirement in all the universities."

"Then, sir, according to these statutes, I qualify on those grounds."

"Perhaps. I must prepare a statute that will keep the apothecaries and the surgeons in their place. I don't want to be interrupted."

But when Sir Edward Stanhope, the Chancellor of the diocese of London, desired his presence, Browne was delighted to visit him.

Stanhope was grossly fat, with a florid complexion. He was the same age as Browne, and he complained bitterly of diarrhoea. He said unhappily, "I'm shocked, Browne, I thought this was an affliction of the lower orders."

"It happens to the best-born. I have treated the Queen for the flux."

"Doctor, what do you advise?" He ignored his assistant, Harvey.

"Your stomach is weak, and you need an enema."

William differed; that would make matters worse. But he was quiet.

Stanhope grumbled, "Do I have to endure such unpleasantness? I can hardly bend over. I hear there are other remedies for gentlefolk."

"Sir, I have some herbs which could suffice."

"Doctor, are the stars in their proper orbit?"

"Yes. As they were when Dee prescribed for the Queen."

Stanhope took the herbs, although with some reluctance.

When the two doctors were back at Browne's residence, William asked, "Sir, weren't you critical of Dee earlier?"

"Rightfully so. Dee has no medical degree. But Stanhope trusts him."

"Sir, won't the herbs you gave him constipate him?"

"Exactly. That will cure his diarrhoea."

William wondered if it was too late to change his mind about practising in London. Browne had changed dishearteningly since Cambridge.

Browne sensed what William was thinking, and he declared, "You have good intentions, Harvey, but they are not sufficient. I have given Sir Edward faith, and that will stop him from feeling bad, at least for the moment."

When Browne was informed that the Queen was very ill and that his presence was required immediately, he told William, "She has been failing steadily ever since she moved to Richmond. I hope she hasn't done anything stupid."

"Sir, she has a great wit!"

"But her vanity drives her hard. She pushes herself beyond her limits."

It was March, 1603, almost a year since William had arrived hopefully in London in search of his future, and by now he felt this time might never occur. He hadn't kissed or embraced Elizabeth, although he continued to visit her regularly, and he was too disturbed to pursue his experiments. But he was excited by the prospect of seeing Queen Elizabeth again.

The journey to Richmond was long and arduous, and they were ushered into the royal bedchamber at once. The Queen was not in bed, as William had expected. Dressed in youthful white silk, she sat regally in an elevated chair while somber-faced ladies in waiting stood behind her.

She looked exhausted, yet he heard her mutter, "I have a hundred things to do. I cannot take to bed. What I know, I know best. Who is there?" She stared unseeingly in their direction, while they waited to be presented.

Robert Cecil—William recognized him from his long, narrow face, his small hunchbacked body—said, "Madam, one of your doctors and his assistant."

"I have many physicians. Which one, little man?"

"Lancelot Browne, Your Majesty, and a young doctor."

"Doctor William Harvey," she said, "that young man from Padua?"

"Yes, Your Majesty," said Browne. "Your memory is as keen as ever."

"He has some common sense. It is a rarity among physicians."

"Your Majesty, I have come a long way to ease your discomfort."

"*Nothing will. I am tied with a chain of iron about my neck, I am tied, I am tied to this throne and I cannot leave it while I live.*"

"You must, Madam," William blurted out, appalled by her pain.

"Young man," she said scornfully, "the word *must* is not used to me."

"I beg your pardon, Your Majesty, but this chair is wrong for your health, it does not permit you to rest properly beneficently."

For a moment William thought her anger would put him in the Tower, but when he didn't retreat, she smiled unexpectedly and asked, "Are you sure?"

"Quite sure, Madam."

But if I went to bed, she reflected, I might never get out of it. And that was not to be borne. Time enough to rest in the tomb. Yet it took all of her strength to sit up straight. Her mind wandered wryly: So my teeth are bad, is that how history will see me? Only a few years ago, at sixty-five, I danced better and longer than all the lively young courtiers and energetic young ladies. Have four brief years eroded me so much? She gripped the arms of her chair to sustain her strength and posture. She asked Browne to offer his diagnosis.

He hesitated, thinking, The Queen was dying but he could not tell her so. She would have his head for such news. He equivocated, suggesting, "If you could rest, then perhaps after you are bled and purged—"

"No!" she shouted, with a flash of her famed vitality. "You have wracked this body of mine enough! Can you find no other remedy?"

"If you could save your energy, Your Majesty, it would be helpful. You do not possess as much energy as you once did and—"

She cut him short furiously. "How dare you question my will!"

Browne trembled as if he had been whipped, and he was ashen.

"I know that my illness is a great inconvenience."

"Madam, I am Your Majesty's most loving subject."

"And your knees ache from kneeling. Harvey, what were you going to suggest? Hurry, while I am still in a mood to be persuaded."

"Madam, if you rested on cushions it would be easier on your body."

Her body ached so, she wondered if she had any choice. Dee hobbled in, and she reminded him, "Good doctor, you recommended I come to Richmond."

"Your Majesty, it is the warmest of your palaces."

But much too cold for her aged body, thought William.

"What do the planets say, Dee?"

He replied, his eyes full of tears because of her emaciated condition. "Madam, I cannot detect any remedies except rest. If you could lie down."

"No!"

"Then use the cushions, Madam. They will be better for your bowels."

They hurt unbearably, and she ordered cushions to be brought so that she could sit upon them. But even then Elizabeth would not lie down.

Now, as the minutes passed, no one said a word. The silence shocked William. She should be in bed, he thought; the devastations of age are evident. He yearned to take her pulse, to observe her blood, so celebrated for its strength and flow, but this was not allowed. He believed that the cause of disease rested in nature, and that nature possessed the instinct to cure itself, but it must have some help, particularly in the form of diet, rest, fresh air, and the air here was foul. In the wish to keep the Queen warm, for she shivered spasmodically, every window was shut tight. And, what is worse, he realized, she is not resting but resisting rest. No one was examining her. That was her wish. Her attitude was: If Dee cannot help me, if the stars are wrong, nothing can help me. Yet William had a feeling that she might still be saved. But the other doctors, even Browne and Dee, accepted her attitude: What happens has to happen. It didn't satisfy William, but it appeared to satisfy them. He thought sadly: So little known, so much to know.

Suddenly Browne asked, "Madam, how can you spend so much time in silence?"

"I meditate." She couldn't move; if she moved, she felt, she would die.

Cecil, who made a virtue out of patience, couldn't control himself any longer, and he said, "_Madam, you must go to bed. To content the people._"

She regarded him with the contempt she had kept hidden until now, and replied caustically, "_Little man, little man, the word 'must' is not to be used to Princes. If your father had lived you would not have dared say so much, but you know I must die, and that makes you presumptuous._"

Cecil flushed angrily and thought, Yes, I am waiting for her to die, but she doesn't have to remind me. It was his duty to provide the country with a proper and peaceful succession, so they would be spared the agony of civil strife. If he possessed an excellent sense of political survival, he had learned from a master: Elizabeth. But now she was eroded by time and exhaustion; she wasn't even a fowl fit for stewing. He knew he was too small to suit her fancy, yet he had served her faithfully; he had put her interests first, as had his father. But Elizabeth wouldn't bow to the inevitable. Cecil started to answer her; then he thought better of it.

Elizabeth wouldn't have heard him; she had fallen into a

reverie as deep as the grave. Time lost its meaning, the faces about her became a blur; she wanted to apologise for her delay in dying; she knew her Lords had other business that waited on this event, especially the welcoming of a new ruler. But she knew her own constitution better than they did. She had to die in her own way, in her own time. This was the final prerogative of her reign. So long as her hands could still move, and thus still rule.

She brushed her hair out of her eyes—that is why I can't see, she thought—but there was no hair there. Puzzled, she told herself she was exhausted by the cure of strong waters, foul purges, and chilling baths. Saddlesore and weatherworn from the English dust. Tired out in the service of her country. If only she could be free of her body, but it had become a coffin as confining as a cell in the Tower. She put out her hand—her lovely hand, all that was left of her youth—to command death to go away until she was ready. She must hold on to her rule until she was prepared to relinquish it. In this, she thought proudly, I am my father's daughter. The Virgin Queen ever faithful to her first love: England.

The last William saw of the Queen was an emaciated old lady, as pale as a ghost, sitting upright on her cushions in a trance, her eyes fixed on the floor at her feet, her finger in her mouth like a little child. Yet still inflexible, he felt, with a strength that had survived immense difficulties. He doubted that he would see her like again.

He heard that she sat this way for four days. Until she fainted from lack of strength, and then her ladies-in-waiting were able to carry her to bed. At her command, no man was allowed to touch her. A few days later she died. But the Queen's command remained in force. Her body was not dissected and embalmed, as was the custom for monarchs, but prepared for burial by her ladies. So no man's hand touched her still. Her secret was still inviolate. But William, even as he mourned for the Queen, had his own secret. He would have given much to dissect her as he had dissected the young woman in Padua. He would have concentrated on nothing but the medical facts. But he knew he must thrust such a heresy out of his mind. The idea itself was treason and could cost him his head. Better, he reasoned, that she died as the Virgin Queen. He decided that if he were admitted to the College of Physicians, he would propose to Elizabeth Browne. He wasn't certain whether he loved her, but she was the most attractive woman he knew, and her father had great influence.

A few weeks after the Queen's death, Browne gave William permission to apply for admission to the College of Physicians. He had not sought approval of his medical degree from Cambridge, and he approached the examination apprehensively. There were four examiners on the committee, and Browne, who spoke for them, presented the questions. They were in Latin, and William's accent was approved. His knowledge of anatomy was judged next, and by the smile of satisfaction that appeared on Browne's face, he felt he had replied appropriately. He was dismayed when, at the end of the examination, he was informed that this was just the first of three to be held before these four Censors.

Everything in William cried out against this postponement. Yet he didn't want to offend Browne. He asked him, "Sir, when will the next examination be?" He could take it tomorrow, in a week, but please God, not much longer. He couldn't be an assistant much longer.

"The candidate can apply for his second examination next year."

William was stunned, but on Sunday, when Browne saw his despair, the Censor explained further, for the young doctor was so distraught he wasn't even attentive to his daughter. "We have to hold some things back, so our candidates appreciate what a distinction it is to be admitted to the College."

"When will I be able to practise myself? Sir, it delays all my plans."

Elizabeth frowned. Now, she thought wearily, he will never propose. "Father, must he wait another year?"

"Yes!" But when he saw her disappointment, he added, "Since his replies to the questions were satisfactory, he is permitted to practise."

"Now, sir?"

Browne nodded.

Elizabeth asked, "He won't be fined or put into prison?"

"Of course not, daughter!"

William asked, "Sir, then why must I wait for official confirmation?"

"No candidate is permitted an easy passage. It would make him weak."

William was silent.

"Don't despair. You will now serve my practice, except when the nobility wish to consult me, and wait to see what opportunities occur."

The next year William modelled his medical views on Browne's. He courted Elizabeth, but he didn't propose, for he still didn't feel qualified to support a family.

His second examination at the College came many months later, and this time he was tested on his knowledge of the urine, and he replied as Fabricius had taught him. He was grateful for his good memory, but he felt far away from the blood, for it was ignored. He had been unable to do any work on it since he had returned from Padua, and he feared that he never would; Browne kept him so busy on other matters. But he felt better a few days later when Browne told Elizabeth: "*Dr. Harvey was examined for the second time for a Candidateship and his replies were approved.*"

"Affairs will move more quickly now," added Browne.

"It is about time," said Elizabeth.

A month after the second examination, William was questioned again. He was asked how he would employ purging, bleeding, vomiting, and opiates. He was no longer hopeful, but when he finished this examination Browne spoke briefly to his colleagues, then stated, "Harvey, you are *approved*."

"Is there anything else, sir?"

"You will be examined for candidateship to the College soon."

This occurred in August, and his answers were approved and he was elected to the College of Physicians, but not officially until October, when he took his oath as a candidate according to the statutes.

Browne spoke pompously to William and Elizabeth the next Sunday. "Harvey, you are now a *Permissus*, able to practise within the jurisdiction of the College. You are deemed fit to be a London physician."

"Good," said Elizabeth. "But, Father, what about a Fellowship?"

"He will have to wait."

"What about St. Bartholomew's Hospital? Are there any posts there?"

"Not at the moment. Be patient, daughter."

"You have told me that a dozen times."

So she is tired of waiting too, William thought grimly, although she makes a virtue of it in my presence. "Sir, is there anything at Court?"

"Not now. King James is a suspicious monarch, and to ease his fears will take time. However, there is a position in the Tower that is available. I could petition Cecil in your behalf. But this is not an easy step to take. It should be appreciated."

"It will be, sir. May I have a moment alone with your daughter?"

"As many as you need. If you are sensible, you could have a bright future." Browne hobbled out, leaning heavily on his cane. Ever since he had been widowed and had been given the care of his daughter, he had sought to do his best for her—his son, Galen, had been away at school for many years, and he

149

had provided for his welfare, but a daughter needed a husband. There was nothing else that was fitting, and his time was short. He could hardly move his arm these days, and his leg was worse.

Once William was alone with Elizabeth, he wasn't sure what to do. He knew he desired her, but he wasn't positive that he loved her. He studied her pretty, high-boned features, as if that would help him make up his mind, while she served him fruit and bustled about him like a helpmate. Her figure was more angular than he preferred, yet he hadn't known any woman since Nina, and the long interval had increased his desire. Only the words came hard. One minute they were talking about her father's gout, which she said was a weakness of his nerves, and the next she was asking him whether he was satisfied with the practice that her father was shifting to his shoulders. Suddenly he felt desperate, and he blurted out, "Elizabeth, dear, this isn't what I wanted to talk about."

"What do you want to discuss?"

"Dear Elizabeth . . ." He paused. He wished he didn't still have doubts.

Hurry, hurry, her heart cried; she couldn't wait much longer.

"Why are we discussing medicine when there is so much else to discuss?"

She thought bitterly, Why indeed! She shouldn't have to wait this long for his proposal. She was neither plain nor poor.

The fine speech he planned came out as: "Will you marry me?"

She was dismayed. She wondered if she would get over the bluntness of his proposal. And he sounded so prosaic.

As he realized her disappointment, he knelt at her feet and cried out, "Elizabeth, dear, I will be devoted to your interests!"

But he hadn't said the magic words: I love you. Yet when

she gazed into his earnest face, his imploring eyes, his out-stretched arms, she couldn't resist him. She bent over and kissed him lightly on the brow.

He leapt to his feet, embraced her, and said, "Then you will be my wife?"

She recoiled instinctively at his touch, although she knew that to resist him could be fatal. She put her hands in his to express her allegiance, but when he started to kiss her on the lips she gave him her cheek.

"Elizabeth, dear, you will marry me?"

She must be sensible. William's parentage was decent, if not noteworthy; he was well bred and educated; they were of the same religion, and thus neither of them would be damned. If they were not romantic, perhaps that was not ill advised. He was virtuous, and she would like being the wife of a physician, as she had enjoyed being the daughter of one. And while he was not the man her father was, with time and her help he might become such a worthy.

"Elizabeth, the sooner we marry, the better."

"You must ask my father."

"And if I obtain his permission?"

"Amen."

Browne considered William's request for his daughter's hand with great solemnity, as if this was a matter which required much thought. He said he would like to meet William's family before coming to a decision, and the suitor arranged for this meeting to take place in London. The two fathers liked each other, for each saw the other as a man of substance. The dowry which Lancelot Browne agreed to provide was large, while Thomas Harvey, not to be outdone, declared that he would give his son a similar sum to establish a practice in London.

On November 24, 1604, William and Elizabeth were wed in the parish church of St. Sepulchre at Newgate. Sir Edward

Stanhope presided, which gave the wedding the importance that Elizabeth craved. William was too nervous to care about his surroundings. He was glad his parents were pleased with Elizabeth. They were proud that he was marrying into an established and worthy family—his mother was even more gratified than his father—and yet he was troubled with a vague discontent. In the time they had been engaged, she had continued to offer her cheek when he desired to kiss her, although he had sought her lips, and they had not embraced. And this caused him to wonder whether she loved him.

They lay in bed in her father's house the night of the wedding, and her body was like a November frost. She was unaccustomed to the nuances of love that he had learned from Nina, and his efforts to express it were unsuccessful. He had assumed she was a virgin, but he expected some response. Instead, she was passive. Yet she was young, of a lusty, ripe age, going on twenty-four, but when he fondled her breasts she recoiled as if it hurt.

She said, "Marriage must be a meeting of minds rather than of bodies."

"But it is God's wish that we increase those who worship Him."

"That sounds like a Venetian heresy," she lamented.

"It is good English common sense. But you act as if love is an inconvenience not to be borne." He got out of bed, although it was cold.

She was afraid that William was leaving her, a humiliation she could not endure. She must hold him, whatever excuse would suffice. Suddenly she was at his side, seeking to warm him with her body even as she shivered from the chill, and she whispered, "I don't want to upset you."

"Yet you do. You want to be wed, but you also want to remain a virgin."

"I can't feel free as long as my father sleeps in the same house."

That had a sensible sound. He decided not to dress and depart. Besides, her father would never forgive such a deed, and Browne had written to Cecil, who was King James's First Minister, recommending him for the post of Physician to the Tower, and hoped for a favourable reply. He thought, He must accept his present condition with good grace. But not forever, he repeated to himself, I am not a saint. He returned to bed and resolved not to make love until they possessed their own quarters and were free of her father's influence. He said, "Elizabeth, dear, you are right. We must move as soon as it is possible."

"But not far away." She felt him draw away, and she added hurriedly, "So you can inherit my father's practice when he retires. This parish is an ideal location, near the Tower, the College, and St. Bart's Hospital."

William sought to please Elizabeth, and he rented a large three-storey house on Ludgate Hill, in the parish she preferred, and took her to view it in the hope that she would approve of his taste. She stood before this grand residence and asked him what it cost.

"Do you like it?"

"I don't know. What is it like inside?"

"Come, Elizabeth, dear, see for yourself."

As William led her through a broad oak front door, she noticed the house was strongly timbered with a sturdy interlacing of red brick. On the ground floor there were a reception room, living room, dining room, and parlour; there were three bedrooms on the first floor; and the top floor contained an attic and spare room. But she felt she had to complain, for he hadn't consulted her in making this choice. She exclaimed, "But it is so large! Probably too large for our needs."

"It is three times the size of an ordinary London house," he said. He showed her the reception room, with its tapestry and painted cloth depicting the diverse histories of England, the Church, and medicine.

He was not finished. He escorted her upstairs to their bedroom. Dominating it was a spacious joint bed with silk hangings and Turkish carpets. There were also wall mirrors and oak cabinets for her wardrobe.

She said, "You will have to practise very hard to afford this."

"I have hopes of obtaining the position of Physician in the Tower."

He is being bold, she thought; my father isn't that certain of achieving this coveted position for him.

"Elizabeth, we can move in whenever you are ready."

She wavered. Now that she faced the prospect of leaving her father's side, it was difficult. She desired her connubial life to be exemplary, but her father had the finest nature she knew, especially if he wasn't crossed. And when he leaned on her arm these days because his legs had become weak and needed support, she felt a warmth she couldn't explain.

"It is the best house I could find."

"It is grand."

"Then why do you hesitate?"

"We will need several servants. Can you afford them?"

"We will have them." He was determined to please her. "You will have whatever you need. Anything that is necessary."

"Do you have any servants in mind? They must be trustworthy."

"I will find servants we can depend on. Elizabeth, when we walk outside we are in the shadow of St. Paul's. I love the ancient cathedral. It is the heart of London for me. Isn't it for you?"

She thought, It was a dark vault of a church, dark in design, dark in depth, dark in feeling. But she nodded. And there was one consolation with this house and its location: She would still be near her father. She kissed William on the cheek to express her approval.

They moved in a few days later, and Elizabeth was more affectionate in their new residence, but he was still dissatisfied, for she was passive. Lying next to her, he wondered if he had the one thing he desired more than anything else: love. On his second effort to make love, he sought to be gentle, but she cried out, "William, be careful! You are hurting me!"

"All you have to do is to respond a little."

"I have a very delicate constitution."

"That doesn't mean that you must abstain."

"This cold air gives me a chill. We need a warmer bed-chamber."

"I've lit the stove, the fireplace."

"And the smoke makes me cough, and the air is foul and hard to breathe."

He had a fear that he had wed at a cost beyond calculation, and he was silent.

She felt his distress and said, "I know a lusty young man like yourself is accustomed to violent exertion, but I have been brought up differently. I must become accustomed to such efforts and practices gradually."

There was nothing else to do but to agree. He lay back in bed, and his shoulder pressed against Elizabeth, and although she had fallen asleep, she unconsciously shifted away from him. He said to himself, I can say no more, for she is proud and I am proud. He resolved that from now on he must not buy anyone's favour; it was too dear, uncertain, and variable.

When Elizabeth awoke the next morning, she saw William sitting on the seat of their oriel window. He was absorbed in what he was writing, and he didn't hear her approach him.

She asked anxiously, "What are you writing so early in the morning?"

"I've been idle too long. I must resume my investigations of the blood." With each word he put down, he felt better. Then he was annoyed. He was out of ink. He needed servants who could hold a key to his imagination in addition to the food larder, wine cellar, and front door. He took out the letter from Silas that had arrived yesterday and that had left him in a state of indecision. This missive, which had been transmitted to him by his father from Folkestone, appealed to him, and yet he felt there was a touch of madness in it. Elizabeth should help him decide. He said, "I want to read this letter to you and get your opinion of it."

"Is it very long? It is chilly here."

"It is from Silas. I told you about him. Remember?"

"I remember."

"He wants to serve me. And this is his plea."

"I thought you said that he couldn't read or write."

"He can't. His sister wrote this for him."

William lit a log in the fireplace so they would be warm and comfortable while he read Silas's letter, and Elizabeth waited attentively, although impatiently. She thought, What can be so vital about a would-be servant's letter? William had told her what had happened at Cambridge, but she didn't believe him.

atisfaction
The blood flows day and night for it
The sun rises every day for it
The wolf howls all its life for it
The flower grows every season for it
Life passes into death for it . . .

He read her Silas's letter.

Dear Master:
 The words are mine but my sister wrote them. She is the only one in my family who can read or write. I found the address of your father at Caius College in the hope that my humble words will reach your ears.

When you brought me back from the dead I swore
eternal allegiance to you. Noble sir, it was not a false
oath, it was spoken with my blood. And now that I
have served a grand house near Cambridge, I am
prepared to serve you. I promise you, I will not be a
burden. I have enough to wear, I eat little, since my
hanging I have not possessed much of an appetite, I
am without any complaints or contagion, I am a
grown man now, and I will be a faithful servant. You
will possess all of my devotion, no dog could serve
you better. In your service I will have a Cambridge
face and an English heart. There is a saying among
my country folk that nothing can equal the devotion
of one whose blood has been saved. It was your
touch that restored life to my body, and so, it is
yours to do with what you will. I have some knowledge of herbs and I know that to cure melancholy I
must use sugar, white wine, and choice maidenhair.

William was silent after he finished, moved by Silas's gratitude in spite of his determination not to be; then he asked,
"What should I do?"
"Is it his service you desire or his devotion?"
"His feelings could be useful. They might be trustworthy."
Now that she was warm and he was distracted from her
failure to please him earlier, she thought, This peasant might
divert him. She said, "I will interview Silas. It is more fitting
for me to do it than for a physician, especially one who may
serve the King soon." When William assented to this arrangement, she felt cleverer and stronger than he.

A few days later she saw Silas in their kitchen. William sat
by her side, but he left the interview to Elizabeth, although
when Silas entered he was glad to see him. He thought ruefully, He could not evade the consequences of his acts. At
the sight of him Silas's face broke into a smile that was like
the sun emerging from behind a dark cloud. But he had not
grown, although he was a man now. He was scarcely more

than skin and bones, yet his complexion was good and his blue eyes gleamed, and he said in a lively manner, "Madam, I understand the ways of gentlefolk."

Elizabeth was pleased that he was clean, that his bright red hair was combed, and that he had taken off his wool cap in her presence with deference.

"Madam, I will be deeply honoured to serve you and Dr. Harvey. I eat very little, I can sleep on the floor, I can—"

"That is not necessary," William interrupted.

"—and I will not cost much."

She addressed herself to vital matters. "Are you devout?"

"Indeed, great lady. I have taken the pilgrimage to Canterbury. I did that after my mother died, to pray for blessings on her soul."

Now she was inclined to favour him, and that would please William.

"Madam, I can make a fire, cut wood, sweep your steps, tend your garden, I have a good hand with herbs and flowers and a broom and a mop."

"You are very small," she said.

"But quick, great lady. Very quick."

"Remember," said William, "my wife is the mistress of this house."

"Of course, noble sir, in my sight as well as the sight of the Lord."

Elizabeth was satisfied until she recalled that she had forgotten one of the most important duties of the household. "Boy, can you cook?"

Silas hesitated, then mumbled, "I can groom your horses, Madam."

"But you have no knowledge of the kitchen?"

"Great lady, I can feed myself. And clean and polish."

"Your manners are adequate despite your want of learning, but there will be occasions when I will need a cook. Your services are not sufficient."

The idea of being dismissed was more than Silas could

endure, and he cried out, "Madam, I know a fine cook. One whom you will esteem."

"Who is this person?"

"My sister cooked for a grand house outside of Cambridge. They found her very satisfactory."

William asked, "Then why do you wish her here?"

"Noble sir, she wants to remain with me. Since neither of us has wed, we are a family. Madam, Squire Foster entertained many of the gentry, and my sister has learned what they favour. Everything she prepares can be digested. We will ease your burdens and serve you devoutly."

Silas was so pale and wan that Elizabeth felt sorry for him. Then she realized that sympathy was weak, and she motioned for him to go.

Instead of obeying, he declared piteously, "Madam, employ us and we will be able to resist the devil, but without your mercy we are lost!"

Perhaps he would even fancy her ahead of William. That idea pleased Elizabeth, and she said, "Fetch your sister and I will decide."

Rachel had become a very pretty young woman, and William hesitated to hire her, but Elizabeth liked her and said she would be useful. His wife thought it helpful that her cook could read and write; this was rare; and thus the girl—as Elizabeth referred to her, although Rachel was only a little younger than she—could keep the household accounts. She was so comforted by the presence of the servants that William complied with her wishes, although reluctantly. And when his wife sought to respond to his amorous demands, he felt better about this new arrangement, even though he still wasn't sure that Elizabeth enjoyed making love.

Both of them relished Rachel's cooking, and Silas served with skill. Meanwhile, Silas assured his sister, who had doubted the wisdom of seeking this situation, that the Madam's severity would vanish with time and that it was a privilege to serve the Master.

But Rachel, while she was grateful that she had her own room and other conveniences she had not known—a mirror, a clothes cabinet, a bed with a mattress, and glass in her window—was not certain that the physician was a temperate man. She thought there was passion beneath his stern exterior, and she wondered whether his wife satisfied him, Madam was so sober. She decided he was not the saviour that Silas worshipped but was using them for his advantage. Rachel felt that the doctor favoured their employment because they were shorter than he was and this made him feel taller. And that he desired Silas's presence to prove what he had done. This made her uneasy, although her brother's happiness gratified her.

Silas was proud that his Master's house was more stone and brick than wood and plaster. He liked the fields to the north and the west, and he enjoyed the walk to Smithfields and Westminster. He didn't care for the men from Yorkshire he met—they acted as if they knew more than anybody else in England, and they ignored the fact that he came from learned Cambridge. But he loved the excitement of London, and that it stirred his senses.

Once the servants were employed, William tried to accept it casually. Browne approved of their hiring, but he was surprised that they were young. He sensed that Elizabeth preferred this; it helped her feel in command. She was so proud he withheld his doubts about her judgement. Then, too, he had vital matters to consider. He had retained a place as doctor to the monarch, and he had obtained an audience for Harvey with James to present his application for the post of Physician to the Tower.

As they prepared for this audience, he advised, "Be flattering. James likes attractive young men about him. Even more than the Queen did."

They were in Browne's home, and William longed to discuss new ideas he had about the movement of the blood. But when he said, "Sir, I believe that the arteries don't contain air, as Galen wrote, but I need an anatomy to prove this," Browne replied, "Perform it privately if you must do it, so no one will know if you are in error." And when William added, "But, sir, I am convinced it is Galen who is in error," Browne retorted, "Leave that to the scholars to dispute. You must be worldly if you want to rise at Court. James is suspicious and superstitious. Be careful what you say to him. Our King maintains there are many strange and mysterious things in the world which are not visible to our eyes."

"So do I, sir." So much about the blood I do not know, he thought.

"He believes in witchcraft. He writes passionately on the subject."

William shrugged sceptically.

"Don't express such doubts to him or you will never advance."

"Sir, do you believe in witchcraft?"

"There is much that we don't comprehend." Browne felt that he had grown old since the Queen had died, but he was determined to advance his son-in-law. His daughter must be left secure. "Although you practise for yourself now, I will introduce you as my assistant. James is still pondering whom to appoint to the Tower. It is an important post. This physician will have many eminent personages to attend."

The Presence Chamber had not altered since William had been presented to the Queen, but as Browne led him towards the King he was amazed by the differences between the two rulers. Elizabeth, despite her age and her ailments, had possessed a dignity and will that transcended everything, but James was awkward, without any of her presence, an ugly, weak figure. He moved with a shambling gait, and when he paused he leaned on a courtier to support the weight of his potbellied frame, as if his knock-kneed legs were too frail to hold his body. He fondled his codpiece to reassure himself of his masculinity, his brown beard was straggly, and he wore a shabby doublet that was heavy for a warm May afternoon, thickly quilted to protect himself from imagined assassins. His voice had a broad Scottish accent that was hard to understand. But his skin was white and soft, and his complexion was good, and his eyes were observant.

Browne knelt before the King, who asked him what he wanted.

"Sir, I want to present a worthy doctor who is eager to serve you."

"What distinguishes him from my other physicians?"

"He has studied at Padua with the famed Fabricius. Sir, a great scholar like yourself could converse with him on many learned subjects."

James looked pleased, yet suspicious, and he asked, "Browne, why else should I favour him?"

"Your Majesty, he has a sound knowledge of physic."

"What is his name?"

"William Harvey, sir."

But as a handsome young courtier approached James, his attention wandered.

"Sir, he is applying for the post of Physician to the Tower."

The King said to Cecil, standing small and pale against the panelling of the Presence Chamber, "Little beagle, you attend their wants."

"Lord Salisbury," said Browne, "we are honoured by your interest."

The King's chief minister didn't reply.

"Great sir, you recall my clever son-in-law. During the Queen's last days she favoured him and found his views pleasing. Remember, My Lord?"

Of course I do, Cecil thought irritably, it had been my business to remember anybody who interested the Queen. And he knew Browne, a clever man at intrigue with some knowledge of physic. But he disliked his persistence.

William was shocked that Cecil, created Earl of Salisbury by the King as a reward for his services, had aged so much.

The chief minister was just forty, but his grey hair and ravaged features caused him to look far older. His back was more crooked and his face was even longer and narrower, and Cecil was all in black, as if this suited his present mood.

Cecil was reflecting bitterly, To what end did all this power lead? The wife he had loved dearly was dead; his son whom he longed to have inherit his situation, as he himself had done, was too foolish to manage affairs of state—only a king was allowed to be foolish and still rule; and now James spoke to him in his hunting voice as if he were a dog to pursue the fox. Little beagle indeed! It wasn't his fault he was born with a frame smaller and more crooked than other men's. Yet he couldn't be guilty of disobedience. He sought to be sensible, saying quietly, "Browne, what do you desire?"

"My Lord, I pray that you heed the suit of my son-in-law."

"Many suits are presented to His Majesty."

"My Lord, Dr. Harvey will perform his duties at the Tower zealously."

Cecil's impulse was still to declare, "I can do nothing!" but James was interrupting him with a strange stare in his eyes, and perhaps this young man appealed to the King after all. He paused, unsure of James's desire.

The King was excited. Now he knew just what to do with this attractive doctor. "Upon my soul," said James, "this physician could serve me."

Browne beamed, but Cecil was puzzled, and William waited nervously.

James asked, "Harvey, do you believe in witchcraft?"

Not truly, thought William, but he felt compelled to say, "Yes, sir."

"Good. Have you read my book, *Daemonologie?*"

William hesitated; he hadn't, yet he feared to admit that.

Browne said hurriedly, "Sir, I have. It is a work of scholarship."

"I wrote it with divine encouragement. Harvey, remember that. It will help you in your duties."

"Yes, Your Majesty," said William, but his uneasiness increased.

"It is a noble work. Witchcraft is an abominable sin."

Cecil sighed with relief. He didn't share James's fervent belief in witchcraft, but that elevated the King's usually moody spirits.

"Little beagle, have you ever thought that Raleigh is bewitched?"

Cecil was surprised. He hadn't conceived of such a charge. James was more crafty than the Court realised. If this could be proven, the fox could be discredited forever. "Sir, if you say so, it is possible."

"I am Europe's leading authority on witchcraft."

"Your Majesty, are you certain that Raleigh is bewitched?"

"It only needs proof. Then he must be burnt with all possible speed."

"Yes, sir. Your law of 1604 makes witchcraft a capital offence."

James turned to William and said, "Harvey, you must keep that in mind."

"Your Majesty, I know very little about witchcraft."

"But you are a physician! And as a physician you are the one who can find proof. If you find evidence of a relationship with evil spirits, it is sufficient grounds on which to condemn and execute a suspect. I drafted this statute myself. Harvey, now you must examine the prisoner."

"In the Tower, Your Majesty?"

"Of course. So virtue can prevail."

As William hesitated, the consequences were evident in the King's scowl. Yet the idea of being tested in this way upset him.

Browne was furious at Harvey for not embracing with instant fervency this chance to please James, but he sought to ease the King's irritation by saying, "Gracious sir, if we had proof it would expedite matters."

James smiled triumphantly and motioned for Dr. Ian Andrews to come forward. William saw the Puritanical Scot,

who had examined him at Cambridge with such righteous
zeal, shuffle feebly to the side of the King. "Dr. Andrews has
served me with great piety for many years."

Andrews's Scottish accent was as broad as the King's, and
his voice had become querulous with age, but he waved a
volume in his hands and found strength to shout with ferocity, "This is a Book of Monsters that says that monsters are
the fruit of relations between women and beasts."

William asked, "Doctor, how does this concern Raleigh?"

"The prisoner has been seen reading it."

"Is that all, sir?"

"It is important. This book tells of abominable practices."

James added, "It is rumoured that Raleigh had a hand in
the writing of it. At the least, approves of it. Little beagle,
don't you agree?"

Cecil was thinking about his dear departed wife, treasuring
the memory that a woman had loved him for seven wonderful
years despite his small, crooked body, and he was in no mood
to argue. So he assumed his public face, and thus his public
mask, when he confided in no one, had no close friends,
remembering his father—Burghley's advice: *By trusting none
with your secrets, none can reveal them.* "I agree, Your Majesty."

William asked, "Your Majesty, is there any other proof?"

"Doctor Andrews, you tell our doubting young man."

"One of the soldiers at the Tower reported that at midnight
he heard a noise in the Bloody Tower, where Raleigh is confined. Then he saw a scroll of paper creep out of the window
without the help of a human hand."

"Doctor Andrews, is it possible that the scroll was pushed
out of the window in an effort to communicate with the
prisoner's friends?"

"No, Harvey! For in the moonshine the soldier saw the
scroll turn into the shape of a monkey, then a turkey cock,
and then fly away. Whereupon the soldier called a gaoler, who
also saw the scroll dance up and down and then creep back

into the window, although nothing held it. This I have had from the mouth both of the soldier and the gaoler."

"Sir, I thought witches were always old women."

James interrupted authoritatively. "Not always. Harvey, your duty is to examine Raleigh to see if he has been infected with witchcraft, or is himself a witch, or a creature of Satan. Then report to my little beagle."

"Your Majesty, what will you consider as proof?"

"You must examine Raleigh carefully for suspicious marks on his body. Any callous spot that is found is to be pricked with pins, and if it is insensitive and there is no blood, that is evidence of guilt."

"Even if a mark should be just a bruise, sir?"

"Satan doesn't make such mistakes."

Andrews added piously, "The devil prefers old women as his instruments, but he could use Raleigh to outwit us and to attack His Majesty."

"Even God has to watch His enemies," James asserted. "I know there are witches resolved to destroy me, for I am God's anointed. It is logical that Raleigh, who has been sacrilegious, is Satan's servant."

"Indeed!" said Andrews. "In Scotland His Majesty was graciously pleased to burn many witches. He spent a whole year sifting them out."

"And many were of good education and standing." When William still wavered, James snapped, "Harvey, are you afraid Raleigh will bewitch you?"

William denied this allegation.

James gave the task of the final instructions to his little beagle. This made him feel clever, for now he wouldn't be blamed but the pigmy would bear the responsibility. Everyone knew that Cecil was envious of Raleigh and had helped to bring him down.

Browne spent the trip down the river congratulating William. "If you find the King's greatest enemy infected with Satan, you could rise high."

William answered apprehensively, "Sir, it is also a terrible test."

"And a rare privilege to serve His Majesty."

But as William glanced at the grand house on the river where Raleigh had lived, then at the ominous grey bulk of the Tower, below their landing at Paul's Wharf, he wished he could practise his kind of medicine.

The next day he arrived at the Tower to examine Raleigh. Browne was with him, to guide him, but his father-in-law was in such pain from an inflammation that had spread to the hip that he had to sit down the moment they entered the prisoner's quarters. William, who was oppressed by the solid square squatness of the Bloody Tower when he viewed it from the outside, was surprised by the space within. And now that he faced Raleigh, he was absorbed by his presence. He had heard about Sir Walter ever since he could remember. Despite his distaste for this task, he regarded him with great curiosity. Yet he was also very nervous.

They had entered through the Traitor's Gate, where a dozen heads were spiked, and were led through the gateway of the inner Ward and into the Bloody Tower, where the ghosts of the slain princes were reputed to roam still. Yet the quarters were comfortable, more like chambers than a prison cell, and Raleigh had a fine walk along the battlements overlooking the Thames, two servants, a large fireplace, a table filled with books, paper, pen, ink, and instruments with which to experiment.

He was introduced to the prisoner by the gaoler as a doctor come from the King to examine him, which caused Raleigh to exclaim, "I suffer only with melancholy, and no one can cure that." Before William could reply—Browne, who had taken opium to dull his pain, had fallen asleep in a chair—Raleigh declared, "Harvey, I have found a cordial that eases pain. Would you like to taste it?" When he saw him waver, he laughed. "Never fear, it isn't poison. See!" He gulped it down to prove his assertion. As he noticed William regarding the dozing doctor anxiously, he added, "I knew him when he attended the Queen. Lancelot Browne was more courteous to me then." He halted, thinking of when he had been one of the most powerful men in the realm.

In this pause William was able to observe Raleigh more closely. His face was better formed than the King's or Cecil's, yet compelling rather than handsome. His beard and hair were carefully combed, and his dress was immaculate.

Raleigh said, "You are young to be physician to the King."

"Sir, this is a special situation."

"But you are an improvement over his old, pious scarecrow, Andrews."

Browne moaned, and Raleigh awoke him and said, "You will ease your pain if you lie down in an inner room, where my wife rests when she visits me."

This done, Raleigh resumed. "Harvey, what is your situation?"

He murmured, "The Court is concerned about your condition."

"They should be. I trust Cecil will secure my removal, for the Tower dampness and river mists have sorely affected my health. I suffer danger of death by palsy, and of suffocation by obstructed lungs."

Yet when William approached Raleigh to examine him, he said, "It isn't necessary. Are you interested in botany? I possess a garden given me by the Lieutenant of the Tower, Sir George Harvey. Are you related? He has been kindly disposed toward me. But, no, I can see it in your face. I also have a laboratory for distillations and analyses. I have concocted a *Great Cordial,* which has cured the Prince of Wales of various humours. It is composed of animal, vegetable, and mineral matter. It will free me from this place if nothing else will."

William wondered. He recalled that when Raleigh had been arrested in 1603, soon after James came to the throne, he had been condemned to death. Only on the scaffold had his punishment been commuted to life imprisonment.

William inched closer to see if there were any marks on his body, as the King had instructed, and Raleigh cried out, "My side often grows cold and numb, and the fingers of my left hand are contracted and stiff."

"Sir, you probably have paralytic symptoms."

"I know. You must tell Cecil to put me into warmer quarters."

"Does anything else trouble you, sir?" William saw a bluish-black spot on Raleigh's arm, and he shivered. Was this the devil's mark after all?

"Oh, that!" snapped Raleigh, noticing the doctor's fascinated gaze. "It's just a bruise. The physician here recommended fried horse dung on it, but I prefer cream and honey. Why do you look so odd?"

"May I examine it, sir?"

Raleigh shrugged and said, "It is of no consequence." But when William's interest increased, he held out his arm for a closer examination.

William couldn't find any other marks, and when he touched it Raleigh winced from the pain. It was a bruise, he decided. He said, "Sir, you should be more careful. And you should take precautions to cure it."

"I will when I have the time. Now I have a duty to the Bloody Tower. These rooms engage my imagination. Every day my mind roams through them and seeks companions. I traverse the passages and staircases and great rooms and enter into the minds of those who have lived here. It is a large and fine company: our Queen, her mother, Anne Boleyn, Sir Thomas More, Essex, the young princes, Lady Jane Grey, Thomas Cromwell—the list is long."

James had said, "*You will see it in his face that he is guilty*," but what William saw was animation and a compelling need to control life rather than allowing life to control him.

"There wasn't even glass in my windows when I was first imprisoned here. I had to stuff them with straw until my demands were heeded."

"Sir, did you ever thrust a scroll out of these windows?"

"Naturally. I have friends who wish to acquire my knowledge."

"Was it done at night, Sir Walter?"

"Probably. I don't remember. How does this concern my health?"

William didn't reply, but he grew red with embarrassment.

Suddenly Raleigh knew. He cried out, "It is a sickly age when a king must resort to such a corruption. Am I accused of consorting with Satan?"

"Not accused, sir, but . . ."

"Examine me, young man."

William refused.

"Are you afraid?"

"No."

"A little ashamed?"

William coughed, then nodded reluctantly.

"I have been accused of many dark thoughts, but never of witchcraft."

"Sir, do you believe in Satan?"

"There is much evil in the world, but nothing is more perplexing than life itself. As a physician, do you share the findings of Aristotle?"

"Not completely, sir."

"I cannot believe that God has shut up all the light of learning within the scope of Aristotle's brain. Not as long as my blood moves freely."

"Sir Walter, how far do you think it flows?"

For once Raleigh was puzzled and at a loss for words.

"There is so much motion in the blood, I believe it flows in a more enlarged, capable manner than we know. But I don't understand enough!"

"Don't be troubled. There is much that none of us understand. But as long as we question and investigate, something is learned. He must awake your companion before he sleeps away the entire examination."

Browne was startled by their presence; he had forgotten where he was. He was upset; William appeared to be exceedingly affected by Raleigh, who was treating his son-in-law with an unexpected and unusual civility now.

Raleigh saw the old man's face contorted with pain, and he said, "Dr. Browne, you must try my *Great Cordial*. It will relieve your pain."

"I can't!" Did the prisoner think he was a fool!

William took a sip and liked that it soothed his own nervous stomach.

When Browne saw that Harvey didn't seem bewitched, while his pain grew worse, he agreed to try the *Great Cordial*. It blurred his pain and revived his spirits. It also convinced him that Raleigh knew practices not common to others. He turned angrily on Harvey and asked, "Have you examined the prisoner as ordered by His Majesty?"

"Yes, sir."

"You must report your findings to the King."

"That I am infected with witchcraft, Lancelot Browne?"

"Do not taunt me, Sir Walter."

"I have many complaints, but the devil's hand hasn't touched me. Like all men, I am the work of God. If I turn over a thousand books to write my own, it is to express His wonders. The world is His, not the devil's."

"And His Majesty's," Browne declared piously.

"Is that why he expects me to acknowledge guilt when there is none to admit? To humiliate me? But I will not be humiliated. Not by anyone."

William said, "Sir Walter, life is an uncertain, risky business."

"A wise thing for a physician to know. I learned that a long time ago. Human nature, what a contradiction that is. Good day, Doctors."

William's last view of Raleigh was of an aging but defiant warrior standing in a shaft of sunlight, as if he were reaching out to it as the source of life. Yet when he decided to report that Raleigh was not tainted by any of the devil's practices, Browne told him this was a grave error.

"James will not favour you then. His belief in witchcraft is fundamental. You must find something sinister in Raleigh's condition."

"Sir, what do you suggest?"

"Mention his *Great Cordial*. It had a strange effect on me."

"Sir, it eased your pain."

"Because it seized control of my senses. As if by magic."

But Raleigh was also one of the most learned, inquisitive men William had met, and he couldn't shorten such a life. He wrote that his medical examination had not found any corruption, but that the prisoner was a fit subject for medical treatment, that Raleigh suffered from paralytic symptoms which would be relieved only if the prisoner was removed to warmer quarters, and he begged Lord Salisbury's indulgence for such findings.

Browne reluctantly agreed to transmit this report to Lord Salisbury, since Harvey would write no other, but he wished his son-in-law had better control of his passions. He waited a month before he was granted an audience with Cecil. Yet, while he was still disgusted with Harvey's obstinacy, he sought to put on his best face for the occasion. He knelt respectfully at the feet of Lord Salisbury, although his body ached so woefully he feared he would cry out in his anguish. He was kept kneeling a long time, while Cecil didn't bother to read the report. Only after the chief minister had contemplated everything in the Audience Chamber but the supplicant at his feet did he say, "Browne, it isn't necessary to kneel to persuade me. Did Harvey find any corruptions?"

"Noble sir, it would be helpful if you read his conclusions first."

Cecil perused them briefly, then dismissed him without another word.

When there was no word from Cecil within the next few weeks, Browne wrote him on behalf of Harvey and received a reply that disturbed him. It forced him to write in a second letter to the chief minister: "*My Good Lord, Although by your own express commandment I am barred from access to you, yet I beseech my honourable good Lord to hear my suit for Dr. Harvey.*" The rest of the plea spoke of the candidate's ability, and added the recommendation of distinguished colleagues in the College of Physicians.

There was no reply. Browne's services were not requested at Court. And Harvey was so absorbed in his practice and medical experiments that Browne wondered if his son-in-law realized how hard he was labouring in his behalf, that he was risking much to obtain a lucrative position at Court for him. He blamed his fading health on Harvey's failure to please. He feared that his daughter had wed an uncertain, precarious future.

Months later, he was summoned suddenly and unexpectedly to Court, and he was commanded to bring Harvey with him. This surprised Browne. It was as if he had been in darkness and then, without warning, he was allowed to stand in the sunlight again. But Harvey didn't want to go.

William had just heard from his father that his mother was seriously ill and that his presence was urgently requested in Folkestone.

"What is wrong?" asked Browne. He thought, It couldn't be that serious.

"My father says that no one seems to know. But her stomach has swollen much. I cannot attend anyone else while she is in danger."

"A few hours at Whitehall won't make any difference."

"It could if she is as sick as my father suggests."

"The instant we are finished with the Court, I will hire the fastest coach to take you to Folkestone. But now you must heed the King."

"Do you think this summons is from James?"

"Yes. No doubt it is about the position at the Tower. Cecil has finally decided to allow my petitions to reach the royal ears. Probably because he wants something now from the College of Physicians."

While William was still doubtful about delaying the trip to Folkestone, even for a day, for his father's summons was urgent, he allowed himself to be persuaded by Browne, and he went with him to the palace.

At Whitehall, despite not having heard from either the King or Cecil for a long time, they were ushered at once into the Royal Presence. Browne could hardly drag himself into the Audience Chamber, his leg hurt so, but he knew that neither James nor Cecil would heed him if he were ailing, and thus he tried to appear healthy and vigourous. And he warned William, "Do not speak well of Raleigh. James doesn't like him praised."

William was startled to see many soldiers protecting the King, who was sallow with apprehension. Then James ordered Cecil to address them.

Cecil asked, "Harvey, did you suppress anything in your report to me?"

"No, My Lord Salisbury, not that I know of—"

"Do not equivocate," James interrupted anxiously. "Doctor, were there any barbarities in the prisoner's mind or on his person?"

"None, Your Majesty. He spoke about his experiments, his *Great Cordial,* his own poor health. Sir, he needs medical treatment—"

James cut him short, imperiously, "Did he mention me?"

"With piety and devotion, sir."

"Not with the devil's tongue?"

"I saw no trace of that, Your Majesty."

"You said piety. Were there any references to the Church of Rome?"

"No, sir."

"None at all?"

"Not that I heard." Yet the King was so eager for him to say yes, he felt compelled to ask, "Sir, what is Sir Walter Raleigh accused of now?"

James said with satisfaction, "Little beagle, inform them what has happened. Perhaps that will help the doctor reveal the guilt we need."

Cecil said scornfully, "Last night an attempt to blow up our King and Parliament was unearthed. It was a gunpowder plot instigated by Papists. Expecting success, they intended to seize power today, November 5."

William was so shocked he stammered, "Sir, I don't know what to say."

Cecil added coldly, "We know that your sentiments and connections are Protestant. You have been thoroughly investigated. Particularly since you went to Padua, which is under the jurisdiction of the Church of Rome."

James shouted irately, "These conspirators are creatures of Satan! When they captured the devil who was to set the match to the gunpowder, Guy Fawkes, they brought him to my bedchamber, and when I asked him how he could conspire against innocent souls, he replied, '*A dangerous disease required a desperate remedy. Sir, it was my intention to blow you back to Scotland.*' Thank God, Guy Fawkes is in the Tower now."

William asked, "Your Majesty, what do you want of me?"

Cecil said, "The King wants to know if Raleigh indicated in any way that he was involved in this conspiracy."

"Sir, I thought he was the Papists' bitterest enemy."

"You did not answer my question. You are not always clever."

"Sir, he didn't discuss political ideas, but medical matters."

"Browne, you were there. Did you observe anything suspicious?"

Browne wasn't sure what to say. He sensed that power lay before him for the grasping. But he didn't recall anything incriminating, and he did desire his son-in-law's respect. "Sir, I saw nothing suspicious."

James left hurriedly then, to hunt where he could kill without fear of his own blood being shed, about which he possessed a mortal dread.

Browne, who felt ill even as he struggled desperately to hide this, mumbled, "My great and honourable Lord Salisbury, my son-in-law could examine Guy Fawkes. And whoever else is confined in the Tower."

"That is not necessary. It is proven that Fawkes is guilty."

"My Lord, may I take the liberty to renew his suit?"

"The appointment has been decided. It has gone to Dr. Gwinne."

No wonder, Browne thought bitterly, Gwinne has better connections.

"Gwinne is more experienced. Harvey is unknown."

William said, "My Lord, perhaps I could assist him."

"With your inability to judge His Majesty's wishes? No!"

"My Lord, suppose I am right and Raleigh is not bewitched?"

"The King thinks otherwise. When you get home I would put Browne to bed. He looks terrible." Cecil said this with satisfaction, as if he had won a victory over a tall, straight-backed man whom he had envied.

At his home Browne refused aid from Harvey. He insisted that William go to his mother's side at once. He ordered his footman to obtain the fastest coach available, and only when his son-in-law was on his way did Browne allow himself to retire to his bedroom, where he collapsed.

By the time William arrived in Folkestone, it was the next day, and he realized that he was very late. He had travelled all night despite the peril on the roads from brigands, and his father wanted to know what had delayed him. Thomas was angry, upset, and very frightened.

"I had to go to Whitehall, on the express command of the King."

For once his father wasn't impressed. He had graver matters to consider. He said, "If you had come yesterday you might have helped your mother. But last night she had a relapse, and today I fear she is dying."

"May I attend her?"

"In a moment. You must know what to expect. What did the King want?"

"He requested my medical opinion of Sir Walter Raleigh."

"Raleigh has strange views. Did the King approve of your findings?"

"I doubt it. Father, are there any doctors in attendance?"

Thomas strode the length of his drawing room to ease his agitation and grumbled. "Now there is. But at first none would come. And you know my opinion of our doctors. Quacks! So when your mother took to her bed, I called our local apothecary, who gave her some herbs."

William asked angrily, "Without the authorisation of a physician?"

"Do they possess better cures?"

"They should. Father, that was negligent."

"Should I have waited for you? The apothecary's herbs eased her pain, but when her stomach continued to swell he recommended a surgeon."

"Was that still without a doctor's permission?"

"Surgeon Mathey saw much service in our wars."

"No surgeon or apothecary should act without the advice of a doctor. They cannot do the right thing if they don't know what is wrong."

"His incision helped your mother at first. But now she is worse. Even as her stomach swells, the rest of her shrinks. She cannot eat."

"What do the physicians say?"

"You will hear for yourself." Thomas led William through the anteroom where four of his brothers waited: John, Daniel, Michael, and Eliab. They greeted William solemnly, with Eliab on the verge of tears. Joshua, the steward, who stood at the door to the bedchamber, said that the doctors in attendance, Pope and Elmhurst, had finished their examination and now it was proper for Thomas and William to enter.

William hardly recognized his mother. Her face was shrunken, and she was swathed in so much bedclothing he thought she could suffocate. She was in a coma, and he saw that her stomach protruded terrifyingly, while Pope and Elmhurst quarrelled about what to do next. Thomas muttered, "As usual, they are too late, we never have them when we need them," but William was more concerned about their competence. He heard Pope's voice rise in anger as the fat, middle-aged doctor asserted, "The wound made by the surgeon should be kept clean with a weapon salve, an ointment compounded of the human tissue, blood, and fat of the wound," while Elmhurst retorted, "Pope, you are in error, we must examine the liver to determine whether her blood is being produced properly."

William interrupted: "Doctors, what about her stomach? From all the evidence, that appears to be the seat of her affliction."

"No," replied Elmhurst, "her heart is the seat of her humours." He walked with a consequential strut, and although he was younger than Pope, he looked older, his face a mass of wrinkles. "The heart has mystic properties. As the Egyptians said. Her stars are in the wrong orbit."

Pope shouted, "I've done the right things! She was purged, bled, took leeches, and I also applied a lotion and plaster to her wound."

She moaned, and William thought irately, The time for being polite was over. He pushed aside the doctors and bent over her. Thomas was shocked when he pulled the bedclothing off to examine her swollen stomach and the incision—

doctors were not supposed to view naked females—but he felt
the situation was too dangerous to heed amenities. The incision had been poorly done, and the swelling looked like a
tumour to him. His father, who averted his eyes, said, "She
has a foulness in the stomach, and much looseness."

"Why didn't you call me sooner?"

"I called you as soon as I needed you. You should have
come yesterday."

At the sight of his wife's blood, Thomas grew faint. Elmhurst, delighted to be a doctor again, agreed to take care of
the sick man, while William continued his examination of his
mother. And Pope, disgusted because he was ignored, retired
to a corner of the bedroom, muttering loudly so he would be
heard, "The Egyptians were wrong. Women are more difficult
to cure than men, for their humours are more contrary and
crafty."

William exposed her body to see it better, and it stirred her
out of her coma. And as she saw her son bending over her
anxiously, and that his gaze was fixed on her breasts, she
murmured, "The mark you see there, between them, I have
had for as long as I can remember, and just your father
knows of it, and he only saw it when I nursed. Why do you
stare so?"

William didn't answer, seeking to understand the mark's
meaning.

"Oh, God!" she whimpered. "Let me go! For God's sake,
don't look!"

"Mother, I must examine you if I'm to help you."

"I'm not a witch! God knows that I'm not a witch!"

Yet he knew that it was precisely this kind of a mark
between the teats that was considered the proof that an old
woman was a witch. But my mother cannot be a witch, he
thought with horror. Not my mother!

"Prick it with pins," she cried. "It is not insensitive. It
hurts."

"It isn't necessary," he said. "You need nature's help, a

good diet, fresh air," but he halted as he realised that she wasn't listening.

His father moaned, "God has made up His mind to take her, there is nothing we can do," and at that the other doctors rushed back to the side of the patient to discover whether that was true.

William felt her pulse. It was irregular, and at his touch she cried out, "Thomas, you tell him that I am a virtuous woman." Her hands covered the mark between her breasts, and she sobbed, "I must die in the arms of God. I am not a witch! Tell him, Thomas, tell him!"

He assured her, "You are righteous, and nothing will change that view."

"Will you put that on my tomb? Please, Thomas, please?"

"Wherever you desire, Joan, dear."

"Place it on the wall of our church. Where everyone can see it."

"I promise."

She appeared less anguished now, and she took William's hand for support, but then Pope, hearing the word "witch," cried out, "We are all sinners, like Adam. Where is the questionable spot? I must prick it with my pins!" Before William could halt him, Pope thrust aside his mother's hand to test the mark, and when, as he pushed his pin against, she didn't respond, he declared ominously but triumphantly, "She could be infected with witchcraft. That could be her illness. She does not stir."

William replied sadly, "She cannot, Dr. Pope. She is dead."

As Joan Harvey had requested, Thomas Harvey erected a brass memorial tablet on the chancel wall of their parish church, ancient St. Mary and St. Eanswythe, so that everyone would be aware that she had been a pious and virtuous soul. When it was in place after the funeral and her family of seven sons and one daughter attended the ceremony, their father read it aloud to them so they could join him in paying her the proper respect.

A.D. 1605, Nov. 8th dyed in ye 50th yeere of her age,

JOAN, Wife of THO: HARVEY. Mother of 7 Sones
  and 2 daughters.
A Godly harmless Woman: A chaste loveing Wife:
A charitable quiet Neighbour: A comfortable
  friendly Matron:
A provident diligent Huswyfe: A careful tender-
  harted Mother:
Deere to Her Husband: Reverensed of her Children:
  Beloved of her Neighbours: Elected of God.
Whose Soule rest in Heaven: her body in this Grave.
To her a Happy Advantage: to hers an Unhappy Loss.

William prayed that this would have satisfied his mother. It did his father. Thomas assured everyone within the sound of his voice that his family was virtuous. He felt the tablet was worthy of a king.

mpurity breeds purity
Else what would it rise to
Purity breeds impurity
Else what would it fall to

  A few weeks later Browne died too. Elizabeth was desolate, and there were moments when William thought she was going to follow her father into the grave. Doctors from the College of Physicians had attended Browne, as befitted his rank, and those worthies had purged his bowels as if they were atheistical and extracted his blood as if it were a dire inconvenience, and ignored William's wish to provide the patient with rest and comfort.

The two deaths that he had been unable to prevent left him sick with despair. He thought bitterly, In spite of all he had learned he had been unable to save either life. His unhappiness increased when Elizabeth wouldn't allow him to touch her the evening after Browne was buried, although he desired only to console her and to ease her sorrow.

She recoiled from him, wept grievously, and sobbed, "It would be lewd of me to indulge in fornication with his body still warm in the grave."

He felt crossly that she thought too highly of herself, but he didn't quarrel with her. He reminded himself that the strain of watching her father die had been shattering, and that she was highly strung.

He waited until he considered that a decent interval had passed, and then, after a month of mourning he sought to embrace her, and she repulsed him. He sat up in bed abruptly, thinking of what the Queen had said:

"My Lords, I have but one mistress and no master."

William wondered: Is virginity my wife's mistress, too, and is she unable to accept a master? Yet his flesh needed fulfillment, and he knew he could not compromise much longer. He turned to Elizabeth, cowering on the other side of the large, canopied bed, and he sought to pull her to him in a demonstration of affection. She began to cry piteously.

"What is wrong now?" he asked solicitously, although he was angry.

"This isn't seemly. You are profaning my sorrow."

"A month later? Elizabeth, how long do you intend to mourn?"

"I wouldn't have to mourn if you had been more considerate."

"I don't understand what you mean."

"Your obstinacy forced my father into efforts that were too much for him."

"It was his idea that I apply for the post of Physician to the Tower."

"But you didn't follow his advice."

"Do you heed mine?"

"And you were away when my father needed you most."

"I delayed my return to London to spend some time with my family. But I didn't criticise you when you didn't attend my mother's funeral."

"That was because of the difficulty of travel. I sent a message of condolence with Silas that conveyed my sorrow over her passing."

Yet he had felt Silas's sympathy more than he had felt hers.

Elizabeth declared he could have saved her father if he had wanted to, and he didn't answer, remembering what actually had happened.

After the funeral William had remained in Folkestone to comfort his father and to share his family's grief. His twenty-three-year-old brother, John, planned to come to London to seek a post at Court, and desired his advice. Thomas, who was twenty-one, was getting experience in the family business. Daniel, Eliab, and the twins, Michael and Matthew, also wanted to be merchants, while the nine-year-old Amy helped in the household.

His father was proud that the Harveys were a closely knit family, and he was determined that his sons become partners.

When it came time to say good-bye, Thomas said, "William, do not be upset about your mother. Nothing could have saved her. It was God's will. And please pay my respects to your eminent father-in-law."

Thus, since Browne had encouraged him to leave London to treat his mother, to find his father-in-law critically ill was unexpected.

Elizabeth reproached him for not returning sooner, and he replied, "Why didn't you summon me?"

"Father wouldn't allow it. He said there was nothing you

could do. But will you examine him? He respects your knowledge and learning."

William hurried over to his father-in-law's home, where Browne lay in an airless bedchamber surrounded by doctors. When he saw Harvey, he ordered that they be left alone.

William was shocked at his condition. Browne's white, set face was like a death mask, and he looked ghastly.

Yet he refused to be examined, saying, "It is too late."

"Why didn't you inform me of your condition?"

"It wouldn't have helped. I've been finished ever since the Queen died. She wore me out. Never devote yourself to rulers, they will squeeze you dry."

"Who has examined you?"

"Colleagues from the College. They told me that my body has been abused beyond recovery, and they kindly gave me opium to afford me an easier passage into my next life. But don't tell Elizabeth. She would never forgive me if she thought I left her of my own doing."

"How can you be sure the end is in sight? Let me examine you. Please."

"No. My colleagues said there might be one chance in ten of success if I allowed surgery, but I am not going to permit a barber to slit me like a worm and perform barbarities on my person. A less painful passing—that honour and courtesy—my profession must grant me."

William noticed that Browne's voice was very weak. But suddenly he said, with an enormous effort, "William, take care of Elizabeth. She has strong ideas, but she needs protection. Promise me." When William promised, Browne rushed on, as if the doctor had to say this before it was too late. "You could have a fine future. You are observant, you have good parts, but in the practice of physic you are too much swayed by your interest in the movement of the blood. It will lead you nowhere, and prejudice many against you. That was of grave concern to Cecil."

William asked anxiously, "Are you certain this is true?"

There was no reply. Browne was unconscious, and he died soon after, of a stone, William suspected, a loss of will, and pain-easing opium.

Elizabeth's tears brought William back to the present. She sobbed, "I am convinced you could have saved him if you had come home in time."

He couldn't tell her the truth; she would never forgive him.

"Your lustful demands at this time could bring about my damnation."

He felt at his wit's end. She had been in an emotional decline ever since her father's death. But he said, "We have our life ahead of us."

"Not mine. I cannot forget how you failed my father. We must have separate rooms." She wasn't sure she meant this, but he must know her will.

He felt as if his feelings were being ransacked. He said, "You can have this room. I will use the bedchamber on the floor above."

Elizabeth hadn't expected such a quick acceptance, and she cried out, "William, are you serious?"

"Since you are more concerned with the welfare of your soul than of my flesh, you have persuaded me to move."

"You are not leaving me, are you?" Her lips trembled uncontrollably.

"This is my home, and we are a family. I promised your father that."

Reassured now that she knew he was not leaving her, and determined to show that she still had the advantage over him, she said, "It is a matter of indifference where you sleep as long as we understand each other."

"Tomorrow I will order Silas to fix the bedchamber upstairs."

She didn't believe that he would go ahead with this arrangement. When he did, she fell ill. Yet he couldn't find anything wrong with her. He stood by her side while she reclined in the large, canopied bed and he said, "There is nothing medically wrong with you. You are not sick."

"I am surfeited with melancholy. You have betrayed me."

He sought to soothe her with a caress, and she pulled away from him. He exclaimed, "Elizabeth, don't you have any natural feeling for me?"

"Shame, William, you are swollen with animal humours."

"You needn't be afraid. I won't trouble you any further. Is there anything you need?"

"I will be content with the calm belief in the path I have chosen."

Nonetheless, since she had been taught Latin by her father and a reverence for the study of religious works, she decided to illustrate her thoughts with a reading of the Bible. By the time Elizabeth reached Leviticus, she felt almost fully recovered, and when she finished Deuteronomy several weeks later she was able to get out of bed. Until then, Rachel brought her food and sought to supply her every want, while William visited her each day to see how she was feeling.

Meanwhile, Silas put a trestle table in the bedchamber upstairs, and fixed the fireplace so it would give off the best possible heat. William also saw to it that Silas furnished the room next to the bedchamber as a laboratory. He was interested in having a large desk to work upon and a comfortable chair on which to sit.

William was surprised when Elizabeth joined him at the breakfast table late in January and asked him, "Are you going to witness the executions at the west front of St. Paul's?"

He was thinking of an experiment, and he looked puzzled.

She said angrily, "Have you no natural curiosity? I've heard that four of the desperate gunpowder-plot conspirators are to be hanged and drawn and quartered there tomorrow. It is a national holiday. Everybody will be in attendance to see the King's orders carried out."

"To see men die? Is there any joy in that?"

"You are a physician. You see death all the time. I wish I was strong enough to see these blasphemers sent to hell. William, do you think my accumulation of melancholy was caused by the devil?"

"You mustn't believe such books, Elizabeth."

"Have you read His Majesty's work, *Daemonologie?*"

"The King commanded me to do so as a form of instruction. But it should have no place in your life."

"When one is close to the shadow of death, as I was, it is important that I know how to avoid the temptations of the devil. It makes the Bible more comforting. I hear Guy Fawkes is being executed soon too."

"I had forgotten."

"No wonder the King didn't appoint you to the Tower. You have no awareness of what service to him requires. Now I realize what my poor father endured seeking to improve your situation. At the least, you ought to support His Majesty by applauding the executions. James is your anointed King, and supposedly you are a learned doctor."

Perhaps she is right, he reflected. The next morning he joined the mob that lined Ludgate Hill as four conspirators were drawn past on a hurdle. Then, with great ceremony, they were placed against the west front of St. Paul's Cathedral, where they were hanged and drawn and quartered. The crowd roared its approval of each bloody step, but he thought it was an ugly sight. These executions at the Church were to reaffirm the nation's allegiance to Protestantism over the Church of Rome, but the truth was, he felt, that they were simply an excuse to indulge in righteous pleasure.

The following day he saw the same rites performed on Guy Fawkes and three more conspirators at Westminster. He sought to observe with clinical candour, as he would have witnessed an anatomy, but he was disturbed by the cruelty with which the men were executed. Yet he found himself assessing what happened to their blood as they died. It spurted forth such intensity when the executioner's knife savagely disemboweled the victims that it flowed as if it possessed a life of its own. But nature also appeared to be violated.

Troubled by what he had seen, he withdrew to his laboratory and reflected, *Sometimes man was nothing but a great mischievous baboon.* He was still sitting in darkness when Silas entered with a candle and asked, "Sir, you haven't had anything to eat. May I serve you?"

"It is too late. It must be close to midnight."

"Master, my sister has kept your supper for you."

"Where is my wife?"

"She went to bed hours ago, sir. After she made her devotions."

"What is there to eat?"

"Rachel will bring it up. Master, we were worried about you."

"I was at the executions. Did you witness them?"

"No." Silas shivered. "I never could witness an execution. Sir, it is not a natural way to die. May we bring up your dinner?"

"Yes, thank you."

Rachel brought a hot meat dish, bread, cheese, and ale. She regarded William warily as she served him, not entering the laboratory until Silas was present, yet she was pleased that he enjoyed what she had prepared. *Ever since Rachel has come to work for us,* thought William, *she has said little, as if her chief interest is simply to be with her brother*—yet he wondered if that was all. Tonight he was especially aware of her luminous blue eyes, exquisite skin, and lovely red hair. Suddenly her appearance stirred him with unexpected feeling. And he was charmed by the gentle simplicity of her manner. For an instant he wished he could strip her bare; then he told himself that this ardent desire was merely a passing fancy. She seemed greatly relieved when he dismissed her.

The next day William returned to the practice that Browne had left him. His first patient was Robert Holcomb, a churchwarden from St. Paul's, whose complaint was that he was grievously lamed by the gout.

William said, "You stand too much on cold stone floors."

"I used a remedy offered me by a young poet, John Donne, who haunts St. Paul's in search of employment. But now my leg is worse."

"His treatment is wrong. You must sit with your leg bare in a pail of water, which is like a frost. Then, when it feels almost dead from the cold, take yourself to your stove, and the heat will drive away the gout."

"That is a harsh remedy. My young friend, Donne, who has experience in medical matters, says that gout often is caused by too much passion."

"And exposure. Especially when it is extreme. Keep your leg warm."

His next patient was an anxious, rawboned merchant, Fred Wells, who complained of a shortness of breath when he climbed steps and said, "I have been purged and bled, but now I am oppressed with diarrhoea."

"It may be your heart."

"I do become exhausted easily. I cannot breathe deeply."

"You must avoid all violent exercise and eat lightly. And try not to become anxious. A calm state of mind will help your condition."

Wells expected magic incantations, Latin phrases, and herbs to make his blood vigourous, and he retired looking very disappointed.

The third patient, whom William had to visit, was Sir Edward Stanhope. At the Chancellor's mansion he surveyed the patient in the places where Stanhope complained of pain. Stanhope, even fatter than before, reclined in a huge four-poster bed, and cried out that his buttocks were afflicted.

They were swollen and pimpled, and William saw a sore like a boil.

"Harvey, it hurts horribly. When my coach bumps, I cannot sit."

"It is a small abrasion. I would recline on pillows."

Stanhope, who really desired Browne, was disappointed by this modest diagnosis. He grumbled, "Doctor Allen, whom I called when I couldn't reach you yesterday, said this is a serious complaint. Where were you, Harvey?"

"My Lord, I was attending the executions at Westminster."

"A Godly occasion. I am sorry I was forced to miss them. But Allen had to purge me, bleed me, apply a balsam, and consult the stars."

"Did his treatment ease you, sir?"

"He was so consoling, I felt better almost at once. But today my pain has returned with renewed severity. That is why I summoned you."

"I will apply a plaster to the boil. It will remove the soreness."

"Is that all you are going to do?" Stanhope was shocked.

"You must give nature a chance to work with rest and a light diet, sir."

"Allen said it was because of a fever and that I must eat heartily."

"My Lord, if you weighed less the abused part would hurt less."

Stanhope was offended, and he sat up abruptly, although that hurt, and said, "Harvey, you lack learning. You are too young."

"Sir, what else did Doctor Allen recommend?"

"He said fried horse dung would ease the pain of the bruise."

"My Lord, it is not a bruise but a sore which has become a pimple."

"When I go to stool, I have much trouble. I must stop my looseness."

"That is nerves, sir. If you will lie at ease and eat less—"

Stanhope interrupted irritably. "Have you nothing else to give me?"

"My Lord, I have offered my remedy."

"It is insufficient. You have no idea how I am suffering. I must find a wise physician who respects my position and understands my humours."

William walked along Paternoster Row later, looking for a book that would distract him from patients such as Stanhope. Most of the titles were religious, and they bored him; then he saw one that intrigued him:

An EXCELLENT conceited Tragedie of Romeo and Juliet.

William had heard that the Lord Chamberlain's Men had done a new version of this old tale, and so he bought it, for a shilling. He was surprised to see on an inside page that it was written by Will Shakespeare. When he noticed that the play was set in Verona, his interest increased; he had visited this town, seventy miles from Venice, several times.

As he read the play, the poetry enchanted him. He was stirred by Romeo's passion, and moved deeply by Juliet's response.

He gave it to Elizabeth in the hope this would end her famine of feeling. Instead, she perused the play briefly, then said, "This poet has no wit, and he writes too freely of tender emotions. There is no virtue here."

Who then shall I love, he whispered to himself as she disdainfully returned his present. She was studying the Book of Job as if it applied to her, and he saw only one remedy for his lack of love. He decided to absorb himself totally in his study of the course of the blood.

A few nights later William needed someone with whom to experiment. It was late; he had skipped supper in his involvement with the structure of the heart, and now Silas stood in the doorway of the laboratory, asking if he was hungry. William became excited suddenly—Silas could be his subject!

He said, "Silas, I'm not hungry, but I need some help with my work."

"To do what, Master?"

"I want to test the sound of your heart."

"Sir, can you hear it?"

"Under certain conditions. Now I want to listen to your heart."

Silas asked apprehensively, "Sir, are you going to use the knife?"

"No, no nothing like that."

"Master, you will not damage my soul?"

"I do not expect to damage anything."

William frowned, and Silas asked anxiously, "What is wrong, sir?"

"I need another person to perform this experiment satisfactorily."

"Master, I will fetch Rachel. She will help us."

"She may object."

"Not if I ask her. Sir, I will return soon."

But it was a long time before Silas did come back, which gave William the feeling that Rachel did not share her brother's willingness to be a subject. Yet, when Silas returned, his sister was with him.

Meanwhile, he reviewed ideas he had been taught about the heart.

Galen had said: *"The right ventricle of the heart, with the blood supplied by the liver, produces the natural spirit. The left ventricle, with the aid of the lungs, begets the vital spirit. And the brain makes the animal spirits. Thus, the blood is supplied by varied sources."*

He felt less sure about this than ever. The blood that had flowed from the executed men had looked the same, whatever parts it had come from. He also felt guilty that he hadn't understood Fred Wells's heart accurately enough. He reflected ruefully, If patients realized how little physicians knew, their practices would fall away to nothing.

Rachel stood before him unwillingly—here only, he felt, because Silas had forced her to come—and she said, "What do you want of us?"

"I want to listen to the sound of Silas's heart, and yours."

Silas said, "Master, I'm so thin."

"That is fine. Your heart is close to the surface. Easy to hear."

She asked suspiciously, "Then why do you need to examine mine?"

"You are more nervous than Silas, your heart could sound differently."

"Is that the only reason?"

"No. I want to test whether your heart and his act the same way under the same conditions."

"We are the same blood," she said defiantly. "Our hearts are the same."

"All hearts should sound about alike. Unless they are diseased."

"Our choice of action is limited. We are your servants."

"You are not forced to consent. I will not dismiss you if you say no."

Silas said, "Sir, I will be honoured to serve you."

She asked abruptly, "Will it benefit me?"

"It will benefit others. Future patients."

"Is it risky?"

"It shouldn't be."

"But you are not sure, Doctor Harvey?"

"No. However, if you are healthy there is very little danger."

"Of course I am healthy."

Silas said, "Rachel, see what happens to me. Then decide."

She waited while the doctor asked Silas to jump up and down, to run in place, and then William listened to his heart. The sound was louder, quicker, but remained regular.

My ear is good, thought William, but I need more practice to trust it fully. "How do you feel after all this exercise?"

"Fine, sir. Rachel, do not be timourous. The Master didn't hurt me."

"Doctor, will you have to touch me?"

"After your exercise, yes."

"You will not take any liberties?"

"I only wish to hear how your heart sounds."

Reluctantly, yet excitedly, Rachel followed William's instructions, jumping up and down, as her brother had done,
then running in place. But when he asked her to unbutton
her bodice so he could listen accurately, she did this slowly
and uncomfortably. William tried to ignore the inviting bulges
of her small but perfect breasts while he listened to her heart.
It sounded louder and faster than Silas's, but still regular.

He said, "To judge from the sound, both of you have good
hearts."

She said suddenly, "Even though we are not gentlefolk."

"That has nothing to do with the condition of your heart."

"Are we done?"

"Once more, if you don't mind. I must verify something."
After they had repeated their exertions, he listened to their
hearts and observed that her heart was more highly in-
tonated than her brother's and possessed a greater audible
range. He attributed this to her more nervous temperament.
He also desired to touch the region of her heart with his
fingers, to judge by touch, but he put that off, not wanting to
upset her. But now he thought of a new experiment.

He ordered them to stand motionless while he put his ear
to their hearts and listened. Then he had them recline upon
their backs, and noticed that the sound was almost imperceptible. Yet when he turned them over onto the left side, the
beat of the heart was more perceptible than ever, but on the
right side the impulse was nearly imperceptible again.

Rachel followed his instructions calmly, convinced finally
that the doctor intended her no harm, and she was full of
wonder that he could hear so much. He regarded the sounds
of her heart with a kind of religious reverence, and admired it
so much that she felt important in a way that she had never
felt before.

When he finished she was disappointed. The experiment

had become intriguing, but she was determined that neither of them would know this.

William thanked them, and he asked if they would mind performing more experiments in a few days. Rachel pretended to waver even as she longed to say yes, but Silas said quickly, "Master, whenever you desire."

These experiments became a regular occurrence. He saw that the beat of the blood was the same wherever he detected a pulse, and it reminded him of how he had realised that Silas was still alive on the anatomy table.

One night, only Rachel came to the laboratory, and explained, "Silas has gone to Whitehall to convey a message to Madam's brother, who is visiting a friend at Court. Galen Browne is applying for a post there."

Poor Galen Browne, thought William. Elizabeth's desire to improve her brother's condition was frantic. Galen, destined for the medical profession by his father from birth, had just received his M.A. degree from Cambridge, but had been unable to pass the requirements for the practice of medicine in London despite his father's reputation.

Even as these thoughts went through William's mind, his interest was elsewhere. He asked, "Rachel, when did Silas leave?"

"Just a few minutes ago."

So he won't be back for hours, he told himself, and we are alone. Yet there was one other thing. He inquired, "Where is my wife?"

"In bed, sir. She is much concerned with her brother, and seems to have apprehensions about him. I helped her with the letter. She says I write a good, firm hand. She should be asleep by now, sir."

Is that a hint? William wondered. The evenings that he experimented had become the most precious of the week, and he could no longer pretend this was only because he wanted to be more learned. Her small-boned, fragile beauty, her fair skin and fine complexion, and her slight but perfectly formed body aroused desires he had not felt since his intimacy with

Nina Robusti. Each time he touched her in the course of an experiment, it afforded him so much pleasure he desired more. Suddenly he asked her to dance.

She bowed, showing the graceful bulges of her breasts, and asked why.

"Dance for the sake of my digestion, and your own. If you know how."

"I think I do. I used to watch at the grand house of Squire Foster. When no one saw me." She whirled about the laboratory with a simple but natural grace. Then she paused, "Sir, do you wish to examine my heart now?"

"May I?"

She stood straight, not quite his height, and he felt her breasts swell as he put his ear to her heart. Suddenly he paused, and she asked with genuine alarm, "What is wrong? Is my heart diseased?"

Her expression was such a touching mixture of gaiety and pathos that he could not restrain himself. William embraced her passionately, but she did not respond, and for a desperate moment he thought, She is as frigid as Elizabeth. And as she shrank from his grasp, he cried out, "Rachel, I count each hour until your appearance here!"

"I am merely a serving girl. You must not forget that, sir."

"I will be a sad and solitary man if you desert me."

"That is a snare. You do not love me, you simply desire me."

He bent over and kissed her, and she did not resist as he carried her to his bed in the next room. He whispered, "You are a gift from God. Angelic and beautiful. When you are close to me, I know nothing of sickness or death."

She lay on the bed, still dressed, and thought, She should be afraid; she must resist the devil—yet she had no desire to flee. She liked his dark hair and eyes, his heavy mustache and small, pointed beard. And as he discarded his doublet and embraced her again, she felt she could hear his heart, too. She could not endure her virgin apprehensions as her blood rushed through her. Ever since the first time she had seen him, years ago outside of Cambridge, she had known that he was unobtainable, yet now she thought passionately, He can be mine. Perhaps he was right—in each other's arms they would know nothing of sickness or death. And what good was her beautiful body if it was never possessed?

When he entered her, she felt torn in half. The pleasure was so extreme she could hardly endure it, but she also felt used— the mistress of the house lay below even as he acted as if he were Hercules.

She sobbed suddenly, "There is no future in this infatuation."

"Nonsense, Rachel. You are even prettier when you cry."

"Not truly. You are married, and I have committed adultery."

"Not really. My wife denies me, and you are my love."

"Or merely her substitute."

"You are too clever to believe that. We must laugh, be happy."

"Doctor, is that what they taught you in Venice?"

"It was a time of love. Rachel, will you visit me again? Alone?"

"I should leave this house tonight."

"Rachel, this has been one of the happiest moments of my life."

"What about your experiments? I cannot endure them now. Silas would know. And your wife. The report would become widespread."

"I understand. Besides, now I should examine diseased hearts, and yours and Silas's are healthy." He kissed her lightly yet warmly on the lips, and gave her a look of gratitude that surprised her. "You are very perceptive. We must arrange to meet so no one will know. What we have experienced tonight is too important to lose."

Silas didn't question the cessation of the experiments, or consider her occasional absences from their quarters belowstairs as something to discuss. William sensed, as their affair developed into a weekly occurrence, that Rachel was in love with him, and his passion for her grew. Their intimacy was natural, while Elizabeth seemed unaware of what was happening. His wife was grievously disappointed that her brother did not receive a Court appointment and had to return to Cambridge and pursue more medical studies.

When William felt guilty, he consoled himself with the reminder that Galileo had lived the same way. He assured himself, If he had taken away Rachel's purity, he had given her a greater gift, and filled them both with joy. Best of all, once again he felt full-blooded.

ee the final boundary
Of a smile . . .
Listen to the last beat
Of a passing heart
Only then can you say
"I was here."

The spring sun was setting, and William, after an arduous day in his laboratory, looked out of his window and wished he could see as much of the blood as he could of London. Two years had passed since the gunpowder had been found in the cellar of the House of Lords, yet he felt uneasy. James was still fervently hunting witches throughout the land, and he had learned very little about the course of the blood.

Yet, he told himself, I must not be dissatisfied. The previous year he had been appointed a Fellow in the College of Physicians, and his practice continued to increase. But his discontent remained. He had spent the entire day studying the motion of the blood, and he had not found anything that was new. If he could only do anatomies he might learn more, but this was forbidden except at the College, and then he needed a special dispensation. Was his interest in these experiments an indulgence? Yet who would speak for the heart if he didn't? No one else seemed to care.

He returned to his studies. He picked up the *Fabrica* of Vesalius and examined his drawing: "*Arterial man.*" The work had been done precisely, and he read carefully what the anatomist had written about this.

"*There are many things regarding the course of the arteries that ought to be questioned. Almost no vein seeks the stomach, intestines, and spleen without a companion artery, and the portal vein takes a companion artery for itself in almost the whole of its course. Many things present themselves here that call into doubt the conclusions of anatomists, but it would take too long to consider them, and I have decided not to alter my account—although at the same time I am far from satisfied.*"

Vesalius had finished in a way that left William more confused. He was trying to decide what to do next when Silas hurried in and said, "Master, Doctor Matthew Ross and Doctor John Hall and a middle-aged man who seems to be suffering from a complaint are below—"

Matthew, who had followed him in, interrupted. "John Hall wants you to examine a patient."

"Who is it?" William asked.

"Hall's father-in-law. William, you are wasting your time here."

"What would you suggest?" Hall stood in the doorway while the tall, big-boned Court physician strode about with a sense of his own importance, dressed more like a courtier than a medical man.

"James is ailing, and none of the doctors in attendance have been able to relieve him. You should examine him."

"I am unpopular at Court since my diagnosis of Sir Walter Raleigh."

"You are clever at diagnosis even if you didn't prove he was a wizard. If you could ease the King's pain, it could be to your advantage. James has little faith in doctors, but if you helped him he could be grateful."

William thought of Browne, who had said, "Never depend on the gratitude of monarchs," and he didn't reply. He hadn't been at Court since his dismissal, and Matthew must feel unable to cure James if his aid was desired. He wished his friend wasn't so ambitious, and a better doctor.

"You should try to please the King. It is the only way to advance, and it could help you obtain the appointment to St. Bartholomew's Hospital that you desire so much. The King's recommendation could do it."

Matthew is wicked in the way he sees a man's weakness, William thought grimly, but my friend is accurate. "Will you take me to Whitehall?"

"Gladly. I will call for you in my coach tomorrow at noon."

"What about the patient below?"

"There is no hurry. He is not a gentleman."

William turned to Dr. Hall. "John, why haven't you examined him?" He knew that this slender, attractive doctor, who was three years older, had developed a fashionable practice in Stratford, although Hall, despite a B.A. and a M.A. from Cambridge, hadn't received a medical degree in England. "Is it because you aren't allowed to practise in London?"

"Partly. And I don't like to prescribe for a member of my family. Then, the patient's complaint may concern his heart. In this respect you are better qualified than I am. But," Hall added proudly, "I possess a medical degree. From Montpellier. Only London doesn't accept it."

"Did anyone question the movement of the blood in France?"

"No. We were taught Galen. Even Vesalius was ignored."

"He shouldn't be! Friends, do you think that the arteries could be the road out of the heart? And the veins the road in?"

Matthew retorted, "What heresy is this?"

John said, "William, you know we are not allowed to question Galen."

"Servetus did."

Matthew said, "And for such views he was burnt at the stake."

William thought, The human body was a wondrous object, but also mysterious and worrying. If he could only find a superior eye to see within the body! He believed now there were vital differences between the arteries and the veins.

He kept these reflections to himself as he followed the other doctors downstairs to the patient waiting in his reception room. Matthew nodded curtly to the middle-aged man, as if this situation warranted nothing else, and left hurriedly for Whitehall and the Court. John introduced the patient, but William didn't catch the name, for the Stratford doctor was embarrassed by Matthew's rudeness, and this clogged his tongue.

Never mind, William decided, it is the patient's health that matters, nothing else. He led the patient into the dispensary, noticing that the man followed him suspiciously, as if this patient didn't trust him.

William asked, "Has any other doctor examined you?"

"No. I do not favour medical men. Most of them are leeches, sucking blood as if it were water instead of the most precious of substances. It was only my son-in-law's insistence that persuaded me to come here."

William was attracted by the resonance of the patient's voice, and saw that he moved with grace and possessed a fine carriage.

"But I may be in error, for you are the only doctor John recommended."

William wished he could be comforting as he noticed the tension in the patient, the quivering of the lips, the sadness in the eyes, but first he must examine him. He asked, "What is the nature of your complaint?"

"Doctor, that is for you to tell me."

"It will be helpful if I know what is troubling you."

"I suffer from headaches, dizziness, and faintness. These discomforts are not imagined. They usually occur after I feel strong emotion."

William observed that this patient was taller than himself, and strongly built, and that his high forehead dominated his countenance. There was a ruff around his neck—more in the fashion of Elizabeth's Court than that of James's—a well-kept mustache, arched eyebrows, large, splendid brown eyes, a sharp, straight nose, smooth, round cheeks, a bald cranium, and a mouth almost feminine in its curve, and sensual, yet also suggesting sensibility. His receding light brown hair was combed carefully down to his ears. But William noted again that the most attractive feature of this face was the powerfully shaped forehead. Then he told himself that he must not allow his examination to be distracted by such details. He asked, "What pursuits give you anxieties?"

"Doctor, how does this concern my health?"

"Your symptoms suggest that you suffer from mental strain."

John exclaimed, "My father-in-law has been working too hard!"

"What activities does he pursue?"

"He is the poet-dramatist William Shakespeare."

William was surprised; the patient had shown no trace of vanity. He said, "I saw *The Taming of the Shrew* and *Hamlet* given for the Queen."

Shakespeare asked, "Did the old Queen express an opinion?"

"They were performed just before her death. She fell into a reverie after *Hamlet*. I was startled by how aged and weary she looked."

"I never heard how she felt about that work. Whether she approved."

"Did you desire her approval?"

"As a member of the Lord Chamberlain's Company, I was

sworn into the royal service as a Groom in Ordinary to the Chamber. Without fee. If I had not become part owner of the Company, I could be penniless now."

"Instead," John said with pleasure, "my father-in-law is one of the most affluent citizens of Stratford. He has acquired considerable land, several houses, and a coat of arms from the College of Heralds."

"Indeed! I can now sign my name *William Shakespeare, gentleman.*"

William ignored the patient's sarcasm and said, "Then why do you suffer from anxiety? Your plays are done far more than anyone else's."

Shakespeare didn't reply. He couldn't reveal how often his passions filled him to the bursting point and threatened to destroy him. Or how deeply he mourned the death of his only son, and, in the last year, the passing of his youngest brother, Edmund, then his mother. And now, when his daughter, Susanna, who had wed John Hall, had a child, it was a girl. Would only women survive him? The two children of his that lived were both girls. Would his name go no further than himself? It would be a grievous sorrow. Yet he liked John, who had some of his feeling, and Susanna had more of his nature than anyone else.

William asked, "Mr. Shakespeare, do you reside in London?"

"When I am working on a play. So I have access to the theatres. I lodge with an old friend, Mountjoy, a tithe-maker, on the corner of Silver Street in the Cripplegate ward. He makes me feel at home."

John said, "My father-in-law has worked very hard. In the past five years, since his Company became The King's Men, he has written *Measure for Measure, Othello, Macbeth, King Lear, Timon of Athens,* and now *Antony and Cleopatra.* It is no wonder that he is exhausted."

If my demon has taken charge, the poet reflected, there is nothing else I can do. And now that I have mastered my skill, it would be foolish not to use it. Yet if I am within the skin of my characters, it is not for anyone else to know. Little enough I reveal about myself in public; my work can speak for itself. It is wise to be secretive, to hide my personal life—otherwise, all men look alike. And suffer from malice. But when I write, I enter a world which is my own. Then I must toil day and night. Then I am true to myself, not halting until I faint or my head pounds unbearably. Then nothing must stand in my way. Yet, while John Hall thinks I have written much the past five years, the previous period was more fertile. Then I wrote a dozen plays. Then I did not become sick from sitting at my desk, or feel my pen become weary in my hand. But now I can no longer work at such a feverish pace. It leaves me dejected and longing to retreat to Stratford and to retire. Yet my mind is still agile, and is filled with many fancies. No one rules me now—except, he thought wryly, Dr. Harvey, waiting to examine me.

He was ordered to disrobe from the waist up, and he felt like an ox about to be slaughtered; he asked if this was necessary.

"It is the most accurate way to listen to your heart."

"Doctor Harvey, do you think it is the cause of my complaint?"

"I'm not sure. Now, if you will be quiet and relax and breathe deeply."

"Few people die gracefully. The time that seems to him to have to come always seems to come too soon."

John Hall said reassuringly, "Will, your time is far off."

"I wonder. But why should we fear it so, when it comes but once?" He followed the doctor's instructions.

William put his ear to the chest of the poet, but the patient, despite his effort to be casual, looked as if the physician were listening to the voice of doom.

"What do you hear, Doctor?"

"A clear beat," said William. But also, if his ear was accurate, a skip. To be certain, he placed his palm next to the heart. The skip remained. He hid his thoughts and asked the patient to jump up and down.

The poet obeyed, but he was breathless quickly, and William halted him, which caused him to ask, "Is there anything wrong with my heart?"

"Mr. Shakespeare, have you indulged in any vigourous activity lately?"

"Often I have run fast and vaulted far and climbed many steps, but these days that tires me."

"You must rest and live more moderately, without excess of feeling."

"I trust I hasten not to my end."

John said, "You suffer simply from fatigue. As I thought."

"I didn't grow exhausted a few years ago."

"You are forty-four now. You must work less."

"Doctor Harvey, do I have ten years left?"

"Perhaps more. If you take care of yourself."

"But you haven't told me what is wrong."

"Each affection of the mind that is attended with pain or pleasure is the cause of an agitation whose influence extends to the heart. In almost every strong emotion the countenance changes and the blood courses strongly. In anger the eyes are fiery and the pupils contract, while in modesty the cheeks are suffused with blushes, and in lust the member is quickly distended with blood. Thus, the passage of the blood can indicate much."

"I have used these devices in my work."

John said, "Many times. William, my father-in-law shares some of your views about the course of the blood and its wide range of movement."

William replied, "So far, all I possess is supposition."

Shakespeare asked, "Then you are not sure what is wrong with me?"

"There is much that we do not know about the body."

But this should not be admitted, John decided, and he changed the subject. He said, "Will, I was interested in the way you had Lady Macbeth cry out in her sleep, '*Who would have thought the old man had so much blood in him.*' You gave this fluid a grand place in your drama."

Shakespeare didn't want to discuss his work; he was concerned about his health. He asked William, "Do you have any remedies to induce sleep?"

"It will be better if you fall asleep naturally. The best prescription for your condition is moderate living. See me again in a few weeks."

"Do you think I will ever free myself of this complaint?"

"Yes. Overwork and tension have put a pressure on the movement of your blood that it is sensible to ease. Most of all, you need rest."

"What is your fee?"

"Pay me when you feel cured, Mr. Shakespeare."

"Doctor Harvey, do you think that the blood returns to the heart?"

"I don't know. It needs much investigation. Do you think it does?"

"I have wondered often about it. Otherwise, it would seem ill-used, wasted. But in this world we go from one uncertainty to another. I will try to employ care and moderation in all things. Yet it will not be easy." At the door he sighed as he said, "Ill health humbles a man so. Sometimes I think it is the worst humiliation of all, especially for a vigourous man. Thank you, Doctor, for your courtesy and consideration."

Shakespeare's bedroom on Silver Street was quiet for a change, but when he was unable to sleep he lit a candle and turned to his desk and read what he had written in *Henry V* about the death of Falstaff.

"*You must observe thus in acute diseases, first the countenance of the patient, if it be like those of persons in health, and especially if it be like its usual self, for this is the best of all. But the opposite are the worst, such as these: a sharp nose, hollow eyes, sunken temples, the ears cold, contracted,*

*and their lobes turned outwards, the skin about the forehead
rough, stretched and parched, the colour of the face greenish
and livid . . . then it is known for certain the end is at
hand.*"

And we will be laid into the earth, his mind ran on.

He stared into his glass and examined the texture of his
flesh. He noted that his eyes and temples were full; his ears
felt warm; he saw that his skin was soft, not taut or arid, and
that his complexion was good. He sighed with relief, put aside
his work, and returned to bed. But his mind refused to halt.
While he was grateful that he didn't resemble a scarecrow,
there was still discord in him. He had read Hippocrates and
Galen, and he had found wisdom in the Greek, but he had
relied on his own observation. He was fascinated by the struggle between life and death. Yet, he reflected ruefully, there are
moments I feel that it doesn't matter.

Shakespeare dead was Shakespeare dead.

But they would probably misunderstand that, too. He was
not interested in idolatry, either side of the grave. Others
could cultivate the myths. Words could create wondrous
sounds, but they could also betray. He tried to sleep but he
kept thinking, The doctor had said he need not be fearful.

William was searching for a better way to judge the
action of the heart when Matthew called for him the next day.
His friend told him what he knew about the King's condition,
which was not much. They were led into the royal bedchamber, where James reclined in a huge, curtained bed that
was draped in silk and damask and had layers of stuffed
woollen mattresses and thick, heavy blankets.

Many doctors were in attendance, and they formed a circle
around James. So, William thought, they make sure that no
one can gain supremacy as they seek to put a name to the
King's complaint. Matthew edged closer, motioned to William
to follow, and waited for the other doctors to finish their
diagnoses, hoping they would be unacceptable to the King.

William heard dropsy mentioned, a chill, melancholy.

James was interested in the last diagnosis. To be melancholy appealed to him as worthy of a monarch. He felt that medicine had failed him. He thought of how the sorrow of Saul had yielded to the harp of David, and he summoned Cecil and said, "Little beagle, I desire some sweet music."

The lutist arrived at once—for Cecil, anticipating the King's mood, had him waiting in the next chamber—but he didn't ease the King's discomfort.

Suddenly James dismissed him, sat up abruptly in bed, and shouted at his physicians, "Can no one relieve me?"

"Sire," replied an elderly, dignified doctor, "I am following Galen precisely, but your stars are not favourable."

James had to run to the water closet. When he returned, William observed, he looked somewhat better but not normal.

The King was irritable, and Cecil hurriedly ushered in Andrews. The elderly physician could barely stand, but the sight of the ancient Scot comforted James.

Andrews said insistently, "Sir, leeches must be used."

The doctor who had diagnosed melancholy replied, "We must use Norfolk leeches"—he came from Norfolk—"and the best are green and yellow."

Andrews, who disliked everything English, and who had a special knowledge of leeches, stated, "Scottish leeches are better."

"Norfolk leeches are stronger."

"But those from Scotland suck better."

Matthew whispered to William, "They are both in error. The horse leech, which comes from the south and is brown, can bear the roughest usage."

"Whatever leech they use, they must be sure it speaks English."

Matthew regarded him with a puzzled air.

"What happens if the leeches do not help the King?"

"I am not worried. Andrews bears that responsibility."

"Then why do you need me?" William asked, but Matthew didn't answer.

Andrews ordered leeches that were contained in special bottles to be brought forth, but when James saw them he cried out, "I do not wish to be bled again. All it does is weaken me. It is my bowels that pain me."

Andrews, disregarding him as if he were a child, applied a leech.

James exclaimed hysterically, "For God's sake, I bleed!" The King looked on the verge of fainting and was terrified.

"No leeches!" William shouted suddenly.

Andrews turned to dismiss the offender but he was halted by the King.

"Let him speak!" But when James saw who it was, he frowned and regarded William suspiciously.

William felt that if he made the wrong diagnosis he could be charged with high treason, yet he was carried on by a wave of emotion. He said, "Your Majesty, may I ask a few questions?"

"How do you expect me to trust your diagnosis after your error with Raleigh?"

"Your Majesty, your health is a different situation."

"Who brought you here?"

"I did," Matthew said diffidently, looking apprehensive.

Ross is an attractive young man, reflected James, and pleasing to have about, even if he doesn't ease my discomforts, which lately have been abundant. He muttered, "Why did you bring him, Ross? When Harvey failed me before."

"Sir, he has sound views on the blood."

"Harvey, there will be no pain?"

"Not in my examination, Your Majesty."

"No bloodletting?" One more sight of his own blood and he would faint.

"None, sir. May I examine you?"

James was still reluctant, but none of the other doctors had eased him, and so he nodded hesitantly.

William carefully viewed his swollen stomach, his pulse, his teeth, which he noted were very poor and probably the reason for his poor digestion. He recalled that Matthew had told him that James had suffered from diarrhoea all his life, but particularly when the King fell into a depression of mind. And now, he sensed, James was oppressed with fear, which added to his melancholy.

James asked, "Harvey, what do you find?"

"You are suffering from strain."

"I know that!" James snapped impatiently.

"Which has affected your digestion."

"What will suffice as a cure?"

"Sir, eat lightly, avoid heavy foods, especially roast meats."

James scowled, but he didn't dismiss Harvey, as Andrews had expected. His pain was worse. He asked, "What foods do you recommend?"

"Substances you can chew properly." He thought, Owing to his want of teeth, James didn't chew his food but bolted it, only this he didn't dare say. "To avoid afflictions of the digestion, you must not drink beer, ale, or wine. What wine do you prefer, Your Majesty?"

"Sweet wine."

"Particularly Muscatel," Cecil said, intrigued by how Harvey went to the heart of the matter.

"What is wrong with that?" James was alarmed; Harvey was so serious.

"It is too heavy, too sweet. Sir, you must avoid it."

"I don't mind if it is strong as long as it is sweet."

"Sir, it is Muscatel's sweetness that troubles you. Heavy draughts give a tendency to an uncomfortable looseness."

"You know my discomfort!"

Cecil thought cynically, Harvey had a sharp eye. This doctor, despite his failure with Raleigh, might prove useful.

James asked, "Harvey, what do you recommend as a remedy?" After the wine wore off, he felt surly and depressed, and often sick.

"Warm water before each meal, sir."

James was shocked. He had the strongest antipathy to water. He cried out, "Doctor, is there no other remedy?"

"Sir, your inner passages must be freed of all irritations. Warm water should cleanse them. Try it for a few days."

James still found this difficult to accept, but suddenly he was seized with a severe spasm in his stomach. He longed to shout for a goblet of wine and to have it pass jovially through him. But he remembered that he had done this earlier in the day and now he felt worse. And he was frightened. He said, "If I do what you suggest, what then?"

"Your Majesty, you should have some relief from your discomfort."

"If I suffer your cure, will I eventually get better?"

"You should, Your Majesty. If you also eat food that is easy to chew and to digest. And avoid strong wine and harsh drinks."

James declared indignantly, "Do you imply, Doctor, that I favour it? A drunkard is a *voluntarius daemon*."

"Sir, I am aware of how you seek to control heavy drinking. Your Majesty, before this diarrhoea did you feel depressed?"

James cut off Andrews's attempt to interrupt, while the other physicians watched in wonder. Even Matthew was startled by William's candour. "Diarrhoea" was not a word to use about the King; a doctor could lose much for suggesting a monarch suffered from such an affliction of common humanity. Yet now James, in his need to ease his discomfort, thought, This illness had begun after a depression of mind, with diarrhoea for the past week. But while Andrews had purged and bled him, his melancholy and diarrhoea had lasted. And his pain had become more severe. "I did, Harvey."

"Sir, your discomfort is caused by a looseness of the bowels."

Cecil said, "Your Majesty, there is much to be gained from moderation. A view I have learned from your gracious lips. Harvey could be right."

"Little beagle, occasionally you are wise. We will see if this doctor is a worker of miracles or merely has a persuasive tongue. Harvey, how long should it take for your remedies to work?"

"Several weeks, sir, possibly longer."

"So long?" The King's eyes flashed angrily, and he was upset.

"Sooner, Your Majesty, if you observe all the precautions."

"William, you were convincing," Matthew said as he escorted him back to his residence. "Yet are you truly certain you will cure the King?"

"No. For there is no guarantee that he will obey."

"You will be blamed if he doesn't improve. You would have been safer if you had done what the other physicians prescribed."

"I should have put more stress on his teeth. They are very bad."

"You may have gone too far as it is."

"He has such a want of teeth. It will make his cure difficult."

"I expect so." Matthew sighed. "What was wrong with the player?"

"I'm not sure." William thought, He must hear the beat of the poet's heart after a period of moderation. "I hope I haven't damaged you."

"That is not likely. My father attended James in Scotland years ago. His cure pleased him, for it eased the looseness of his bowels."

"What was your father's remedy?"

"Cheese."

"But that would give him much wind!"

"Yes. It also hardened his bowels. And James had just heard from Cecil that the English nobles were receptive to his succession to the Queen, who was failing, and that ended his depression and, thus, his diarrhoea. He regarded my father as a magician. To him, we can do no wrong. But you could. He still sees Raleigh as a thorn in his flesh."

"Suppose I do cure him?"

"You will be excused your sin with Raleigh, and I will be thanked."

Several weeks later, William was summoned to Whitehall by the King. At the palace he found that James's discomfort was gone. James was in good spirits. The King was relieved that he could get out of bed, and he was pleased with his complexion, which was fine again.

No other physician was in attendance in the Presence Chamber, and Cecil was the only member of the Court who was present. James greeted William with a smile and asked, "What reward do you desire, young man?"

"Physician to St. Bartholomew's Hospital, Your Majesty."

James was shocked, and he cried out, "To tend the poor and the sick?"

"To learn my trade as a physician, sir."

"It is a mean parish. I thought you would desire a post at Court."

"I do, Your Majesty. But that is for you to decide."

James stared at Harvey and thought, Whatever this doctor was, he was not a raucous crow hungry for rewards. His pain and fear had forced him to follow Harvey's cure despite his antipathy towards it, and now he felt much better. He asked Cecil, "Is the post available?"

"I will find out, sir."

"Your Majesty," William ventured, "I have heard that the present holder of the office is gravely ill."

Cecil asked, "And you desire the post to revert to you?"

"If the diagnosis of my colleague is correct. Meanwhile, My Lord Salisbury, if I could be in the situation of assistant?"

"You will feel amply rewarded? Even more than a post at Court?"

"As I said, My Lord, that would be a great honour, but at the moment—"

James interrupted, "If the post is available, you will be considered."

"Thank you, Your Majesty."

"I may send for you, too. It is useful to keep you in London. I have a firmness in my bowels for the first time in years."

Cecil said, "Your Majesty, this is a matter that will take some time."

"I am not unreasonable. Doctor Harvey will be patient."

Shakespeare returned to be examined and said, "I have been sleeping better since you advised me. I try to live these days with moderation."

It was just a month since he had seen the poet, and he was even more pleased when this examination revealed a regular heartbeat in the patient; there was no trace of a skip now.

"Then I am cured!" the poet cried, sensing the relief in the doctor.

"I think so."

The patient smiled. Now he could become a Stratford gentleman and enjoy his coat of arms. "Doctor, what was the nature of my complaint?"

"The heart is a strong instrument, but stress can injure it. And the supply of the blood can be affected adversely."

"I thought the liver was the cause of the flow, not the heart."

William told the patient to put on his doublet, which he had taken off without hesitation for this examination. He noticed that the poet, for all his calm, was sweaty. He said, "The fibres of the arteries are so resistant to pressure, yet soft enough to have a high degree of absorption, it would appear, with such characteristics, that their properties permit them to bear a heavier substance than vital spirits like air."

"What, Doctor? Life itself?"

"I haven't been able to see an artery yet in proper detail, but they are reinforced in such a way they may carry the abundance of the blood."

"At least you didn't feel compelled to examine my urine. Most physicians use that to judge all symptoms."

William watched the poet depart, thinking, He had tried to be accurate, but he felt he had improved the poet's health only for today. He hurried up to his laboratory to resume his experiments.

Shakespeare walked to his rooms on Silver Street and felt happy and relaxed, like a man relieved of a heavy burden. Until he recalled the doctor's warning: "Be careful. Do not allow yourself much passion." He grew grave now. This would be difficult. Passion was the heart of his work. "Consider," he said to himself, "what I am writing for *Cymbeline*."

By medicine life may be prolong'd, yet death
Will seize the doctor too.

orty centuries later
Man will still be trying
To swim like a frog
Remake nature's colours
Dance like a cloud
Only a parrot
Will be trying
To talk like a man.

King James directs that Mr. William Harvey, Doctor of Physic, shall have the Office of Physician of St. Bartholomew's Hospital after the decease or other departure of Mr. Doctor Wilkenson who now holds the same with the yearly fees and duties thereunto belonging.

This letter was given to William six months after he cured the King. When he presented it to the Governors of the Hospital, he was appointed assistant to Wilkenson. The following year, as he expected, Wilkenson died of overeating. Several months later, on October 14, 1609, William was named to the Office of Physician.

William examined James regularly during this time; the King was relieved that he remained free of pain and discomfort without the anguish of bleeding and purging. Yet he wasn't sure he should trust Harvey, remembering that Raleigh was still alive in the Tower, and so he didn't appoint him to the Court; at the Hospital the doctor could be watched and judged.

The admission to the Office of Physician to the Hospital possessed William with a new excitement. He thought, St. Bartholomew's was his house now. His knowledge of medicine should grow greatly. He didn't tell anyone of this feeling, but he was proud that St. Bartholomew's, which had been founded by Rahere in 1123, was not only one of the most ancient of hospitals but was also considered one of the best.

He surprised Silas by disdaining his servant's suggestion that he go to the hospital by coach or horse. "It is close enough to walk," William said, amused that Silas regarded such a modest method of travel as a problem.

Walking was useful. He liked the air in his face, and he needed it to awaken him. And as he strode along with short, precise steps, this aided his reflections. Often this was when he planned his experiments.

Today, although it was a cold, damp November morning, he set out for St. Bart's on foot and by himself. He wore thick leather boots to navigate the mud and a broad-brimmed hat to protect him from the showers. The streets were narrow and wound between timber-framed houses. At the entrance to the hospital, he paused to survey Bartholomew's Fair, which was being held outside of St. Bart's in the great plain of Smithfield.

Pedlars harangued him, not recognising him as a doctor because of his modest livery. "Man, what do you lack? Drums, eggs, fiddles, rapiers, daggers?"

He was jolted out of his reverie, thinking, He needed a new dagger.

"What would your worship buy? Pears, onions, a parrot from the Spanish Indies?"

That could please Elizabeth, he reflected, or Rachel.

"I have a drum to make you a soldier."

But now he was late, and he hurried through the arched brick gateway of St. Bart's and into the Great Hall.

As Physician in Residence, he sat at a table once a week and examined the patients who lined up to use him. They were the poor who were harboured in St. Bart's because they had nothing else, and the Matron supervised them while William wrote prescriptions for each one. This reminded William of the Charge of his Office: *"You shall not for favour, lucre, or gain write anything for the poor but such good and wholesome things as you shall think with your best advice will do the poor good. And you shall take no gift or reward of any of the poor of this house for your services. This you will promise to do as you will answer before God, and as it becomes a faithful physician."*

When this duty was finished, he visited those in the wards who were too ill to come to him. There were twelve wards, two hundred bedsteads, one apothecary, and three surgeons. There were also a number of students who worked in the wards, but no one was allowed to make a decision, perform surgery, or write a prescription without William's approval.

Often he was so tired he ached, but he never neglected a patient. A young beggar, who reminded him of the Silas he had saved, died because he wasn't called in time, and he was furious. The student in charge of the ward said that no one else had had the authority to act. Chief surgeon Joseph Fenton, a stout, middle-aged man who expected things to go wrong, added, "It was God's will. The boy was too clever to live long."

William replied, "The patient was slain by neglect and indifference."

"Sir," said the apothecary, Roger Gwynne, "the student was right. When the sun rises, the disease abates. If the lad could have only held on until dawn."

William lost his temper, and in his anger he raised his hand to strike the student who had failed to call him when the patient had had a convulsion, controlling himself only when he heard a boy whimpering in the next ward. The boy, who was ten, had a stomachache, and as he eased it he had second thoughts about his temper. And he realised that he was learning much.

"How much are you earning?" Elizabeth asked, irritated by the large number of hours William was spending at St. Bartholomew's Hospital. They were eating breakfast, which Rachel had cooked and Silas served.

"Twenty-five pounds a year for my services."

"Considering what they ask of you, that isn't much."

He was glad to see her at the table; many days she preferred to stay in bed and have the servants bring the meal there. "I'm satisfied."

"I'm not. If you were like Matthew, you would be recognised as a doctor of distinction."

"Sometimes he is more of a courtier than a physician."

"That is fitting for one who attends the King. But you consider that beneath you, except when you are ordered to do so by His Majesty."

"That is not true!" His exasperation grew; he had lost two patients the day before, and he was still exhausted from his fruitless effort to save them. And it was just a week since the boy had died of convulsions. "I'm honoured to serve the King. But that is only part of being a doctor."

"Then these endless experiments of yours? Will they never end?"

He sighed and said, "I wonder too. They are very difficult."

"You spend almost all of your free time upstairs. What

do you really do there? I can't believe you give all that time to your experiments."

He didn't know what to answer. Usually she didn't question him, but this morning something potent appeared to be causing her to suffer. He wished, If she was going to be religious, she would be more joyful about it. Instead, the more devout she became, the more fleshless she became, a grey, gaunt, perpendicular presence who had lost most of her prettiness.

"William, there are evenings I don't hear your footsteps."

He was surprised. "Can you hear me?"

"Of course! Your laboratory and bedroom are directly above me. But occasionally the footsteps do not sound like yours."

Rachel's, he thought worriedly, but he said positively, "It is Silas you hear. He helps me frequently. Do you hear anything else?"

"Why?" she asked suspiciously.

"I don't want to disturb you."

"You are very generous," she said sarcastically.

"Do you hear much? Many sounds?"

"Naturally. I have excellent ears. The best in this house."

"What do you hear, Elizabeth?"

"You are insistent today. Floors creak, I hear you get into bed. What in the world forces you to make so much noise sometimes? There are times I think you are having a nightmare." Silas served her a fried egg, but now she wanted it boiled. He retired to the kitchen to inform Rachel of this, and Elizabeth blurted out, "William, you never talk to me any more. I can't converse with the servants. Silas only wants to talk about you, and Rachel fears me. Every time I open my mouth, she grows pale. Has she done something wrong? Her brother did commit a crime."

"Elizabeth, he stole a scrap of bread when he was starving."

"We cannot trust them. I should have a housekeeper whom I could converse with. You should dismiss Silas and Rachel and hire new servants."

He was appalled at the thought of losing them, and he said, "Silas is very considerate of your wants, and you like Rachel's cooking."

Elizabeth's reply was interrupted by Rachel, who entered and asked, "Madam, how long would you prefer the egg to be boiled?"

"Long enough so I can eat it comfortably."

"Do you desire it soft or hard?"

"Girl, you know what I prefer."

"Madam, you eat fried eggs most of the time."

"You are insolent. Tell your brother to bring the rest of my breakfast to my room. You are a fool not to know what I wish. Good day, William."

A moment later, when Elizabeth had gone to her room, Rachel whispered to William so no one else would hear her, "She knows, she knows."

"Nonsense. She knows nothing about us. Where is Silas?"

"He went to the market to buy more eggs. That was why I came in, to distract your wife from the delay. Instead, I upset her."

Rachel was plainly dressed in sober black, but her blue eyes glowed and her long red hair was carefully combed, and her small, fine-boned features were especially attractive by contrast with his wife's sombre appearance.

I am the devoted wife, Rachel thought, not Elizabeth Harvey. She said softly, "Sometimes I think our life together is too difficult."

"Please, no reproaches now."

"I must talk about it. We are only half-hour people, never whole-day folk. And everything must be conducted in whispers. Then, your wife wants me dismissed. The egg was just an excuse to find fault."

"It was a triviality. We mustn't waste our time arguing about her."

"She will find out eventually if she doesn't know now."

"I told you, she knows nothing."

"William, you mustn't be too sure. It could lead to disaster."

"Rachel, don't you think our love has been worth it?"

He always comes down to one thing, she thought sadly. But she no longer felt immature. She could consider leaving him. Yet where would she live? The only road open to her was to serve in another house, and she would need his recommendation. She felt trapped, then. She was so tired of being discreet. And suddenly he was embracing her passionately, and her resolve to be distant dissolved and she agreed to come to him that evening.

She was startled when he said she must walk in the bedroom in her bare feet so there would be no sound. She whispered, "Your wife does suspect."

"She does not. But why give her a chance to find out?"

He ended her shrivelled feeling by carrying her to his bed, and then, as he made love, she felt marvellous. He said soothingly that he could not live without her, he must get a woman to take care of his wife while she ran the house, and she fell asleep, a luxury she rarely allowed herself.

It was his touch that woke her. He was listening to the beat of her heart, and she complained, "You are always observing me, even when you are caressing me. It is shameful." Now that her sensual moment had passed, she felt bullied by vulgarity. Yet as he jumped out of bed and hurried from the room, her anger passed and she was unhappy. A minute later, as she heard his returning footsteps, she felt her blood rushing joyously through her, but she whispered, "I must go. Someone could find us here."

"That is unlikely. My wife has locked her door."

"Is that why you got out of bed?" Ecstasy by stealth, she thought.

"I was curious. And I sent Silas to Folkestone, and he won't be back until tomorrow. I may spend some time there on my father's farm."

"Will you take me with you?"

"Aren't we straying away from our reason for being here,

Rachel, dear?" Before she could reply, he was making love to her again.

Or to the smooth sensuality of my nakedness, she thought critically, as he caressed her skin amourously. I will not be pitiful, she decided, whatever he intends. Meanwhile, she sought, as her own emotions demanded, to work good medicine with a romantic and merry abandon.

A few days later William brought his wife a parrot from Bartholomew's Fair. The pedlar informed him, "This bird from the Spanish Indies speaks a clear English," and to prove his contention he turned to the bird and addressed it, and the parrot cried back in a loud, sharp voice, "What do you lack? Buy it here! Half the value of anywhere else!"

Elizabeth was pleased with the parrot. Each time she approached the bird to feed him and to fondle him—they assumed the parrot was a male because of the bright plumage— the bird preened his feathers and favoured her, for she insisted on being the only one to attend him. She made a pet of the parrot and named him Arthur, after King Arthur, and cared for the bird with a devotion that she gave to nobody else.

Soon Arthur grew so familiar and tame that she permitted him to wander at liberty through the entire house. He did this when he missed his mistress, calling for her by name when she was absent. Then he searched for Elizabeth with a persistent determination, and when he found her he greeted her cheerfully and courted her with a display of his plumage.

If she called him, he flew to her, and he grasped her garments with his bill and claws and, using them, climbed up her dress to her shoulder or settled on her hand. This amazed William, for Elizabeth disliked being touched. But she loved the parrot's grip, and she encouraged the bird to sit on her shoulder or on her hand. She took a great delight in commanding Arthur to talk, and words that she would not endure or excuse from anyone else, she enjoyed from the parrot.

What gratified Elizabeth most was that the bird became her

inseparable companion. She encouraged him to sit on her lap, playful and impudent, and he adored her scratching of his head and stroking of his back. Then he expressed his contentment with gentle movements of his wings and soft murmurs, while she accepted this affection with triumph.

So William was even more certain that Arthur was a cock parrot. He assured Elizabeth, "Because of his excellence in talking and singing."

She agreed, "Arthur has lively conversations with me. He repeats everything I say."

Rachel wasn't sure the parrot was a male, which called to William's mind what Aristotle had said, and he wrote it out for her edification:

"If Partridge-hens stand over against the cocks, and the wind blow from where the cocks are, they conceive and grow big and for the most part, they teem even by the voice of the cock, if they be at that time wanton and lustful, and this may also fall out from the cocks flying over them: namely if the cock do transmit a fructifying spirit into the Hen."

Rachel thought sadly, We will never have any children, even if it is possible; he has seen to that with his devices from Venice. She was relieved that his wife was distracted by the parrot, but William was waiting for her response. She said, "Silas has set the table with pewter plates and knives and spoons. Should I put a place for Arthur?"

"I thought you would be grateful that he occupies Elizabeth so fully."

"I roasted two pieces of meat and baked white-flour bread today. Do you want Silas to carve and serve it, or wait until the bird is ready?"

She sounded contemptuous, and he replied quickly, "Rachel, you make cooking a craft. You should be proud of your skill."

"Your wife doesn't eat eggs since you gave her the parrot."

"You are observant."

"I can see clearly." His wife entered with the parrot on her shoulder, and Rachel thought, The bird was more like a lover than a pet.

Elizabeth said, "Girl, I will attend to Arthur's feeding my-self."

Satisfied that Rachel and Elizabeth were content with their situation, William devoted himself to his medicine the next year. He worked harder than ever at the hospital, in his prac-tice, and with his investigations but he felt he learned too little. It was not enough to study Vesalius, to draw the heart as he knew it, to use the patients who visited him as a way of learning about the heart and the motion of the blood. He felt he was observing the wrong facts. Perhaps Galen was right after all, he reflected in a moment of despair, and the venous blood is supplied by the liver. Yet when he saw Rachel's cheeks flush when he kissed her and felt the quick beat of her heart when he embraced her, he returned to the notion that the heart supplied the impetus to the movement of the blood. This distracted from his lovemaking, and only her sudden withdrawal brought him back to the sensual instant. Yet he still was driven by a need to solve what had become a great mystery to him.

He sat in his laboratory after Rachel left and resolved to examine the arteries closer. He knew that when a corpse was dissected, arteries were empty of substance, and so, as Aris-totle and Galen maintained, it was assumed they carried only air. But the more he thought about this view, the less he believed it. Yet he must have proof. Whenever he suggested his suppositions to other physicians, he was regarded with suspicion. There was just one place that dissections were al-lowed, the College of Physicians, and that was the sole privi-lege of the Lumleian Lecturer of Anatomy.

But when he had questioned the present holder of the Chair's view that the liver was the main organ in the move-ment of the blood, he had been ignored. Yet he had felt compelled—and, as a Fellow of the College of Physicians, he was permitted to speak—to express the value of examining the

great artery, the aorta. Then he had been ordered to keep
quiet or be evicted from the anatomy hall. This had added to
his conviction that one thorough dissection of the heart and
the arteries was of more value than a dozen lectures. Nothing,
however, encouraged him in this direction. Silas had returned
from Folkestone with the news that his father was unwilling
to allow him to use the family livestock for such purposes.

His discontent remained even when he was called to examine the King again. This time James was convinced that he
was seized with a dangerous melancholy, but his symptoms
were still a looseness of his bowels and excessive diarrhoea,
and William told him so.

The King was disappointed—he desired a more interesting
complaint—but he agreed to follow William's instructions,
although reluctantly.

Now a year passed before William was summoned to
Whitehall Palace. It was the autumn of 1611, and it was to
see the performance of a new play.

Matthew informed him, "This invitation is an expression of
the King's favour. He is in better health since you treated
him. He doesn't like your remedies, but he appreciates that
you ease his discomfort."

"What play are we to see?" The Great Hall was crowded
with courtiers.

"A comedy called *The Tempest*. James has been fond of
Shakespeare's work since *Macbeth*. He is particularly pleased
with the witches in that drama. He thinks the dramatist expressed discernment. But this man's work is a passing fancy.
No one will view it when he is gone."

William was seated in the rear of the audience, and he saw
the poet and John Hall nearby. He nodded to them, and
they acknowledged his greeting.

Whitehall Palace was quiet when *The Tempest* ended. William heard Prospero's renunciation of his magic and his
withdrawal from the practice of his art with the feeling that
the poet was saying good-bye. He joined the poet and John

Hall, standing by themselves, while everyone else concentrated on the King and *his* views.

John said, "Will, it was successful. Everyone was quiet at the end."

"Everyone is," he replied, "at the end. Doctor, I didn't choose the subject, it chose me. Consider, I am only eleven years older than my son-in-law, and yet there are times that I feel twice his age."

William said, "With your wit, sir, you should not bear such a cross."

John said, "Will has decided this is the last play he will write."

"Mr. Shakespeare, what will you do without writing?"

"Tidy up my life."

"Do you have a new complaint?"

"No. I rarely get headaches since I've become more moderate, and my body bears its burdens better. But this is not an age to trust. Death is everywhere, and no one can evade its clutch. I cannot say to it, 'You cannot touch me!' Even the King knows that and fears its coming."

John asked, "Will, are you certain about the feelings of the King?"

"When I mounted the boards as a player, I played kings. I have written much about them. I am acquainted with their nature and their mortality."

"You should be satisfied, you have achieved your ambitions."

"And have perceived that when men seek to cure mortality by fame, the grinning skeleton beneath the slab mocks their pretensions to grandeur. I find it difficult to contemplate the loss of life. It is the only thing I know. Doctor Harvey, are you troubled by the deaths you experience?"

"A physician cannot afford to be, or he will end prematurely in the grave. But I am disturbed when it is unnecessary. As it is so often."

"Often I think life is just a dream, and death the only certainty."

"Yet your work expresses a strong allegiance to life."

"Sometimes. But when I see the barbarism about us, and know that our mortality is as frail as an eggshell, I have many doubts about its worth. A pin can puncture us so the air comes out like a burst balloon. There are many moments when I think the world is mad."

"Whatever happens, avoid such pressures."

"Then will I possess ten more years?"

"No physician can be sure. Do not push too hard."

"I should have played Prospero."

They were halted by an elaborate ceremony. Sir Francis Bacon was presenting a new edition of his book, *The Advancement of Learning*, to the King, to whom it was dedicated. As the solicitor-general approached the throne, William wondered: What sort of man is this courtier with his eloquent voice and elegant style? Bacon was regarded as a crafty intriguer, a brilliant scholar, a writer of polished aphorisms, a mordant wit. Yet William felt this didn't tell him why Bacon strove so to climb the ladder of kingly preferment. Cousin of Cecil's, protégé of the beheaded Essex, rival of the powerful Coke, cool in discussion but passionate in ambition—William recalled the many ways that Bacon was viewed, and he wasn't sure which to believe. Bacon knelt before the seated King, clad from head to foot in gold lace, purple satin, and silver brocade, second in splendour only to James, who motioned for him to rise and to speak, which he did.

"*Gracious sir, you have blessed us with a happy country, your people content and obedient, fit for war, used to peace. Your church fertile with good preachers; your judges learned and learning from you; just, and just by example. Your servants in awe of your wisdom, in hope of your goodness. The fields growing from desert to garden; the City growing from wood to brick. All, Gracious and Almighty sir, due to you.*"

William saw a sardonic smile on the poet's face, and approval on Matthew's. He couldn't accept the solicitor-general's view of James's reign; he thought it false.

James nodded in acknowledgement of Bacon's wisdom, and dismissed him so that he could talk to his favourite, the handsome young Robert Carr.

Bacon joined the courtiers who were congratulating the poet on *The Tempest*. He was accompanied by Ben Jonson, the dramatist. William had seen several of his plays, and he had heard that this writer was apt to be irascible. But now Jonson was jovial, a strongly built man, not quite forty, with powerful hands, dark hair, a broad forehead, piercing eyes, and a pointed beard. He and the poet greeted each other familiarly, but they were formal with the courtiers.

William expected Bacon to compliment the poet, even if it was just a gesture, but he merely said, "We are fortunate to have the protection of the King."

Shakespeare nodded, but he did not speak.

Jonson, who cared for few mortals, liked both men, for Shakespeare had supported him by acting in his work, and Bacon had expressed his esteem by attending his dramas. He hurried to say, "Sir Francis, your words were well chosen, as were Will Shakespeare's."

"My essays are fragments of my conceits," said Bacon. "Like halfpence, while the silver is good, the pieces are small."

As he had expected, Ben Jonson retorted, "Sir, small only in size, but large in vision. I know no other public figure with such grand views."

"Yet I have my infirmities."

"With your able and active mind, sir?" Jonson appeared surprised.

Matthew introduced William to Bacon, who said, "I know who Harvey is. I have heard that he healed the King."

Matthew said, "Sir Francis, you have many interesting ideas about the practice of medicine. But sometimes are you not too sceptical?"

"Not sceptical, but rational. Too often doctors are so pleasing to the humours of their patients, they do not press the cure of the disease."

228

"Not Harvey, sir," Matthew replied. "Usually he is too direct."

The poet added, "He cured my complaint."

"You are fortunate, but I am often ill with colds, rheums, light fevers, dyspepsia."

Matthew said, "Sir Francis, I am sure Doctor Harvey can help you."

"I doubt it. A good doctor is rare. Most of the time, I have to cure myself. But illness gives me the privacy to read, ponder, and to write."

William noted that Bacon glanced away from the one he addressed, more interested in his own ideas than in the person to whom he spoke. Yet when he smiled his soft mouth and round cheeks were attractive. In the next moment, looking sombre, he appeared old for fifty. The lines in his face were deeply etched, his long hair was grey, his features were thick with age. What dominated were his eyes. They were hazel. And penetrating and cruel, thought William, *eyes like a viper*.

Bacon said, "However, I desire the services of a competent doctor."

William replied, "Sir, you said you have no faith in physicians."

"Very little when it comes to the practice of physic. But I am concerned with philosophical speculations about the nature of the body, and I require several physicians to verify my conclusions, and you appear to have good eyes. In that capacity your services could prove useful."

"I'm sorry, sir, but I'm already committed." The idea of leaving his own explorations for someone else's was too much to endure.

Bacon regarded William as if he were insufferable—did he not realise his importance?—and so he had to assert his superiority somehow. He turned to Shakespeare, who stood silently but observantly, and declared, "I would have written *The Tempest* differently."

"So would I, sir," replied the poet, "if I were you."

229

hen you leave the last fact
you have only begun
Then chisel out the essence
its only lasting power
and carve it into an immensity
larger than time
for all impartial generations
to see and know again.

"My Lord's complaint is regrettable, but nothing more can be done."

William stood by the bed of his newest patient, and as he said these words to himself, he realized that his judgement was a minority one. It was six months after the performance of *The Tempest*, and the many physicians who were in this sumptuous bedchamber in Whitehall Palace were optimistic about the patient's recovery. James had commanded them to cure his failing chief minister. And William knew that he was under the same obligation; he too was here because the King had demanded his presence.

Cecil, the best procurer of money that James possessed, was ill and growing worse. So the King had summoned any doctor who might restore him to workable health. With Cecil's illness, affairs of state were ill too.

The chief minister lay in a huge bed that was draped in satin and gold, and his pallid skin betrayed the sickness of his body. Yet even as William observed this, he listened to the other doctors in the hope that they would say something that would help the patient.

Matthew said, "It is the stone. I have extracted his urine."

Andrews stated, "I have let his blood with my Scottish leeches, but the poor worms have difficulty finding his veins."

"My Lord requires more purging," declared Wilkins. His voice dropped so Cecil couldn't hear him. "Hunchbacks always do. That affliction drives a black and malignant vapour to his liver and affects his blood."

"No," retorted Scrope, "purging will awaken his disorder. His vapours have reached his heart. He needs oil of ants to soothe his blood."

William winced at the remedies they suggested, and then he heard a new voice. This physician, who spoke with a French accent, was an immense man, with huge shoulders and a belly as wide as a large barrel.

Matthew introduced him as Sir Theodore Turquet de Mayerne and added, "Our distinguished colleague was born in Geneva and studied at Montpellier, and the King has just appointed him a royal physician. Mayerne has been in attendance to Cecil for some time, and offers interesting observations."

"What are they, sir?" asked William.

Mayerne said, "My diagnosis reveals a large abdominal tumour."

That is possible, thought William, there is a large swelling.

"The symptoms are evident."

"Yet you believe that Cecil may recover?"

"Yes, Harvey. Cecil is not an ordinary man."

"What are his chances?" Must he amend his own dire conclusions?

"While his hydropsical affliction has been complicated with scurvy, the patient's courage may bring him through his illness."

"Do you possess a remedy?"

"Care and a rigid diet may force the disease to yield to treatment. I cannot despair of a case where the patient's will is so strong."

"Has there been any improvement recently?"

"I have seen him constantly the last few weeks, and occasionally his strength revives. It is melancholy and heavy spirits I fear the most."

William was eager to discuss this case further. But the patient wanted to speak to him, and he returned to Cecil's side.

231

Cecil said, "Harvey, the King thinks you are a conjuror since you cured him. But my doctors contradict each other. As you will, no doubt."

"My Lord, I believe that Doctor Mayerne is closest to the truth."

"He is persuasive, but he doesn't ease my pain. I feel I'm near my end. Oh, I do not fear it," he said sharply as he saw Harvey regarding him with pity. "I will not be sorry to go. I'm not seduced by the lust of power, as some say, but I will be happy to be relieved of the heavy burdens I have borne. Do not protest. I see death in your eyes."

William did not answer.

"But you can serve me."

"How, My Lord Salisbury?"

"I'm interested in Raleigh's health." Cecil reflected, I never thought he would outlive me. "Harvey, they say he has the stone."

"Sir, I'm a doctor of physic, not a spy."

"I desire you to examine him as a physician. The present holder of the Lumleian Chair of Anatomy is ailing, and a successor will have to be found soon. A word in the right place could be useful."

"Sir, Raleigh will refuse to allow me to examine his body, as you did. If I could view your abdomen, I could be of more assistance."

Cecil thought, He couldn't permit this. No one had ever seen him naked, not even his wife, who had viewed him in the modesty of darkness. If he had been tall and straight, he would have made a virtue of nakedness, but, while he had been overworking, he had not lost his mind. The precise form of his misshapen body was a secret he intended to carry to his grave. God had constructed him rudely, but now he must make his peace with Him and prepare for heaven and pray for divine mercy. He said, "Harvey, you have a sharp eye and an agile brain. Whatever your examination of Raleigh discloses, it will be of value." When he saw the doctor hesitate, he

232

added, "This affords you a priceless opportunity to examine the most important prisoner in the realm. And judge the effects of confinement."

It was too tempting to resist, and William replied, "I will do my best to give you an accurate medical report. But nothing else, My Lord."

"As you wish. The weakness of my body leads me to believe that I am stricken with a mortal illness. Is that your judgement too?"

"Sir, you could recover." If he gave Cecil a pessimistic view, it would destroy the one weapon the patient still possessed.

"I don't know who diagnoses better than Mayerne. But his person is so untidy and extravagant, it is difficult to expect caution from him."

"My Lord, why did you summon me?"

"If you could ease James's discomfort, you are more able than I thought. Do hurry with Raleigh. I doubt I have much time left. But one thing consoles me. Death is not the end but the beginning of a better life."

Cecil's authority admitted him to the prisoner's presence the next day; Raleigh sat in his cell as if it were the centre of a stage. His doublet was off, his shirt was open, to demonstrate his good health, yet William noted that time had pillaged him too. Raleigh's hair was grey, his frame was bent, he warmed his hands to remove their ache, and he looked like an elderly man. Suddenly he shivered from the April chill, and his glance was uncertain. He ordered his servant to put logs on the fire and said, "It will not make much difference, Harvey, the Tower is a cold place, but I must work on. Work is my medicine. It keeps my flesh firm. What is your purpose here? I'm a busy man, not to be interrupted."

William stared at the great sheaf of papers on which Raleigh was writing.

"My *History of the World*. It will teach much. Who sent you here?"

"The Earl of Salisbury, sir. He is concerned about your condition."

"He fears I will outlive him. I hear he fares poorly these days."

"Not well, My Lord, not well. May I examine you?"

"No." Raleigh was emphatic. "I'm still properly made. I don't foam at the mouth. I reason still with life. Although death is always with us. As any doctor should know. But I don't fear it, since it is natural."

"Sir, I could ease your chill, and your ague and gout."

"Doctor, you interfere with my labours."

"What about your medical experiments, sir? Have they progressed?"

"Everything I do progresses. I don't need a doctor, I need freedom. Did Cecil speak of this? That cunning and cautious vulture."

"He is more interested in making his peace with God, sir."

"So he is dying. I hear that he has the pox."

"That is false. His nose is as sharp as a pen, and there are no scabs. Sir, his affliction is probably a tumour. He has a great swelling."

"Rotten from an excess of craftiness. But I will not join in the general celebration. He is a skillful minister, if without friends. Harvey, I do not speak from satisfaction but from truth. What does Cecil truly want to know about me? I'm still a loyal subject to James."

"I told you, sir. He is interested in your health."

"Tell him that it is like everybody else's. It is the final fact before death. But now you waste my time." Raleigh stood up impatiently and strode over to a makeshift shelf that had been built against the grey stone wall of the cell—for the moment Raleigh's intensity and eloquence had caused William to forget that they were in the Tower—and took a paper from his Bible, which he held up for the physician to see. "I carry this book wherever I go. And they say I am an heretic. This paper contains my argument. Give it to Cecil." As William took it slowly, he added strongly, "You can read this poem. It is not a secret."

William read:

> *Even such is Time! who takes in trust*
> *Our youth, our joys, and all we have,*
> *And pays us but with earth and dust;*
> *Who in the dark and silent grave,*
> *When we have wandered all our ways*
> *Shuts up the story of our days,*
> *But from that earth, that grave, that dust,*
> *My Lord shall raise me up, I trust.*

It had begun to rain, and William heard it patter on the prison wall, and he thought of the river outside. At this instant there seemed to be no one else in the world but the two of them. But the sudden silence suggested the grave. Then he heard noises from the river, as if to tell him that he was still alive. He said, "Sir, the poem is quite moving."

"I wrote it as a love poem. Years ago. Except for the last two lines, which I have added. Show it to Cecil. It will provide him with a proper exit, since we are all players on this stage, the earth, and we face death from the moment we are born. And when he asks how I am, tell him that I have lived with death so long that it has become my constant companion. And often, I think, my friend. Just. Mighty. And eternal."

He walked William to the door so there would be no more delay. It was dark outside except for the flicker of the torches along the battlements, where guards stood with a silent solemnity, and for a moment neither of them said anything. Then Raleigh looked back at his *History of the World,* which lay on his table in a vast profusion of sheets, and said, "Tell Cecil that when I make my exit, it will be a more fitting one."

The ailing minister had left Whitehall by the time William reached the palace the next day. He heard that Cecil, rising out of bed with an extreme effort, had decided—on Mayerne's advice—to see if the waters of Bath could cure him. The first news was that the waters had produced good results, but, as William had expected, they didn't suffice, and Cecil grew worse again. Finally, in his desperation, the First Minister turned back to London. Matthew told William, "He said, '*to return to Court to countermine his underminers and cast dust in their eyes.*' But I hear that his disease is out of control."

Several days later, Cecil died, between Bath and London.

It was a relief for William to return to his practice at the hospital and at home, for he was oppressed with the preoccupation with death that was everywhere. There was so much more he desired to know, and he decided that was what sustained Raleigh, despite his affection for death. He didn't show the poem to anyone, but decided to keep it for himself. He was just beginning to feel comfortable again when Elizabeth came to him in great distress.

She said anxiously, "Arthur is ill. He refuses to eat even when I offer him food. And his plumage droops and looks so shabby suddenly."

William felt on difficult ground. His wife assumed it was his duty to cure the parrot, but he didn't know what to do.

She put out her hand for the bird to rest upon, and for the first time he didn't leave his perch. Then Arthur began to shiver, and William had a feeling that he was suffering from an acute fever. Elizabeth took him into her lap and caressed the parrot, but instead of preening himself or welcoming this affection with gentle murmurs, he plucked at her garments, picked hairs from them, scratched her, and, worse for her, when she reproached Arthur, he didn't answer, as if he had lost his voice.

The thought that she might never hear Arthur speak to her again was too much to endure, and she collapsed on the couch, dropping the bird on the floor.

After William had put Elizabeth to bed and ordered Rachel to attend her, he returned to the parrot, who lay inertly on the

floor where he had fallen. As he examined Arthur, the parrot
was seized by many convulsions, and then, as William feared,
when they ended a freezing numbness stiffened his joints, his
pulse beat poorly, his breathing became slow and suddenly
ceased altogether.

His wife refused to believe that Arthur was dead. She insisted on picking up the limp body, and tried to massage life
into it. This failed, and she cried out amid her tears, "Arthur
was poisoned."

"Who would do that?" asked William. This is preposterous,
he thought.

"You know many prescriptions. You were jealous of him.
And so was Rachel. I know Arthur was sound and healthy.
He had no fever."

"I don't know what he had. That was the trouble."

"You should feel guilty. You couldn't even provide a satisfactory cure. Because you didn't want to. Because you wanted
Arthur dead."

How could he console the inconsolable? It was a question
that he couldn't answer. He waited until Elizabeth fell asleep
from exhaustion, and then he took the parrot to his laboratory. He dissected it with great care and came upon a womb
and an almost completed egg.

"*But, for want of a cock, corrupted,*" he told Elizabeth
after she woke up and appeared able to hear such news.
"*Which many times befalls such birds, that are immured in
cages, when they covet the society of a cock.*"

"What are you trying to tell me?"

"Arthur, poor dear, was a hen, not a cock, and was impregnated."

"Who could have done that?"

"Elizabeth, you allowed the parrot to fly in the garden,
where there were other birds."

"You are only seeking to prove that Arthur wasn't poisoned."

"I'm only trying to find out what happened. No egg is made

without a hen." He sought to console her, and she recoiled from him and buried her head in her pillow, looking ill, frightened, and hostile. He had an impulse to react violently, then told himself, This was really a cry for help. "I will buy you a new parrot."

She sobbed, "I don't desire a new parrot. I desire Arthur."

He returned to the laboratory to bury the bird in the yard. He thought, I must renew my dissections of animals. I must gather more information from them about the process of life.

Silas joined him to dig the grave and said, "Master, do you think the bird was bewitched? Changed from a cock into a hen by the devil?"

"No. It was my error. I should have known that the bird was a hen."

"Sir, it wasn't your fault. You know so much."

"Not enough."

They buried Arthur under a tree on which the parrot had loved to roost.

ll I knew
yesterday
I know today
but differently

The arteries do not take air from the lungs but blood from the heart.

This idea awoke William in the middle of the night while Rachel slept next to him, and he eased out of bed to jot it down. At this moment it seemed right to him, although he had puzzled about it for years. He wondered why it was clear to him tonight when it never had been previously. Perhaps, he felt, this is because I am stimulated by her love. And that it was possible. There was a touch on his shoulder, and he recoiled, afraid that it was Elizabeth who had come to pry, although since the parrot had died she had kept to herself so that she could mourn without interruption.

It was Rachel, whispering, "What is wrong? Have I offended you?"

She had clutched his hand until she had fallen asleep.

"No." It was a few weeks after the death of the parrot, and she was the one ray of light in the house. But he felt it was risky to praise her.

She couldn't make herself mean and inferior in his presence, and she was sorry she had asked. She turned to go downstairs, and he halted her.

He said quietly, "Rachel, dear, we have many senses, and we must use all of them. Especially in physic. Otherwise, we are impoverished."

She liked being included in his work, and she asked, "What have you learned this evening?"

He told her, but added, "Yet this possibility is just a speculation. I need proof. I must use my father's farm for dissections."

"Silas told me that he refused to allow his animals to be touched."

"I must change his mind. He is stubborn, but he is not a fool."

Rachel had never heard him so determined. She lit a candle so that he could verify what he had written. But his mind had moved beyond that with an impatience and insistence she knew too well. She stood as if paralysed.

After his sensual satisfaction he brimmed with energy, and he was nauseated by the passion for death that had absorbed Cecil and Raleigh, and even the poet and, in a way, Bacon; he wanted none of that.

"You are drunk," Rachel said. "Not with love, but with the blood."

"I cannot wait any longer. I will be thirty-four soon."

"And I waste your time?"

"You give me the happy moments of my life." He led her back to the bed, and yet in their movements towards the culmination of love, he was thinking that even in his erection it was the blood that made this possible.

Anatomies, anatomies! They dominated his mind as he came to the conclusion they were the proper pursuit of a physician in search of the solution to the mystery, and that took him to Folkestone a week later.

Thomas was startled to see his oldest son. Usually William informed him when he was arriving, but on this June day the father saw that the son wanted the advantage of surprise.

William said quickly, "Sir, I require the use of your farm and livestock. I will pay liberally for any of the animals I dissect."

Thomas thought, It was wise to kill for food, but what William desired wasn't sensible. And it would be costly. Yet he was proud that his son served the King and had attended Cecil. Searching for an excuse that wouldn't offend him, he said, "I'm thinking of selling the farm."

"After it has been in the family for generations?"

"None of your brothers likes to farm except Eliab, and he wavers. John has become a gentleman footman at Court, and the others intend to be merchants in London. I plan to move there myself. I would have done so by now if I hadn't been reelected Mayor of Folkestone."

"Then I will buy the farm!" declared William, although he had no idea how much it would cost or where he could obtain the money.

"You will ruin your chances at Court. The King will never use you."

"I must possess its resources when I need them."

"What about your duties at the hospital and the College of Physicians?"

240

"I will be at the farm only occasionally. How much would it cost?"

"More than you can afford. It is no longer essential to my fortunes. I have decided to become a gentleman, and I have applied for a coat of arms." William realized that his father was very serious, although he had called himself a yeoman when he had entered his son at Cambridge. "Your dissections are a great folly that could ruin your reputation. Would you give up an assured income for a few drops of blood? Whitehall Palace for a hermit's life? Your doctor's garb for a butcher's gown?"

Did his father think he was so easily and quickly discouraged? William said abruptly, "Then I must find another farm to use."

Thomas sensed that his son meant it. If William had inherited anything, it was his strength and stubbornness. Yet he had to say, "If you use the livestock, I will expect a strict accounting of the cost."

"Certainly. Eliab can keep the books. I will pay you to the farthing."

On his return to London, he sought to arrange his affairs so he could spend time at the farm. Matthew promised to defend his situation at Court; Mayerne assured him that he would be available at St. Bart's and would serve any patients who required immediate attention.

Believing that he had solved his problem, he asked his wife to join him at the farm, and she refused. Although it was noon, she was lying in bed, where she spent most of her time mourning, and she added, "I'm too ill," giving him a look he knew, a mixture of melancholy, self-pity, and scorn. "You are a fool to think you can alter anything. All you will accomplish is to destroy your practice and career."

"At the farm I could find you a pet to replace Arthur."

"No one will ever replace him," she sobbed, and hugged her pillow.

"Arthur was a hen," he reminded her. "And suffered an affliction."

"He was not. You should not have dissected him. No wonder he died."

William didn't understand her reasoning, and he said so.

Elizabeth cried out, "I lie here ill and you do nothing for me!"

"How can I when you don't permit me to examine you?"

"It is unseemly. Impious. But if you insist on deserting me . . .?"

She didn't finish, and he didn't ask her to do so. Her moods were becoming a constant irritation, and it was difficult for William to control his temper. And Rachel, too, became exasperating.

She desired to go to the farm with him, and when he said that was impossible, that it would create suspicion, she threatened to leave him.

While William hesitated, Rachel slipped out of bed to depart.

He said, "It will cause a scandal if I take you and not my wife."

"If I stay under these circumstances, I will grow old and unwanted."

"That is not true. But I cannot get rid of my wife just because she doesn't give me love. All I can do is to treat her like a patient."

"You are wrong. She uses her illness to keep you tied to her."

"If I take her to the farm, I will take you."

This is a concession, she thought with satisfaction, and she returned to his side and said, "I will stay now, but not forever."

Silas and Eliab went to the farm with him a few days later. It was a mild day in July, and his twenty-three-year-old brother introduced him to their father's hired man, Ned Barr, who took care of the farm.

Eliab was fair-skinned and smiled often. Ned was weather-beaten, grim, and dark. His brother was short, while the hired man was tall and burly.

Eliab, as the son of the owner, slept in the house, while Ned rested in the barn with the animals, and took care of them in return for shelter, food, and a shilling a month. His words were mostly grunts as he showed William the sheep that grazed in the pasture, the chickens, and the ducks.

William asked, "Ned, is there much wildlife about?"

"There is game enough to eat. And plenty to store for the winter."

"I may want frogs and mice, too."

"What for?" The hired man was puzzled, and he frowned.

"For my physic," he said, and saw that Ned didn't understand.

Silas said, "Master, I will catch them. I did that often as a boy."

Ned said abruptly, "We also have some seagulls and goats."

William wasn't sure what the hired man meant, but he was pleased that the main house was sturdy. Although it was timber-framed, the base was a solid stone, and the space between the wood was firmly filled with wattle and daub to resist the weather and to hold the parts together.

Ned said, "It won't crack. The plaster is lime and cow dung."

There was also glass in the windows, and comfortable rooms. William sensed his father had considered living here, and as Eliab showed him around he felt exhilarated and saw the farm as nature's laboratory.

Eliab asked, "Brother, how long do you intend to remain here?"

"Just long enough to see what I can use. Is there an empty shed available?"

"There are several. What do you need them for?"

"I will require one for my laboratory."

"Do you intend to dissect many animals?"

"As many as are necessary. But I will pay for any I use."

"Father said that I'm responsible for the farm. I will be here when you are. If I know you, once you start work you won't eat much."

Anatomies, anatomies! He had so much energy for them that now his life became a time of feverish activity. He performed his duties at St. Bart's; he participated in the administration of the College of Physicians; he served his own practice conscientiously; he appeared at Court so that James remembered he existed; but it was the work he did at the farm that absorbed him the most. The assistance of Matthew and Mayerne permitted him to visit it several times a month. While he felt that his wife and Rachel resented his absences as an affront against themselves, they did nothing to alter this situation. Elizabeth remained in a state of piety and invalidism, and Rachel came to him regularly, apparently satisfied with Silas's report that there were no women at the farm.

His first dissections were on dead flies, slugs, bees, and snails. After weeks of this kind of work, he found nothing new. He turned to larger animals, and his confidence ebbed as he saw that the hearts of frogs and turtles had only three chambers. This caused him to dissect dogs, cats, and snakes, and he felt better when he saw that their hearts had four chambers, divided into two auricles and two ventricles, similar to man's.

Encouraged, he assured himself this justified these experiments, and he ordered Silas to bring him live snails. "As many as you can find."

"Sir, I've seen some beautiful violet snails on the beach."

"The colour doesn't matter. The slower motion of their heart should be easier to observe. And then I should be more accurate."

"Master, they are so small, do they have a heart?"

"Yes, although they are coldblooded. You must be sure they are alive." He arranged the table for his dissections and brought out his instruments. This time he intended to labour until he found something promising.

Silas returned with four freshly caught snails from the shoreline, carefully kept alive, and William took them as if they were a treasure.

He put the first snail on the table, reminding himself that its heart had two auricles and two ventricles—the same as the human heart—and he decided to cut to this part at once. But for a moment he felt sick at the idea of cutting a living animal. Then, as he realised that such feeling stood in his way, he sought to ignore the writhings of the snail as he exposed its heart while it was still alive.

Yet for an instant he felt the snail's pain, and the dying heart went on beating, as if it were reluctant to relinquish life. He told himself that this feeling was stupid. As it was, he had forgotten to be observant.

He cut the second snail quickly and stared at the pulsating heart with his magnifying glass and saw that the two auricles moved together, as did the two ventricles. Then, as the light grew dim, he wasn't sure. He took the third snail, and when he did this experiment he felt the beating heart with his fingers. The pulsation was as he had seen it. His fingers were a second pair of eyes. He enjoyed this sensation. But what had he learned?

He was thinking this when Silas said, "Sir, I have a fourth snail that is still alive." Grateful for such foresight, when he cut this time he saw that, while the auricles moved together, and so did the ventricles, they didn't act simultaneously. The contraction of the auricles had precedence, the ventricles following after a brief pause. And as the snail died the auricles beat last. Life lingered longest in the right auricle.

All the snails he dissected alive confirmed these findings.

On his next visit to the farm he decided to dissect a live dog. Eliab thought he was inhuman; Ned acted as if he were sacrilegious, but he couldn't endure the uncertainty. He gave the dog opium to ease its pain.

Only Silas assisted him, and his servant couldn't look when he cut the chest to survey the beating heart. William felt sick too, but he knew that wasn't the issue. Facts were. And he must not waste them.

The dying heartbeats of the dog were the same as those of the snails. He did a similar experiment on a cat and a lamb. He was relieved to find that the auricles and ventricles of all the animals whose hearts had four chambers behaved in the same way. This indicated an order in nature.

Questions remained. Why did the auricles seem more vigourous? Why did they live longer? Silas brought him a dying dove, and he hurried to cut to its heart before death became final. But the bird died even as he held it in his hand. He moistened the motionless heart with saliva on his finger, and it began beating.

"Look!" he cried. "It contracts like a muscle."

"Master, you have brought the bird back to life! Like you did me!"

"No. The dove is dead, but its heart goes on still."

"Perhaps it is a miracle. Perhaps the bird will not die."

"That is not possible. The heart has stopped, and the bird is limp."

He followed this experiment with one on a dying frog; the motion of its heart was easily observable. Even as the animal's life withered away, the heart pulsated for some time afterwards. It was like a muscle that had strength so long as there was blood in it. But he needed more proof. Silas was cleaning up the shed, for it was spattered with blood and his father was expected and his servant wanted things to be tidy.

It was almost spotless when Thomas arrived with Eliab and Silas bowed humbly and left, hiding the remains of the frog behind his back.

Thomas surveyed the shed with distaste and said, "Eliab tells me this is where you spend most of your time. It isn't healthy or fitting."

"Father, I must make the decision what is fitting."

246

"Have you learnt anything?"

"A few uncertainties. I go from uncertainty to uncertainty."

"And neglect your London duties! I should forbid you to use my farm."

"Then I will find another."

Eliab said, "Father, William has learnt more than he admits. He wants to be sure before he says so. He is like you in that respect."

Thomas acknowledged that grudgingly, but he was pleased by what Eliab said and he asked, "Son, what have you learnt?"

"That the heart of an animal can beat even after death."

"That is God's will. Do not tempt Him too far. Satan is always near."

William didn't reply, but blew out the candles so the others had to retire to the outside, where they could see. In this instant he saw better without the light. The darkness stimulated his imagination.

Matthew thought he was pursuing his work at the farm with a fervour that was fanatical, and that this was insane. His view didn't surprise William, but he was distressed when Mayerne agreed with his old friend. They stood in the anatomy theatre of the College of Physicians after a dissection and lecture. Everybody else was gone, and he yearned to turn over the cadaver and examine its heart. The lecturer had spoken only of the wounds, ulcers, and broken bones of the back, and had kept the corpse's face downwards.

He begged them, "Help me persuade the College to dissect the heart."

Mayerne wavered, but Matthew said, "It is not fitting. Only the official lecturer is allowed to dissect. You could be considered sacrilegious. You will be disturbing the passage of the soul."

Mayerne nodded in agreement, but, William felt, more reluctantly, for the stout, cheerful doctor asked, "What have you learnt at the farm?"

"Why should the auricles and ventricles contract for the sole purpose of nourishing the lungs? That is wasteful of the structure of the heart."

Matthew replied, "Don't judge. That is God's will."

"It could also be His will that the blood may move differently than we have been taught. I need a human body to investigate this possibility."

William turned to the candle-lit corpse and started to turn it over so he could examine the heart, but Matthew stopped him and said, "You could lose your post here if you disobey the rules. Come, leave such matters to the barber-surgeon who is to dispose of the cadaver. I have a bleeding to perform, and you will see that I have a rare skill."

On their way to this chamber Mayerne lagged behind Matthew so he could ask William, "Harvey, are you sure about the movement of the auricles and the ventricles in the animals you have examined?"

"Yes. I have performed many experiments on this subject."

"You must be quite clear about what you find. If you attack cherished beliefs, your path will be difficult enough as it is."

It required influence for a patient to be examined at the College of Physicians, and William wasn't surprised to find that he was a nobleman, Lord Carew of Clopton, which was near Stratford. William knew this adventurous soldier, who was a friend and neighbour of the poet's.

George Carew, who was approaching sixty, was proud of his physique, which was that of a younger man, and he disrobed for the doctors, all of whom he knew, and said, "I attribute my complaint to a swelling of my hip, but I lack wind, and I would be grateful if it could be restored."

William thought, No wonder the patient has exposed himself. *Carew's member was a pretty bauble, a whale as big as his middle.*

Matthew bled the patient from a vein at the bend of his elbow, saying, "My Lord, this bloodletting will remove the poisonous vapours."

While Carew dressed William asked him if he had seen the poet recently.

"Yes. He has become a gentleman, and he has acquired a coat of arms."

"My Lord, how is his health?"

"Indifferent, I fear. He complains of headaches and vertigo."

"I should examine him again, sir."

"That isn't necessary, Harvey. His son-in-law examines him now. I use John Hall myself. He has excellent cures for distemper and convulsions."

Before William could discuss the poet's health further, Carew drew Mayerne aside to discuss the King's condition, for Mayerne had become James's favourite physician.

Then Matthew whispered, "William, how can a clever physician like you go against everything we have been taught for centuries?"

"I see a possibility of motion in the blood that could be vital."

"How can there be motion without an adequate moving power?"

"The heart may supply such a force. It could be a muscle."

"Galen denied the muscularity of the heart. An empty sack cannot fill itself. The time you waste on experiments could be better used at Court. While Raleigh still languishes in the Tower, James frets about his health."

"I have found many errors in Galen. Especially about the heart."

"Nonsense, William. As he wrote, veins hold the blood that originates in the liver. The wise doctor accepts that and doesn't speculate. But you risk your career, and in the end you will have no place or influence."

William didn't heed Matthew. But during the next few months, despite the many dissections he tried, he learnt nothing new. He did so many he grew sick of them. There were gloomy moments when he wished he were a boy once more,

free of ambition and anxieties, and he recalled the Armada
and how he had been sickened by the boiling oil used to heal
the wounded and their anguish, and how he had been unable
to face this and had fled. Yet these methods were still being
used on the wounded even as he believed there must be a
better way to treat wounds, although he didn't know of any.

One night while he was in bed with Rachel—it was 1614
now—he was so troubled by his failures that he was unable to
culminate their sexual joining. He felt dreadful, but she didn't
reprove him as he expected, only fondled him and said, "William, you are not pleased with yourself, are you?"

He muttered, "I go in a circle without arriving anywhere."

"Maybe so does the blood."

"No. It must have a purpose. But I have become so concerned with the auricles and ventricles, I cannot think of
anything else."

She handed him a slip of paper and said, "I've saved these
words ever since you wrote them. Read them. Please?"

*"The arteries do not take air from the lungs but blood from
the heart."*

He felt embarrassed. He had forgotten these words. His
heart raced. They could explain the action of the auricles and
the ventricles.

"William, is this idea of any value?"

"Yes!" He stared at what he had written until she asked
him what was wrong and he replied, "Do you understand
what this idea could mean?"

"How can I judge? But if it helps you, I am grateful."

"So am I, Rachel, dear." He kissed her with a fervour that
he rarely displayed. "What made you hold on to this scrap of
paper?"

"I treasure whatever you have written when you are with
me."

He returned to his dissections with a renewed vigour. At
the farm Ned took ill with a muscle complaint, but when

William offered to treat him the hired man declined suspiciously. Later Silas told him that Ned had used sheep dung and had been cured, but William believed that rest and time had sufficed, for the hired man had remained in bed for a few days.

He was more excited by the live snake that Silas brought him. Now he could test what he had written about the arteries. Then he admonished himself, Observe carefully, read each sign, however trivial, nature has its plan. I am not trespassing, as so many think, but exploring.

He cut open the snake and saw that its heart continued to pulsate. He repeated this experiment, and as the snake's heart contracted and dilated, he compressed the artery between his finger and thumb at a place above the heart. The heart became distended and looked as if it would burst. He withdrew his finger and thumb from the artery and the heart became normal.

Growing more excited, but still unsatisfied, he did the same thing with the vein below the heart, to arrest the incoming flow of blood. He saw that as the part which was between his fingers and the heart became empty, the heart became smaller, paler than it was before, beating more slowly too, as if it were about to die. He asked himself, Is it because of a lack of blood? He removed his obstacle to the flow of the blood, and noted that the colour and motion of the blood became normal. He wrote:

"Here we have evidence of threatened death from two opposite causes—extinction through deficiency, and suffocation through excess."

He sat under the great oak which had been on the farm for centuries—Eliab said since the Norman invasion, and did he know that Hastings was nearby? He had forgotten this, and ostensibly he was seeking shelter from a shower, but actually he was using this pause for reflection.

He thought of the coach he had bought because of his many trips to the farm. It was a large, square box that swayed precariously on leather straps, crude and springless. It jolted him uncomfortably, with only thick flaps to protect him against the rain, wind, dust, and sleet.

His buttocks ached so at the end of the journey! Did that have anything to do with the motion of the blood? He had tried his new experiment on dogs, cats, and frogs, and the marvellous thing was that the same thing happened to their hearts, arteries, and veins. He said to himself:

The blood enters a limb by the arteries and returns with the veins is proved experimentally in animals. He wondered: Is this true in man?

He decided to try this experiment on Silas, who obeyed reluctantly. He assured him, "There is nothing to fear. I'm not going to cut you."

Nonetheless, Silas was dubious, and while he couldn't say no to anything his master asked, he felt he was becoming a sacrificial goat upon the altar of the doctor's religion, and he was afraid. He prayed to Jesus as his master tied the bandage about the upper part of his arm.

William said, "It may give you some discomfort when I tighten it, but you won't be hurt," but Silas remained apprehensive.

Yet he felt his life was worth only what value William put on it, since he owed it to him, and so he tried to obey his master and to stand quietly and submissively as the doctor adjusted the bandage. Even so, he had to explain, "I don't have as much blood as stouter folk do."

"I will manage. The fact that you are lean and have large veins makes you the best subject for such a trial."

Silas didn't agree, but William ignored his nervousness. He drew the ligature as tightly as the subject could bear it. He was excited when he saw that the artery didn't pulsate beyond the bandage. Yet the artery throbbed violently and was preternaturally distended above the ligature. Examining the whole limb, he saw that when he kept the bandage on for a few minutes, Silas's hand grew livid. The servant looked at him appealingly, as if he were on the verge of death, but William couldn't halt.

When he made the bandage less tight, Silas was grateful, although William reminded him this was merely the next step in his experiment. The veins swelled, and there was an immediate colouration of the entire hand.

Silas's imploring look begged for relief, but William was busy writing down his latest observations: *"The difference in the effect of the tight and medium bandage is this. The tight bandage not only obstructs the veins but the arteries also; whereby it comes to pass that the blood neither comes nor goes in the member. The medium bandage obstructs the veins, the more superficial among them especially, while the arteries, lying deeper, are not obstructed but continue conveying blood to the limb."*

If this is true, William thought, the arteries do carry blood and not air or spirits, as is believed. This experiment also indicates that the blood passes from the arteries to the veins at the periphery of the body, not from the veins to the arteries, as was stated by Galen.

"Then it is possible, from the unusual fullness of the veins, that the blood flows incessantly outwards from the heart by the arteries and ceaselessly returns to it by the veins." Even as he said this to himself and the possibility elated him, he realized it was just a supposition.

Silas interrupted him. "Sir, do I have to wear this bandage any longer? I can hardly breathe."

Is it air in the arteries after all, he reflected unhappily, as Galen said? Or fear? Or something I don't understand? He ran his hand through his thick dark hair, wishing the body were not so complicated.

"Sir, the bandage is very uncomfortable."

He took off the ligature and saw that as the binding on the veins was released, the blood that had accumulated in them emptied toward the heart.

This caused him to investigate their structure, and he discovered that the coat of the arteries was thicker, stronger, and more resilient than that of the veins. *Was that because the arteries had to sustain the shock of the propelling heart? Could their purpose be dependent on a pumping action of the heart?*

Next he found that in all the large animals he dissected, the nearer the arteries were to the heart, the stronger they became. And then they differed even more from the fabric of the veins. The veins were less stiff in texture, more yielding. This convinced him that they served quite different functions. He was even more sure of this when he saw that the aorta contained both elastic tissue and tough, inelastic tissue.

His common sense told him that this large artery was constructed in such a manner for only one possible reason: to accept blood in varying amounts from the heart, sometimes in large quantities, sometimes in small—a flexible channel adjusting to the changing demands of the body. Yet, he wondered, if the blood leaves the heart by way of the arteries and returns through the veins, what about the valves of the veins?

He ordered Silas to exercise vigourously so that his veins, which were large and stood out because of his leanness, would cause his valves to knot. Ignoring Silas's dread—by now, he thought impatiently, Silas should know better—he had him place his forearm on the table. He bandaged the limb and with his finger pressed the vein at its knotted valve so that the blood would be pushed in the direction of the heart and beyond the next valve. He was grateful that Silas, despite his fear, had sufficient faith in him to stand still. William pressed on the vein until he had emptied the blood between the two valves. Then he lifted his finger from the vein and stopped pushing the blood. The result was as he had hoped. The vein he had emptied had stayed empty. He cried out in his joy, "The valves prevent the return of the blood! Fabricius was wrong!"

Silas said, "My heart hasn't been the same since the hanging."

"Your heart is fine." William felt a heavy burden lifting from his shoulders. His newest discovery almost convinced him that the blood did return to the heart, and possibly left it, also.

"Master, was I able to help you? Did you learn anything?"

"Indeed! The blood in your body may circulate."

"Sir, what do you mean by that notion?"

"The blood may move about the body in a circle. Out of the heart through the arteries and into the heart through the veins." Then he sought to control his excitement, adding, "But I need more facts."

He could hardly wait to return to the farm to resume his experiments. Usually several weeks passed between visits, so he could perform his London duties properly, especially at the College of Physicians, where, it was said, the post of Lumleian Lecturer of Anatomy, which he coveted, would soon be vacant. Now, however, feeling he was close to the solution of the mystery, he decided to come back to the farm the following week.

Elizabeth, who was devoting herself to a new version of the Bible authorised by King James, wanted to discuss it with him. In this English translation she was finding a true comfort for her sorrows.

She was disappointed when William said, "I will read it later."

He was equally brief with Rachel, who had seen little of him lately. He apologised, yet he felt he had to confine his energy and emotion to his experiments, even as she acted as if he regarded her with indifference.

If we cannot agree on how to spend time together, Rachel reflected bitterly, it confirms my original fears. Taken in lechery, she told herself, it is no wonder that his infidelity is my folly. She felt in a situation of discomfort and duplicity, and she wasn't sure what to do next.

* * *

William pushed all these matters out of his mind when he reached the farm, for there, he was certain, nothing would interrupt him. Then Eliab stood in the doorway, frowning.

"What is wrong?" William asked irritably, angered by this distraction.

"You owe Father a considerable amount of money for the livestock you have used. He wants to know when you are going to pay it."

"Calculate it. To the penny. And I will bring it with me next time."

But Eliab didn't depart, as he expected and wished, but said, "Ned is upset by the number of animals you have killed. I tell him that he is wrong, but he regards you as a murderer. He has become very difficult."

"He is a wretched, ignorant fool. And insolent."

"Perhaps, but he thinks you are committing terrible wrongs. He has been talking in the village about you. He says you consort with Satan."

"By God, are you suggesting that I stop?" William was furious.

"I'm warning you to be careful. To dissect a little less. Insects, mice, frogs, but not lamb or sheep that people eat. Or dogs."

"Why not dogs?"

"The villagers love dogs."

"When they don't have to eat them. Eliab, are you finished?"

"For the moment. I hope you will be soon. Before there is trouble."

William fondled his dagger and said, "I can defend myself."

After Eliab was gone he locked the door of the shed—so I won't be disturbed, he told himself—and he worked more feverishly. He sent Silas to fetch him a sheep, when Ned wasn't looking, and then he sought to concentrate on the heart to find out if it were capable of performing as he hoped. He dissected a live frog, and as he felt its heart with his hand

256

the tissue became harder. He told himself, This hardness must come from muscle tension. He itemized the evidence that indicated the heart could be a muscle: It contracted, it generated force, its fibre was sturdy and vibrant. Minutes later, the frog's brain cut off, sensations gone, its heart continued to beat. He shredded the heart; the shreds beat. He cut up another heart, and he saw that each fragment beat. Fascinated by the possibility that the heart might be a pump, he examined the heart of a four-chambered creature, a rabbit that Silas had caught for him.

The servant was uneasy, for he had heard Eliab's warning, but his master was drunk with blood; he thought, Nothing would deter him.

William observed that the wall of the right ventricle was much thinner than the left's. He held up both to the sun and saw that the light came through the right ventricle, but not the thicker left ventricle.

He decided that the wall of the right ventricle was thin because it delivered blood only in and out of the lungs, while the left delivered it from the head to the toes, and so needed to be thicker and stronger.

Silas was so restless after he brought the sheep he needed next that William commanded him to go to bed. "I can do whatever I have to do by myself." Silas hesitated, but the doctor was so insistent that finally the servant departed, apparently for bed.

William thought, The great thing is: So much was falling into place.

He locked the door again—this next experiment was a precious one—and he bound the sheep, gave it opium to lessen the pain and so it wouldn't resist his knife when he opened it, and cut to the heart so he could observe that while the animal was still alive. He saw, contrary to what he had been taught, this heart emptied when it contracted, and became tense with the expulsion of the blood. Then, as the heart relaxed, it received blood.

Now he was almost convinced that this heart was a muscle, and was in all the animals he had examined. And could be in man. But he needed human anatomies to prove this possibility. And that the heart was a pump.

He pondered for many hours, seeking to find a way to verify these views. The candles burnt out, and he sat in darkness, where he could contemplate best. To suggest that the blood circulated through the body, and that it was propelled by the heart, was to take a great risk.

He was startled by a loud knocking on the locked door of the shed. It sounded hostile, and his hand went instinctively to the dagger at his side.

It was Silas, inquiring, "Have you eaten, sir?"

"I forgot. Bring me water-cider." It was yeast, sugar, and apples fermented for forty-eight hours, and it was his favourite drink.

"Master, there is none left. You have drunk it all up."

"Then bring me coffee." He unlocked the door and thrust his fingernail caressingly into the groove of the coffee bean he kept in his pocket for comfort. "This little fruit is the source of happiness, wit, and energy."

Now that Silas was inside, he could say what was actually on his mind. "Sir, you haven't slept at all, and it is almost dawn. And it is Sunday, and the villagers will not like you violating the Sabbath."

William shrugged and declared, "I will work whenever it is necessary."

"And there is a message from London, sir."

William took it but he didn't read it, saying, "We need more wood. If it rains, as is likely, the heat will help avoid melancholy, and keep us warm. Beware of catarrhs. Drink the best coffee. And avoid ignorance."

"Sir, aren't you going to read what Dr. Ross wrote? It is urgent."

William regarded the message reluctantly, sensing it would force him to halt when he felt at a vital part of his experiments. Matthew had written:

258

"A new Lumleian Lecturer is about to be chosen at the College, and if you are interested in the post, it will be useful to show yourself at Court, since the King could have the last word on that situation. A new performance of *Macbeth* is being given at Whitehall, which should put the King in a favourable humour, for he likes this drama. Thus, it would be advisable for you to attend, a view that Mayerne shares."

When Silas saw his master hesitate, he said hurriedly, "Sir, you could return to London today. With rain, there will be less dust on the roads."

"Yes." He sighed. "Clean up the shed so there is no sign of blood." He must not neglect the King. "You will stay here until I return." He ignored Silas's protests. "Which will be as soon as possible."

Who would have thought the old man had so much blood in him . . .

William sat at the rear of the great hall of Whitehall Palace a few days later and those words reverberated through his mind. Did the poet understand the movement of the blood through the body? He must ask him when he got the chance. The poet was in attendance this winter day of 1615, and William wondered what was on his mind, Shakespeare looked so grave.

His attention concentrated on him, although he saw Matthew, Mayerne, and most of the Court hovering about the King. He was concerned about Shakespeare's health, for the poet had aged since he had seen him last.

Shakespeare seemed pleased to see him, but not interested in discussing his work. But when he realized that the doctor's interest in his views of the blood were genuine, he said, "I did write this tragedy at James's request. He wanted a drama that would support his dynasty. Yet I was told to avoid the death of any King onstage, this would offend royal sensibilities. And he wanted to see more of the witches. The use of the blood . . ." He shrugged. "I trust it didn't injure your feelings."

"I am curious where you found your ideas about the blood."

"They are all about us, and my son-in-law is a physician."

"You dwell so much on the blood. Have you ever thought it may circulate?"

"How?" Shakespeare looked puzzled and sceptical.

"From the heart into the arteries and then back through the veins."

"I thought the arteries carried the vital spirits."

William wasn't sure it was prudent to pursue this matter further.

Shakespeare said suddenly, "I believe the blood flows like a river, but it is the liver, not the heart, that causes this flow." He added sadly, "I lack vigour. In 1606 I was able to perform in my play, but no more. Hippocrates says, '*Weariness without apparent cause indicates disease.*'"

Before William could examine the poet, which he wanted to do, he was summoned by the King in the person of Matthew, who whispered, "None of your outrageous ideas about the blood or he will never consider you."

When James ordered him to speak, he said, "Sir, I told Dr. Ross that your good health is indispensable to the health of the realm." He disliked himself for indulging in such flattery, but he told himself that as Lumleian Lecturer on Anatomy he could further his work—and James smiled.

Matthew said, "Sire, Dr. Harvey is a fine anatomist."

Mayerne added, "Possibly, Your Majesty, the best in England."

James said, "Harvey, you are rarely at Court, yet you want this post?"

"Sire, I would be happy and honoured to be at Court whenever you desire. But Dr. Mayerne and Dr. Ross assure me that your health is sound."

"I hear that you pursue strange experiments."

"Not strange, Your Majesty. I simply search for knowledge."

"Do not declare anything that is contrary to our established opinion. That could be used against my divine authority."

James turned to Bacon to discuss financial matters with him.

William told Matthew and Mayerne that his newest experiments indicated the arteries contained blood instead of air, contrary to Galen, and that the heart might be a muscle that pumped blood around the body.

Matthew replied, "Do not declare this in public."

Mayerne asked, "Have you any proof?"

"How can he have any proof?" Matthew cut in. "Galen proved that it is *the liver which generates food-enriched blood which passes up and down the body through the great veins until it is consumed or evaporated. The heart is merely the generator of heat and the vital spirits, the cistern of the blood, and the arteries contain air, because they are empty at death.*"

Mayerne still wanted to know what experiments he had performed, but Matthew's lack of faith disheartened William, and he changed the subject. He asked, "Do you think I have a chance for the post?"

Matthew said confidently, "As I told you, if you don't offend."

"You are qualified," said Mayerne. "You are a fine anatomist."

"It is an inferior skill," Matthew stated. "Fit only for surgeons."

He saw that Shakespeare was alone, and he excused himself to talk to the poet. But when he reached the poet, Bacon engaged him in conversation, saying, "Men pretend to ignorance because they are lazy."

"Sir," said William, "men are ignorant because they lack imagination."

Shakespeare said nothing.

"For myself," replied Bacon, "I find that my industry and wit fit me for the study of the truth. When my uncertain health doesn't hinder me."

William stared at the poet's throat and saw his pulse beating rapidly. Too rapidly, he felt, and surely I should examine his heart.

Bacon was determined to be the centre of attention, and he said, "Doctor, you inspire some confidence in the King despite your frequent absences from Court. And your work at St. Bart's is commended."

"Thank you, sir. You are kind."

"I am never kind! Only accurate! I find in the afternoon I need a comforting drink to support my spirits. Is that an advantage?"

"Sir, I could determine this if I could examine both of you."

Bacon looked offended, as if such a situation were beneath him, and strode away, while the poet smiled sardonically and shrugged.

William asked, "Mr. Shakespeare, what troubles you now?"

"My headaches have returned."

"Have you been moderate?"

"As much as is possible. But my difficulty is the human one. All things tend to their end. Some sooner than others. But why should I fear to leave this world, when men defile it so?"

A hand on William's arm pulled him away from the poet into the privacy of a corner of the great hall. He swung around to protest such liberties being taken with his person, and he was startled to see that it was his thirty-three-year-old brother, John, dressed in the livery of a Yeoman of the Bedchamber. John was proud of his wide, fluted white ruff and his velvet doublet adorned with the royal emblem of a Tudor rose, and he said, "For a sensible man, brother, you can be reckless."

"You look quite shapely. I don't know why you should be anxious."

John's short, pointed beard matched his long, pointed face, and he said, "I have reason to worry about you. There are tales in the village that you practice witchcraft at the farm. I know that isn't true, but if it reached the King's ear it would be unfortunate. Now that I have attained the post of Yeoman of the Bedchamber, I have a privileged position close to his person. But he is quickly suspicious. Why don't you devote yourself to St. Bart's? To the care of the sick poor? In the name of God."

"My object is to find the truth. Is that so hard to endure?"

"New ideas are not regarded favourably here."

"I know." Was he, like a poor, floundering fool, merely dreaming?

"The family is glad to aid you, but we don't want to see your career injured. You have good prospects at Court. If you are careful."

I must be very careful, he thought, in all my experiments. When I am in London I will be a London doctor, but when I was inside the chambers of the heart I must understand how it works.

"I saw you conversing with Lord Bacon. I trust you listened carefully. He has great influence now, and comprehends the craft of medicine."

"Thanks for your advice, John. I will try not to harm you."

He arrived at the farm to find an agitated Silas. A note scrawled in black capital letters had been put under the door of the shed. He read:

DO NOT PROFANE OUR LAND AND SABBATH WITH YOUR SLAUGHTER OF INNOCENT CREATURES OR YOU WILL SUFFER. YOUR PRACTICE OF THE EVIL ARTS IS KNOWN AND WILL BE PUNISHED IN HELL. WE ARE GOD-FEARING FOLK.

For an instant he felt sick at the stomach, and afraid; then he was angry and disgusted. How could he fight what he could not see? He asked Silas, "Have you reported this to anyone?"

"No, sir. I was afraid. Do you think they will kill us?"

"We mustn't heed it. This is merely an idle threat."

"Ned didn't write it. He can't read or write. Sir, what will you do?"

"I require a full-grown sheep. One that weighs a hundred pounds."

"Now?" Silas was shaken by his master's determination to continue.

"Of course." He felt he could be hurrying toward the gallows, and yet he couldn't allow himself to be intimidated, it was against his nature. He was possessed now, too, with a fierce rage that he didn't know whom to strike back at, and that was the worst feeling of all. "Get it right away."

"Aren't you going to tell your brother, sir?"

Why should I, he thought, Eliab will only try to halt me. "No," he said, "Silas, we mustn't tell anyone of this foul note. It is the work of a disordered mind. Now, fetch me a sheep without Ned knowing it."

"He must know it, sir. He keeps count of his flock."

"Don't worry about it. He may think it strayed. After this one I may not need another one for a while." Silas looked so relieved he was annoyed, but he said, "Hurry, so I can complete this experiment today."

"Master, it is Sunday."

"I know it is Sunday!" he shouted. He wished those damned bells from the village church would stop pealing, they were so distracting.

Once he sought to learn how much blood there was in the sheep that Silas brought him—Ned was in church, and the flock was in the care of his dog—William forgot everything but the experiment he was doing. He concentrated with emotional immediacy as he cut so that he could observe the beat of the heart while it was still alive, and he drained the sheep of its entire store of blood. The animal weighed one hundred and four pounds, which was satisfactory, for it was close to the body mass of man.

When all the blood was drained from the sheep, it totalled

four pounds. It had taken an hour, yet during that time the heart had beat sixty times a minute and had expelled two ounces of blood with each beat. He wrote:

"Since two ounces of blood are projected by each contraction of the heart at the rate of sixty times a minute and the beats in an hour are three thousand and six hundred, the quantity expelled by the heart would be four hundred and fifty pounds. Yet when the body of the sheep is drained of blood it amounts to just four pounds. Thus, the amount pushed out of the heart in an hour is far greater than is in the sheep. So, it must be assumed, that it is the same blood flowing through the body, that the fluid which flowed out through the arteries now returns by the veins. It is a simple matter of necessity that the blood performs a circuit, returning to the place from whence it came forth."

Yet even as he was greatly excited about where these views led him, he reminded himself, he had not proved that these facts were true of man.

When William returned to the farm two weeks later and nothing had happened, he decided that the anonymous note was an idle threat. He told no one about it or about his deductions, although Rachel sensed he was pleased with his work, for he was attentive, and Elizabeth was glad that he was willing to discuss the new version of the Bible with her.

He decided to measure the amount of blood in an animal larger than man, and he found a butcher who lived near Folkestone, and arranged to view a bullock as it was slaughtered. Silas insisted on going with him, and since it was a short distance and they had to ride over fields instead of roads, he left the coach at the farm and went on horseback.

It was a lovely spring day, and Silas recognised many of the flowers in the fields, but his master looked so serious that he didn't mention them, asking, "Sir, do you know this countryside?"

"Most of it. I walked some of these paths when I was a

child. But I preferred the leas along the cliffs. I was fascinated by the sea."

"And now, sir?"

"I am possessed by a different sea, the blood. I am paying this butcher a goodly sum to witness what he would be doing anyway."

Yet he was pleased with the butcher's efficiency. Roger Ward was a tall countryman with wide shoulders who wore his bloody apron with pride, and at William's request he slaughtered a bullock in prime condition by driving a great spike into its heart. William noted, It had an immense effect on impact, for the heart contracted and dilated like a gigantic muscle.

The butcher, taking every precaution to secure accuracy, found that the total amount of blood was thirty-eight pounds for a body weight of eight hundred and fifty-two pounds. William calculated that the amount of blood to the total weight of the body was about the same as in the sheep.

This suggested to him that the same fact could be true of man.

The sun was setting as they returned to the farm, and suddenly he had to reach it quickly. It is on fire, he thought agitatedly, there is such a bloody glow in the sky, but as he galloped up to the door of the shed, Silas close behind him —Silas was afraid to follow him, yet more afraid not to—he saw that it was his coach that was ablaze. Silas cried out about the cost, but William was concerned about the cost of time. They couldn't halt the fire; the wood had been ignited from a bonfire that had been lit beneath the vehicle, and soon it was a burnt wreck.

He found a note on the shed door that said in an ugly black scrawl:

TAKE NOTE HERETIC. IF YOU CONTINUE TO VIOLATE GOD'S WAYS YOU WILL DIE AN EQUALLY UNPLEASANT DEATH. AT THE STAKE AS BEFITS AN HERETIC.

He hid this and faced Eliab, who had just arrived, attracted

266

by the blaze, which could be seen in Folkstone, several miles away.

Eliab asked anxiously, "Brother, what happened? The coach is gone."

"I lit a fire to get warm, and a spark ignited the vehicle."

"You are less than candid. The bonfire is under the coach."

Silas said, "Begging your pardon, sirs, but the—"

William halted him. "Take care of the horses. They are frightened. Hurry, before we lose them too." As Silas obeyed him, although reluctantly, he asked Eliab, "How much money do I owe you for livestock?"

"Pay me later. You will need it for a new coach."

"Eliab, I would appreciate if you didn't tell Father about this."

"He is bound to find out about the fire."

"Tell him that it was an accident. As it was."

Eliab didn't answer, but examined his brother to make sure that he hadn't been hurt in trying to put out the blaze. Then he sighed with relief and said, "Do you truly think your experiments are worth this?"

William pretended that he didn't understand what Eliab meant.

"I know you have been threatened. I have heard that they are afraid of you in Folkestone. It is no secret. Were there any notes?"

"No. I told you, it was an accident."

Eliab didn't object this time, although he didn't lose his sceptical look. He felt closer to William than to his other brothers, for William had encouraged his learning and had never treated him like a child. He said, "Perhaps the heart is the kind of vessel you think it is, but no one else cares. In the village all that matters is the land owned, the crops, the harvest of fish from the nearby sea, the houses built to protect against the wet and the vermin. You should leave well enough alone."

William replied, "At least the coach will make firewood for cooking."

Eliab said abruptly, "I am dismissing Ned."

"I have no proof he did this."

"He has talked against you in the village. I will get a new hired man. But be careful, William, they are afraid of you in Folkestone, and I don't want to have any bodily harm come to you. They could make a bonfire out of you. As you told me, Calvin made one out of Servetus for his new ideas."

William nodded, even as he bubbled with ideas. He said, "Eliab, you must be more cheerful. Our hearts beat a hundred thousand times a day. By heartbeats, life is not short." His brother was incredulous, and William added, "I calculated that fact carefully. At the rate of seventy-two times a minute, in the course of twenty-four hours our hearts beat one hundred and three thousand, six hundred and eighty times."

"Then you do believe your theories about the movement of the blood?"

"All the evidence I've found in animals indicates that it circulates."

"Do you expect to continue experimenting on the farm?"

"That depends."

"Depends on what?" Eliab asked anxiously.

"On what I need to know."

Someone shouted from the darkness, "Heretic! You are possessed with odious, depraved peculiarities!" William said they must disregard that, and ordered Silas to ride into Folkestone and hire a coach, and when Silas was afraid, he agreed to go with him, and Eliab joined them.

He liked to ride, and his new discoveries exhilarated him. He thought, as he mounted his horse, He was not an heretic; the blood was immune to taunts, its movement was God's creation, there was much that was natural and elemental about what he was learning. It would be stupid to stop. Nature was teaching him now. Nothing must interfere. But he kept the note.

As they rode through the night air, he felt his blood moving faster.

I can only be
as great
as I am
You can be
greater
If you like
But be sure
you are
yourself

"Will Shakespeare is dead. Harvey, we have lost a patient."

William heard John Hall's words with dismay, but he was not surprised. Whilst a year had passed since he had seen the poet, he recalled vividly their last conversation, and that his patient had felt the onrush of death even as he had sought to minimise it. He paused in his preparations for his anatomical lecture at the College of Physicians—he had been appointed recently to the Lumleian Chair—and asked, "John, why didn't you inform me sooner that he was ailing?"

"I told Will you ought to attend him, but he refused. He seemed weary of life, and, I think, desirous of leaving it. He ignored my warnings to be careful and said I mustn't consult any other doctors, even you, whom he respected. He said that if nature couldn't heal him, nothing could."

"Did you observe his symptoms?"

"He had difficulty with his breathing, and he was seized with a pain in the region of the heart. Soon after, he was gone."

"What do you think was the cause of death?"

"Will was proud of his heart. He regarded it as a source of his strength. So I am saying that he took cold, sweated, and died."

"Do you have his manuscripts?"

"They are the property of the companies he wrote them for. He never clasped them to his person, as I thought he would, but was more interested in becoming *'Will Shakespeare, gent.,'* which he did, ceremoniously."

William longed to examine the body to determine the cause of death, but when he suggested an autopsy, John said, "He forbad it and ordered the following inscription to be put on his grave." John read it to him:

> *Good friend for Jesus sake forbeare,*
> *To digg the dust encloased heare,*
> *Bleste be ye man yi spares thes stones,*
> *And curst be he yi moves my bones.*

And thus, William reflected, the poet has gone into the earth and no one will ever know for certain the cause of his death. He turned back to his duties. He arranged his knives, probes, and other instruments in the proper order and made sure they were sharp and spotless. There was a mat at the foot of the dissecting table so his feet wouldn't become cold, silver rods for him to touch the body with when it pleased him, and an upright skeleton for illustration. But he felt that the anatomy room, a square hall of moderate size, with the seats adjusted so that everyone attending could see, was not marvellous, as his colleages assumed, but, compared to Padua, old-fashioned. Today's anatomy was listed as a visceral lecture, but he intended to go straight to the heart. It was his second anatomy; he had used the first for general observations, but now he planned to reveal what he had learned. Since the threats against him months ago, he hadn't returned to the farm, but he told himself that he would—as soon as it was essential for his experiments.

The audience settled into their chairs, and he saw Wilkins, Mayerne, Scrope, Matthew, and doctors such as John Hall, who, while they were not members of the College, were allowed to witness this anatomy lecture.

Two felons who had been hanged the previous Friday were brought in, although it was now Tuesday. William disliked this practice, but it was the custom. He thought that to examine accurately he should have the bodies right after death. He was glad there were two and that they differed. He had asked for a middle-aged man and a youth if possible, and the surgeon in charge, John Woodall, had sought to please him. One of the cadavers was the poet's age, and the other was hardly older than Silas had been when he had saved him.

Woodall was a renowned military surgeon, and William felt this stern-faced, sixty-year-old chirurgeon, with his white ruff, thick white beard, and florid cheeks, desired a recommendation from him for an appointment to the staff of St. Bart's. A curtain was put around the anatomy table so that the cadavers were decently hidden before the lecture began. William knew the bitter controversy in the College about whether the genitals should be shown, and he had decided on his course of action. He ordered the curtains removed so he could start, and the bodies to be turned upwards.

Woodall passed these instructions on to his assistant, although with distaste. The surgeon operated in any position that was necessary, but he saw no point in stressing the genitals; he preferred modesty.

William began by drinking to the King's good health out of a gilt cup which had been given the College by Henry VIII. It was the custom, as was his bowing dutifully to a portrait of that monarch by Holbein which hung over the table. Then, he spoke in English, although most doctors lectured in Latin— for surgeons understood only English, and physicians preferred to stress their superiority by showing their familiarity with Latin. While William's Latin was good, his English was better, and he wanted no misunderstanding of his words. He cut the cadavers himself instead of ordering Woodall or his assistant to do so, which was the usual method.

He saw the audience stiffen, but he had to find out for himself. He felt like a young teacher speaking on behalf of the body, although he was thirty-eight and he could be close to the end of his life. He knew that the average mortality was estimated to be thirty-nine.

He said, "I shall proceed to the heart, arteries, and veins."

Then, with his silver rod he pointed to the exposed organs in both cadavers, and stated, "The heart has two ventricles, a right and a left. I am amazed at Aristotle, who described three. This fact is true of many animals."

"But we are not animals," protested Wilkins. "We are created by God."

"All animals in His kingdom are His creation." He ignored Wilkins's horror and returned to the cadavers. He made sure each corpse's heart was laid open so its entire mass could be examined closely and clearly. Then he fixed the four parts of the heart and declared that this structure was the same in all men. No one protested openly, although he heard restless stirrings in his audience, and he continued, using the cadavers to prove his findings. "You will see that the walls of the arteries, such as the aorta, are more resilient in the young than in the old." He recalled how this had been brought to his attention when Silas had dashed into his house without breathing hard, while the elderly widow next door had puffed heavily, although she walked slowly. "And the arteries have a thick coat, especially the pulmonary artery, carrying the right ventricle's blood."

Scrope shouted, "It carries only air, as stated by Galen."

"Contrary to Galen," he replied, "I have inflated the lungs with air and I have found that, whatever the force I used, air could not be driven from the air tubes into the heart. Thus, I must conclude that the arterial system is filled with blood, nothing else."

He paused in the hope his findings would be accepted, and heard a storm of criticism that was violent and outraged.

"Lord God," he answered, "if what I have found is true, it is Your grace and truth. The heart, arteries, and veins are Your creation. Fellow physicians, to examine them is not impious. I have incised the trachea of a living dog, filling its lungs forcibly with air by a bellows, and seen that no trace of air could be found in the heart or the great vessels."

Matthew said hurriedly to calm his irate colleagues, "And

you give thanks to our Lord for revealing to you His goodness, mercy, and wisdom."

"Indeed! That is why I perform these dissections. So that you can reliably witness my observations and reasonably accept His truth."

Wilkins said, "I give thanks to our Father that I don't believe you. I pray for your soul before it is seized by the devil."

Scrope said, "You know we have been taught that the liver is the laboratory of the natural blood. What you say is not possible."

Mayerne wanted William's assurance that he was sure he was right.

William hesitated. He was grateful that Mayerne seemed eager to support him, and Mayerne had considerable influence, but he wasn't sure.

"What's wrong?" Matthew asked when he didn't reply.

Nothing has to be wrong, William decided, so long as some doctors listen to me, and Mayerne and Hall are doing so. He pointed to the heart of the cadaver and said, "As you can see, it is shaped like a muscle that could push the blood in through the veins and out through the arteries."

Wilkins sneered. "You involve us in futile, sacrilegious speculations."

"The heart's action is like a fist clenching and unclenching."

Wilkins ignored this explanation, and as he rose to leave, most of the doctors joined him. At the door he declared, "You don't know what you are talking about. *The heart's substance is thick flesh, red, not musculous, its motion not voluntary as muscles have.* Harvey, if you continue to talk nonsense, no physician will attend your lectures."

"If that is so, why don't you demonstrate your views on the cadavers?"

"Surgery is a foul trade, fit only for barbers! Harvey, you appall us!"

The majority of the doctors agreed with Wilkins and left
with him, but William was grateful that Mayerne, Hall, and
Matthew remained. He dismissed Woodall and his assistant,
saying he had private matters to discuss and that they should
return later to dispose of the cadavers. Then he stated, "It is
likely the old theories about the heart and the blood are in
error."

Mayerne repeated, "But we do need more assurances, Harvey."

Mayerne still sounded anxious, and before William could
answer him, Matthew said, "If you cannot prove you are
right, you may be forced to resign. All my colleagues are
convinced that the blood is generated by the liver and then
consumed at the periphery of the body."

"My experiments indicate that the periphery is where the
blood could travel from the arteries to the veins," William
replied.

"Have you seen any links between these vessels?"

"No," William said regretfully.

Matthew's tone grew positive. "If you are not sure, you are
wrong."

William doubted that he was wrong. He had found so much
evidence that the blood moved around the body, he felt there
must be a link between the arteries and the veins. If he only
had an instrument to see better—but his magnifying glass was
just strong enough to see a snail's heart.

Matthew stated, "My views have existed for centuries.
Since Galen."

"Perhaps the body has changed since then."

Mayerne said suddenly, "That is possible."

"Come, Mayerne," said Matthew, "the King is ailing, and
he needs us."

Mayerne joined Matthew, but Hall wanted a minute more
with Harvey.

"Suit yourself," said Matthew. "William, what makes you
so stubborn?"

"The amount of blood I have found in animals indicates it is virtually impossible that the blood could be produced over and over, as Galen declared."

Matthew asked, "In what kind of life?"

"In sheep. Dogs. Bullocks."

"But not in man. You have not found that in man. Have you?"

"No. Not yet."

"You see!" Matthew cried triumphantly. "Our friend rushes to his conclusions without the proper evidence."

William was shaken by this charge—it was possible that man differed from the living animals he had dissected—although the evidence he had accumulated indicated that the structure of sheep, dogs, bullocks, and man were the same, and thus they should function the same way.

After Matthew and Mayerne left for the Court, John Hall wanted to discuss his father-in-law. He felt guilty about his sudden death, and he said, "I didn't know that Will was in a serious condition until it was too late. Do you truly believe that the blood goes around and around?"

"It is possible. Perhaps even likely."

"And that it can harm us by rushing too hard, too fast?"

"Yes. I thought that was your father-in-law's complaint."

"So do I. Now that I have heard your lecture." John sighed. "Too bad."

"Then you think that you could have saved him?"

"Oh, no! He was quick to use my medical knowledge when it suited him, he took a keen interest in bodily ills and how they influenced behaviour, but he was a reluctant patient. I had great difficulty in getting him to see you, and he had a feeling of fatality about himself. When I noticed he wasn't well, just before he died, he refused to go to bed, as if that was a condition he couldn't suffer. He said to me, 'We live today—tomorrow—yesterday. That is our history. So why should I fear death when it will come when it will come.' And it did for him. On April 23. Quietly."

"John, I'm sure that you did what you could for him."

"I wanted to. He was a good father-in-law." He was proud that Will had made him his chief executor and had left him and his daughter, Susanna, *All goods, chattels, leases, plate, jewels, household stuff whatsoever.* It was a great compliment, and it eased his guilt. "But when I advised Will to rest, as you did, he replied, 'Rest is for the weary, and the dead.' "

William said impatiently, "Would you excuse me, please?" He had seen something in the cadavers that he wished to examine further.

"Are you going to look at the corpses again? They are rotting!"

"Thanks for attending my lecture. And staying. It is appreciated."

William was even more grateful when John left, for now he could continue before it was too late. The marks about the neck of the youthful corpse were such that he concluded the boy could have died because the circulation of his blood had been stopped. He wondered what Silas had felt. The older man excited him, too, for he saw that his ventricle was ruptured with a rent of such size, it easily took one of his fingers. It indicated that the stress of the blood had been too great for his heart.

He wrote his notes and inscribed the title page in Latin and red ink:

"Lectures on the Whole of Anatomy by me William Harvey, Doctor of London, Professor of Anatomy and Surgery, Anno Domini 1616, aged 37. . . .

"The inner parts of men are uncertain and unknown, wherefore we must consider those parts of other animals which bear any similarity to those of man. Yet this lecture reveals the arteries have a thicker coat, and especially in adults whose heart beat is stronger, because the artery sustains the impulse. W-I Hence a thing which none have mentioned, the pulmonary artery is thicker for it sustains the pulse of the right ventricle in adults and of the . . ."

Woodall was at the door with his assistant, asking if he could dispose of the corpses, and William was glad he was writing his notes in Latin, so they couldn't read them. He hesitated to relinquish the bodies, but Woodall regarded him suspiciously, and he didn't want to antagonize the surgeon; then, perhaps today there was no more to be learned.

"I'm finished," he said. "But Woodall, it would be helpful if you could get me a recently strangled cadaver, within an hour of hanging."

"Why, sir?"

So all the blood might still be in the body and I could measure it more accurately, he thought, but he said, "So it will be less injured."

"I will try, sir, but it will be difficult. The custom is for the College to take cadavers on Tuesday that have been hanged on the previous Friday, and this has never changed. Doctor, why are you so concerned with these dissections when you have such a fine practice?"

Because, he reflected, I can't help myself. But he said, "The more I know about human anatomy, the better I can practise physic."

Woodall looked dubious, but he removed the cadavers, as was his duty.

William put again at the end of his notes his medical signature: "*W-I.*" He liked that feeling, as if it verified his suppositions.

His need to confirm his findings about the amount of blood in animals took him back to the farm now. He liked his new coach better than his old one. It was painted blue, with small yellow front wheels and large rear wheels, and he cherished its colours even though it was uncomfortable.

Silas drove it, proud of his skill, although he was reluctant to return to the farm; he felt like a fox caught in the chase again.

The farm looked unchanged in the months that had passed

since the burning of his old coach, and yet, as they drove up
to the house where Eliab and the new hired man, Albert
Hoag, awaited him, he recalled the hours after he had been
threatened. They were still vivid in his memory.

It was dark when they reached Folkestone, and William,
Eliab, and Silas went to the church where his mother was
buried, for Eliab said the weekly coach to London stopped
there and they could learn its schedule. But he felt Eliab
wanted to hear the gossip.

The evening prayers were ending, so it was too late to
attend services, as Eliab had intended—to prove that his
brother wasn't an heretic—and now Eliab wasn't sure what to
say. He saw the Reverend Ira Wood standing under the
torches that were lit outside the ancient grey Norman towers,
and, taking William by the arm, he approached the clergyman.

William tried to ignore the angry glares of the congrega-
tion, but when Eliab told Wood that he was sorry they were
too late for services, the elderly, gaunt minister snapped,
"Your brother is the oddest man who ever was born in the
village! Isn't he aware he profanes God's ways?"

William's effort to explain was ignored. Wood's attention
focussed on the procession approaching him. Twenty villagers
dragged an old woman behind them and wanted Wood's blessing and to be delivered of evil.

The aged crone was in chains, her grey hair hung in wisps
about her scrawny face, and her toothless mouth gave her
skull a death's-head look.

"What has she done, Eliab?" William asked, while Silas
shuddered.

"She is a witch. Two children saw her cat fly, although she
insists it was a black raven and that it wasn't summoned by
the devil."

"Is there any other proof?"

Eliab shrugged. "She is old, has dark eyes, and keeps a black cat."

"I don't consider that evidence. What does the local doctor say?"

"He found callous spots on her body that are insensitive to pain. According to King James, this identifies her as a witch. Now they have to decide whether to hang her or burn her. You must be more careful. If Father wasn't Mayor, you would have been attacked long ago."

William edged closer to the old woman, who was surrounded by sneering villagers, but all of them stayed a safe distance from her, keeping her at the end of a long chain. He thought, It was possible her skin had become calloused by usage and age, but he had no chance to establish this fact. Wood regarded him as as unwelcome as the witch; he was sure she must be one, for misfortunes had fallen on Folkestone: poor crops, two ships lost at sea, a dozen villagers dead from the plague. He ordered her condemned before she could infect anyone else with Satan.

Wood was glad to give Eliab the schedule of the coach to London; it was the quickest way to be rid of his brother's unholy influence.

William didn't think anyone was possessed by the devil, but he knew it was futile to object, no one would heed him; Silas believed in witchcraft, and so did Eliab. He was grateful the coach left early the next day for London before the old woman was put to death as a witch.

Millions of heartbeats have passed since then, he thought now, and he sought to feel at home on the farm. Silas told him, "The old crone was burnt. The Reverend said, 'To exorcise the devil from the village.'"

Everyone had accepted this. He decided to devote himself to animals.

Because of his long absence from the farm and because he wasn't sure how much longer he could work there without interference, he crowded in as many experiments as he could. He gave the hired man two shillings to fetch the animals he needed, and the red-haired, middle-aged Hoag did so, although he sensed that the hired man disapproved of what he was doing, despite the persuasive money, and could cease helping him at any moment.

After two days of incessant labour, he decided to summarise his newest findings. He used large candles so they would last the night, he had water-cider for his thirst, and he locked the door of the shed.

He recalled how he had cut to the heart of a living dog and felt the pulse with one hand and the heart with the other to determine whether the arteries were compressed when the organ was dilated, or whether—at the same time—they also had the same movement as the heart. He saw how the heart of the dog seemed to bound upwards, and when it no longer moved the dog died instantly. *"Was it that the whole of the body responded to the artery as his breath to a glove?"* As he said that aloud to himself, he wrote it down and signed it, *"W-I."* But the question remained.

"Here! Here!"

He turned at the sound of these words and saw Eliab standing in the doorway. He was startled and annoyed. "How did you enter the shed?"

"Silas gave me his key. He was worried when you didn't come to bed."

"Silas should know better. He is aware I often work until midnight."

"It's morning." Eliab drew the curtains away from the windows so the bright morning sun could enter the shed. "Is your work that important?"

"I don't know. But it might be." He held the heart of a sheep up to the sharp light of the sun and exclaimed, "Look, these valves of the mitral are among the most beautiful tissues in the body!"

Eliab hid his revulsion and asked, "What is the mitral?"

"The valves between the left auricle and the left ventricle of the heart. If I only knew how they worked, it would be easier to understand the movement of the blood. It is a lovely part of the body. In sheep it closes many times a minute, and despite its tender appearance it is extremely strong. Whoever designed it was a master."

"William, you are drunk. The blood intoxicates you."

"What I have shown you are facts. Eliab, why are you here?"

"Father is coming to the farm this morning, and he wants to talk to you."

Thomas liked his sons to be dressed as befitted a gentleman who had just acquired a coat of arms. So William put on his best clothes, his brown velvet doublet, his silk stockings, and his silver dagger. Now that he was no longer absorbed in his work, he was very tired, eager for sleep, and it didn't ease his fatigue when his father informed him later, "William, I've sold the farm." Thomas said that abruptly. He knew that an accomplished fact couldn't be changed.

Yet William, once he was over his shock, exclaimed, "How could you?"

Thomas felt he had endured much from his son. Despite William's work at St. Bart's and the College of Physicians and his fine practice, his experiments had caused consternation in the village. Thomas was sure his good will and patience had led him to be generous to a fault, but he was not passive by nature, and enough was enough. He gripped the hilt of his sword and stated, "Now that my office of Mayor of Folkestone is ending, I'm moving to London. To join your brothers. John has excellent prospects at Court, and the others are in business. I've no need of the farm."

None of William's protests moved his father. Then he decided to try another tack. "I will give you fifty pounds for the livestock."

"That is two years' earnings. That isn't necessary!"

"I insist on paying."

For a moment Thomas appeared ready to change his arrangements, but then, as he saw a delegation of villagers approaching, he said, "I've given my word to sell it. The purchaser is coming with the money now."

William arranged for his equipment to be transferred to his home on Ludgate Hill, hoping he could continue his experiments there, but when he arrived at his London residence, he wondered if that was possible, there was such a savage quarrel erupting between Elizabeth and Rachel.

He entered the kitchen and heard his wife screaming at their cook, "You've made a mess of the floor! You know this house must be kept clean!"

Rachel, who was on her knees seeking to wipe up the spilled water, replied angrily, "I just dropped some coffee. You were in such a hurry, you rushed me and made me nervous. You shouldn't interfere with my work."

"You have worms. That is your trouble. No wonder I'm ill."

"You are ill, Mrs. Harvey, because it suits your purpose."

"What do you mean by that? You're no better than a scullery maid."

"Your husband is one of the best physicians in England, yet you do not allow him to treat you. Because there is nothing actually to treat."

"How do you know about my husband's physic?"

"Goodness, his patients tell me."

"You? An ignorant serving girl?" Elizabeth was contemptuous.

William was stunned by the viciousness with which his wife scolded Rachel. But before he could intervene, Rachel retorted proudly, "I'm not ignorant. I can read and write as well as you can, Mrs. Harvey."

When Elizabeth saw William, she cried out, "I won't suffer her cooking any longer. She could be poisoning me. And she is unclean." Before either William or Rachel could disprove her charges, she clutched her husband's hand and whimpered, "Help me back to bed. I feel faint."

He did, for she couldn't reach it without his aid. Then she sobbed, "I haven't been well since my father died." Yet when he went to examine her, she wouldn't allow it, adding, "It is immodest. What did you do at the farm?"

"I was investigating the movement of the blood in animals."

"You till the wrong garden." She reached for the Bible, which was always at her side. As she had told William repeatedly, this version was authorised by King James, and it comforted her that she had his attention. She said, "Your lust for success blinds you to the laws of God. I hear that the Reverend Wood accused you of violating God's spiritual precepts and that you ignored his warnings. You could come to an untimely end."

He took the Bible from her and quoted: *"There is nothing covered that shall not be revealed, neither hid that shall not be known."*

Elizabeth fell asleep, enervated by her burst of emotion, but he found Rachel in tears. She sobbed when he returned to the kitchen, "I've got as good manners as your wife, even if she was born a lady."

"Of course you have. You have splendid blood flowing in your veins."

"But you said last week that blood is just blood. The same in all."

"In a medical sense. My wife is so nervous, she speaks hastily."

"She knows, William. That is why she shouted at me. She knows."

"Rachel, you are as unreasonable as she is. It doesn't flatter you."

"You are clever, but she isn't stupid. At the least, she suspects us."

"I will employ a cook. That will satisfy Elizabeth."

Rachel was petrified. It was fine for her to leave of her own accord, but to be dismissed by him was cruel. And she was angry that she had aged in his service. Just this morning she had seen new lines around her eyes and mouth; that was why she had spilled the coffee. In this instant she hated him and felt that he had taken away her youth, her one precious possession. She said, "I will go. As soon as I can pack."

"What are you saying? Are you out of your mind?"

"I'm no bitch to be dispensed with because I'm worthless now."

"Rachel, I'm promoting you to the position of housekeeper."

She was relieved and pleased, but she said, "Your wife will misunderstand it."

"Then it will serve her right. If she wants to spend most of her life an invalid, so be it. Come, we mustn't waste any more time."

"William, she won't accept me as a housekeeper."

"She will when I hire a woman to take care of her needs."

He sounded so positive that he had found a solution to her difficulties that she said irritably, "You're always so sure!"

If she only knew! Now that he had disposed of the immediate crisis and his excitement had evaporated, he felt so tired—he hadn't slept for several days—he could hardly think straight. Yet he knew he must go on. So many times he had felt like stopping his explorations, but now he was too close to discovery to quit. He didn't answer her.

He looked so strained that Rachel couldn't stay angry. She followed him upstairs, and as he lay beside her and was unable to make love, she sensed his fatigue and sought to comfort him with a gentle lullaby.

There was no proud swelling of his member, as he craved, but her song soothed him. Just before he fell asleep, he thought of how sweet it would be to be sure, but truth was concealed behind so much blood, flesh, and bone, he doubted that he would ever find it.

* * *

He told his wife he was making Rachel their housekeeper, and she said he was extravagant and foolish, and he added, "It is to please you. You need a lady to attend you properly. I'm employing Mrs. Clara Lang to attend you as a companion and a nurse. This middle-aged widow is a lady who fell into poverty when her husband died unexpectedly."

Clara was modest, pious, and eased Elizabeth's loneliness. Soon the two women were reading the Bible together and comforting each other.

Recovered from his fatigue now, he hired a country girl—whom Rachel recommended—as the new cook. He was glad that Mabel was plain; he felt he must avoid any further jealousy in his wife. Then he employed another country girl, Ruth, to clean the house. He put Rachel in charge.

The next year he believed he had brought sanity into his house. There were still times he feared his wife knew about his affair with Rachel, and that his mistress was unhappy with her situation, but he couldn't see any alternative to what he had done. He couldn't leave Elizabeth, as Rachel asked; his wife needed him. He couldn't dismiss his housekeeper, as his wife wanted; he couldn't imagine living without her. So he kept them apart as much as he could, even as he knew that neither Elizabeth nor Rachel was satisfied. It is the best I can do at the moment, he rationalised; his attention had returned to the heart and the blood.

Little was learnt. His mind was sluggish. There were too many diversions. Most of his family lived in London now, and while he was fond of them, he resented that they expected to see him often. He tried to compensate for his discontent by working hard at St. Bart's; he lectured regularly on anatomy at the College; he gave his practice more attention; he did his experiments in the laboratory in his home. But he missed the resources of the farm. Silas got him dogs, cats, and sheep to dissect, but the sheep were awkward. It was so difficult to bring such a large animal into his house he stopped doing it. What he wanted most of all was a newly hanged cadaver, but Woodall had done nothing about his request. Although he had recommended the surgeon to the staff of St. Bart's, so far no one had been appointed to fill this vacancy.

William was in the anatomy room of the College, exploring the possible ways the blood could move, when he was interrupted by Matthew.

"William, the King has had a relapse, and my presence is ordered." He drew Harvey aside so no one else could hear him. "But I am puzzled by his complaint. I've bled him, I've taken his urine, I've purged him, but even Mayerne, whom he likes, has been unable to ease him. You must examine him. Please, at once! He may have an affliction of the blood, and he remembers your previous cure."

This was a request William couldn't refuse, although he was upset by the distraction, and he accompanied Matthew to Whitehall Palace.

There was a variety of physicians in the royal bedchamber. Six were from James's personal staff, while six had been called in for consultation. Despite his relapse, they were unanimous in their optimistic view of his condition, although they disagreed on how to treat him.

Mayerne whispered to William, "Read what I have observed."

William examined Mayerne's observations: "*Colic, diarrhoea, jaundice, fever, haemorrhoids, nephritis, arthritis, ague, rheum, and melancholy.*"

"Most serious, I believe, is his melancholy. Look!"

William saw a James who was thinner, greyer, and paler than he had ever seen him, and he realized that James's complaint was serious, for Bacon and the privy council were in attendance.

As he approached James, he reviewed Mayerne's diagnosis of the King: "*He demands freedom and relief from pain, little considering the causes of his illness, yet the King laughs at medicine and holds it so cheap that he declares physicians to be of little use and hardly necessary.*"

James was so afraid of the possibility that he was dying he couldn't think of anything else. Every time he lay on his left side, his heart thumped so loudly it terrified him. He couldn't sleep, he was afraid to fall asleep, afraid he would never wake up, yet the less he slept, the worse he felt. The more he worried about the sound of his heart, the more breathless he became. He missed Andrews, who had died. In his melancholy he would even have borne the Scot's leeches, although they bit harder than any others.

And now Harvey was asking, "Your Majesty, may I examine you?"

No, he longed to shout, all you doctors are no better than gravediggers, but he nodded because the thought of dying had made him sick at the stomach, and Harvey, at least, had relieved him of that complaint.

"Sir, what are your symptoms?"

"Headaches, breathlessness, and nausea."

"Sir, may I examine your heart?"

James agreed reluctantly, although he doubted this would ease him.

The King's heart beat faster than normal, and William told himself, If I am right about the motion of the blood, his fear has created such a force in his head that it has caused his brain to ache. And this could give him an upset stomach, and his breathlessness is another symptom.

James mumbled, "I tried the waters of Bath, but they didn't help me any more than they helped Cecil. "But no more bleedings, no more purgings. They do not comfort me."

"Sir, I am concerned with your heart."

"It is stout, Harvey, the stoutest in the realm."

"I know it is, Your Majesty, but it also carries a great burden."

He sighed. "That is true." He was pleased by the doctor's sympathy.

William noted that James lay on his right side despite a

painful boil there. "Sir, wouldn't it be easier to lie on the other side?"

"I hear my heart beat then! It sounds so loud . . ."

James halted, aware of what he was revealing, and now William was sure that fear had given him headaches, and breathlessness. William listened to his heart again, and its rapid beat convinced him that he was right. "Sir, your heart has had to struggle to move your blood instead of easing it through your body, and this has led to your other symptoms." James was doubtful, but William, believing he was on the correct path, continued. "You must worry less, and exercise the same moderation with your mind and emotion that you did with your food and drink years ago."

James asked, "Then will even my nausea go away?"

"Yes, sir, for it is caused by the faster action of your blood."

"Harvey, do you think my life is in danger?"

"Not if you live moderately, sir, and avoid anxiety and aggravation."

"How can I? My reign has been oppressed with ominous portents."

"Favourable ones, too. Your Majesty, you've kept England free of war."

"That's true." Yet he had been born in violence, and his mother, Mary, Queen of the Scots, had died a bloody death, which he could not forget. It is no wonder, he shuddered, that I suffer at the sight of blood. He asked, "Harvey, if I heed you, will I have ten more years?"

William shrugged.

"You are not sure?" The King was offended.

"Sir, you could have many years, but you have large and heavy duties."

"I know. Doctor, what do you recommend?"

"Change the air every day, and new flowers will serve you well. Take a deep sniff of them often, especially in the morning—they will remind you of your native Scotland. Do not allow yourself to grow weary. And rest more. Then, sir, you should be able to walk outside soon without discomfort."

James obeyed him, for nothing else had cured him. As his fear ebbed, so did his breathlessness. This dissipated his panic, and his nausea. Reassured now, his heart was less noisy and emphatic, and he slept more soundly. The day he was able to walk in the palace gardens, two weeks after Harvey's visit, he was glad he had heeded him, although he still distrusted doctors. He wasn't as sure as Mayerne that Harvey was clever, and he had heard gossip about strange practices this physician performed in his laboratory with the heart. But he was no longer ill, and perhaps this physician had healed him because Harvey was a magician. This made James suspicious, but then he thought, He was sensible, I am suspicious of everyone; at least Harvey's magic and craft are in my service.

When Bacon ordered William to attend him, the doctor felt that the King was cured, for the Lord Keeper, recently appointed to the highest law office, was in many ways in charge of the government. Yet he was wary as he arrived at Bacon's great mansion in the Strand. He knew Bacon was supposed to possess the subtlest mind in England, but also the slyest. He wasn't sure what to expect, so he paused to view Bacon's town residence. It was close to Whitehall Palace, as befitted the official home of the Lord Keeper, and was the former residence of the Archbishop of York and Wolsey.

He was escorted into Bacon's presence at once. In the elegant gallery, whose splendour the Lord Keeper expected him to admire, he saw him sitting in a chair almost as grand as the King's throne. Bacon dismissed his liveried servants, saying, "They have to appear before me in Spanish boots. The smell of English leather offends me. No wonder I am ill."

This is hardly the place or circumstance to examine him, William felt, but he asked, "Sir, what is your complaint?" He was surprised that Bacon, supposedly luxuriating in his hour of triumph, looked discontented.

"I have given out that my infirmity is gout. But the truth is, I have so tender a constitution of body and mind that I wonder if I will be able to undergo the burden of so much business as my place requires."

"Sir, I would think that you would be happy with your great place."

"The greater the place, the greater the responsibilities. And the greater the enemies, and the envy. I suffer much."

"My Lord, may I examine your foot?"

"No. I have my own cure for the gout. I use a poultice, then a bath of fomentation, and lastly a plaster. These remedies rarely fail."

William hid his irritation—this was not a cure he used— and asked, "Then, sir, why did you request my presence?"

"I'm obliged to you for having healed His Majesty."

"What about yourself, sir?"

"As you may know, I do not have a high opinion of physicians."

"I know, My Lord," William said wryly, wishing he could depart.

"*They are not accurate. They do not rely enough on remedies. Medicine is a science which has been more professed than laboured, and yet more laboured than advanced.*"

William flushed angrily, but was silent.

"*Too much attention is paid to anatomy and not enough to philosophy.*"

Unable to restrain himself any further, William turned to go.

"Wait."

"Sir, you do not need my practice or my physic."

"Most physicians are superficial, but you have spirit."

"My Lord, what is wrong with you?"

"I've constant pain."

"Where is it worst, sir?"

"In my groin. Lately I have pissed blood."

"My Lord, it sounds like an attack of the stone."

"It is a possibility I have considered. I drink many draughts of strong March beer to ease the passage of my urine."

"It is no cure. Sir, you should be cut for the stone."

"No. Too many die from such an operation."

"Then why did you summon me, My Lord?"

"You are observant, and you could be useful to the King. Come, you must see my beautiful gardens."

While Bacon limped as he led William to the superb gardens that sloped to the Thames, he grew more animated as he expressed his feelings.

"I was born here when my father was Lord Keeper. My return to York House has been the most cherished ambition of my life. My first memory is of the watermen rowing my father to Whitehall to attend the Queen. As a child, I saw her sail by in state, surrounded by many courtiers."

"Sir, I saw the Queen before she died, but it was too late."

"That was so." Bacon stood in his garden, halfway between the river and his magnificent town residence, and while he dearly loved York House, he was determined to make it even more grand, as an example of how a nobleman should live. His meditation was interrupted by the approach of two men. "Harvey, do you know John Donne and Ben Jonson?"

"Donne only by reputation, sir, but I met Jonson at Court, when you presented *The Advancement of Learning* to His Majesty."

"You have a good memory, Doctor. Have you read my work?"

"Some of it, sir."

"You do not approve of my writings?" Harvey had not praised them.

"My Lord, some of your views about medicine are harsh."

"Aren't yours, Harvey?"

Ah, he thought, but I am a doctor. He observed Donne curiously, for he had heard that this poet had written passionate poems, yet had entered the Church recently. Donne was dark, with a long, sharp nose and chin and a pointed black beard cut as decisively as his lean, angular features.

Jonson had gained weight, and there was grey in his hair, and his usually boisterous manner was humble in the presence of the Lord Keeper.

Donne said, "Doctor, I've some interest in physic. My stepfather was a physician, and I am interested in attending your lectures. I'm curious about your views of the blood. My own conclusions have caused many speculations in my mind. As I have written. What do you think of this?

*"Know'st thou how blood, which to the heart doth flow,
Doth from one ventricle to th' other goe?"*

William exclaimed, "But, sir, that is only a beginning!"

"I know." Donne's expression grew sombre, and he added bitterly, "My wife died a few months ago in childbirth, although several doctors attended her. None of these physicians or their physic was worth much."

"Sir, how many times was she brought to bed with child?"

"Twelve. But she was only thirty-three."

"And worn out with childbearing, although scarcely beyond her youth."

Bacon disliked this conversation; he had a fastidious distaste for talk of illness, except his own. He preferred what he was thinking. Even in good fortune, he was plagued with ill spirits, with the ghosts of the past, Essex, Cecil, the Queen, as if the persons to whom he most desired to demonstrate his advancement were gone. I must make a greater show of my grounds, he decided, and as he thought of this he found a new justification of this idea, and, liking the way he phrased it, he repeated it to remember it: *"God Almighty first planted a garden, for without one a building and palace are but gross handiworks."* He had invited Donne and Jonson, as literary men, to ask their opinion of a work he was contemplating, but their talk of medicine bored him, and now Harvey was asking Jonson about Shakespeare, which he found fatiguing.

"Jonson, I understand that you visited the poet just before he died. Did he complain of any affliction?"

"No. We drank some, we talked a bit, and for a night he discarded his air of respectability. But he lived so much in his imagination, it was hard to know what he was thinking. I was surprised to hear he had died."

"I was told that it was sudden—"

"Doctor, what is the difference!" Bacon interrupted irritably. "We dig our own graves, one way or another."

Donne was not interested in discussing Will Shakespeare, but he resented Bacon's tone. He excused himself, pleading business at St. Paul's, and when he heard that the doctor lived nearby, he offered him a ride in his coach, although he warned, "It may be uncomfortable, Doctor. The road from here to the cathedral has a very bad character. It is full of pits and sloughs, and hasn't been repaired since the time of Henry VIII."

William accepted, thinking, The suddenness of the poet's death suggested that it could have been his heart after all.

o be a dot
Entire
Is as much
As being any planet
From afar

Sir Theodore Turquet de Mayerne requests the pleasure and the privilege of your presence at the Cock and Bull Ordinary to honour our distinguished colleague and physician, Doctor Matthew Ross.

This invitation delighted William, and he put on his best garb for the occasion and arrived at the inn at midday; he liked to be prompt. It was a rendezvous for medical men, conveniently located between the College and the Court. The Cock and Bull was on the north side of the Thames, near the great mansions of the nobility, with a landing place on the bank of the river so that the guests who lived in Whitehall could come by way of the Thames, which was more comfortable than travelling along the muddy, unpaved Strand, although William had gone that way on horse with Silas escorting him. He strode upstairs to the first floor, where Mayerne, as the host, was greeting the guests, all of whom were physicians.

"No women have been invited," Mayerne said. "So we can talk freely and eat and drink as much as we please."

Matthew asked, "Is Elizabeth still ill?"

"Yes."

"That is a very pretty cook you have."

"She is my housekeeper now. Mayerne, this chamber is spacious, with its high ceiling, long gallery."

"I'm glad you like it. I've done my best to make the day festive."

After the seating with Mayerne at the head of the long table as befitted the King's Physician in Ordinary, and Matthew at his side as the guest of honour, waiters brought in roast beef, then wild fowl, many vegetables, cakes, fruit, and wine. Mayerne addressed the physicians.

"It gives me great pleasure to announce that His Majesty has graciously admitted Doctor Ross into the place of Physician in Ordinary."

The announcement, although anticipated, was received with applause.

"This honour has been given him because he has cured the King."

But I did, thought William—or is it that my ideas about the blood upset James and ended my prospects? His head spun,

and he realised that he had drunk too much wine. As soon as
Mayerne ended his speech, William walked over to a window
and opened it. The cool air cleared his head, but he was still
puzzled by Matthew's elevation to the highest medical post at
Court. Mayerne, Matthew, and Wilkins were involved in an
animated discussion, and he joined them to find out why that
actually had happened.

Wilkins said, "Matthew, you are right. I never talk physic
with my spouse. It is enough that she is healthy and bears
sound children."

Matthew replied, "My wife knows her place. It is Mayerne
who is indulgent to females. Both of the wenches who attend
him are voluptuous. William, how do you think they please
him? You have a household of women."

"They are used to serve my wife."

"Do you need four women for that purpose?"

Mayerne said, "Women are good for the blood. William,
don't you agree?"

"That depends." He wondered how much they assumed
about Rachel.

Wilkins said, "Mayerne, you can be proud. But Harvey's
women are plain except for his housekeeper, and she is too
thin for my taste."

Mayerne, angry that Wilkins was taunting Harvey, said,
"Wilkins, I heard that just as you were going to examine a
cadaver, he rose from the table and walked away, while you
fainted from shock and fear."

Wilkins grumbled, "That was exaggerated. The rogue
wasn't hanged efficiently, but the next time I supervised it I
made sure he was dead."

Matthew said, "That isn't as upsetting as the doctor who
felt for the stone, and when his finger came out of the rectum
he found that his patient had syphilis. The doctor had his
finger cut off immediately."

William wished he could return to his experiments. He saw
York House, at the bend of the river, and then Woodall

entered and hurried over to Matthew. The elderly, dour surgeon was smiling and excited, which was unusual. Perhaps
Woodall has found a cadaver for my dissection, he thought,
and so, while he felt like an intruder, William joined them.

"Forgive me, sir." Woodall addressed a triumphant Matthew. "I would not have invaded your banquet, except that I
have been appointed to the staff of St. Bart's, and since our
two appointments are in conjunction, I feel safe in assuming
that you are responsible. Thank you, gracious sir."

Matthew beamed while William asked, "What about the
corpse I need?"

"I haven't found one." Woodall's indifference was plain.
"Doctor Ross, may I congratulate you. You are an honour to
the medical profession."

Mayerne said, "It was Harvey who recommended you, not
Ross."

Woodall was stunned, and he regarded Mayerne with disbelief.

"It is true. Ask the governors of the hospital."

"Sir, does he have sufficient influence to be heeded in such
a matter?"

"He does now. He is appointed Physician Extraordinary to
the King."

William exclaimed, "Are you certain? It is not a jest?"

"It is the reason I invited you to this celebration. His Majesty has given you that position officially, and has ordered me
to inform you."

"I find it hard to believe. You know that he is suspicious of
me."

"He is suspicious of everyone. But the King is not a fool,
although he sometimes seeks to give that impression to throw
people off their guard. James knows who cured him. If Matthew was rewarded for it too, it was because he was wise
enough to call you in for consultation."

Matthew grumbled, "I would have cured him myself, given
more time. He wants us to serve him together—with me in

command. He was reluctant to appoint you because of your views on the blood, until I assured him that I would control your physic. And Mayerne spoke in your favour, too."

William asked, "Mayerne, why didn't you tell me sooner?"

"I wanted to be certain. At first James was hesitant. You will receive fifty pounds per annum, and your first duties will be to the King."

Even as William was deeply gratified by this appointment, he was oppressed suddenly with a new fear. He asked Mayerne, "Will this tie me to daily attendance on the King?" This could be too high a price to pay.

"No. Only Physicians in Ordinary are tied to daily service."

"Besides," said Matthew, "when there is a crisis the King always consults Mayerne first. But while he is still dubious about your character, William, he thinks you have a gift for physic. He was pleased with the quickness of his recovery from his latest complaint."

Mayerne turned to the surgeon and stated, "So you see, it would be advisable to heed Doctor Harvey's requests."

"Of course, sir." Woodall was obsequious now, although William still didn't trust him. "Doctor Harvey, I will search again for the proper cadaver. I will keep an eye on Newgate and Tyburn, where I am most apt to find one. Sir, what age, size, and shape body do you prefer?"

"A man in his twenties and thirties. In his prime. Before too much exertion has hardened the walls of his heart and made them smaller."

Woodall nodded, mumbled a reluctant "Thank you, Doctor Harvey, for the appointment to St. Bart's," and bowed his way out of the chamber.

Mayerne proposed a toast, "To our most efficient pulse taker," and as he filled William's glass, then refilled it, William felt strange. He was grateful he had a strong head for drink, but now the combination of circumstances came upon him in such a rush he felt intoxicated. Physician Extraordinary was a situation he had desired ever since he had begun the study of medicine. Only Physician in Ordinary was a greater honour, and as Hall and Wilkins congratulated him, although Wilkins did it hesitantly, it was as if they spoke about somebody else. I have drunk too much wine, he thought. His body was heavy, his head spun. Mayerne, who saw his state, summoned Silas, who had eaten heartily of boiled beef and beer on the floor below, and ordered him to take his master home.

The fresh air cleared William's head, and the canter of his horse jolted him so much it kept him awake. Yet, when he dismounted, he was so drained of energy, he could hardly climb his steps. Inside, he sat down quickly on a sofa in his reception room, feeling on the verge of collapse.

Silas asked, "Sir, who should I call? You need a woman's attention."

His desire was for Rachel, but his duty was to Elizabeth. Yet if he called his wife, his mistress would be hurt; if he asked for his housekeeper, his spouse would be offended.

"Silas, you won't have to call anybody."

"Sir, I can't put you to bed myself. Should I call Mrs. Harvey, or would you prefer that I summon my sister?"

But Rachel's presence is dangerous, he reflected. He said, "Call my wife. She will be proud that I am a Physician Extraordinary. As her father was."

The wait seemed interminable. He longed for the sound of Rachel's voice. He doubted that his wife would come, yet he was sure that his housekeeper would have appeared immediately. It was many minutes later when he heard footsteps approaching, and even as he wished that it were Rachel, he knew it was Elizabeth, for they were loud and emphatic.

She stood in the doorway and said, "Your servant informed me that you wish to speak to me. Ordinarily I wouldn't have come, I was in the midst of my devotions, but he said it was urgent. What is wrong?"

"Elizabeth, I have been appointed Physician Extraordinary to the King. I wanted you to be the first to know. I hope you are pleased."

She smiled, then remembered her grievances and declared, "You should have had this appointment years ago."

He put out his hand to embrace her, and she recoiled from him.

"You have allowed my father's memory to rot until now."

He was sick of her allegiance to her father but he didn't reply.

"He gave his life to see you in this post. But you didn't heed him."

"Let's not quarrel. I want this to be a happy time. Medicine is such a part of your family. It is in your blood."

"It is good news. Now you can help my brother."

"When he applied to practise in London, he was turned down by the College. He failed their examination. I cannot change that."

"You should have more influence now. At the least, you can have him come down from Cambridge and be accepted at Court."

"I will try."

"It will help if you give up your vain pursuit of the blood."

He gazed at her, expressionless, although he felt weary and dizzy.

"You will speak up for Galen?" she asked, urgently and anxiously. When he nodded, she added, "What else do you want? I haven't finished my devotions."

"I need help to get up the stairs. If you could help me, I would appreciate it."

She said contemptuously, "You are drunk. That is why you want my attentions."

"If you don't aid me, I will have to ask someone else."

"Use your servant. He waits on you like a dog."

"Elizabeth, I need a woman's attention."

"Where is your housekeeper?"

"You don't mind?" He was wide awake abruptly, fearing a pitfall.

"How can I? You are the master of this household. I know that she tries to please you. Like her brother."

"Elizabeth, you have your personal servant, as Silas is mine."

"After a fashion. If you get Galen admitted into the College, I will make the best of my afflictions."

He wondered what would happen if he sought to kiss her, but her stern visage dissuaded him. He said, "Don't worry, I will manage the stairs myself. As I always have."

"Now I can finish my prayers and thank God that your appointment as Physician Extraordinary has recompensed my father's efforts."

After Elizabeth was gone, it cost William a desperate effort of his will to reach the landing on the first floor, but he managed by holding on to the railing as he climbed the winding stairs. At this instant he wished his house were smaller, but now at least he could afford it. He started for his quarters on the next floor, stumbled, and fell with a loud crash.

Silas and Rachel were at his side quickly.

They lifted him up as soon as they ascertained that he wasn't hurt. Then Silas and Rachel placed his arms over their shoulders and helped him climb the stairs. He noticed that the three of them were virtually the same height. He felt lightheaded, blithe-hearted as his arms embraced their warm flesh. Rachel's touch gave him a youthful, vigourous strength. No longer worried about his intoxication and fatigue, he felt these things were only momentary. Yet when they put him on his bed, he lay there like a scarecrow, his arms spread out, and tears came again to his eyes. Whatever he professed, he had desired passionately to be Physician Extraordinary, and now it was as if he had no one to celebrate it with. They had retired to the hallway, and he felt dreadfully alone.

He heard Silas say, "The Master needs a woman's attention," and Rachel reply, "That is his wife's duty," and then their voices dropped to a whisper, as if they didn't want anyone else to hear what they discussed.

He wondered if Silas knew of his intimacy with Rachel, and, afraid that this was what they were discussing, he cried

out, to halt such a possibility, "Is no one going to attend me?
Am I without service in my own house?"

Both of them were at his side instantly, and Silas said, "Sir,
I must take care of the horses." Before they could halt him,
he was gone.

William asked, "Rachel, does your brother know about
us?"

She wasn't certain, but since it was a possibility that upset
her, she changed the subject and said, "You can't even stand
straight. What has affected you so severely?"

"I am Physician Extraordinary. I celebrated, and this is
the result."

"You didn't tell me first. Now I know that you don't love
me."

"I wanted to. But it was impossible under the circumstances."

"So you told her first." She pulled away from his out-
stretched hands.

"I had to. Otherwise she would have been suspicious of
us."

"She is anyhow. She is very rude and disagreeable to me."

"I know what you mean." He sighed. He tried to sit up in
bed and undress himself, but the effort was too much for him,
and he fell back on the bed. Rachel couldn't endure the anguish on his face.

She whispered, "You must work less. You drive yourself
too hard."

"Rachel, dear, the heart is like England, an island created
in a great sea by God Almighty, not as a punishment but as a
grace."

"I understand."

"You are what I must hold on to. You, more than anyone
else."

She started to undress him now, carefully and tenderly, and
at her gentle touch he felt better. She was mumbling, "You

are right, you must keep the peace. God, give us our daily bread and forgive my trespass."

He kissed her soft hand as it fondled his black hair, and she whispered lovingly and proudly, "Physician Extraordinary. You should be happy. It is a great honour. One that you deserve."

He wasn't sure what he deserved, but he was grateful that she cared.

 would not be Fate
I would not be God
I would not be
whatever has to strike
life down

I would be a beautiful
colour
that would allow a
clover
to live forever

William resumed his exploration of the course of the blood and the action of the heart. He dissected a large variety of animals that were small enough to bring into his laboratory at home without difficulty. These experiments confirmed his conclusions that in all these creatures the blood circulated and the heart functioned as a pump. But he was still uncertain about man. None of the corpses that Woodall brought him was satisfactory, and he felt he could still have a long journey ahead of him.

His position as Physician Extraordinary was verified by an official notification from the Lord Steward. He visited James in that capacity, as a consultant to Matthew, but he didn't believe that his views were essential. There were a dozen other physicians in the royal retinue, and the King's ailments were minor. James accepted Mayerne's diagnosis that his chief complaint was arthritis, regarded Harvey's presence with indifference, and was preoccupied with Sir Walter Raleigh.

William felt it didn't matter what this prisoner said or did, that Raleigh was doomed by the King's implacable hatred, and that his death waited only until James found the proper excuse. Yet it was evident that Raleigh was not a common felon to be executed for a triviality.

He discussed Raleigh's situation with Mayerne, who said, "Ever since James met Raleigh, when this courtier greeted him as the new ruler after Elizabeth's death, he has hated Raleigh. I have often wondered why."

Perhaps, thought William, the King had been envious, for that time Raleigh had possessed a tall, commanding presence, while James's thin, poorly shaped figure had been insignificant by comparison.

Mayerne added, "And now the King has found an excuse to put him to death. It is because of what happened in Guiana. Did you know that?"

"Yes. The reports are everywhere." After Raleigh had been in the Tower for thirteen years, James had freed him—but not pardoned him—to search for gold in Guiana. But when he had returned without any treasure, and with four Spaniards dead—Raleigh had given his solemn promise that no Spaniards would be harmed—James had decided this was sufficient reason to condemn him to death. William asked sadly, "So Raleigh is to die?"

"It is inevitable. He is a victim of the King's Spanish policy. Since Raleigh is the best-known foe of the Spanish, James is using the Guiana tragedy as the excuse. He wants the Prince of Wales to wed a Spanish princess, and he feels that Raleigh's death will convince King Philip that such an alliance is advisable and England is his friend."

"I saw the Armada. We cannot trust the Spaniards. Bacon is Lord Chancellor. Doesn't he realize it is a mistake to condemn Raleigh?"

"Bacon never opposes the King. Although he is supposed to be a judge, he will act as James's spokesman. It is the custom and his nature."

"I see no reason to justify such a verdict. Doesn't Bacon realise the execution of Raleigh will deprive England of one of its best minds?"

"Possibly that is why our Lord Chancellor doesn't oppose his death. But the King is making one concession. Raleigh is to be beheaded instead of being hanged and drawn and quartered according to the original sentence of 1603. While the trial isn't finished, everything has been decided."

"Raleigh in many ways is the King's most distinguished subject."

"That may be the trouble. James wants no other star in his firmament. He has advised me that he desires his doctors to attend this execution."

"Why? He will not need any confirmation that his prisoner is dead."

"The King will view our attendance as an expression of loyalty."

"Is he going to attend?"

"No. Personally, the sight of blood makes James faint."

One week later he went to the Old Palace Yard at Westminster, where the execution was to occur. The early-morning chill was penetrating, and he shivered as he pushed his way close to the scaffold so that he could observe accurately. He assured himself that he had come not to approve of James's judgement, but to express his respect for Raleigh. Now that he was here, he wondered whether there would be an unusual effusion of blood at the stroke of the ax, even as that thought made him shudder.

A great crowd had assembled, including many of the most

powerful men in the realm, and William saw Mayerne, Matthew, and most of the royal doctors, as if they couldn't afford to be outdone in their devotion to the King. The hubbub that prevailed on such occasions became a vast hush as Raleigh limped in with his escort, as if everyone had to hear his final words. This execution was different from any other William had seen. Raleigh, who had strode through life as if he were on a stage and he one of the leading players on it, was making his death a fitting occasion for his farewell.

As Raleigh climbed the scaffold, he was the most cheerful person present. The condemned man stood before the ax with such composure that William felt that everybody was as moved as he was. Raleigh had risked death so often he was no longer afraid of it. The prisoner, who had aged since William had seen him last, looked like a weather-beaten Devon oak, yet he faced the ax peacefully. Then he spoke.

His words reminded William of the poem Raleigh had given him, which he had come to treasure—and he listened intently, desiring to fix them in his memory as his remembrance of this man. But as Raleigh used this moment to vindicate his behaviour, what he said became a blur to William.

The prisoner, in spite of his condition, was seeking to control his situation. Yet as he ended his speech and reached the final heartbeats of his life, his voice conveyed a new dignity, and now William sought to remember each word.

"What is death but an opinion and an imagination. Though to others it might seem grievous, yet I would rather die so than of a burning fever."

The waiting crowd, which had begun to stir uneasily during his speech of justification, fell utterly silent again.

"Now I have a long journey and must bid the company farewell."

Then, after the sheriff had removed everyone except the executioner and Dr. Robert Tounson, the Dean of Westminster, who was present to administer God's mercy and charity, he started to blindfold the prisoner.

Raleigh said this wasn't necessary and asked to view the ax, "*I prithee, let me see it. Do you think I am afraid of it?*"

The ax was handed to him, and he ran his thumb along the edge and said, smiling, "*This is a sharp medicine, but it is a sure cure for all diseases.*"

The Dean of Westminster prayed solemnly for the prisoner's soul, but William wanted to hear Raleigh's words. Although the air was chilly still, and Raleigh suffered from the ague, there was no shivering in him now. Instead, he turned resolutely towards the block as he was told to lay his head on it. William heard the executioner ask, "*Sir, would you prefer to face east toward the land where the Lord had risen?*"

"*What matters how the head lie, so the heart be right.*"

Yet, to please his friends, he faced east. The executioner begged his forgiveness, which Raleigh gave kindly, and when it was suggested again that he should be blindfolded, he refused contemptuously, declaring, "*Think you I fear the shadow of the ax, when I fear not the ax itself.*"

There was a moment as still as death while Raleigh prayed silently. Then, as he stretched out his hands to signal the executioner to act and the headsman wavered, stricken by the gallantry of his victim, he cried out, "*What do you fear? Strike, man, strike!*"

The blood gushed out of the severed body, and William was astonished by its extraordinary flow. For an instant he wished he could measure the quantity and verify his suppositions. But he couldn't be the impersonal physician. He heard weeping, and he consoled himself that Raleigh had not wept, that by heartbeats his life had not been brief. As the executioner held up the bloody head to signify that the King's justice had been done, there was not the usual applause, but a shudder went through the crowd.

Someone shouted, "*We have not another such head to be cut off!*"

He reached the side of his friends, and Matthew said, "William, did you ever see so much blood! I have never witnessed

such an effusion. It flowed from Raleigh like a torrent. That
should satisfy even you."

Raleigh's body was wrapped in velvet and put in a coffin,
and blood continued to drip from it. The moment was a few
minutes after eight in the morning, on the twenty-ninth of
October in the year 1618, and the sheriff repeated that the
King's justice had been done.

William left the other doctors and walked reflectively to the
Thames. The river moved slowly and seemed to mourn for
Raleigh, as he did. Yet the physician part of him kept remembering how, at the stroke of the ax, Raleigh's blood had
flowed copiously and in a great rush. There was so much
death about him that he had to think affirmatively to keep
himself going. He wondered: How much blood is needed each
day to live?

He was still pondering this question when Woodall asked to
see him. A month had passed, and he sat in his office at St.
Bart's and tried to be peaceful, as Raleigh had seemed to be at
his death, but it was impossible. Yet he was glad that Woodall
wanted to talk to him. There was much he had to discuss with
his chief surgeon. William was unhappy with what he had
found this morning in the wards. There were many poor
people in them who were afflicted with diseased arms and legs,
and he feared that they couldn't recover without the loss of
these limbs, yet he doubted that many would survive an amputation. Several had died recently from these operations. He
told the matron to admit Woodall.

Before the surgeon could state his business, William said,
"Many are dying from sheer loss of blood during amputations."

"Not from mine, sir. Since I've come to St. Bart's, I have
taken off, and helped to take off, more than one hundred legs
and arms, besides many fingers and hands, among all of
which not one of them has died."

"Has any other surgeon performed amputations?"

"Fenton and Collston, sir."

"No one must operate without my approval."

"Sir, you are often elsewhere. And some of the cases need immediate attention. If patients have been lost, none of them have been mine."

"I will supervise when I am here. When I am not, if the situation is immediate, you must be strict. Cut only when it is essential."

Woodall was surprised. "Sir, I thought you favoured surgery!"

"Not indiscriminately. What did you wish to discuss with me?"

The surgeon glanced about to be sure he couldn't be overheard, then whispered, "Doctor, I think I have a suitable body for your purpose."

"Has it been hanged recently?"

"Not yet. The subject is confined in Newgate and is to be executed in a week. If you could examine him, you could decide if he is suitable for your needs. If you meet me at the entrance to the prison, one of the gaolors, whom I know, will allow us to view him. It is a great favour."

"Examine him while he is still alive?" William was shocked.

"He is in a cell. He will not know your intention. He will think you are from the Crown, deciding the time of his execution. It is the custom."

Even as William was repelled by this idea, he was interested.

"He is thirty, in his prime, very healthy, of moderate height, weight, with no imperfections and no risk of error. He is condemned to die."

"Why is he to be hanged?"

"I don't know." Woodall shrugged. "Sir, there could be a hundred reasons. He could have taken a sixpence from a washerwoman, refused to serve on a frigate, been a highwayman, anything that opposed authority."

"What is his name?"

"I didn't ask. It doesn't matter. Sir, if you want to be certain that he fits your needs, you must examine him."

The surgeon was persuasive, and while William was reluctant still to examine a man he intended to dissect, he agreed to meet Woodall that night at the entrance to Newgate. To ease his own feelings, he sought to ease the afflicted in the wards so they wouldn't require an amputation.

Newgate was just around the corner from the hospital, and night came early during November. By the time William reached the entrance, he saw many stars. There were some old women in rags at the old iron gate, and most of them were sobbing. It was known as the Holborn side, the west, and he stared at the stone statues: Liberty, with Whittington's cat at her feet, and Peace, Plenty, and Concord. He waited, and the longer he waited, the more reluctant he was to enter. He was about to depart when he heard Woodall call him. The surgeon stood before the city side, the east, and its stone statues: Justice, Mercy, and Truth.

Woodall said, "Sir, this is the main entrance. And I have a key."

Now he couldn't enter. He asked, "Why are the women crying?"

"They are waiting to find out when their men are to be hanged."

"Is that so critical?"

"It is if the women wish to claim the bodies. Otherwise, the corpses will be taken by the mob, or thrown into the garbage fields of Tyburn."

"Perhaps they are waiting for the man you want me to examine."

"No, sir. I made sure of that. He has no kin. But this situation is costly. A number of people will have to be paid."

"How much will it cost?"

"Two pounds, sir." As William wavered, he asked, "Is that too much?"

Nothing was too much if he found out what he wanted, but he said, "It isn't the cost that concerns me. It's other things."

"Is it that we are going contrary to the authorities, sir?"

"Oh, no, we mustn't allow our respect for them to be over-done!"

"I won't as long as you take the responsibility. You are my superior. Sir, as Physician Extraordinary, you do possess special privileges."

Woodall went to open the prison gate, and William cried out, "I can't look at him! It will affect my knife! I would remember his eyes!"

Woodall was stunned. He told himself, The condemned man was damned, and that was God's will; ten men were to be hanged this week, and he couldn't afford to care—that was weak. He hid his disgust with the vacillating doctor, for Harvey could harm him, and said, "Sir, if you don't view the body, you could be dissatisfied with the subject."

William thought passionately, But if I meet him, I cannot dissect him. My cadavers must be without identity. Otherwise, dear Lord, it is impossible, and there is no wonder in Your creation. In the next moment the physician part of him cried out, God has given me a gift I cannot ignore. I cannot halt now, I have come too close to allow anything to halt me. This search is the best part of me, I must pursue it to the end whatever the consequences and be grateful that I can. He said, "I cannot examine him. I must take the chance that this man you have chosen is right. If he isn't, I will not blame you."

"When I was a lad, sir, I saw burnings at Smithfields. Hanging is an easy way to die. Almost as swift as the ax. What should I do?"

"Obtain the body you have recommended. When will it be hanged?"

"Within a week. I will act as a friend to the condemned man and, with the proper warrant and authority from the College, claim the cadaver for it. I will make sure that you have the body within an hour of the hanging."

Relieved, William nodded. Then he remembered a possible disaster. He said hurriedly, "You must alter the circumstances. Instead of having him hanged, have his neck broken. A quick, sudden drop will do that."

"Sir, it is the custom to strangle."

"Strangling will disturb the respiration and lessen the amount of the blood in the body. Dry up the arteries. There must be as much blood as possible in the body. A broken neck will be quicker, less painful."

"Sir, that will require a special gallows, with a sudden drop. And the authorities frown upon this method. It will be very costly."

"I will pay." Whatever happens, he thought, the passages of the blood must not be bare. "Bring me the body as soon as it is dead. Unless it is mangled." He must take positive action before it was too late.

He put everything else out of his mind while he waited to measure the quantity of blood in a newly deceased body. Woodall obeyed his orders, and the following week, when the surgeon brought the corpse to him, soon after the neck was broken, he was excited yet nervous. The surgeon had worked speedily, since William had given him an extra pound for his services and said he would speak to the King in his behalf. Woodall sought to be as helpful as possible and asked, "Sir, is the cadaver satisfactory?"

"I will find out in a moment."

"It is the rogue I asked you to view. Sir, do you have enough blood?"

"I think so." His excitement grew, for, as he had surmised, there was blood in the arteries. If the cadaver had been strangled, he thought, it would have suffocated, and thus there would be none. Now he understood why air was usually found in the arteries after death, and not blood.

Now the blood possessed a natural flow as he washed it out of the veins to measure the quantity in the entire body.

As Woodall drained what had become a precious fluid,

William weighed the blood in the auricles, where it lingered longest after death. It is a wonderful sight, he thought, and his pulse raced with exhilaration.

Woodall asked, "Sir, is the heart sound?"

"Yes. It is splendid. It hasn't any fat. It is large, strongly developed. Woodall, how does the draining go?"

"Fine, sir. I'm almost done."

"You should complete it quickly. The butcher drained off all the blood in a massive bullock in a quarter of an hour."

"Doctor, I'm finished."

Then they measured. They found that the amount of blood in this cadaver was in the same ratio to body weight as it was in the sheep and bullock. He thought, So even if the cadaver has lost blood between death and draining—which is unlikely, since I have moved swiftly—my conclusions are correct. It was right to break the neck. But there are other facts to be learnt.

Woodall said, "Sir, a preacher assured this rogue that a merciful God would forgive him, and he died with a peaceful smile. Did you notice?"

"No!" William couldn't notice anything that would divert him. "How much blood did you find in the auricles, where it lingers longest?"

"Two ounces, sir."

"So did I."

"Then why did you ask me, sir?"

"I must verify my own findings. I cannot hazard any guesses."

"Sir, should I put your instruments away?"

"Yes. While I make my calculations, will you dispose of the cadaver? Bury it reverently. It has served me well."

After this was done, when the surgeon returned he found the doctor strangely still. "Sir, did you find what you were looking for?"

"A far greater quantity of blood is ejected by the heart in the course of one day than can be found in the entire body."

"I don't understand, sir."

"Our measurement of the auricles proves that each time the heart beats it ejects two ounces of blood into the arteries. We also know that the heart of a man at rest beats seventy-two times a minute. Thus, the following calculations are true. At such a pulse rate the heart ejects a vast amount of blood. Seventy-two times two comes to one hundred forty-four ounces of blood a minute, five hundred forty pounds an hour, more than six tons in twenty-four hours. Yet it is impossible that the body produces that much blood each day."

"Sir, the heart must be powerful."

"More powerful than believed, but not that powerful. Don't you see, far more blood is driven out of the heart in one day than could be produced by the body. Six tons is an impossible quantity. Such a quantity cannot be supplied by any amount of food and drink consumed within the time specified. The conclusion is inevitable, Woodall, that blood ejected from the heart can do nothing but return to the heart."

"No one will agree with you, sir. It is contrary to our teachings."

"I have proof. We must not cling forever to our old ways."

"If I were you, I would be practical, and keep your views to yourself. Sir, it is not worth your career."

William didn't reply but sat in deep thought.

"Besides, sir, suppose it does move about the body—not that I believe the blood does—how does that happen?"

"I have some suppositions about that, but I'm not sure."

Woodall smiled triumphantly and exclaimed, "Sir, unless you are, nobody will believe you. And all your other activities will be discredited."

Woodall must be sure he would not find out how the blood circulated to be so candid. Then William sought to drive his own doubts out of his mind. Yet he knew that unless he could prove *how* the blood circulated, no one would believe that *it did* circulate. When the surgeon was gone, he wrote down what he had learned. But for the moment, he decided, I mustn't show my findings to anyone.

He thought, The world cannot accept the movement of the

blood as it is; they can accept it only if it is as they desire it to be. Yet he felt that part of his struggle was over. The body was a noble creation, and he saw a new order in it. Although he had reached forty, he no longer felt old. The circulation of the blood could be so simple, it was incredible that no one had thought of it. But no one had.

His mind returned to Raleigh—this man would have heeded him—then he sought to continue his calculations. He realized that if he suffered his patients' pain, he would not have enough strength to survive.

Yet, he felt that Raleigh was by his side as he wrote down: *"It is a simple matter of necessity that the blood should perform a circuit and return to the place from whence it came forth. W-I."*

As he sat in the dark, too absorbed in his calculations to think of lighting the candles—and besides, he reasoned, I often think best in the dark—he exclaimed to convince himself: *"The heart must be a pump! The blood must circulate! But how?"*

 elf pity
is the warden
that puts the lock
on action

Exercitatio anatomica de motu cordis et sanguinis in animalibus.

He read this title to Rachel, who stood next to him in his laboratory, then remembered that she didn't know Latin. He translated for her: *"An Anatomical Treatise on the Move-*

ment of the Heart and Blood in Animals." He had laboured two years on this study, and he desired her approval.

She replied, "Will this title satisfy other physicians?"

"I hope so. However sceptical they are about my conclusions."

"Are you far advanced in this work?" William had been so distracted he had spent very little time with her lately, and that worried her.

"Not far enough." He sighed. "I still have much to learn."

"When will you publish your findings?"

"When they satisfy me." And when, he thought, it is less risky.

Rachel wondered if it was his nature to delay. She felt that in the years she had served him she had given him her youth, her most precious possession, and yet she felt like a person only part of the time, and that was not enough. But he hated to be distracted while he was working, it made him bad-tempered, and so she said, "I wish I knew Latin."

"What do you need it for?" He laughed. "Very few women know it."

"Your wife does. And I could help you more with your work."

"Latin is overdone in physic, and my proficiency in it is overpraised."

"William, what have you learned?" She had come upstairs to tell him that his dinner was ready, and she was afraid that he was overworking.

Pleased at her interest, and relieved that she had changed the subject, he stated, "*The blood is continuously and uninterruptedly transmitted by the heart into the arteries in such an amount it cannot be supplied from the ingest, and in such a way the whole mass must pass through the organ.*

"Rachel, do you understand?" If she does, he thought, many will.

"I think so." She wasn't sure, but if she tried she would be included.

"But I haven't been able to determine where the blood moves from the arteries to the veins. It is beautifully logical how the blood goes in many branches to the very tip of the body, but the way back is puzzling."

"You told me that it probably returns through the veins."

"That seems logical too, but I cannot discern how. Not even by sight or by touch. Until I can prove my suppositions that the blood moves from the arteries into the veins, I cannot be certain that I am right."

As he paused to reflect, Rachel decided that she couldn't ask for a better moment to express what troubled her most. She said, "William, we can't go on this way for the rest of our lives."

"What do you mean? Has Elizabeth been difficult lately?"

"No more than usual."

"That is a normal complaint."

"William, my complaint goes far deeper."

He walked over to the window and looked out on the garden below, which Silas tended with devotion. She had, as they both knew, made her own bed, and sometimes she had to lie in it alone. He loved her, but she must recognise the attraction of his medical explorations. He said, "You must be patient until I am not so fully engaged."

Easy for him to counsel patience, she thought sadly, he is living the way he desires. But it isn't easy for me, and she said, "You see me as a pale, fair, red-headed girl, but I haven't been that for years. Do you realise I've been in your household a long time? And now it is 1621."

"It has been a happy time for me."

"Yet I am still your servant belowstairs, whatever I am above."

He asked sharply, "Rachel, what do you really want?"

"I want to eat with you, walk with you, and go to church with you."

"You know that is impossible." He felt she was provoking him, and his irritation grew. He hadn't known any other woman since she had entered his house, and he had given her a large part of himself. But now, he thought, she pities herself until she is wretched instead of sensible. He added, "I cannot desert my wife. She needs me. She is an invalid."

"Which she uses to her own advantage. You know that she doesn't love you, and probably never did. Yet you stay attached. I am not sure I want to continue in this manner."

His impulse was to shrug and to say, "Do as you wish," but even as he didn't want to be tied irrevocably to her, he did not want to lose her. He said suddenly, "Rachel, dear, I am working for life, not death."

"What has that to do with my situation?"

"You are the beneficent influence in my life. But you worry too much about aging. Your complexion is still fair, you are still youthful."

"I won't be forever," she replied grimly. But she was grateful that he was concerned about her. She compromised, hoping he would give in too, saying, "If I were more a part of your life, it would be a comfort."

"You are," he assured her. "I discuss my work with you freely."

"I am flattered and interested. That is why I want to learn Latin."

"I will write my notes in English so you can read them." And because he thought better in that language.

As he returned to her side and put his arm around her waist, she asked, "How do the arteries get rid of the blood if not through the veins?"

"They don't, I believe. I am convinced that there must be connections from the arteries to the veins, but I haven't the means to detect them."

He looked so distressed that she suggested he have his dinner, her ostensible reason for coming upstairs. When he declined, saying he wasn't hungry, and looked annoyed, she caressed him and said he should rest.

Her touch excited him, and as she assured him that everyone else was asleep, he longed to return her affection. Then she would realise that his desire for her was undeniable. Yet even as he possessed her, he was thinking, The blockage in his explorations was due to the failure of his own imagination; he must be more strict with himself.

He walked to St. Bart's the next morning, feeling vigourous because of their lovemaking. The matron, sisters, and students waited to serve him, but it was Woodall who requested his immediate attention. The surgeon said, "Sir, I have an urgent and remarkable surgery. It is difficult and needs your approval."

William asked, "Matron, are there any other emergencies?"

"None at the moment, sir. There are no deaths, and no one else is critical."

"Woodall, what kind of an operation do you wish to perform?"

"Sir, the patient is a poor serving woman who was accused by her master of pilfering. In her defense she swore that if she had committed the crime she was accused of, then her legs and hands would rot off. And that has come to pass. This wretched servant, because of the Providence of God, has had parts of seven fingers rot, and both of her legs almost to the gartering place, and she has been referred to me to be cut, by God's mercy. If the mortified parts aren't removed by noon, she will die. She will anyhow unless a master operates. But I need your permission."

William viewed the patient and agreed with Woodall's diagnosis. The mortified parts were gangrenous, and he gave the surgeon permission to operate, for nothing else could save her.

The patient was stricken with remorse and fear, and Woodall gave her a draught which contained opium to dull her pain and to relax her. She was in her thirties, and gradually her contorted, thick features lost their tenseness and she stopped trembling. The surgeon placed his instruments and assistants with great care, and he stood where the light was best.

William watched intently while Woodall examined his fingernails to be sure they were neither too long nor too short. Then he felt his fingertips and said, "Doctor, I have practised all my operations with each hand and with both together. To obtain ability, speed, and readiness."

"Where will you start?"

"The legs, where bleeding is profuse. It is vital to be quick. I can cut off a leg in a minute. Otherwise there is a great risk. I must be careful not to sever an artery, for then she will bleed to death, sir."

So Woodall, whatever he professes, William thought gratefully, acknowledges that the blood flows from the heart through the arteries.

Woodall ordered his two assistants to hold the patient's body so that it would not disturb his knife. Then, as she prayed, he ordered an assistant to stuff her mouth with a thick cloth so she wouldn't cry out and distract him. He felt her flesh, muttered, "A tough fowl, hardly fit for stewing," and cut off her gangrenous legs with sudden swiftness. At the same time he ordered his assistants to place ligatures about the stumps. They used twine, and he said in an aside to William, "To staunch the flow of the blood and to stop haemorrhage. It ties shut the ends of the bleeding vessels."

When the patient fainted from shock, William wondered, Is it a special kind of vessel that moves the blood from the arteries to the veins?

Woodall said, "Now she won't upset my knife. I use an ointment of oil of roses and turpentine to prevent swelling and inflammation."

He followed the same procedure with the seven rotting fingers, and as he dressed them afterwards, while the patient still lay in shock, he said, "Doctor, I do not fear dangerous bleeding from the veins, especially in the extremities, for they do not bleed as much as the arteries."

William observed that when the vein was slit the blood flowed out with a mild pulsation, unlike the gush of a cut artery. He decided, This must be because in the veins the blood had only to drop to the heart and required very little pushing. Thus, it appeared that it was returning to the heart through the veins—as he had supposed.

After the patient was put back into the ward, Woodall said, "Doctor, I made sure there would be little loss of blood. Whenever possible, I pull the blood out of the veins. I am certain that she will heal."

She did recover. William congratulated Woodall, who replied, "Sir, so merciful is God to us vile creatures, when we are most unworthy of His mercies. She has confessed her guilt, yet she is still living. I am grateful that God has given me a great gift." But William noted sadly that she had become a permanent occupant of the hospital. She couldn't walk; she couldn't afford artificial limbs; she had no money. There was no provision for such assistance for someone who had sinned. And now, he was told, she would not be able to steal again.

Lord Robert Worth came to him soon after, in great distress. But William could only wish him peace and mercy, for as he observed in the notes he kept of his patients: *This patient, a Judge and a Baron of the Exchequer, has a retraction of the penis to such a degree that he illustrates the belief in some people that men can degenerate into hermaphrodites or women. He has no string tied to nature. W-I.*

Mary Sage was eighteen, and she was brought to him by her parents because she had lost sensation in parts of her body. They were worried that she would be regarded as a witch and exorcised. As he examined her and wished she were not so plain, he advised her parents that her *strange Distemper* was a *Uterine* condition which could be cured by *Hymeneal Exercises.* They didn't understand his diagnosis, and he added, "*She should find a husband.*"

Then a fierce controversy involved him at the College of Physicians about the publication of Dr. Helkiah Crooke's *Anatomy.* At the same time this anatomist offered his book to the College for publication, he applied for admission as a Fellow. The twenty-one Fellows of the College were ordered to consider his application and his *Anatomy,* and William, as a Fellow, was one of those at this meeting on Amen Corner.

Matthew declared, "Crooke's *Anatomy* is indecent. It is improper to describe the human generative organs in an anatomical treatise. And it should not be written in English, as he has done. His illustrations of the generative organs are shocking and must be removed and the text censored."

"How can we understand the human body if we don't view all of it?"

"Harvey, that doesn't relate to the question," said Wilkins. "You know it is against the custom to write about medicine in anything but Latin."

"It is useful that this book is written in English. That will help our patients and surgeons to understand the body better, too."

Matthew said, "It will corrupt them and lessen our prestige."

"And lower our standards," Wilkins added. "Crooke is guilty of disrespect to our College. I move that this book be condemned and, if it is published anywhere in its present form, that it be burned."

William's protest was overruled, and everyone agreed with this motion except Mayerne, who was silent. It was decided that Crooke's *Anatomy* should be submitted to the Bishop of London for his official suppression, thus uniting the Church with the College, and Crooke's application to be a Fellow of the College was rejected by an overwhelming majority.

"A wise decision," Matthew said with satisfaction. "The flesh is weak, and we must not tempt it." Led by Wilkins, most of the other doctors crowded around him to congratulate him for having conducted this crusade.

Shortly after this meeting, Mayerne submitted a book which he called *Pharmacopoeia,* for publication by the College. It was approved unanimously, and Matthew informed

William, "We will publish this book. The College is the sole guardian of medical learning in England."

William didn't share this view—the references he made to his new findings in his Lumleian Lectures were ignored or derided—but he thought Mayerne's *Pharmocopoeia* a fine work. It was the first comprehensive and accurate compilation of drugs that had been published in England, and they were arranged in order of their usefulness. He realised this was why Mayerne had not supported Crooke, although that had been his impulse.

Later Mayerne told him, "While you were away Crooke apologised to the College for criticising it, and he has been admitted as a Fellow."

"So his *Anatomy* has been banned?"

"No! The Bishop refused to suppress the book, and it has appeared in English, with nothing changed. But without the College's approval."

William was reading the *Anatomy* to see if Crooke had enlarged on Vesalius's *Fabrica*, the best work on the human body he knew, when his wife interrupted him. It was rare for Elizabeth to come to his laboratory. It must be important to her, he thought, and he put the book aside with a sigh. As far as he had gone, Crooke's work was disappointing, a summary from other writers, except for one thing the writer had said: "*Surgery alone is still uncultivated in our language.*" That was quite true, but there was nothing about the blood and the heart except the ancient views.

"What is it, Elizabeth?" She looked uncomfortable yet determined.

"You promised to speak on my brother's behalf."

"I did. But when Galen presented himself for examination at the College of Physicians, although it was the third time, he failed."

"He could be admitted to Court. Now that you are a Physician Extraordinary, you must have some influence there. My father did when he held that position. He tried valiantly in your behalf."

"I will always be grateful for his efforts. But no doctor can practise in London unless he is licensed by the College. That rule is absolute."

"You have influence at the College. You could make him acceptable."

"He cannot pass the examination unless I take it for him."

"You could tutor him."

"That is impossible. I'm very busy these days."

"Galen could live here while he studies with you."

"No!" William was shocked. That prospect was frightening.

"Why not? You virtually lived in my father's house when you needed him."

"To tutor him isn't enough. His knowledge of physic is faulty."

"I've already told him to come in from Cambridge tomorrow and discuss his situation with you." She glanced around the room, and as she saw the written pages on his desk, she asked, "Are you writing a book, too?"

"I may. These are some notes I have compiled."

"What do you call them?"

"*Exercitatio anatomica de motu cordis et sanguinis in animalibus.*"

"I prefer '*De motu cordis.*' It is shorter."

But does she have any feeling for it? he wondered.

"When you finish this work, do you intend to publish it?"

"I haven't decided yet. Do you like the idea?"

"If you get Galen into the College, I will appreciate your knowledge of Latin." Rachel had entered, and Elizabeth asked, "Girl, what do you want?"

"Madam, Dr. Harvey's brother John is below."

Elizabeth said, "Remember, Galen will be here tomorrow, and I expect you to help him. Girl, prepare the spare room to accommodate Dr. Browne."

After his wife was gone, Rachel said with alarm, "Her brother intends to move in?"

"I won't allow it."

"Your wife is insistent. He will suspect us. He has a lustful eye."

"Have you kept my notes in order?"

"Yes. If he is in the house, I cannot remain." She thought anxiously, I must look for a new situation now, while I can use the fact that I am housekeeper to an eminent doctor and can also cook, sew, and garden.

"Rachel, I assure you, Galen Browne will not remain here. I cannot force the College to admit him. He will have to return to Cambridge."

"That is not inevitable. I don't trust your wife. She may want her brother in the house to spy on me. She feels that is beneath her."

"She suspects nothing. Will you tell John that I will be down soon?"

His brother wanted him to see their father. Elizabeth served them tea and cake in an animated manner, for John had risen in the King's household and possessed influence. He admitted that he had put a word in James's ear about William's skill with physic, and that it had encouraged the King to advance his brother to the position of Physician Extraordinary.

William doubted this was the reason for his promotion, but he didn't argue; he was concerned about their father. "John, what is his complaint?"

"I don't know, but he thinks he can cure himself. But lately he has been in bed, which is not like him. Could you visit him tomorrow?"

Elizabeth said, "John, couldn't it wait a day or two? My own brother is seeing William tomorrow, and it is urgent."

"I wouldn't want him to wait long. I'm worried about our father."

"Just a day or two," she pleaded, looking almost attractive now.

John nodded, for he knew that she was infatuated with her brother.

Galen was dressed in the height of fashion, and Elizabeth eyed him as if he were a treasure, but William observed that his round, thick face had grown pudgy, and that he was fat and overdressed. And while he was two years older than Elizabeth and it was not the custom, he deferred to her as if she were the head of the family.

She said, as Rachel supervised the dinner and Silas served them, "Galen, tell William about your work at Cambridge. So he can know how to aid you."

He said, "My practice is uncertain. I had a nobleman last year as a patient, but an indiscreet diagnosis of syphilis led to my dismissal."

William asked, "Was it a correct diagnosis?"

"I wasn't sure. But his nose was inflamed, and he had ulcerous sores. Now I tutor students in the rudiments of physic when any of their tutors are ill. But either my pupils are poor or they are noblemen's sons whose riotous behavior is impossible to control. It is a sorry situation."

Elizabeth said, "William, that is why Galen must practise in London."

Galen said, "I didn't leave my wits at Cambridge. I'm a devout Galenist. But in Cambridge I earn only forty pounds a year, while in London a doctor can earn two hundred, and much more if you cure a nobleman."

"That is exaggerated. Have you done any anatomies?"

"I don't believe in them. They are a bloody business."

"He is right," said Elizabeth. "Dissection is an offence against God."

"Do you know any surgery?"

"Of course not! That is for barbers. I do not soil my hands with such a foul occupation."

Galen was so pompous, William wanted to dismiss him. But my wife, he thought, would never forgive me, and would fall into an even worse decline. Yet he couldn't tutor him, and when she suggested this he shouted, "That is impossible! I haven't the time!" Elizabeth looked prepared to faint, and he softened his manner and added, "However, I will take Galen to Court next week. A masque is being given in honour of Prince Charles, and it will be a good time for him to meet other doctors, and perhaps the King himself."

Elizabeth was pleased; she was sure an exceptional thing could happen. Galen was busy devouring a third portion of roast beef and washing it down with his fourth draught of beer, and he was startled when Rachel entered to remind William that the doctor planned to visit his father today.

Galen hadn't remembered that their housekeeper was so attractive. After she was gone and William stood up to indicate he had to leave, Galen grinned and said, "William, that is a fair wench. Elizabeth, I would keep an eye on him. She could keep me from growing weary."

"Rachel has been with us a long time," William replied angrily. "She runs the house very efficiently."

"I can understand that. Elizabeth, your companion is quite plain by comparison."

"William doesn't consider my wants, except when they fit in with his own. I have wondered often whether we should keep this housekeeper."

This comment nagged at William while he visited his father. Thomas lived in Hackney, which was just outside of London, to the northeast. He was in bed when William arrived, but as he saw his physician son he got up.

"There is nothing wrong with me," he growled, and stood to prove it. "John worries too much. I want to discuss other matters with you. William, have you made any impression on the King? Now that you have been honoured?"

"It is difficult to say. I attend him occasionally."

"Do not press your views. You are not as diplomatic as you should be." Before William could respond, his father clutched his stomach and had to rush out of the room to relieve himself, then returned, looking drawn.

William asked, "Is your stomach very painful?"

Thomas shrugged and changed his posture to ease the ache in his rectum. "It is like an old friend who sometimes indulges me and sometimes doesn't. I wanted you to come when we could be alone. I have a private matter to discuss. I have decided to make you my executor."

The thought of his father's death struck William as unreal, although he was seventy-two and had outlived almost all of his contemporaries.

"Don't be difficult, William. I have drawn up my will, and you are best suited to be the executor. Of all my children, you care the least for money, and thus you will be the most trustworthy with it."

"Father, I don't know what to say. I am honoured but . . ."

"Don't say anything. My mind is made up."

"Now may I examine you, Father?"

Thomas grumbled that it was not necessary, but William insisted. He found that his father's rectum was inflamed, and he gave him an ointment to ease the pain, while Thomas said, "I don't trust doctors, most of them are butchers. Do you truly believe that this salve will help me?"

"It will give you some relief. But what you need most is a soft diet that will put as little strain as possible on your digestion."

"Don't tell me how to behave. You are still my son. Don't be rude."

"You may also have the stone. You may need an operation."

"I'm too old for the knife. You will execute my will faithfully."

"If you follow my instructions faithfully."

Thomas agreed, although he muttered, "I expected to be punished for your experiments. They are mad, you know, but you have risen high despite them."

William returned home, thinking that it was only a matter of time with his father. All the evidence indicated his chief illness was old age.

His laboratory was spotless, and there were flowers on his desk, and he realized that Rachel was responsible. Stimulated by her consideration, he wrote: *The proper function of the auricles occurs when they relax, for then they are filled from the veins which end in them. Contracting, they throw the charge they have received into the relaxing ventricles and these, contracting in turn, propel the blood into the arteries.*

But there were still gaps in the road. Suddenly he felt overwhelmed with fatigue and an increasing impatience with the activities that were diverting him from what he desired to do most. He picked up his notes, which Rachel had arranged so carefully, and his impulse was to tear them to shreds. Then he would be free from this pursuit that possessed him so passionately and sometimes so painfully. At the same time, living in a landscape without his experiments would be like being an exile.

Rachel was at the door, asking him if his notes were in order, and he replied, "They are fine. Has my brother-in-law left?"

"Your wife wanted him to stay, but he said he would be back next week."

"Rachel, how old are you?"

"I'm not sure. There are no records for people of my station. My mother told me that I'm a year older than Silas, but it may be more."

"Then you must be going on thirty."

"More like forty," she said mournfully.

"Good Lord, you don't look it. Your person is a charming thirty."

"You must be tired to make such a mistake. What is worrying you?"

"I doubt my father will live much longer."

"I never knew mine."

"It makes one appreciate the heartbeats we have. Whatever happens, you will want for nothing. Now, if you could jump up and down, it would be helpful. There is something about the heart I must explore."

For an instant she longed to flee, but he looked so imploring she couldn't resist him. I never can, she thought wryly. And as she did as he asked, she told herself that she must not feel sorry for herself. He did love her and need her, and the last, in a compelling way, was the most important heartbeat of all. She jumped as vigourously as she could.

ithout a last word
there cannot be a first word
Without a first word
there cannot be a next word . . .
Let us listen to all the words
in whatever order
And avoid silence
that unexpressed slave

After the plays of Will Shakespeare, the masque bored William. He sat in the gallery of Whitehall Palace, with Galen at his side, and as they watched the elaborate entertainment created to honour Charles, the Prince of Wales, he waited impatiently for the pageant to end.

News from the New World was an allegory about America, written by Ben Jonson and designed by Inigo Jones. It was a mixture of florid prose and topical references, lavish costumes and ornate settings, and he did not believe any of it. He thought, The poet's work often was disorderly and violent but it was suffused with passion and vitality, while the masque was lifeless and synthetic, and he wished that something that he cared about would happen on the stage.

His mind wandered as he wondered why he was wasting his time here when there was still much to learn about the body. He yearned to be excited, as the poet's plays excited him, and Rachel's presence, and an accurate medical diagnosis, the marvel of a newborn baby, and the heart and its expression of God's purpose. There must be some kind of vessel that carries the blood from the arteries to the veins, he assured himself, and he wished he had an instrument with which to look for this link.

His brother-in-law said, "William, it is over." Galen sighed with relief. "You will introduce me to the King? As you promised?"

If I cannot see any vessels conducting blood from the arteries to the veins, he reflected, how can I be sure? How can I trust this conclusion? He felt squeezed in by his ignorance.

"James should remember my father. He served him with distinction. As Physician Extraordinary, you should have preferential treatment. Aren't you listening? You are not going to break your word, are you?"

Galen's anguish shook William out of his reverie, and he replied, "Of course not." He noted that Buckingham was by the King's side, not Bacon, and Charles was on the other side, but there was no sign of the Lord Chancellor. He had heard that Bacon had been accused of bribery, but until this moment he had thought this merely rumour. He took Galen by the arm and said, "I will introduce you to some of my fellow physicians, too. That will be useful."

Galen was disappointed, and he replied, "I am told Buckingham has the greatest influence at Court. Even more than the Prince of Wales."

"So it is said."

As they started towards James, someone called, "Wait a minute, William!"

It was his brother, anxious to know about their father. John was dressed in the livery of a Yeoman of the Bedchamber, and Galen envied John's elaborate Tudor garb.

John nodded to Galen, whom he had known a long time, although only casually, and he said, "William, I'm still concerned about our father. As soon as you left him, he took to his bed. Yet you didn't treat him."

"It is too late. The only thing I could do was give him an ointment to ease his pain and a mild diet to lessen the strain on his digestion."

"What do you think is wrong with him?"

"He may have the stone, but to cut now will only cause him much pain without any chance of a cure. He is too old, worn. Father was right to refuse the knife. It would only give him needless anguish."

"Did he discuss anything else?"

William didn't want to lie, yet his father had sworn him to secrecy. He said, "John, the King looks poorly."

"His health becomes more difficult daily. He is so weak he has to be strapped into the saddle when he hunts."

"It is unfortunate that his infatuation with Buckingham makes the King try to act half his age. He is fifty-five. And aging fast."

John was shocked. "I hope you don't express those views publicly. The Lord High Admiral has become the most powerful person in the realm."

Galen said, "William, you are rude. Buckingham is a beautiful man."

And that is the reason for his rapid rise, thought William. Even now, at twenty-eight, his heart-shaped features were finely framed by his light brown hair and illuminated by his vivid blue eyes. It is no wonder, William's mind ran on, with the King's predilection for handsome young men, that George

Villiers has gone swiftly from a gentleman waiter at Court to Cup Bearer to the King, Master of the Horse, Marquess of Buckingham, and Lord High Admiral.

By contrast, the Prince of Wales, who stood hesitantly behind his father, looked insignificant. He was much shorter than Buckingham, just five feet four, with bowed legs, prominent eyes, and while Charles had pleasant features, they were commonplace next to the beautiful Buckingham's. And now, as if aware of that, Charles was remote and ill at ease.

The King linked his arm in Buckingham's to keep from falling and fondled his codpiece with his other hand, ignoring his son's presence.

William said, "Your Majesty, may I present Dr. Galen Browne to you?"

James said irritably, "I have too many physicians as it is."

"Sir, his father, Lancelot Browne, served you with distinction."

"I don't remember such a physician."

Galen said, "Sir, that was in the first years of your glorious reign."

James didn't like being reminded of his age, especially when his favourite was present, and he indicated that they were dismissed.

Galen was so stunned that William replied, although he knew this was risking his own situation, "Your Majesty, may I present Dr. Browne to the Prince of Wales and the Earl of Buckingham?"

"Why, Harvey?" James scowled and was suspicious immediately.

"Sir, they may be pleased to allow him to serve them some day."

"Steenie, what do you think of these doctors? Do you trust them as little as I do? Although Harvey has eased my complaints several times."

"He has a considerable reputation because of his work at

St. Bart's and the College of Physicians, but it is marred by his need to explore the heart. I am unacquainted with Browne. Or his qualifications."

"Galen Browne, My Lord," he corrected. "My father, as I said—"

Buckingham cut him short. "How is your Latin?"

"May it please my noble Lord, I know many magical remedies."

The Prince of Wales, who stood shyly behind his father and the favourite, asked suddenly, "Browne, what are they?"

"Sir, I have an herb rue that stirs the spirits and sharpens the wits."

"I don't need anything for my wits!" the King snapped furiously.

William stepped between them before James could chastise Galen and said, "Sir, no one is more loyal than Dr. Browne. It is his concern for your health that makes him express such sentiments."

Galen said, "Sir, you must be careful for the sake of the country."

"I don't need physic," grumbled James. "I can still hunt."

William asked, "Your Majesty, may I examine you?"

"Mayerne did. He gave me pills for shortness of breath and asthma."

William still felt the King needed an examination now; he looked so pale. But James refused; the thought of admitting weakness before his adored Steenie was too much to endure. He started for his bedchamber, but he halted when Buckingham asked Galen, "Where did you study physic?"

"My Lord, at Cambridge, as a member of the learned professions."

"When were you licensed by the College of Physicians?"

Galen blushed and mumbled, "Sir, I haven't had time. But I will."

Buckingham lost interest, and so did Charles, and the King cried, "My bowels are loose, it is the evil purge my royal apothecary fed me," and as he fled to his bedchamber they followed him.

Galen wanted to know how old the Prince of Wales was, and William replied, "Charles is about twenty-one."

Galen stated, "He looks younger. Did you notice that he stammers?" As if that made his own failure less.

William saw Mayerne, Matthew, Wilkins, and Scrope in another part of the gallery. They were engaged in an animated discussion, and because he had promised to help Galen, he took him over to the doctors and introduced him. Mayerne and Matthew were cordial when they heard that Galen was William's brother-in-law, but they continued their avid conversation.

Mayerne asked William, "Are you aware Bacon is charged with bribery?"

"I heard talk about it, but until now I thought it was merely rumour."

Wilkins said gloatingly, "It is more than that. He has many enemies."

Galen said, "But Sir Francis Bacon holds the highest post in the land."

Scrope retorted caustically, "So the greater the fall."

When Galen had learned that William was Bacon's physician, he had memorised his titles in the hope that they would be useful, and now he listed them for the others so they would be impressed by his knowledge. "Sir Francis Bacon is Lord Chancellor, Baron Verulam, and Viscount St. Albans."

Scrope added disdainfully, "And now he is found corrupt."

William interrupted. "Henry, that hasn't been proven."

"It will be. The important thing is, he is charged."

"Are you certain?"

"Yes. Sir Edward Coke, who hates Bacon ferociously and always has, with his clever lawyer's mind has resurrected the ancient mediaeval device of impeachment. He intends that Bacon will go on trial before the Lords on the basis of articles of impeachment drawn up by the Commons."

Scrope's joy at Bacon's possible collapse struck William as a shabby attitude, for, whatever the Lord Chancellor's flaws, and he was aware of many of them, Bacon had written and striven greatly. But his reply was interrupted by a fierce quarrel between Ben Jonson and Inigo Jones.

Jonson yelled, "Jones, this masque was my idea!"

The middle-aged Jones, whose commanding figure towered over the shorter, bulky Jonson, flared back, "I shared equally in the devising. Yet you begrudge me equal place as the inventor."

"That is not my provocation." As Jonson saw he possessed the physicians' attention, he gripped the title page of the masque and showed it to them, adding, "I admit that you toil hard on my masques, and I am agreeable to allowing your name beside mine. But not ahead of it."

William and the others read the title page that offended Jonson:

The Inventors
Inigo Jones   Ben Jonson

Jonson's fury grew as he shouted, "Next time I will solve this problem in my own way! I will omit your name from the title page completely!"

Jones's handsome features became hawklike, and he went as if to draw his sword. Then he thought better of it, remembering that Jonson was a skilled brawler and had slain a man in a duel. He said, "I am the King's Surveyor. Leave my name off and there will be none of your masques at Court."

"At least you acknowledge they are mine." Jonson's intensity increased as he saw his audience increase. "Apart from myself, no one knows how to write a masque. Dispense with mine and there will be none at Court."

"I have some gift for words. I could combine all the elements."

Jonson laughed, and now he was speaking more to the others than to Jones. "I dislike romantic drama; it is usually

335

false. My good friend Will Shakespeare put a seacoast in Bohemia when there was none for a hundred miles. Such carelessness and lack of scholarship is sad. And that is characteristic of surveyors, who do what they know not."

Jones thought, As a mature and honoured artist, there is no reason to be lectured like a child. He snapped back, "All this is to no purpose. You do not know Italian, the cultivated tongue, with all of your vanity about being learned. Your masques are just bits and pieces pasted together."

William observed that neither of them was listening to the other. Then, as Donne approached, the recently appointed Dean of St. Paul's by the King's grace and mercy, the surveyor became stern and quiet. Jones was hoping to design a new west front for the cathedral, and the last person he desired to offend was the Dean of St. Paul's.

Jonson felt he could indulge himself with Donne, for they were old friends. He declared for anyone willing to listen, but particularly for Donne, who might use his words in a sermon, "Money is the god at Court. It controls everything. I work for a stupid, greedy Court, and no one cares that my masques are grounded on solid learning. They would prefer a ballad about dancing beats." Then he strode off as if he had triumphed.

Unable to allow the writer to have the last word, Jones said, "Masques are devised to appeal to the eye as much as the ear." He bowed to Donne and turned back to the stage to take care of his precious costumes.

Donne said quietly, "Ben is one of the most learned men in England. But sometimes it is better to whisper than to shout. Mayerne, I'm deeply concerned about Bacon's health. Have you attended him lately?"

"No, Harvey is his personal physician."

William said, "The Lord Chancellor hasn't requested my services."

"I should attend him," Donne said thoughtfully. "He must be much troubled these days. Whenever he is attacked, he falls ill."

336

Matthew said, "Your Grace, I would not interfere. In your present position it could offend the King. William, you shouldn't attend him either. It could damage your prospects at Court."

William replied, "If Bacon asks me to attend him, I will."

Donne hurried to say, before another quarrel erupted, "Harvey, I have attended two of your dissections. They are interesting. My stepfather was President of the College of Physicians, and I spent my youth there."

Wilkins grumbled, "Harvey, I hear you dissect without permission of the College. Use criminals who are still alive. Such practices are heretical. Matthew, as chief Censor, don't you think he should be investigated?"

Matthew had heard rumours that Harvey had ventured into forbidden fields, but his colleague was useful to him, and he did not relish losing his services. He shrugged and said, "Wilkins, nothing is proven."

Donne said, "I find his views on the blood plausible."

Encouraged, William said, "It is a delusion to think the liver creates the blood. It would have to make six tons a day, which is impossible."

This evoked a chorus of dissent from everybody but Donne and Mayerne, who were silent, and William stated:

"Each time the heart beats it ejects two ounces of blood from the auricles and ventricles. Since it beats seventy-two times a minute, it ejects one hundred forty-four ounces of blood a minute, five hundred forty pounds an hour, six tons in a day."

Wilkins sneered, "You are wrong. The auricles ventilate the blood."

"No. The auricles are active instruments, and the charge of blood they receive from the veins, they project into the ventricles, by which, in sequence, the blood is caught on the move and thrown with force into the arteries. The ventricles act like a tennis player, who strikes the ball to best advantage when he takes it on the rebound."

Mayerne, uncomfortable in the sullen, incredulous silence

337

that fell upon them, said abruptly, "No more talk of physic, except for pleasure."

This reminded Galen of his reason for being there, and he said, "I would serve His Majesty faithfully."

Matthew asked, "What makes you think that you are worthy?"

"My father, Lancelot Browne, served King James and Queen Elizabeth."

"That is not a sufficient qualification. What remedies do you know?"

"I have found an herb rue which preserves chastity. I have also cured people who suffer from dizziness by having them run naked through a field of flax. But always after the sun has set."

"What else have you cured?"

"Syphilis, agues, gout, ulcerous sores, and impotence."

"Then why do you petition us now?"

William, remembering his promise, cut in, although he felt ridicule in Matthew's tone. "My brother-in-law is eager to obtain a license to practise physic in London."

"You know the requirements."

Mayerne asked, "Dr. Browne, why don't you apply to the College?"

"I have, sir."

"Three times," Wilkins reminded him. "I sat in on your third failure."

"Sir, I have studied Aristotle, Galen, word for . . ."

Matthew interrupted, "Apply again for examination."

"Thank you. When, sir?"

"As soon as possible. This is a courtesy to Dr. Harvey."

Galen told Elizabeth not to worry, that he had impressed the medical men he had met and that some of them would be considering his application for a license to practise medicine in London. She was uneasy that he didn't have time to improve his Latin, but he was certain it would suffice.

He was examined the following week at the College of

Physicians. Galen was disappointed that he didn't know any of the five Fellows who examined him—William had been excused at his own request—but he was certain he would pass.

His certainty never wavered, even when the chief examiner insisted that he must reply in Latin. Criticised for his faulty use of the language, he replied, "I lost some of my Latin by want of using it." This was regarded with scepticism, and he added, "I trust you will excuse my lack of Latin, noble sirs, a fractured skull has caused me to forget it."

He admitted he had no idea how the bones were formed, but he insisted he was an authority on the urine. Then he grew tired as the questions continued—he had expected a shorter examination—and he could not remember.

Told that he was rejected, when he recovered from his indignation he was proud he had the presence of mind to ask, "When can I apply again?"

"You have applied enough."

"Despite Dr. Harvey's recommendation?"

There was a brief conference between the five examiners, who then informed him, "To please Dr. Harvey, you can apply next year."

Galen assured a grievously disappointed Elizabeth that he had been courteous, but that the Fellows' lack of civility was appalling. She accused William of not keeping his promise to help her brother, and she was even angrier that he was not surprised by this rejection.

He replied, "The College stated that Galen's knowledge of physic is insufficient, especially in anatomy and in his inability to use Latin."

Galen retorted, "Did you speak to your colleagues at Court?"

"Yes, but I've been told that James is so involved with Buckingham, he feels the Lord Admiral is the only physic he needs at this moment."

"Lord Fancy Steenie, the Earl of Maidenhead," Galen said derisively. "Does he think tickling his codpiece will make him feel younger? Fool!"

339

"Besides, no one can serve the King unless licensed by the College."

William's finality dismayed Elizabeth. Weeping hysterically, she rushed off to her room, shouting that her father's memory had been profaned. "Her companion will comfort her," William assured Galen.

He escorted him to the door—for there is no reason for him to stay now, he thought gratefully—but Galen paused to ask, "When did you bring that pretty housekeeper into your employ?"

"Her brother did. They want to be together, for they have no other kin."

"I could use such an attractive wench. Is she warm-blooded?"

"If I can assist your practice in Cambridge, I will do so."

"Your housekeeper would help. Do you realise that her presence could add to Elizabeth's poor health?" Finally, however, aware that William had no intention of discussing Rachel any further, he grumbled, "My gifts would have been recognised if London physicians weren't such snobs."

After Galen left, William thought, He is the greatest snob of all.

A week later his services were requested by Bacon. Elizabeth, irate about Galen's failure, blamed William and told him that if he treated Bacon, who was under attack, he would have even less influence. By now he was in no mood to be criticised, and he lost his temper and shouted that she should mind her own business; if she didn't, he would never speak on her brother's behalf again. This silenced her, and she retired to her bed.

As William prepared to visit Bacon, he recalled that Matthew had said that Browne's presence was demeaning to the practice of medicine, and that he was an ass.

The Lord Chancellor lay in his bed at York House, quite ill, but so located that he commanded a view of the Thames, and Whitehall Palace. This was the most coveted situation of all the great houses on the Strand, and he was determined to retain it. Despite the charges of corruption against Bacon, he was surrounded with splendour. Liveried servants were everywhere; his table was strewn with flowers of the most expensive kind; a cabinet of jewels was by the side of his bed; three coaches stood outside; there was a great barge at his water gate, and many watermen. Yet his wide forehead was wrinkled, his brown eyes were sunken, and his complexion was ghastly, his skin drawn and taut.

When William finished his examination Bacon asked, "What is wrong?"

William hesitated. The patient's rectum was inflamed, but that was no wonder, Bacon gave himself so many purges. And his stomach was swollen, but that could be from gas brought on from nerves.

"As you know, I have little faith in doctors."

"I know, My Lord. I have treated you before."

"Unless they are philosophical. Do you know the estimable Dr. Anthony?"

"Very well. He has been fined several times by the College of Physicians for practising physic without a license."

"You have been too severe with him. He has discovered a universal physic, of potable gold, which he mixes with mercury. It has an affinity to the philosopher's stone, and this tincture of gold has had surprising effects."

"My Lord, has it relieved you?"

"It has helped persons of great note."

"Then why have you summoned me, sir?"

"Anthony was unable to find the right mixture. What is my affliction?"

"Your infirmity lies in your digestion, sir."

"I thought I had the vapours. I possess skill in physic too."

"Sir, your troubled state of mind has affected your stomach also."

Bacon cried out, "This is no feigning, but a sickness of my heart, caused by these terrible charges that have been brought

341

against me. This talk of impeachment has ruined my nature. Yet I have done nothing that has not been done by everyone else. All men in public office accept gifts. It is the custom. Whoever I have judged, I have judged fairly. Is it any wonder that I have fallen ill? With my sensitive physique! What do you prescribe? I have written prescriptions for my apothecary to fill, but these mixtures upset me."

"My Lord, you should have consulted me first."

"I am consulting you now!"

"Easing of your mind would be useful, sir."

Bacon was upset. He had expected a much more severe and frightening diagnosis. He wondered, Is Harvey a fraud, like so many doctors? "I have frequent fever, attacks of gout and ague, which I have inherited."

"I know, sir, but at the moment you have a gastric disturbance, and dysentery, probably accentuated by your temperament and strain."

"It is no wonder. I am sixty, and I have suffered much. But I am not dishonest. Careless, perhaps, I have never been able to keep account of money. If I live splendidly, I live as a nobleman in my position must. But no one visits me now. Jonson, who wrote a birthday ode to me two months ago, has not seen me since I have been charged, and even Donne has forsaken me."

"My Lord, they are concerned about your well-being. But they feel it is more fitting that you are attended by a physician. You must stop treating yourself."

"But I know many remedies. I have written much about medicine."

Like a Lord Chancellor, William thought derisively, but he said, "Sir, I cannot take any more responsibility for you unless you heed me."

"You are quite right." At the thought of being impeached a stomach spasm had just attacked him, and suddenly he felt contrite.

"My Lord, rest, do not worry—"

342

"How can I not worry?" Bacon interrupted with an anguished cry. "When I am threatened with deprivation of all I have desired. When I face the humiliation of being stripped of all my offices and perquisites."

"Sir, you will have to control yourself if you are to recover."

Such plain speaking shook Bacon. No doctor spoke to him like this. In his annoyance he forgot his pain and languor. He thought angrily, Perhaps I can confront my accusers in the House of Lords, or at the least influence James and Buckingham, who with their power can still save me. Preoccupied, his mind on that new possibility, he dismissed Harvey as he got out of bed to write a letter to prepare his approach to the King. He composed it carefully:

"Sir, I am as innocent in my heart as any born upon St. Innocent's Day. I confess I accepted gifts after judgement, but I conceived it to be no fault, I judged as justice said; if I am in error, inform me, Your Majesty."

Donne told William that this was what Bacon had written the King. "He sent it to me for my approval, but I doubt it will alter his danger. Important witnesses have come forth to testify against him, and the charges of corruption increase. I am going to preach at Whitehall on April eighth for the King. I think you will find my sermon of interest. Do you think you cured Bacon? He has sickly inclinations."

"As much as he would allow me. His worst affliction is in his mind."

William invited Elizabeth to attend this service with him. At first she refused; she said it was absurd that a poet who wrote erotic poetry could express the divinity of God. But when he pointed out that the King would be in the audience at Whitehall Chapel, she agreed to accompany him.

He was relieved; now he could invite Rachel. To avoid any difficult consequences, he did this through Silas. He told him, "I am allowed two servants to attend me, so I desire that you and your sister be there."

"Thank you, Master," Silas said. "Are you going to be honoured?"

"That's not likely. But it is possible that my views may be mentioned."

Later, when Rachel told him that she couldn't go, that it would appear unseemly, he reminded her that this was one of the things she had requested.

"By your side," she replied, "not as a servant to sit in the rear."

"I cannot sit with you, it would expose our situation, but I think the Dean is going to support my views, even if it is only by implication. I thought this would make you happy. You have helped me with them."

Now she no longer felt wretched but devoutly religious at the idea of being in the same church and at the same service with William, especially when he was to be praised, and she admitted she had said yes to Silas.

The next Sunday he sat in the chapel and decided there would be no mention of him; this was a royal occasion, for, as Donne had predicted, the King was present. Rachel was in the rear with Silas and the other servants, as prim as anyone. Elizabeth sat by his side, dressed soberly in black, like a Puritan, and prepared to disapprove of Dr. Donne.

Then, just as he felt drugged by the sonority and solemnity of the Dean's voice, his words aroused him. He cried to himself, Donne really is supporting my views of the motion of the blood. His sermon was saying:

"We know the capacity of the ventricle, how much it can hold; and we know the receipt of all the receptacles of the blood, how much the body can have; so we do of all the other conduits and cisterns of the body. But this infinite hive of honey, this insatiable whirlpool of the covetous mind, no anatomy, no dissection has discovered to us. When we look into the vessels of our body for drink, for blood, for urine,

344

they are pottles, and gallons. When we look into the furnaces of our spirits, the brain, and the ventricles of the heart, they are not thimbles. For spiritual things, we have no room; for temporal things, we have no bounds."

So, he thought gratefully, Donne, despite some scepticism, is inclined to believe me. Elizabeth said, "The Dean disappointed me. I expected more from the Dean of St. Paul's and a graduate of Cambridge."

He couldn't find out what Rachel felt, for she and Silas were gone by the time he reached the rear of the chapel. The King had halted him to inquire about the health of the Lord Chancellor, and he had replied, "Your Majesty, better, I believe, as long as he can rest."

Then he heard James saying to the Venetian ambassador, *"If I were to imitate the conduct of your republic and begin to punish all those who take bribes, I should soon not have a single subject left."*

At home he felt a new attitude in Rachel, as if, for once, she was pleased with herself. But he had no time to discuss the sermon with her, for Bacon wanted him again, even more urgently this time. He found the Lord Chancellor in great distress, retreating even deeper into his bed, reading a lengthy bill of particulars and crying out hysterically, "The Parliament has brought forth twenty-eight articles of impeachment against me. They are a terrible indictment. The Commons drew up these charges and have sent them to the Lords for inquiry, but this means that I will be convicted. I am dying, swollen in body, stricken with a mortal fever."

"Easy, My Lord," said William, as he reexamined his distraught patient. "It is still rest that you need most."

"I am writing my will. Do you think I have time?"

"Sir, you have nothing to fear, except what is in your mind."

"I must submit. To relieve my afflictions. Don't you think so?"

William felt that Bacon desired agreement rather than a medical diagnosis, but perhaps, considering his situation, this would help him. He nodded and said, "Now be sensible, My Lord, and try to sleep."

"No! Now that I know what I must do, I must do it now! I will plead guilty! His Majesty implied that I should, then all would be forgiven."

Once again Bacon forced his aching body out of bed, so that he could express to the King in his most obsequious manner how he sought the royal favour by his extravagant profession of loyalty. He believed this would save him, for he knew no one wrote more wisely than he did.

The King did not answer. It became evident that the Lord Chancellor was going to be convicted, for the evidence against him was overwhelming.

Then, although he did not appear in the House of Lords to respond to the charges—he pleaded that this was impossible owing to the gravity of his illness—he managed to find the strength to go over all the charges.

Next to each count he wrote, "*Confessed . . . Confessed . . . Confessed.*"

Still contrite, he wrote to the House of Lords that he was willing to submit to their judgment. He admitted he had been negligent, but that he had not intended any bribery or corruption, and he begged for forgiveness and a merciful verdict of censure rather than removal from office.

This didn't satisfy either House. They didn't agree with his suggestion that he should lose his Seal and nothing else. He was ordered to appear in Parliament to hear his sentence pronounced. When he still pleaded that he was too ill to attend, four Lords came to York House and took the Seal of his office from its treasured place by the side of his bed.

A few days later the House of Lords voted without dissent that the Lord Chancellor was guilty of all the charges.

Soon after the Chief Justice prepared to pass sentence.

Degradation was recommended, but two votes, one of them Buckingham's, averted this.

As William waited in Westminster Palace for this sentence to be passed, he thought of Bacon lying in his bedchamber, surrounded by his wealth of possessions, although thousands of pounds in debt. The Chief Justice said:

"The Lord Viscount St. Albans to pay a fine of £40,000. To be imprisoned in the Tower during the King's pleasure. To be forever incapable of holding any office, place or employment in the state or commonwealth. Never to sit in Parliament nor come within the verge of the court."

Now, William observed critically, a wave of sentimental sympathy swept through the kingdom for the fallen Lord Chancellor. Bacon's fine was remitted; he spent just one day in the Tower; he was allowed an annual pension of twelve hundred pounds from the government—an amount, thought William, larger than most noblemen could count on—and continued to live far beyond his means. But he hadn't yet paid William for his services, although Bacon admitted that they had helped him recover. This prodded William to put his own affairs in order. He was forty-three, and while he felt in good health, he told himself that he must make provision for the future. Since Rachel had attended the services, she had blossomed as if reborn, and had encouraged him to work on his studies as much as he could.

He summoned his solicitor so that he could draw up a will —his first. He was pleased to find that he had accumulated a thousand pounds in his years of practise and that he owed no money; he hated being in debt.

His solicitor, Christopher Brooke, was a friend of Donne's, Ben Jonson's, Michael Drayton's, with a keen interest in poetry. The slim, tall, fair lawyer, who was the same age as the Dean, and who had helped Donne in his clandestine marriage, was trustworthy and could keep a secret.

William willed a third of his estate to his wife, a third to be divided among his brothers, although he favoured Eliab, and then, he told Brooke, he wanted to take care of his manservant and housekeeper in his will.

Brooke wasn't surprised but asked simply, "How much, Doctor?"

"How much is the custom?"

"That depends on the circumstances. Usually, ten pounds is generous."

William hesitated, then said abruptly, "They have been with me a long time. It has been almost a lifetime. Put down fifty pounds."

The solicitor's eyes widened at the size of this bequest, but he did as he had been told. Then he asked, "What about the rest of this third?"

"I'm not sure." But of one thing, he was. Now, at least, Silas and Rachel had the protection of a family, too. And he could return to his work on *De motu cordis* with a free mind.

 o complex is truth
The only time I know
What to do or say
is when I am at work . . .

Two years of intense exploration followed. Then, late in 1623, William decided to summarise his findings. It was a Sunday afternoon in November, and as he sat in his laboratory and waited for Rachel to bring him more ink and paper so he could write out what he had learned before the sun was gone—he liked to work by daylight—he grew reflective.

He was glad his household had attended morning services at St. Paul's to hear his favourite preacher, Dr. Donne. Since the sermon at Whitehall, regular attendance at Sunday services had become a weekly occurrence whenever possible. He sensed that they shared his surprise and disappointment that the Dean had been absent today. Donne must be ailing, he decided—nothing else would keep him out of the pulpit— and he hoped it wasn't serious, for the Dean was troubled with frequent ill health.

He was gratified that this routine pleased Rachel and even appeared to satisfy a need in his wife. Now her companion and the two other servants also sat in the rear of the cathedral like a tightly knit family, although he knew that Rachel preferred to keep apart from the others. He was relieved that his household seemed to have settled into some stability.

Only two things had upset him during the past two years: Galen had failed another examination, and his father had died a few months ago. The first had been a minor irritation, but the second had been a painful shock in spite of his belief that it was inevitable. He recalled his father's final days as if they had happened yesterday.

He stood by Thomas's side on a lovely afternoon in summer —the rest of the family were sitting in the sun to enjoy the unusually fine weather—and he wondered if he should have done more. His father wasn't complaining, but he could tell that Thomas was in severe pain. William thought, Perhaps he should operate. But when he suggested this, his father refused with a finality he couldn't overcome.

Thomas motioned for his son to come closer and whispered, "Although I made you my executor, I left you nothing in my will."

"That doesn't matter, Father. It is your health that concerns me."

"It matters to me. I take care of my own. On my instructions, Eliab put the money you gave me for the livestock into the business. Now it has doubled, and you will have that, more than a hundred pounds."

"Thank you."

"You don't have to thank your own kin. We are a closely knit family. It has been my greatest joy." Thomas reached out for him, and William felt that in his frantic clutch he was crying out in anguish. Then he asked harshly, "Do you have anything to ease my pain? It is cruel."

It was so unlike his father to complain that he replied, "I will give you some laudanum. Take it carefully, too much can be dangerous."

His father smiled wryly, yet nodded weakly as he took it and hid it under his pillow, as if its presence must be kept a secret, unworthy of a Yeoman who had become a gentleman with a crest and a coat of arms.

A day later his father was dead and all the laudanum was gone. William had left enough for a week's dosage. He felt Thomas had put an end to his life because it had become too painful to endure, but he told no one of his suspicion. He considered himself a free thinker, who believed it was right to put an end to one's life if one tired of it, but he knew this was a view that few shared, and it could deny his father a consecrated grave.

His brothers asked him to witness an autopsy on his father, and it was found that Thomas Harvey's colon was swollen and his spleen abnormally enlarged. When the others were gone, he extracted blood from the heart. He wasn't sure that laudanum had penetrated it. Yet, he thought, if the blood circulates, it must have done just that.

Voices in the hallway brought him back to the present. Rachel and Silas were quarrelling, and this annoyed him, for it distracted him from finishing his notes. And he was curious, for this was unusual.

Silas said, "You like to think the Master prefers your services only, but you are wrong. You cannot do everything for him, and you shouldn't try."

Rachel asked, "What have I done that offends you?"

"I should fetch him the ink and paper he needs. I'm his attendant."

"But I help him with his work," she answered proudly.

"I could help him, too, if you would teach me to read and write."

"Silas, you are too old. You could never learn now."

"I'm not too old. I'm only a little past forty."

"How can you learn figures when you don't even know your own age?"

"You don't know yours. But I'm old enough. I'm forty, at least."

"I'm older. Our mother told me that."

William sensed that Rachel was proud that she held advantages over her brother and that she had become very possessive about them.

"Rachel, there is no guarantee you can do everything for the Master better than I can. If you teach me to read and write, I can help him with his work too. When he works late into the night, as he does so often."

"No!" William felt terror in her response. "That is impossible!" She had striven too long and hard for this privilege to lose it now. "The time I need to teach you, I need to help him." There was an uncomfortable silence, and then she said softly, as if she realised now they could be overheard—and William had to ease quietly and unseen into the hall so he could hear them—"Why aren't you satisfied? You go with the doctor on most of his calls, you are paid a pound a month, when a groom, coachman, and gardener, all more skilled, earn only ten shillings."

"It isn't the money, and you know that. As it isn't for you."

"And even though he has become the King's physician, he has kept us."

"Rachel, he knows that we serve him better than anyone else."

She thought, Lechery is not always enough, or even fidelity, but she said, "No one can measure their value to someone else, and you shouldn't try."

"You are the one who worries about how much he needs you. But that is not the issue, and you know it. I told you something is wrong with Ruth and that she should be attended by the Master, but you don't want him to examine her, although she is clearly ill, her belly has swollen so."

"She is probably pregnant. A midwife should see her."

"I doubt that Ruth is with child. She is a good girl."

"Naturally she will try to brazen it out. Incontinence is a sin."

Silas didn't reply, and William wondered if he knew about them. He had never indicated that he did—and they had been careful—and yet Silas was so critical of her that he could be suspicious. It caused him to step forward to make his presence known and to ask, "Is Ruth in much distress?"

After they recovered from their surprise at his sudden appearance, she shrugged, but Silas said, "Yes, sir. I think you should examine her."

William took the ink and paper from Rachel. He thanked her for fetching them and put them on his table with a sigh, preferring to finish his notes rather then to examine a servant girl who probably was pregnant. By the time that is done, he thought irritably, all the light will be gone. But Ruth was in his service, and so she was also his responsibility.

The maid was moaning, and when she saw the doctor she was startled—he had never ventured belowstairs before. Until now, he had not seen her as a person, just as an appendage to help Rachel. This afternoon, however, he noted that Ruth's breasts bulged, that she had a lusty figure and regular features.

She cried out that the Master must not examine her, it wasn't seemly.

He ignored that and asked her, "How old are you, Ruth?"

"Twenty-eight," she whimpered. "My body has swollen to excess, sir. But I'm not pregnant, although if I were married I would want to be. Perhaps I have the vapours."

Most of her symptoms suggested pregnancy, yet doubt remained in his mind. He ordered the others out of her room, and then he examined her belly. There was the bulge that indicated that the woman was pregnant, but he still wasn't satisfied. Next he put his hand there, and nothing stirred. Then he heard her stomach rumble. Good God—he smiled to himself—it is her vapours. Part of her yearned to be with child, and so she had felt the symptoms of a pregnant woman, yet another part of her knew she wasn't, for she was muttering, "I'm still virginal."

Elizabeth, aroused by the commotion, rushed in and stated passionately, "I always said these girls are not to be trusted. This slut must go!"

"Why?" he asked, annoyed by her interference and her views.

"She is pregnant. A physician who examines servants is a fool."

"You are interrupting me. Keep out of this. You have no knowledge of physic, only ignorance, and you must not go busybodying in affairs you do not understand. This girl is ill, not pregnant."

"You can't fool me. She should be put out this instant. The whore."

"Ruth will stay here. Now go back to your own bed, where you belong. Before I lose my temper. All she has is a bellyache."

She almost spit in her rage, but she obeyed him and left.

Ruth sobbed, "Sir, my stomach swells, yet I eat virtually nothing."

"Because your flesh desired to be pregnant, it took on some of those symptoms. But your spirit was troubled by this, for it knew this was a delusion, and so your agitation caused your stomach to swell. Once you ease your mind and accept your true condition, you will recover. I will give you a preparation which will lessen your vapours."

She nodded, but her face was still so contorted with

anguish he wasn't sure that he had eased her or whether she was less tormented or more.

It was dark by the time he was able to return to his notes. He had begun them excitedly, for he had new comments to record, but now he felt so exhausted he doubted they would make sense. He had asked Silas to bring him extra candles, for he expected to work late into the night. He had done this deliberately, to give Silas more to do and to lessen Rachel's possessiveness. But as he waited, he wondered if she would come to him at all this night. When he had turned to Silas for his request, she had flushed angrily and walked away.

So he tried to forget her as Silas brought him a large store of candles. He told himself, He didn't wish to purchase anybody's love, not even Rachel's; to do so was to bribe, to have what had no true value.

Nothing came from his pen the first hour he sat, and he was stricken with sadness at the thought of Rachel not being there, of how empty his life would be without her; he was charmed by the pertness of her walk, her smile, her wish to be with him always; she enjoyed his company whatever he did, and perhaps that was what it meant to be in love.

Annoyed with himself—he rarely permitted anything to distract him—he opened the window and walked about his chamber in his shirt until he was cool and wide awake. Then he began to work on his notes again.

"*W-I. Most hearts weigh a little less than three-quarters of a pound. But my father's was larger and weighed more. It beat about 42 million times a year. And since he lived to the age of seventy-four and his pulse rate was a normal 72 beats a minute, his heart beat over three billion times during the span of his existence. It provided a change of blood about once every minute and moved at least 250 million quarts of blood during his lifetime. Yet, I hold it to be true now, there were only about six quarts of blood in his body, as in the average human body.*"

If his father was typical, and the evidence indicated he was, this verified that the heart was a pump and it pumped blood in a continuous flow. Grateful for what his father had taught him, he reviewed what happened when he compressed the artery leading from the heart.

"*W-I. The artery between the point of compression and the heart becomes distended with blood. When this is relieved, the artery dilates. This is caused by the contraction of the heart which discharges blood into it. And as this organ dilates, it draws blood into the cavity from the veins. So we must view the heart as a muscular sac, contracting and driving out the blood, expanding and sucking the blood in.*"

His elation ceased as he realized he wasn't sure. He was wide awake now, although it was midnight, for he believed he was on the right course after all. His new conclusions convinced him that the blood did return to the heart through the veins. He decided to trace the path from the veins to the arteries. That link should be more discernible than the one bridging the gap between arteries and veins. He turned to notes that were relevant.

"*W-I. I have, in a recently strangled cadaver within two hours from its hanging, opened up the chest and pericardium (before the redness of the face had disappeared) and demonstrated the right auricle of the heart much distended and infarcted with blood, this auricle swelling to the size of a man's large fist so that you would think it would burst.*"

No longer feeling as if he were talking only to himself, he said aloud, as if to answer his critics: "*This proves that the blood must be continually moving somewhere, otherwise the system would burst or choke the heart by distending it.*" His own heart seemed to beat faster with excitement, and he felt he spoke to Hippocrates, Aristotle, and Galen. "*This dissection should convince the doubters the blood does return to the heart from the veins and into the right auricle. From there, it goes into the right ventricle and as this vessel contracts, it forces the blood into the artery-like vein and*

355

towards the lungs." He paused, recalling that Galen had taught that the septum allowed blood to ooze through it from one side of the heart to the other. "*But damn,*" he cried aloud, arguing with this ancient authority. "*There are no pores and this is impossible!*"

He wrote with intensity, as if fate pushed his hand:

"*Galen's theories are incongruous, obscure, and impossible. In man the blood definitely goes from the right ventricle of the heart through the artery-like veins into the lungs. Then it moves from there through the vein-like artery into the left auricle and then into the left ventricle, which contracts and sends blood out to the arteries.*"

Relieved, as if he had lifted a heavy burden off his mind, he thought, *The heart is a simple and beautiful place. The auricles act as collecting chambers. The ventricles act as pumps. It is the right side of the heart which gathers the returning blood from the veins and forces it through the lungs. It is the left side which takes the blood from the lungs and pumps it, refreshed and purified, into the rest of the body.*

Suddenly he felt guilty. He had forgotten to sign his name to his last set of notes. Or perhaps, he thought, I have been afraid.

He wrote "*W-I*" at the end with an especially dominant flourish.

The night no longer was long or hard, and although he was disappointed that Rachel didn't appear, when he went to bed he slept as soundly as he had for many weeks. Whatever the heart was for others, it was a wonderful thing for him, and, in his new view, a superb and remarkable creation.

The next day Rachel told him that Ruth had fled. This proved to her that the maid was incontinent, a judgement his wife shared. He didn't agree with them, but he didn't argue; he felt this was futile, and he asked Silas what had happened to Ruth and where had she gone.

"Probably to the dungheaps of London, sir. The women made her feel shame, and that drove her out. Too bad. No doctor will look at her now."

His notes were interrupted by a summons from Mayerne. It was a week later; Rachel had hired a new maid, but she had stayed away from him.

He was surprised that he was asked to attend Donne. The Dean liked his doctor, Simeon Fox, the youngest son of John Fox, the author of the *Book of Martyrs*, the most widely read work in the kingdom.

What surprised him even more when he arrived at the Deanery was to find Donne acting as his own doctor. Although Fox and Mayerne were at his side and he looked ghastly, he ignored their attentions, sitting upright in bed and busily putting pen to paper with passion.

William asked Mayerne, who drew him aside to discuss the situation, for there seemed no point to his examining Donne, "Why did you summon me?"

"I want your support. Donne respects your views. He is intrigued by your experiments with the blood, and he is inclined to agree with you."

"Not that I do," said Fox, "but John has a vivid imagination, and your ideas indulge it." The sober, stocky doctor, who was in his forties, had joined them so they couldn't conspire against him. "He is quite sick."

"He looks dreadful," said William. "As if he prepares for the grave."

Before they could discuss the patient further, he ordered them to come to his side. He desired to speak to them. Donne sat as straight and stiff as a ramrod against his pillows, although William noted that he was as thin as a scarecrow and his features were sunken. He stated, "I am using this leisure to put in order the holy meditations I have had about my illness, so I can use these devotions in the service of God."

357

Fox protested, "You are still very ill. You could have a relapse."

"Composing my *Devotions?* They are no strain, but a great relief."

William said, "Even so, now that I'm here I should examine you."

"I've been examined often lately. I know what is wrong with me."

"I don't. However, if you don't desire my services, I will go. I have many patients who do need them."

Donne realised that Harvey meant exactly what he said and replied, "Be as thorough as you wish." After all, he thought, if I desire to discuss the experience of my illness with Harvey, I must acknowledge that the man is an observant physician—that is why I called him.

William examined Donne with great care. Then he took Fox and Mayerne into a corner where the Dean couldn't hear him and said, "Most of the symptoms indicate a severe fever. But he appears over the worst now, and seems to be on the way to recovery."

Fox said, "John is out of danger if he heeds my advice."

Mayerne added, "I'm not sure that is enough. He should be allowed to work, it is possible such an involvement may help him more than any medicine. Then, at least, he will be at peace with himself."

Fox whispered, "John will never achieve that, it is not his nature."

Donne shouted, "Have you decided when I am to die?"

Fox hurried to his side and said, "You have much life left in you."

Mayerne added, "If you favour your flesh and do not scourge it."

When William didn't comment, Donne turned to him and declared, "You don't share their views, do you? You are more pessimistic."

"Not if you take better care of yourself. Worry less, rest more."

358

"I have much to do, and little time to do it."

"That is still no reason to overwork," William reminded Donne.

"I have a scattered flock of wretched children, and I must sustain them as long as my infirm and aged body permits."

"Then how can we take your body seriously when you don't? You violate its needs until it cannot serve you, yet you regard it as faithless."

"No, no, no! It is my body that has inspired these *Devotions*. It is true my preaching often exhausts me, but the King dislikes to hear of my poor health, it reminds him of his own. This time I have recorded an accurate account of my illness, so perhaps, like the ancient adage, '*Physician, Heal Thyself,*' I will accomplish this worthy end."

"You have failed," said Fox. "Not only did you have to call me," he added, aggrieved, "but you had to call Mayerne and Harvey, too."

"The King sent Mayerne on his own wish and as his own physician. And I respect Harvey. Now that I am convalescent, I have used my observations of my illness for my *Devotions*. The first part, *Meditations*, is almost finished, and I want you to hear them. So you can tell me if they are as correct medically as they are spiritually."

William, Mayerne, and Fox listened intently as Donne read to them.

"*Variable and therefore miserable condition of man: one minute I was well, the next I am ill. I am surprised with the sudden change and can impute it to no cause, or call it by any name. But I can scarcely see, my taste is insipid, my appetite dull, my knees weak, I take to my bed, I call my physician, I observe in him the same diligence as the disease. I see that he fears; I fear the more because he disguises his fear. I see it with more sharpness because he would not have me see it. Then he desires another opinion. Upon their consultation they prescribe cordials to keep the venom and malignity of the disease from my heart. They apply dead pigeons to my feet to draw the vapours from my head.*"

William wanted to interrupt him, upset by such a mediaeval remedy, but Donne, enraptured by his words, rushed on solemnly yet passionately.

"What will not kill a man if a vapour will? What have I done to breed these vapours? I do nothing upon myself, and yet am mine own executioner."

He paused, faint for a moment, then spoke more slowly and emphatically.

"The sickness declares the infection and malignity thereof by spots. The Doctors observe these accidents to have fallen upon critical days. I sleep not day or night. From the bells of the church adjoining, I am daily reminded of my burial in the funeral of others. Now this bell tolling softly for another, says to me, 'Thou must die.' Perchance he for whom this bell tolls, may he be so ill, as that he knows not it tolls for him."

Donne was losing what little vigour he had, but he avoided their advice to halt. Either way, he thought, I will be dead soon, and he resumed:

"The bell tolls for him that thinks it does. Who can remove himself from that hell which is passing a piece of himself out of this world. No man is an island, entire of himself; every man is a piece of the Continent, a part of the main; if a clod is washed away by the sea, Europe is the less. Any man's death diminishes me, because I am involved in mankind. Therefore never send to know for whom the bell tolls, it tolls for thee."

Donne's brief flurry of strength was gone, and he sat hunched over in his bed, and Fox reminded him, "John, you are not dead. You are better."

"For the moment."

"For a reasonable time, if you listen to me. You must build up your strength and put flesh on your bones by drinking milk for twenty days."

"I dislike milk passionately. It curdles my stomach."

"Try it for ten days. It could add years to your life."

Mayerne said, "Dean, I agree with Dr. Fox. And you must work less."

Donne turned to William and asked, "Do you favour milk, too?"

"I favour whatever will nourish you. Thank you very much for granting us the privilege of hearing your *Devotions*. I will remember them."

"I always prefer my words spoken. It was one of Will Shakespeare's virtues. I must get better so that I can preach what I have written."

No one replied, as if the gravity of his *Devotions* reminded them of their own mortality.

As William started to go, Donne said, "Harvey, you are the only one who hasn't offered a cure. Is it because you think this is impossible?"

Donne is preoccupied with illness and death, thought William, but his eloquence should be treasured. "Sir, you spend too much time in study and prayer, omitting all exercise. It is no wonder that you have fallen into a great sickness. You must take moderate walks for exercise and renew cheerful conversation. In my practice of physic, more people die of grief than of any other disease. It is your studious and sedentary life that causes you to contract frequent illness. Follow these instructions and you could lengthen your life beyond your present expectations."

"Have your investigations of the blood led you to any new learning?"

"Recent experiments have reiterated to me that the veins return the blood to the heart and the arteries take it out."

Mayerne said, "Harvey, why don't you propose your views to the College and find out what our estimable Fellows think?"

"What do you think?"

"I'm inclined in your direction, but I would prefer more proof."

William turned to Donne for his view, and he said, "I share Mayerne's position. You may be right, but it would be helpful if you produced more evidence. You feel as strongly about the heart as I do about the gates of heaven. Your passion is commendable. And thank you for your services." The Dean sighed with relief. Now that he had expressed his emotion through his *Devotions,* he felt much better, for he would not die barren.

It was the blood in Donne's veins that prevented a relapse. William came to this conclusion when the Dean continued to recover. While he had no proof, he felt that the passage of the blood had driven out the disease whose infection had been manifested by the fever. He also reflected on Donne's words so he could relate them to his own work, and he wrote: "No heart is an island, entire of itself; every heart is a piece of the Continent, a part of the main. Each pulse that tolls, tolls for me."

He was less satisfied with Rachel. Since her quarrel with Silas and his treatment of Ruth, she had avoided his laboratory and bed. She did her household duties carefully and regarded him with a frozen face. He felt that she was perverse, and he was lonely and unhappy without her, but he was determined not to be the first to give in.

He sought to confirm his suppositions about the veins so that he could present them, with the proper proof, at his next Lumleian Lecture. He was determined to avoid any errors, and he felt that the secret of the veins depended on the nature of their valves. They had fascinated him ever since Fabricius had revealed their existence to him in Padua. He reviewed what he knew about them, and his renewed interest in the valves clarified his thinking about them, and he came to the following conclusions:

"*W-I. The valves in the veins of many parts of the body are so placed that they give free passage to the blood towards the heart, but oppose the movement of the venal blood the contrary way. Thus, it is logical to believe that the blood is*

sent out through the arteries and returns in the veins, whose valves encourage its course in such a manner."
Now that Rachel no longer read his notes, he wrote them in Latin.

His enthusiasm dwindled as he prepared to present these views to his colleagues at the College. It was a month later, a grey afternoon in January, and as he arranged his Lumleian Lecture, the elements weighed on him like an oppressive burden. He had heard much criticism in advance.

As he entered the anatomy theatre and he saw that Woodall had put everything in order, he had to proceed. On his instructions, the cadaver was recently executed, a thirty-year-old man in good health, with the neck broken so there would be sufficient blood. The circle around him was confining, and the physicians' faces seemed to hover over him like a ghostly jury. The chamber was crowded and in the gloomy light it was as if they were about to impeach him and convict him of heresy. He was ill at ease; he saw no encouragement in any of them. Even Mayerne, who sat in the front row, appeared more curious than believing, and everyone else looked sceptical. Yet he couldn't halt—that would betray him. He put his rod on the valves that Woodall's surgery had exposed and said, "These cusps of the valves of the vein exist to stop the backflow of the blood."

"What happens then?" Wilkins demanded.

"The blood returns to the heart," he replied.

Scrope said, "Then you insist that Galen is wrong?"

"That is possible."

"But you are not sure."

"As these valves of the veins are constructed, there is no alternative."

"But you are not sure." This time it was Fox who repeated the query.

So the fact that Donne gave me more attention has offended his personal physician, he thought sadly, but he tried to reply impersonally. "Doctor, if the direction of the blood in the veins is interrupted, the valves become distended, abnormal, strained."

Wilkins declared, "Harvey's practices bring the College into disrepute. We must halt such heresies."

Woodall stopped dissecting, and William shouted angrily, "Don't you understand anything? *Is man nothing but a great, mischievous baboon?*"

Scrope yelled back, "You are impious!"

He stepped forward to halt any further demonstration, and William, irate enough to use the dagger at his side, clutched his colleague and pulled him to the side of the table. Grimly, while everyone was too stunned to stop him, he declared, "I will demonstrate. Scrope is lean enough, his veins are large enough, and they stand out. He is an excellent subject."

Scrope was amazed by Harvey's strength, and stood as if paralysed.

William examined him and added, "Good. You have been active. Your blood is moving fast, and your valves are like knots. They are working."

He bandaged Scrope's arm, and he placed the forearm on the table and pressed the vein with his thumb so that he milked the vein in the direction of the heart until he had pushed it beyond the next valve. Then he paused and pointed out that the emptied vein remained empty. "You see. The blood does not slip back. The valves prevent that. The blood has to flow forward, to the heart."

"You flout our authority," said Wilkins. He strode out of the anatomy theatre, and many of the doctors followed him. But William noticed with gratitude that Mayerne stayed, and Matthew and Scrope, and several others. Yet he felt there was no true acceptance of his views. Matthew said he was persuasive but that proof was still lacking; Mayerne praised his ingenuity in contriving an intriguing answer; Scrope regarded him with wonder, as if he were a magician.

This is nonsense, he thought wryly. In repeating this experiment he had convinced himself that he was right about the veins and the valves.

When he returned to his laboratory late that night after dining at the Cock and Bull Ordinary with his friends, he was intoxicated. They had drunk copiously, and while he doubted they would support him publicly, Mayerne and Scrope had drunk several toasts to his work.

He glanced at his desk—before he went to bed he always made sure his notes were in order—and suddenly he was sober. Under his recent notes was written: "I do not understand them. Please do them in English."

It was Rachel's handwriting; he knew it too well to be mistaken. He was joyful. She had missed him as much as he had missed her. And while he had come home with no intention of writing any notes, he had to reply.

"W-I. Convinced again when veins are tied it proves they carry blood toward the heart and are a vital link in the circular passage."

He wrote in English so that Rachel could read it.

At their reconciliation a week later, they didn't discuss their separation, but sought to make it a happy occasion. After he had expressed his love and she had responded passionately, she lay in his arms and asked, "When do you intend to publish your conclusions?"

She looked so youthful tonight he found it difficult to believe that she was past forty. Her colour was high, her skin smooth, and her face had lost its recent tautness. He realized that he had known her more than twenty-five years, yet she still retained her freshness.

"William, you seem almost convinced that your views are correct."

"Almost. But not quite."

She wondered if he was afraid to send them forth for the world's appraisal. Certainly, she thought, he is not too old or weak to face criticism. He is in his prime; he takes excellent care of himself, and follows the advice he gives his patients, except in his passion for work.

He said, "While I'm convinced there are links between the arteries and the veins, I still haven't been able to prove that."

"I believe you," she said, and kissed him. "Do you need more paper?"

"What for?" He was in no mood to work. Her warm body was inviting, and he leaned towards her to embrace her, but she was talking.

"You should put down what is in your mind. I'm sure it is useful."

"You are more eager that I publish than I am."

"I don't understand everything you tell me, but I know that it is remarkable. You should publish. As soon as possible."

"I will when the time is ripe. I'm not sure James will approve, but Charles might. The Prince of Wales has a fancy for learning."

"William, you would wait until the King dies?" She was shocked.

"It might not be long. He fails daily. The more he seeks to keep up with Buckingham, who is half his age, the more he ails."

"Are you afraid of how your colleagues will receive your doctrine?"

"Not afraid," he retorted. "Just concerned."

"Enough physicians will support you. Besides, you are right."

"How can you be so sure? You only hear my side."

"If your views are logical to me, they will be to others."

Then he was her lover again, and she responded with a warmth that was even more intense than before.

The next day he was working with renewed vigour on his notes when she interrupted with a letter for him. Despite his feeling for her, he was annoyed; he felt he had found new evidence, and he read it to her.

"W-1. When I cut parallel arteries and veins it shows how the blood from the cut ends flows in different directions. Thus, they work . . ."

He halted, for this was as far as he had gone, and now he had forgotten what he had intended to write next. His annoyance grew, and he frowned.

"I'm sorry, I know how much a distraction can distress you, but this letter bears the royal arms. And a messenger waits below for a reply."

He took it unwillingly and perused it quickly. It was, as he had feared, a summons to attend the royal family—not the King, as he had expected, but Charles, the Prince of Wales—and a coach was waiting to convey him.

At Whitehall Palace he was admitted into the royal bed-chamber at once, and he was startled by what he saw. Charles, after a sickly childhood, had become healthy and, at twenty-four, was thought to be in the most vigourous part of his life. But now he lay in the huge four-poster bed, haggard and drawn. He was drenched with sweat, and shivering with a chill.

William realized the situation might be serious, yet there was no sign of the King or of Mayerne, the senior doctor at Court. He did see Matthew, Elsingham, and Moore, who were Physicians in Ordinary, but he didn't respect the last two. The elderly Elsingham, who had been personal physician to James, resented that Mayerne had supplanted him in the King's regard, while the younger, pedantic Moore prescribed by the book and his astrologer.

He asked Matthew, "What are the symptoms?"

"A severe fever. Charles requested your services. I have told him how highly I think of you, and since no one else had been able to ease him, the Prince of Wales thought you might. As you did his father."

"Where is the King?"

"Hunting at Windsor with Buckingham. Although he is in no condition to endure the saddle. But he is determined to express his virility where he shines. Mayerne is with him, should a physician be needed."

Elsingham interrupted, "I am responsible for the Prince. I have bled and purged him. The vapours press on his stomach and must be released."

"The stars are unfavourable," said Moore. "It is no wonder he ails."

Matthew said, "Charles has grown worse. William, examine him."

As he approached Charles, he heard Elsingham and Moore say scornfully to each other, "This quack will never cure him. *Circulator.*"

This reminded him that they had been at his Lumleian Lecture and that they had walked out with Wilkins. Then he ignored them as he examined the patient. Some of his symptoms resembled Donne's, and he followed the same procedure while Charles murmured, "My head burns."

"I know, Your Highness," William replied. "It is your fever. Our first task is to lessen it. You must drink plenty of warm potions and swallow an opiate which will enable you to sleep. Rest is essential."

Matthew agreed, but Elsingham and Moore sought to demolish his remedy with their learning, warning Charles that Harvey was unreliable.

Charles hesitated, almost convinced by the intensity of their words; then he remembered that their remedies had made him feel worse. He gave William permission to prescribe, and when Elsingham and Moore continued to protest, he said, "The King ordered you to heed him. He cured my father."

Elsingham replied, "Sir, how could he? This doctor has dared to differ with Aristotle and Galen. Such a man is not to be trusted—"

"Sir, William cut in, "it is not incantations or secret potions or astrology that you need, but care and medication. Were you exposed to rain or chill lately, especially when you were exhausted?"

"Yes!" exclaimed Charles. "I caught a chill after I rode all day in the rain at Windsor." He didn't add that he had done this to prove to Buckingham, whose affection he craved, that he could outdo his father. Perhaps Harvey is a magician, as some say, he thought, there is a skill in him that is worth heeding. His mind made up, his voice took on a royal severity as he commanded, "Elsingham, Moore, do whatever Harvey recommends. I am prepared to try it."

They nodded humbly even as William felt their enmity grow.

William said, "Sir, you must avoid water for the moment and drink warm wine. The water supply of the palace is liable to pollution and may have infected you. And you will recover sooner if you can leave London. At the moment the air of the city is dangerous for your condition. The fog, the rain, the smoke from the fires form a humid and harsh element that fills the air with heavy particles that damage your health. You should convalesce at Windsor, where the breathing is much better."

Charles liked the idea even as he wasn't certain about the cure.

"Most of all, you must perspire. But under the proper conditions. When you travel, keep warm and dry. Then, as soon as you are in your bedchamber of the castle, have a hot fire and wrap yourself in blankets so that the heat will force the poisons out of your body, sir. And there you will have the services of Mayerne, who is just the man you need."

"What about yourself, Harvey?"

"Sir, you won't need me then." Good God, he thought, I don't want to desert my notes now. "When your chill goes and you stop sweating, walk in your gardens when the weather isn't foul and keep dry and warm."

Elsingham acted as if Harvey were mad, but Charles liked the idea of Windsor—he loved the castle and the hunting park—and already the thought of being there and away from dreary London had lifted his spirits.

"Of course," the Prince of Wales said, "I will do what you suggest."

Matthew added, "Sir, if I may, I could accompany you to Windsor to make certain that Dr. Harvey's instruction are properly supervised."

"Thank you, Ross. A fine idea. I know you are a virtuous doctor."

Matthew kept William informed of Charles's condition, and when he heard that the Prince of Wales was free of his fever and walking in his garden and about to hunt, he was not surprised. He wrote his friend that he was gratified, and he continued to push ahead with his work on *De motu cordis*.

He was absorbed by a new discovery. He was working on it in his laboratory when Rachel said, "You haven't eaten all day!"

"I beg your pardon."

"Aren't you listening? You know I don't interrupt unnecessarily."

"Rachel, you worry too much. The less I eat, the better."

"I'm concerned, not worried. Did the Prince of Wales express any appreciation of your cure? It is only a month since he was so ill."

"More than I expected. Ten pounds and a fine circular clock."

"Silas heard he was pleased with your treatment. When he becomes King, he could appoint you a Physician in Ordinary and his personal physician."

"I can't think of that now. I have something vital to tell you."

She expected it to be personal, and she was disappointed when he read from his notes, although she listened attentively, he was so passionate.

"*W-I. I have observed the first rudiments of the chick in the course of incubation, and in the midst of it there appeared a bloody point so small it disappeared during the contraction and escaped the sight, but in relaxation it reappeared and was red and like the point of a pin."*

She was puzzled and she said, "I don't understand what this means."

"This blood is forming the heart. The blood is thus, I believe, in itself, the first trace of life to appear. It is the difference between being and non-being. And represents the first sign and principle of life."

He was as excited as she had ever seen him, and so she nodded, although she still wasn't sure she knew what he meant.

He sensed this, and he exclaimed, "Rachel, I'm saying that if my facts are correct, and I am almost convinced they are, that life begins with the blood and the formation of the heart."

She was awe-struck with the wonder of it and was silent, while he wrote:

"W-I. The red capering point, that is, the beginnings of the heart in the chick embryo causes me to conclude (against Aristotle) that the blood is the first Genital Particle, and that the Heart is its instrument designed for its circulation."

ury your hand in the sand
and walk away
How far
can you get from your hand
or man from man

Blood is the difference between being and non-being, it represents the first sign and principle of life, the first Genital principle.

371

This concept fascinated William, and he repeated it until it had become as vital to him as the heart itself. The more he reviewed this idea, the more it aroused him to further studies and experiments. Encouraged by his findings, by Rachel's help and support, by his explorations and discoveries, by his passion for fuller knowledge of the human body, he pushed on vigourously to complete the circuit of the blood. Several links in the chain were still missing, but he was convinced that if he pursued his course firmly and persistently he would find the answers he needed.

He put his views into *Exercitatio anatomica de motu cordis et sanguinis in animalibus.* He was determined to use this title, no matter what anyone else said.

This book took definite shape during 1624, and the year was spent planning it. Each month was measured by how much work he did on it, and by 1625 he felt that a published work was possible; most of the chain of the circulation seemed sound, even though he hadn't found a link between the arteries and the veins.

But when Rachel, who aided him frequently these days, asked, "When do you intend to publish your book?" he shrugged and replied, "Soon."

He was sitting at the dinner table—Elizabeth was visiting Galen in Cambridge—and she was serving him instead of Silas, who had escorted his wife in their coach, while the other servants were busy elsewhere.

She thought that any time in the next few years would be soon enough for him, and she wasn't sure she could wait. Now it was a strain to climb the stairs to the laboratory, and often it left her breathless. But she tried to move energetically when William was about. He didn't like weakness, and she didn't want him to suspect that anything could be wrong with her.

Then he looked troubled, and she asked, "What is upsetting you?"

"I will have to write in Latin. Or no physician will read it."

That is a small price to pay for its being published, she decided, and she replied, "I assumed you would. It must be a learned work."

"I want it to be so clear that any doctor can understand it."

"Even your brother-in-law, Galen?"

He smiled and said, "I would like him to learn too."

"You are wasting your time there." Rachel sat down at the table.

This was unusual, and he asked, "Don't you feel well?"

"Just tired. With Silas away, I have more work to do than usual. Your wife seems to fancy Silas's services lately. I wonder why."

"Perhaps she desires his regard, too. She is not utterly devoid of feeling. Would you like part of the roast chicken? You like the wing."

"I should eat with you?" Rachel looked shocked.

"Isn't that what you wish?"

"Not this way." She felt a sudden stab of pain in her chest, but she disregarded it; she had no intention of seeing a doctor, least of all him; she was resolved to keep out of bed. "You look contemplative."

He stood up, put his arms around her joyfully, and exclaimed, "I have just had a fine idea. I should have thought of it sooner."

"You have found the bridge between the arteries and the veins."

"No. My magnifying glass isn't strong enough. Rachel, I must invite my friends who can advise me how to publish *De motu cordis*. Mayerne, John Hall, Matthew, my brothers Eliab and John, Ben Jonson, and maybe Inigo Jones. All of them have been published or know something about it."

"Your wife will want you to invite her brother."

"Why not? He may have some ideas."

She shook her head in disapproval, but she didn't say anything.

He hesitated. Rachel's fragile features were pale and taut, and he saw lines that he had never seen before. He asked, "Are you sure that you can supervise such a party? Do you have enough strength and servants?"

I must find the strength, she thought, publication is too vital to be hindered by any weakness on my part. She nodded energetically.

"I hope it is sensible to write my findings in Latin. While it is regarded as the best tongue for learning, I'm more at home in English."

While she prepared for the party and he sent the invitations, he was asked by Bacon to attend him in a new illness. Bacon had been pardoned by the King, but only after a desperate struggle to keep his beloved York House out of the covetous hands of Buckingham had failed and he had been forced to sell it. Now he was staying in his old rooms at Gray's Inn.

William was ushered into the study—and not the bedchamber, as he had expected—by a footman in a splendid livery. It was a richly furnished room, and Bacon sat at a desk, writing. But William observed that he had aged, and sat with one foot in a small tub of steam water.

Bacon continued to write until he was finished with what he was doing. Then he addressed William. *"Much can be learned by careful recording of the anatomies of defunct patients. Do your eyes ever blur from overwork?"*

"Occasionally, sir. What is your complaint?"

"I have lived much of my life here. My father possessed these chambers before me. I inherited them from him when I was eighteen. When I thought the law was mine to own and the world would move in my direction. How confusing is time. I was happy then. Now the future is forsaken."

William wondered why he was there—there was such a

natural and inevitable antipathy between them. Yet, while he doubted that Bacon would agree with him, he had written in his notes: "*W-I. I cured him.*"

Ghosts appeared in Bacon's mind: Elizabeth the Queen, Lord Essex, his cousin, Cecil, Raleigh. Friends, he reflected, who were enemies in their failure to advance me as high as I had expected; I, who have been one of the great minds in the realm, perhaps the greatest, as my work shows.

Tired of waiting, William turned to go, but now Bacon halted him.

"I am not well, Harvey. I suffer from many complaints."

"What is the nature of your pain, My Lord?"

"My head throbs, my eyes grow dull with use."

"What about your foot? It looks swollen."

"*It is an attack of the gout that I take pleasure in treating myself.*"

"Sir, I would use a different remedy."

"*No. My remedies usually drive away the gout within twenty-four hours.*"

"Then why have you summoned me, sir?"

"I have a tender constitution and suffer much from colds."

"It is no wonder." William motioned to the windows, which were wide open, although it was February and bitterly cold, and shut them. When Bacon protested, he added, "My Lord, you were sitting in a draft. That is why you catch so many chills and have frequent colds."

"But if I don't have fresh air I will die of suffocation."

"It is not likely, sir. And the dampness outside makes you worse."

"Harvey, I like the snow. It has a purity that I admire."

"No doubt, and at your age, My Lord, it could kill you. And now, if you will excuse me, since you have cured yourself."

"Wait! Heaven help us if two learned men like ourselves quarrel. I hear you are considering issuing a report that the blood circulates."

"Who told you, sir?"

"Our friend, Donne. Do not argue narrowly. As Galileo has done."

"I studied with him, sir. He didn't share your regard for Aristotle."

"Unfortunately. He stops with just a few discoveries, when he should relate them to all learning. He is not universal enough for my taste."

"Galileo has proven that his support of Copernicus is correct, sir."

"Not actually. You must not use this astronomer as an authority or express views that are incompatible with those held by Aristotle or Galen."

William changed the subject, thinking, If he couldn't help Bacon, perhaps Bacon could help him. "Sir, I hear you publish much these days."

"Indeed. One book after another. When my poor health permits."

"Sir, it is the custom to publish in Latin, but I prefer English."

"No learned man should. English is too private a tongue, excluding many readers, it cannot endure as a literary language. I publish in Latin, which makes my books citizens of the world, as English books are not."

Bacon listed the remedies he used, to prove that his knowledge of physic surpassed Harvey's. William marvelled that Bacon was still alive after the purgings, bleedings, and drugs he had given himself. As he expressed his prodigious learning, he forgot his gout and the tub of water, which was cold now. And as William bowed out, he realized that his patient had not asked him one question about his own work, or mentioned the money owed him for his medical fees, although Bacon still lived sumptuously.

Rachel ignored her fatigue and uncertain health as she supervised the other servants while they waited on the guests at the party. She thought, It was a group proper for William to have invited: Dean Donne, his friend, Christopher Brooke, Dr. Matthew Ross, Dr. John Hall, Dr. Galen Browne—the only one of whom she disapproved—Ben Jonson, and Eliab and John Harvey. Dr. Mayerne was abroad, and Inigo Jones had declined on the grounds of poor health, but actually, William informed her, because of Ben Jonson's presence.

She was annoyed that no women were present except his wife, but when she called this to his attention, he replied, "The wives aren't interested in our views," but she felt this was unfair, although it was customary.

Good food and drink are a solace, William reflected; it is the one need everyone has in common. Silas took their capes, hats, and walking sticks and served with skill, yet when he brought in coffee, which had become William's favourite beverage, not everybody agreed with his taste.

Galen had never heard of it, and he didn't like its smell.

Eliab said, "It is new in England, but common in Turkey. My four brothers who are merchants in the City of London have begun to import it. So far, it has been almost impossible to sell, people are afraid of it, but William likes it so much he calls it *Milord Coffee.*"

William added, "While it is not in general use, it will be some day. I find that this drink comforts the brain and the heart and helps digestion. I drink it daily now."

"No one else does," said Matthew, "it is too strange a drink."

After the guests were served a drink they preferred, they settled around the oak table to chat. A large fire warmed the dining room, which was illuminated by great, wide candles. Rachel had seen to every detail with care and ability, and he was proud of her. Then she retired to the kitchen to manage the cleaning, and his wife was the only woman in the room, a privilege accorded her as the wife of the host.

Everybody spoke at once until Galen said loudly, "William, I hear that you are publishing your views on the blood."

William asked, "How did you find out?"

"Elizabeth told me. Why else would you invite all of us?"

"You are my friends. It is natural that I would ask your advice."

Donne said, "I presume you advocate that the blood circulates."

"Yes."

No one spoke for a minute, and then Matthew asked, "Are you serious?"

"As serious as you are when you treat the royal family."

"That is different. You are a fine anatomist with great manual dexterity, you are Professor of Anatomy at the College, you are principal physician at St. Bart's, and consultant physician to many noble Lords, but if you go ahead with your mad plans to publish, all this could vanish."

"Perhaps," said William. "Dr. Donne, who published your *Devotions?*"

"The Church authorities. They were entered in the Stationer's register by the printer and read and approved by the official licenser. But while I incline towards your views, you will not be able to get Church approval."

William turned to John Hall and said, "I observed that your father-in-law's plays appeared in print recently. How was that done?"

"This folio of Will's plays was published by Heminge and Condell, who were his colleagues, but Jonson knows more about this matter than I do."

Jonson said, "I added my appreciation. It helped the publication."

"What about the actual publication of the plays?" William asked.

"Indifferently, in my view. My collected works were published in a thousand-page edition by William Stansby, a prominent London printer."

"Do you think he would consider my work?"

"He only publishes plays and romances. And you will need approval."

Matthew said, "I don't think you will find a London publisher."

Galen said, "Possibly the College of Physicians will publish you."

William felt Galen was being spiteful, but he asked Matthew about that.

"It embarrasses me to tell you, but you remember what happened to Crooke. And your work is more scandalous."

"So I am an heretic because I do not hold with all the old views, but write about the blood as it is."

Eliab was unhappy at his brother's distress. William's spare face had grown grim as Brooke said, "Dr. Harvey, I dislike offering an adverse opinion on a work I have not read, but from what your friends say, I must caution you. Booksellers will not sell an unauthorised work, and you, without the licensing privilege, will be summoned to appear in court for libellous statements, and the punishment is harsh."

"But there cannot be any libel against the dead."

"You still must be licensed by the Censor and the Stationer's office."

"Then the privilege of those people is a very great hindrance to the advancement of learning," William said angrily.

Eliab, no longer able to endure his brother's unhappiness, cried out, "I will support you. And you will too, John, won't you?"

John wavered, and then, remembering his father's credo that the family must support one another, he nodded, although slowly and reluctantly.

"Thank you, Eliab, John. But I must bear the responsibility. I will find a publisher. When I finish the work. Then I will have time to look."

Donne said regretfully, "I wish your views weren't so revolutionary."

William was surprised. He said, "They are simply the truth as I see it."

Now, however, Jonson was more interested—he liked a

good quarrel as much as any man—and he stated that he would try to find a publisher.

A new argument broke out over whether it was better to submit the book in English or Latin, until William cut in, pleading, "For the sake of our digestions, please, let's change the subject. Bacon prefers Latin."

A few days later, deep in *De motu cordis*, he was interrupted by Rachel with the news that he was wanted at Court. "When?" he asked angrily.

"Now! The summons is urgent and comes from the Lord Steward himself! The King has fallen gravely ill, and he has been taken to Hampton Court, and the messenger says that no excuse will be accepted. Please be careful. If the King dies after consulting you, you could suffer."

The ride to Richmond took a long time, and Matthew greeted him anxiously, saying, "The King needs all the medical attention he can get."

Thus, William expected to examine James immediately. Instead, as he started towards the huge bed in which lay the King, Matthew halted him.

"You must wait your turn. James consults a different doctor in turn, and when they do not ease him, he has the next one examine him."

"But everything indicates that his condition is desperate. Where is Mayerne? He knows James's ailments better than anybody else."

"He is abroad. He will not be back for months."

"What do you think is wrong?"

"James has so many ailments, it is hard to know which is the worst."

William knew James feared crowds almost as much as he feared death, and realised that he must be very sick to permit so many doctors to attend him. There were a dozen in the royal bedchamber.

At the moment James was consulting Elsingham, his former favourite.

William heard Elsingham say, "Your Majesty, your condition is quite complicated. But most of the doctors agree with me. I will cure you." He gave James barley water, absinthe, and anise, and assured him this would end his ague, but the King shivered violently and dismissed Elsingham.

The pedantic Moore was startled and astonished that the King was concerned about his health. "True, sir, it is a sickly season, but your stars have improved, and I will pray for you devoutly and earnestly."

The King was more interested in Craige's remedy, for he was a Scot, and a Scot should be trustworthy. He applied pigeon dung to James's feet and stated that would ease the difficulties in his legs.

Then the royal apothecary had to be rushed in to give the patient perfume and rosewater, for the stench of the dung made the King faint and weak.

The next doctor to examine the King, the elderly Bedwin, said, "The old have more ailments than the young," which upset the already distraught James, and he dismissed this physician abruptly.

Then he saw William waiting, and he cried out, "Harvey, examine me! You have eased me before, and you helped my son."

William thought that James looked awful; the King had aged years in the last few months. And after he examined him, he was convinced that the King had caught a severe chill from exposure, which had been made worse by his low spirits and his other ailments. There were signs of a urinary infection and a possible stone, and evidence of a general debility of his entire system. He felt that there was nothing that could be done to cure the King. The only thing left was to make James comfortable.

James asked, "Is it critical?" Harvey was frowning.

If he told the King the truth, it would only make matters worse.

James sobbed, "I fear that I shall never see London again."

William said, "Sir, you are depressed. It is natural with a chill."

"A tertian ague, Matthew Ross told me. I was right never to trust doctors. There is too much gloom. Bring me fruit. It makes me cheerful."

But his greed for fruit had worsened his condition, William had heard, and he said. "Sir, fruit is contrary to the needs of your digestion."

"Then where is Steenie? He will know what to do. He loves me."

This outburst was too much for James's feeble body, and, greatly stricken by his favourite's absence, he fell back, inert. The Earl of Warwick, who was the ranking nobleman in attendance, ordered the doctors to retire to quarters that had been prepared for them and to await a further summons.

The next morning all the doctors were ordered to the bedside of the King, but William refused to struggle with them for the King's attention. James wasn't listening to any doctor, but asking for Steenie, and only when he was told that Buckingham was on the way did he feel better.

Even with this moment of improvement, William thought that James had grown worse overnight. But he realised that none of the other doctors would say that. They believed that so long as they did nothing, they could not be blamed. He tried to place himself so he could point out that there were specific remedies that would ease the patient's pain, but he was ignored. Missing his studies very much, he asked the Earl of Warwick for permission to return to London, and it was given, since now James asked only for Buckingham.

Matthew told him that to leave would end whatever opportunity William had to become a Physician in Ordinary, but he was so eager to return to a constructive situation that he brushed aside his friend's warning.

He had just turned on to the road to London when he was halted by the Lord Keeper of the Great Seal, John Williams, who was also the Bishop of Lincoln. The Bishop, who was coming to the sickbed of James to keep away the Church of Rome, exclaimed, "I am surprised that the King's own doctor, a Physician Extraordinary, is leaving in a time of crisis. When the King needs you most. His condition is critical."

"Your Grace, he doesn't need any of us. I serve no purpose now."

"You can advise me. I will need you to judge the King's ability to act. You are an honest physician."

William felt in an awkward position. The Bishop had succeeded Bacon as Lord Keeper, and he knew that the King heeded him more than he did anyone else, with the exception of Buckingham. So he turned back, in the hope that he might still be of some help to the King. But when they reached the bedside they found Buckingham and his domineering dowager mother had arrived and were attending James.

The King's spirits had lifted at the sight of his beloved Steenie. The Duke said that the Bishop would be useful for spiritual advice, but that he intended to cure the King with his own hands; he knew just the remedy.

Buckingham called Hayes, the King's surgeon, to apply a plaster after he gave James a special potion.

When Buckingham saw the doubt on the faces of the doctors, and even the Bishop and Warwick looked hesitant, although James appeared eager to try anything Steenie suggested, the Duke said, "I used it on myself."

But Buckingham is half the age of the almost senile King, thought William, and he wondered whether he should question these remedies.

The Duchess added, "I'm the same age as the King, and it cured me."

The Bishop turned to the doctors and asked them their opinion.

Two new physicians who had been called during the night, Chambers and Atkins, said nothing. Bedwin withdrew, refusing to commit himself, while Elsingham, Moore, Craige, and Matthew declared they couldn't assent.

Yet, William realised, no one has asked what the remedies contain.

The Bishop asked, "Harvey, what is your opinion?"

"What does the potion contain? That is the chief consideration."

Buckingham replied, "It is a white powder compounded of a mixture of milk and ale, hartshorn, and marigold flowers."

"A well-known potion, sirs. I doubt it will help."

"But it won't harm James," said the Duke, "and it could relieve him."

James's pain had grown, although he had felt better when Steenie had arrived, and that reminded him how happy his favourite's presence made him feel, and he cried out, "I desire it! Nothing else has helped me!"

Then, as the royal apothecary was called to administer the potion, the King muttered, "It pleases me that Steenie attends me."

Elsingham grumbled, "Sir, he is not skilled in physic. It is risky."

What is even more risky, reflected William, is for a doctor to commit himself—for when the Bishop asked them their views, none of them would say anything. Finally, he was asked if Buckingham was going too far, and he felt, James was so miserable and melancholy, anything which would ease his mind without damaging his body might be advisable. So, while he didn't approve, he didn't object. At the worst, he decided, it won't hurt the King; at the best, it might lessen his anguish and permit him to die more easily. He said, "Sirs, the ingredients of the potion are harmless."

Buckingham said, "If that little perpetual movement called Doctor Harvey, a most learned physician, assents, I am confirmed in my physic."

At the same time James called out, "Hurry, my gentle Steenie, before it is too late! I desire anything that you prescribe!"

So, while the other doctors stood in sullen silence, the King drank Buckingham's potion. Although William still did not have a high opinion of the white-powder mixture, which James had taken with a goblet of warm wine, he was pleased that the King fell asleep for four hours—the longest rest James had enjoyed in several days.

Meanwhile Buckingham commanded the physicians to remain while the Bishop sat by the King's bed. The Bishop, although he hadn't disputed the Duke's remedy, doubted that the King would live, and he was even more determined that his soul must be protected from the Church of Rome.

The next afternoon James was worse, and the Duke declared there was only one cure, a plaster that must be applied to the King's side. Elsingham said he couldn't assent; the majority of the physicians still in attendance supported him; the rest said nothing.

Buckingham turned to James, who was in such misery that he could hardly speak, and when the Duke said, "My dear James, I have had this plaster prepared for the express purpose of saving your life," the King asked piteously, "Steenie, will it give me any relief?"

"The application will remove your pain."

"Put it on. Quickly. Before I expire."

Buckingham ordered the King's surgeon to apply the plaster to James's side. As this was done Elsingham strode out of the sickroom, followed by Moore and Chambers. Matthew looked unhappy, as if he didn't approve but was afraid to say anything, while William felt ill at ease. He thought the plaster would soothe James but in the end alter nothing. And to protest would be futile, he realised, for James was determined to heed Steenie and only him. James muttered, "*I need no advice from doctors to take it. They are seldom necessary and support their physic by mere conjecture and uncertainty and are usually useless.*"

A little later the Prince of Wales was summoned to join the Bishop in the bedchamber, and now it was evident that the King was dying.

The air was filled with the sound of prayer, which the

Bishop led, followed by Charles, Buckingham, and Warwick. No physicians were consulted—as if finally, William thought, James's fatal sickness is realised. Late that day, just as night was coming, Charles and the Bishop knelt by the side of the King, who raised himself for a moment on his pillow, muttered, *"Veni, Domine Jesu,"* and then fell back on the sheets emblazoned with the royal coat of arms and died.

When William returned home he found two messages. One, from Ben Jonson, said he had been unable to find a London printer who would publish a book that suggested the blood circulated; they felt such an idea was heretical. The other message was from Galen, who said that Cambridge could not consider such a doctrine, it would create controversy and put the university into disrepute.

Elizabeth and Rachel were waiting for him in the dining room, and his housekeeper was helping Silas serve his wife. He sensed that this was merely an excuse to greet him as soon as his wife did, but he greeted Elizabeth first.

She was dressed in a plain black dress, and she said, "I am in mourning for our late King."

Rachel asked, "Doctor, were you consulted about his fatal illness?"

"Yes. So were many other doctors." Why was she so concerned?

"Sir, there are rumours that the Duke of Buckingham poisoned him."

"They are nonsense. The Duke's remedies didn't matter either way."

Elizabeth asked, "Girl, why are you so interested?"

"The doctor could lose much if he approved of the Duke's remedies."

"What business is that of yours?"

"I don't wish to work in a household afflicted with ill will."

"If he publishes his observations, he will arouse much more ill will."

386

William became tense. His wife regarded Rachel suspiciously, and he hurried to say, "Obviously, anyone in my household will be affected if my situation is. Elizabeth, the girl's concern is natural."

"Has your situation been affected?"

"Not that I know of. I was one of the physicians who performed the autopsy on James at the request of the new King, Charles. There was no doubt that he died of natural causes. The rumours of poison have been spread by people who hate Buckingham. He has many enemies."

"So do you," grumbled Elizabeth, and he saw Rachel nod in agreement behind her back. He longed to retort, "These fears are old women's fears." But they existed, and he decided he couldn't do anything about them; moreover, he had important matters to fight for, and so he was silent. "If you publish your views on the blood, you will lose your practice and your privileges, and could be tried for heresy."

"That is a chance I will have to take if I publish."

After he gulped down his dinner, only sipping his favourite coffee, for the longer he was away from his studies the more he missed them, he hurried up to his laboratory to write down the new conclusions he had come to during the many hours he had waited at Hampton Court.

It was midnight when Rachel tiptoed up to the laboratory to give him a further message. She had waited until she was sure his wife was asleep.

He read what Ben Jonson had also written: "London printers prefer to publish books about second sight and other supernatural matters, particularly the fancies of astrology, for which there is a great demand. If you are determined to publish, you will have to seek a printer abroad."

Rachel whispered, "I didn't want your wife to know this. It would have only made her more critical of you and given her more cause to complain."

In the shadows of the doorway, where she had remained, her white, set face was startlingly frail, and he said affectionately, "You are sensible."

"I hope that you were equally sensible at King James's deathbed."

"My dear Rachel, I came up here to obtain a bit of peace and quiet. I don't want to spoil it by worrying about gossip and slander."

"William, you are preaching to me again."

"I know I'm not the easiest person to be with, and there is still much to learn. But I'm almost sure about the link that is missing."

"Between the arteries and the veins?"

"Yes. At Hampton Court there were many waiting periods when my mind didn't have to hurry. Do you realise that there are vessels that contain blood in all parts of the body? Even in the extremities?"

"Is that important?"

"Nature tends to perfection, even if man doesn't, and we ought to consult more with our sense and instinct, than the fashion of the country."

Her absorption stimulated him, and he added, "This inclines me to believe these vessels take the blood from the arteries to the veins."

"Why don't you prove that with your magnifying glass? You used it to watch the hearts of snails and other small objects."

"It isn't powerful enough. It doesn't reveal nearly enough of what I need to see." He picked it up, then threw it down regretfully. "If I could only see such vessels, my proof would be irrefutable."

Happy that she was personally involved in his life again, she said, "If you think so, you must be right. You have discovered many things."

"I have not discovered enough."

"Then you are not going to publish?"

"What I have begun, I will finish."

Rachel embraced him to express her congratulations, and then she remembered a possible difficulty and danger, and she shivered fearfully.

William asked, "Dear, what is worrying you now?"

"I hope you are not persecuted for Buckingham's remedies and failure."

"I see no reason why I should be. Any physician who examined James honestly should testify that he was sick unto death. The autopsy proved that. His final convulsion was caused not by the potion or by the plaster, but by infection and the damage to his kidneys. As it is, I will face enough difficulties if I publish *De motu cordis*."

"But you will publish it, won't you?" Here, she felt less afraid, for she believed this was the best of him and should be preserved.

"If I find a publisher, I will publish."

"And if you don't?"

He hesitated, that decision still suspended in his mind.

She whispered passionately, "You must publish. You have discovered so much, you can't halt now. You can overcome the difficulties."

Her faith gave him the resolution he needed, and he nodded.

"How will you do it, William?"

"If no one else will publish me, I will do it myself."

he Rock of Gibraltar will be destroyed by a fly

"Buckingham has been impeached by Parliament."

Matthew stated this as if it were the end of the world, and William looked up irritably from his desk. "For God's sake," he longed to shout, "it is not that important," but his friend obviously thought it was. Matthew knew that he hated to be interrupted, yet had rushed upstairs without being announced. William was working on *De motu cordis* with a rigourous discipline, and in the intervening year the book had taken final shape. Now he was writing letters to people abroad in the hope that they would help him publish it—his efforts to publish it himself had failed—for no one in England would support his belief that the blood circulated. He realised that he could not get rid of Matthew quickly, and he put his letters aside with a sigh and asked, "Why are you so concerned? Your position as physician to the new King is safe?"

"I'm not certain yours is."

"Why should that be? I'm not publishing *De motu cordis* here."

"You are going to be involved in Buckingham's impeachment."

"I don't see why. I'm not a political creature."

"It is implicit in the charges that Parliament has brought against him."

"I doubt that."

To prove his point, Matthew read from the paper he was holding:

"*The Duke of Buckingham has bought some of his offices; he has sold places and taxes for corrupt practices; he has procured many titles for his family to the prejudice of the nobility and damage to the Crown; he has received vast sums of money for his own private advantage, he has—*"

William interrupted, "None of this concerns me."

"One charge does." Matthew read each word of it with solemnity: "*Lastly, the said Duke, without sufficient warrant, and contrary to the law safeguarding the person and health of the Sovereign, did unduly procure certain plasters and a potion and gave them to his late Majesty in his last illness contrary to the will of the Royal Physicians, which divers ill symptoms did appear upon his said Majesty.*"

"James was not poisoned. And you know that, too."

"I was more careful than you. I didn't agree to the administering of the Duke's remedies, but you did."

"I simply didn't object. I knew, as you did, that they wouldn't harm James and that they could ease his mind."

"That is not what Parliament believes. While poisoning isn't stated explicitly because of King Charles, it is very much implied in reference to Buckingham and anyone who supports him. I have come to warn you that if you defend the Duke you will be in grave danger."

"Despite the fact that James was dying anyway, and that he begged for the potion and plaster himself."

"Nonetheless, the consequences could be grave. The Duke is hated. Whatever goes wrong, and some of it is his own fault, is blamed on him."

"I suspect that Buckingham's greatest sin is his incompetence."

"Compounded by his vanity and arrogance."

"Matthew, do you think that the Duke is going to be convicted?"

"If Parliament has its way. They regard him as the cause of all our miseries, _the grievance of grievances,_ and they attack him ferociously."

"Bacon would have been amused. He felt he would not have been convicted if Buckingham had supported him."

"Could you have saved the Viscount St. Albans's life?"

"No one could. He insisted on prescribing for himself. Bacon played the physician, and it killed him."

"Are you sure, William?"

He nodded and told him why.

"Two months ago, after a severe winter during which Bacon suffered much from many colds, for he was afraid of suffocation and he exposed himself to fresh air unnecessarily, he decided to perform an experiment, although there was snow on the ground and the air was raw. But the snow was part of his experiment, and so he was not to be dissuaded. He took a ride in a coach with Dr. Witherborne, and it came into his mind that he had wondered if snow would preserve flesh from putrefaction, as in salt. So he got out of his coach with Witherborne and went into a woman's house at the bottom of Highgate hill and bought a hen. He made the woman open it, and then they stuffed it with snow. But the snow so chilled him that he fell ill, and he couldn't return to his lodgings at Gray's Inn. He went to the Earl of Arundel's house at Highgate, where he was put in a bed that the servants warmed with a pan of coals. But they forgot that the bed was damp, and this made his condition even worse. By the time I was summoned by Arundel, for Bacon had called Hobbes, the philosopher, instead of me, so that his final words could be properly put down for posterity, it was too late. There was nothing that anyone could do. He grew weaker daily as his lungs congested. On April the ninth, Easter Day, he died."

"You never did have a high opinion of Bacon."

"*I esteemed him for his wit and style, but I cannot allow him to be a great philosopher. He wrote Philosophy like a Lord Chancellor.*"

"You are derisive because he didn't use your physic."

"*When he allowed me, I cured him.*"

Matthew was curious, too, about the letters that William was writing, and he wanted to know to whom they were addressed.

"I'm inquiring of our friends from Padua about having *De motu cordis* published in their countries. I have corresponded with them through the years to exchange views— Giovanni Cattaro in Venice, Caspar Hofmann in Nuremberg, Jean Riolan in Paris, and Baruch Mendoza in Amsterdam."

"Mendoza is a Jew," Matthew said contemptuously. "Didn't you know?"

"No."

"You will surely be accused of heresy if you allow him to help you."

"Mendoza is sympathetic to my views. Good night."

Matthew had no intention of being dismissed yet; he wasn't finished. He peered at the sheets piled up on a corner of the desk and said, "So, in spite of all the warnings, you are still determined to publish?"

"If I can find a printer when the book is finished."

"When do you expect that to be accomplished?"

"Most of the text is done, but I have to write my introduction and conclusion."

"William, be careful when you are called before Parliament to give evidence about James's death. Or I have wasted this visit."

After he had sent off his letters to Mendoza, Cattaro, Hofmann, and Riolan, he reviewed the facts of James's last illness and death. It had happened over a year ago, and he was determined to be clear on his evidence. Much as he disliked Buckingham, he couldn't testify inaccurately.

When he was ordered to appear the following month before a select committee of Parliament, he felt prepared, although he was uneasy about what he might face. The Duke was so hated these days most people were eager to believe the worst about him, the more scandalous the better.

As he started out, with Silas accompanying him, his wife was waiting for him at the door to release her own feelings.

She said, "The Duke has no friends. Everyone is against him now."

"The King will support him. More strongly than ever, I hear."

"That is not what I have heard. Elsingham has accused the Duke of murdering James. I read his pamphlet, *The Fore-Runner of Revenge*. It is convincing. Everyone is reading it and believing it."

"So convincing that this doctor fled to Brussels after writing it."

Silas said, "Master, it is advisable to be cautious. They say on the street that the London mob builds a scaffold for the Duke on Tower Hill."

Rachel joined them; her excuse was that she wanted to be

sure that her brother was properly attired, but William saw concern on her face.

Elizabeth added, "And you mustn't mention your experiments, it could fatally prejudice Parliament against you. Irretrievably."

He was watching Rachel walk. She still moved gracefully even though she was in middle age, but he noticed also that she paused often in what she did. He wondered if that was her age; she was in her middle forties. He said, "I'm grateful that all of you are concerned, but it is the Duke who is being tried. I'm simply a medical witness."

Elizabeth retorted, "You will suffer if you support him. And you should have dressed more modestly today. It would have been more fitting."

Rachel thought William looked just right. His large white ruff was an appropriate frame for his broad forehead, with his dark hair carefully brushed back, his penetrating brown eyes, his high cheekbones, his sharp, resolute jaws and chin, and his short black beard and mustache, which was wide and thick. He didn't appear forty-eight, even in the sun. His sturdy body gave her a sense of relief and the feeling that he would defend himself ably if that had to be done. Then he left in his coach, with Silas to attend him, as befitted the King's Physician Extraordinary.

There was a mob outside Westminster Hall, clamouring for the Duke's head, and some of them made threatening gestures against William. He ignored this, although his hand went instinctively to the dagger at his side. He strode through the old Palace Yard and under the Roman arch that led to the Court of Requests that housed the Lords, where the trial of Buckingham was to occur.

He was admitted by armed guards into the oblong chamber that served the Lords, and he waited impatiently until the trial was called to order.

Buckingham stood before the judges, dressed modestly, as if that would refute the accusations of extravagance. But while he answered the charges with eloquence, William sensed that he was not making much of an impression on Parliament, that they were more determined to punish the Duke than to judge him. He had divorced himself almost completely from the charges and the Duke's replies, although Matthew sat beside him now with a number of other physicians whom he knew, when a thunderous voice shook him out of his reverie.

"I suggest, My Duke of Buckingham, that you did not intend to cure our late King with your potion and plaster!"

William looked up at the speaker, Sir John Eliot, who glared as he spoke.

Buckingham cried out, "How dare you accuse me of such a calumny?"

The stout, middle-aged Eliot retorted, *"Sir, your giving a physic to King James in his last illness was an act of transcendent presumption."*

"I was supported by several physicians."

"Who?" Eliot made that sound as if they were guilty too.

"The Earl of Warwick's physician, and the King's physician, Harvey."

William wanted to deny this—he didn't know of any doctor who had advised the taking of the potion or the plaster, for Buckingham had controlled the situation and all he had done was to raise no objections. But none of the members of Parliament who were sitting in judgement on the Duke heeded his effort to get their attention.

Eliot said, "Yet you knew that the King was failing."

The Duke replied, "I knew that he was in a very distressed state. But the potion and plaster were applied at the King's command."

"Elsingham's pamphlet, *The Fore-Runner of Revenge*, takes a different view. My Lord, he accuses you of having poisoned the King."

"That is outrageous, sir. This doctor doesn't dare face me."

Eliot called out, "Harvey, did you know of these remedies

395

and that they were being applied? You can answer from where you sit."

"I knew they were being applied, sir. But I didn't recommend them."

Eliot returned to the Duke, who still stood before the heavy trestle tables where the judges sat, and said, "My Lord, you are not an expert in physic, yet you believed you were competent to prescribe?"

"Sir, I used those remedies on myself and on my mother."

"Nonetheless, My Lord, His Majesty grew worse."

"He was dying. I was trying to save him. And to ease him. There wasn't much hope from the moment the King fell ill. Sir, why should I harm the person who did more for me than anybody else in the world?"

"That is not the question, My Lord. We are here to determine whether your physic hastened the death of our late King."

Windows were opened because of the June heat, and William heard the mob in the old Palace Yard shouting for Buckingham's arrest. But no one moved in the chamber. The Duke was silent while Eliot consulted with the other seven members of the select committee. William wondered where Charles was and what he would do about these charges against his servant, who had become just as much his favourite as his father's. Some said the King was at Windsor, hunting; others thought Charles was in residence at Hampton Court, trying to decide what to do.

The Court of Requests was full, and William felt confined. Matthew shifted restlessly, and William saw anxious looks on the faces of the other doctors who were waiting to testify. He told himself that he must not be afraid, his sanctuary was the truth, yet he doubted that was desired. Most of the judges regarded the Duke with open hostility. Matthew whispered, "His excessive power and his abuse of this power is the cause of the evils happening to the King and Kingdom."

Before William could answer, This isn't what he is accused

of, Eliot said, "My Lord, have you anything else to say in reply to the charge you hastened his Majesty's death by negligently administering an injurious potion and plaster without consent of his physicians?"

The chamber stirred. This was virtually a charge of murder.

The Duke seemed about to explode with rage. Then, with an intense effort of his will, he regained his self-control and said, "I begged the King not to take the physic unless advised by his physicians."

Eliot retorted sternly, "My Lord, no doctor has said that he did."

"They did, sir. As I told you, Harvey."

So Buckingham is a liar too, William thought indignantly.

"Moreover, sir, the physic was applied by the King's own command. And some of his doctors tasted the potion, and none of them disliked it."

"That isn't true either," William longed to shout, feeling damaged.

"When I heard rumours that my physic had hurt the King, I told him, in his last hours, and he said, '*This is not true. They are worse than devils that say it.*' "

The judges ordered Buckingham to stand down, and they called on the medical witnesses to testify.

Bedwin struck William as a poor witness; he had left before anything had been done. This doctor said, "I heard that the potion and plaster were administered without the assent of His Majesty's physicians."

Chambers agreed, and added, "We were against the Duke's physic, and we did not agree to his treatment. When it was applied, the King soon became progressively worse."

Eliot asked, "Chambers, who was the chief doctor attending the King?"

"Harvey, sir. He was with His Majesty during his last hours."

"Were you consulted?"

397

"No, sir."

"Do you recall anything else that was significant?"

"Sir, I heard the King cry out, '*Will you murder me and slay me?*' "

Yet Chambers had been afraid to commit himself, and he had said nothing while the Duke's physic had been administered, but had withdrawn.

Moore said, "I was at all the consultations but one, sir. I was treating the King successfully until Buckingham and Harvey intervened. The use of the potion and the plaster was not approved by me, or by the other physicians, except Harvey. He saw it given, he should be blamed."

The fact that Craige was the next witness convinced William that the judges were determined to convict the Duke, and that anyone who supported him was in peril. Buckingham's enemies must be powerful if they could disregard the late King's banishment of Craige. He wondered if he was being attacked by these doctors because he believed that the blood circulated.

Craige repeated the assertions that Elsingham had made in *The Fore-Ruuner of Revenge*. "*After the Duke gave our late Majesty the white powder, which only Harvey consented to, it was done without the other physicians' advice or consent. Furthermore, when he applied the plaster to the King's heart and breast, the King grew faint and short-breathed and anguished.*"

William shouted, "Sirs, this isn't true. Craige left before the plaster was applied, and so did Elsingham. They don't know what happened."

Eliot rapped on his desk and snapped, "Harvey, you are out of order!"

"My reputation is being attacked, sir. Quite unfairly."

"You will have your opportunity to reply. Craige, continue."

"*As my colleague wrote: 'The Sunday after his Majesty died, Buckingham desired the Physicians who attended His Majesty, to sign with their hands a writ of testimony that the*

*powder which he gave him, was a good and safe medicine;
which they refused.'* "

"Except for Harvey?" Eliot prodded.

"Except for that Physician Extraordinary," Craige
sneered.

"Thank you, Doctor," said Eliot. "Your testimony has been
helpful."

The Duke hadn't done this, but William felt hopeless,
for much of this false testimony was being accepted by the
judges. Parliament was using the law to suit itself, and now
they listened avidly to Eliot, their leader and spokesman,
nodding in agreement with what he was telling them.

Eliot ordered, "William Harvey, rise."

He approached the marble bench and concentrated on Eliot,
who leaned ominously towards him as if to intimidate him.
The harshness of his countenance was unsettling. When he had
risen Matthew had whispered, "Do not defend the Duke, it
could be fatal," and he wasn't sure what to do. Buckingham's
testimony, which had implicated him unfairly, added to his
dislike of the Duke. But whatever he felt, the facts were . . .

Eliot stated, "Witnesses on opposite sides of the question
agree you consented to the final treatment of the King? Do
you admit that is so?"

"No. As I said, sir, I didn't approve."

"But you didn't disapprove."

"Sir, I simply stated that the potion and plaster were
harmless."

"All the other physicians disagreed with you."

"Not all, sir. And those that did, didn't know what was in
the physic."

"Yet it is reported that this physic had an ill effect on the
King."

"Sir, it had no effect on him. Except to ease his mind and
spirit."

"Then you do think the potion and the plaster should
have been given?"

"That isn't the issue, sir. Other things caused his death."

"We will decide what is the issue. It was natural for the Duke to assume that your failure to object to the treatment was assent."

"Sir, His Majesty was dying, and in the end nothing was altered."

"Do you think he was poisoned?"

William hesitated, and he saw Buckingham grow pale, as if, with all his vanity, the Duke was frightened that this doctor—the only one who had supported him—would attack him now too. He said, "In a way, sir."

Eliot said triumphantly, "Then you do agree with this charge!"

"The poison in the King's system was there for a long time. Sir, it was a urinary infection that must have affected his kidneys."

"How can you be sure?"

"The autopsy of His Majesty was conducted thoroughly, sir."

This was ignored by Eliot and the other judges; they were conferring about something else. Then Eliot said, "Harvey, you are in grave difficulties. Your evidence is contradictory. I'm sure the Bishop of Lincoln will help us to establish the truth."

The Bishop added, "*I was so involved in saving the late King's soul from the Church of Rome, I was unable to judge the medical situation, but Harvey argued that His Majesty's former vigour of nature was low and spent, and I believed so learned a doctor's observation, although I never heard that opinion from anyone else.*"

That is untrue too, William thought bitterly, but his spirits rose as Matthew was called. He was grateful his friend refused to admit he had made a mistake, but he was distressed when Matthew said that he might have been injudicious in his failure to object to the Duke's treatment.

Eliot said, "So the Duke wasn't able to enlist your cooperation?"

"That is correct, sir."

"Do you think the King suffered from the Duke's physic?"

"I don't know, sir. I opposed the posset drink, but I wasn't heeded."

"But you do think it could have harmed His Majesty?"

Matthew shrugged. He didn't want to hurt his friend, but he didn't want to hurt himself either. He sat down without another word.

Buckingham was called back for his final response, and he said, "I must add for the learned judges a letter sent to me by our Majesty, Charles." He read, *"My father asked for the Duke's treatment, for he knew that the Duke loved him."* He paused, then added with tears in his eyes, "Noble Lords, I had nothing to gain by our late Majesty's death. If anyone was negligent, it was the physician who attended him last, William Harvey."

William was summoned to answer this charge, and he heard the crowd in the old Palace Yard crying out in a mocking chant:

"Who rules the Kingdom—the King!
Who rules the King—the Duke!
Who rules the Duke—the devil!"

"You are right," he was tempted to say, but he had the facts in writing now. As he faced Eliot, he read his record of James's last illness.

"His Majesty desired the physic, thinking it could do no harm. No physician consulted or asked for his opinion, since the King desired it, and because the physic had been used by the Duke and his mother. Now the King was determined to take it, although no doctor had advised it. And it was impossible to stop this, for the King took diverse things, whether doctors advised him or not, for he undervalued physicians."

Craige and Moore cried out that this report was irrelevant.

William went on to his notes about the autopsy of James.

"The King's heart was found to be great but soft, one of

his kidneys good, but the other shrunk so little it could
hardly be found, wherein there were two stones, his gall
bladder judged to be melancholy, and many signs of a
urinary infection, renal calculi, and general debility."

Craige declared, "That is only a matter of opinion."

"Quite so," Moore agreed, "His Majesty could have lived
longer."

This was more than Matthew could endure, and he rose
quickly and said, "My Lords, Doctor Harvey's account of
the autopsy is accurate. The King was dying, and there was
nothing that could save him—"

Eliot interrupted, "That is not the issue. The charge is:
Was His Majesty's death hastened? Harvey, we have all the
facts we need."

"Sir, don't you want to hear the cause of his death?"

"That has been decided. Sit down."

Since the inquiry focussed on how James had died, none
of the other articles of impeachment was considered at this
time. The discussion among the judges was so brief William
realised they had made up their minds in advance. Eliot,
speaking for all of them, stated: *"This select committee*
finds that the Duke of Buckingham has been, in administer-
ing his physic to our late Majesty without the proper advice,
guilty of transparent presumption and dangerous conse-
quences."

Buckingham's attempt to reply was silenced.

Eliot said curtly, "The other charges will be considered
later."

Harvey was ordered to stand apart from the other physicians.

Eliot declared, *"This inquiry finds that William Harvey,*
Physician Extraordinary to our late King, was remiss in his
duties and he is censured for negligence and his failure to
save our Majesty's life."

William's first feeling was of outrage. Then he resolved to
be indifferent. He thought, The world can bestow honour or

dishonour, but only the man himself can decide whether either matters.

He refused to discuss the verdict of the inquiry with anyone. He ignored his wife's reminder that she had told him censure would occur if he supported the Duke; he was grateful that Rachel had the decency not to reproach him. Instead, she sought to absorb him in *De motu cordis*. But he couldn't work on it. He was numbed by the lies and his mind was blank, and he put aside his almost completed book while he waited for replies to the letters he had sent to his foreign colleagues.

When Parliament submitted a remonstrance to Charles, demanding that he dismiss Buckingham—which was equivalent to conviction—the King angrily dissolved Parliament, thus ending his chief minister's trial.

William noted that Charles acted swiftly in defense of his favourite—just a week had passed since the inquiry. But when he heard nothing from the King, he wondered if he was still a royal Physician Extraordinary.

At the College he observed that most of the doctors were careful to stay apart from him, but he was pleased that Matthew defended him, and Scrope, and Fox, who, he felt, was influenced by Donne, and Argent.

Argent had been elected President of the College, and he was grateful that Harvey had not fled from London during the plague of the previous year, as had most of the doctors, but had remained in the centre of the city and had continued to practise and to treat victims of the plague.

Woodall told him that he had gotten a male cadaver, newly hanged and in perfect health, but outside the normal ways. Excited, for William felt he needed this involvement, he hurried towards the College of Physicians, although it was dark and he was alone, and in a narrow alley two strangers attacked him with cudgels. His anger overcame his fear, and he drew his dagger and ran at the leader to drive his sharp steel into him. The burly assailant fled, and the smaller accomplice followed him hastily.

What troubled William most was that he learnt nothing from the anatomy. He was preoccupied, wondering who could have known where he was going. He doubted it was Woodall, yet only the surgeon and his assistants had known where he would be going. And he had failed to get a court appointment for Woodall. Full of suspicion, he couldn't concentrate, and the cadaver blurred in his sight.

He told no one of this ambush, but from then on he travelled by daylight, accompanied by Silas, and wore a sword with his dagger.

Another shock came with the letters he received from Riolan and Hofmann. They denounced his view that the blood circulated. They added that his opinions were immoral and they couldn't help him publish them.

He was surprised that he hadn't heard from Giovanni Cattaro, for Venice was the most learned community in Europe. Impulsively, for the more he was rejected the more he must respond by acting, he found Nina's address. He had held on to it, for he had intended to return to Venice some day. He wrote her, asking about her health and life, and did she know Giovanni Cattaro's whereabouts? Still driven by his new vigour, he obtained Galileo's address and wrote him also. He doubted that his old teacher would remember him or reply, but in the hope that it would spur the astronomer and interested in his opinion, he added that he was convinced the blood circulated and he intended to publish these views.

After he posted these letters, he felt better; he was fighting back.

He sat down with grim determination to finish *De motu cordis,* but his mind refused to function as he desired, and he was unable to write anything of consequence the next month. Much as he believed that he was right about the movement of the blood, the knowledge of the completion of its passage was blocked to him now. He was relieved there were no more attacks on him; instead, his situation had gone to the other extreme, and he felt isolated. He hadn't heard from the King since the trial, and that bothered him. He was glad Elizabeth was spending more time with Galen—it made matters at home easier—but Rachel worried him. She didn't look well, yet when he wanted to examine her, she refused, and changed the subject.

He was feeling particularly irritable when Matthew appeared in the doorway of his laboratory.

Matthew said, "I was starting to wonder if it would happen."

"You have heard of a publisher who will print my book?"

"No, no, that is not something that I can support!"

"Then what bad news have you brought me now?"

"It is not bad news. You are still a royal Physician Extraordinary."

"What makes you so positive?" William asked sceptically.

"Charles has generously recognised your services to his father." He was annoyed that William wanted proof, but he was proud that he had had the foresight to bring the official document with him. He read it:

"By order dated 28 July 1626: Unto Doctor Harvey the sum of 100 £, as of His Majesty's free gift, for his pains and attendance about the person of His Majesty's late dear father, of happy memory, in time of his sickness. By writ, dated 27th of May, 1626 . . . 100.0.0."

Instead of being appreciative, as Matthew had expected, William exclaimed angrily, "Why did he wait so long if he had decided before the judgement of the inquiry that I had served his father honourably?"

"Perhaps he didn't want to commit himself until he was certain. What does it matter? Soon you will be pardoned too."

"Why should I be pardoned when I have not committed any wrong?"

"Parliament stated otherwise. And times are difficult. Despite our testimony, it is still generally believed that Buckingham poisoned James. Indeed, since the King dissolved Parliament and elevated the Duke even higher, there are more grave rumblings of discontent in the country."

"Yet you expect me not to be disenchanted?"

"You will recover. You are too energetic and enterprising. I have more good news. You have been appointed one of the four Censors of the College."

But while he felt better, he did not feel festive. No one had appeared to publish *De motu cordis*. He turned back to the book.

Matthew noted with surprise, "You are writing it in red ink!"

"With my blood. Do you want to read it?"

"Why should I? I know your views. But it doesn't circulate."

here can she go to know
Is all of life only an attempt
Should that be enough for her

Many months passed as Matthew's disbelief prodded William into renewed efforts to find the final proof that the blood circulated. Most of this time was spent searching for evidence that it moved from the arteries to the veins at the periphery of the body. He had hardly any doubts about this link now—he felt it was such a *reasoned necessity*—but conclusive verification was still lacking. So he didn't put these views into *De motu cordis*. He was waiting until he was absolutely certain.

Meanwhile, he attended the King when Charles caught a chill and had an upset stomach. There was no mention of the trial or of his role in it on either visit, but Charles heeded his advice, and these minor ills were cured. Matthew and Mayerne, who had returned from abroad, attended the King also, but there was no sign of the other doctors who had been witnesses at the impeachment, while Buckingham's presence still dominated the Court—the Duke was even more the King's most trusted servant.

William had given up expecting a reply to the last letters he had written, when there was a reply from Nina. He thought hopefully, This could be good news. Giovanni Cattaro had taken chances; he was counting on him and his enthusiasm. He pushed aside his almost finished book, and prayed that Nina knew where his old colleague was. He read eagerly,

> It was strange to hear from you after so many years and I hesitated to answer you for a long time. Then I reflected, why not, and once I began I had to finish. Cattaro left Venice a decade ago, and I haven't heard of him since. As for myself, I have fallen on evil times. Carlo Labia always desired me, and finally, after my father died, I succumbed, I married him. And now that he has me, I doubt he desires me. I trust that you have been more fortunate. I have heard that you serve your King and St. Bartholomew's Hospital as their physician.

After his disappointment with Nina's reply, when there were letters from Galileo and Mendoza, a week later, he sought to restrain his excitement. Yet he couldn't completely contain himself as he turned first to Galileo's answer. He

thought gratefully, If the astronomer had taken the trouble
to reply to him, it must be encouraging. He read with
anticipation.

I cannot judge whether your suppositions are true,
since I have not examined them myself, but your evidence indicates that you could be correct. If you
publish, I am sure that I will find much that is excellent in it. Certainly it is possible that the blood circulates, many things in nature circulate. But I am
pessimistic when you speak of publishing in Italy
because it is a learned country. There is much fear
here of new ideas, and those who print the books are
frightened men. When I published my support of
Copernicus, although I proved it was right, I provoked the censure of the ecclesiastical authorities.
I was forced to promise that I would restrain myself,
as if one could restrain the motion of the blood, and
abstain from advocacy of what is called *"condemned
doctrines."*

My dear Harvey, what you must realize is there
are so few who seek the truth. But I must not mourn
over the miseries of our time.

I recall you clearly. You were a rare student. You
didn't accept only the past, or approach physic with
closed ears and eyes. You used your own resources.
I remember we agreed: *"How absurd to believe God
shut up all light of learning within the lantern of
Aristotle's brains."*

Yet you must be careful. You differ with views
held for centuries, and to question orthodoxy is to
risk grave consequences.

I taught the old Ptolemaic astronomy for years,
although I knew it was wrong, and now I refrain
from publishing my findings to avoid being imprisoned and ridiculed. Yet if one sees through the darkness, it is because God has lit our way, what we
teach is in praise of Him.

So while I cannot help you publish in Italy, my
good wishes go with you. Remember, dear student,

what I taught you and that *I can listen only with the
greatest repugnance when the quality of unchange-
ability is held up as pre-eminent in contrast to vari-
ability and change.*"

William reviewed Galileo's words until they were fixed in
his mind. He wondered, is discovery of new ideas always to be
subject to adversity? There was much in this letter that
moved him, and some of it discouraged him, and he hated
being stifled. By the time he started Mendoza's reply he had
lost his excitement, and he didn't expect anyone to publish
him.

Dear Esteemed Colleague:
I am sorry I am slow in answering, but I was waiting for an appropriate reply from a printer in Frankfurt. I have read your view that the blood circulates,
and there is much in it that appeals to me. You may
have found the true path of the blood, but here they
still teach that the blood forces its way through the
septum, an opinion I do not share. But I wonder
about the movement from the arteries to the veins. I
cannot detect any passage. Work is being done in
Amsterdam on glasses in the hope of finding a lens
that will help us find such passages. But so far, while
we can make distant objects nearer, as our old Master, Galileo, has done with the heavens, we cannot
yet make near objects bigger.
And I fear that your view that the liver cannot any
longer be regarded as the centre of the vascular system will be attacked violently. Yet you support your
opinion with much evidence, and I'm inclined to
believe you.
If you can establish the link between the arteries
and the veins, as I think you will, you should convince many that you are correct.
I am pleased by your interest in my opinions, and
I am happy to inform you that Fitzer, a Frankfurt
printer, will read your work. I cannot guarantee that
he will publish it, although I stressed that he give

your book the most serious consideration. That he
will read it is encouraging, since other printers I
spoke to about it would not even read your words.

Write Fitzer in English, he is an Englishman who
succeeded to this Frankfurt printing firm when his
father-in-law, a German, died recently. He is young,
in his middle twenties, and he is interested in estab-
lishing a reputation even if it involves some risk.

Please forgive my presumption, but I trust you
wrote your book in Latin. No one on the continent
can be expected to read English. And communicate
promptly with Fitzer, before he forgets your name
and purpose.

William was jubilant until he recalled Galileo's warnings.
Infected by them, when he wrote Mendoza his thanks he
said he would consider submitting his book to Fitzer, but that
at the moment it was not ready. He told himself that this
delay gave him time to show how the blood moved from the
arteries to the veins, and to add to his conclusion and
introduction.

The next night Rachel came upstairs to help him with
his work, and he said hopefully, "I may have a publisher for
De motu cordis."

She replied triumphantly, "I knew you would find one."

"We mustn't become too excited. The printer has agreed
only to read my work. I have no assurance that he respects
truth."

She wondered if he knew that she was racked with a
severe cough and that her chills were growing worse. She
hadn't told him of either complaint, and in his absorption
with his work he hadn't noticed them. When she coughed in
his presence these grey, dreary January days of 1627, she
blamed it on the smoking fire and hid her frequent chills.

He whispered, "I told you first. Rachel, you are a great
blessing."

His affection revived her old vivacity, and she said happily, "I pray often for the day that will see you published."

"Not yet. Not yet. I have much work to complete."

"William, you are not afraid?"

"No! No!" But he realized that he was.

"The doctors will swallow your words if you make them clear enough. How long will it take you to prepare your book for publication?"

"I cannot measure it in such a way. But most of the pages are done."

"I will help you day and night if necessary." Her eyes shone.

"You are not that young or strong enough for that now."

"Silas will take care of most of my duties. You must not delay."

Her sense of urgency echoed in him as he told his wife at breakfast the following morning about the letter from Mendoza. He was tired, for he and Rachel had worked late, and she looked exhausted as she supervised the meal. Then Elizabeth said, "I hope you can take care of yourself."

"What do you mean?" he asked indignantly. He took care of her.

"Your attack on authority will be regarded harshly."

"What has given you such a cheerful attitude?"

"There is no need to be sarcastic. You are such an advocate of the truth, you should listen to it from me. As you want me to listen to you."

Perplexed, he said, "Elizabeth, you speak in riddles."

"Not really. Now that you are going to be pardoned, you may avoid punishment even if you attack our medical authorities."

"Pardoned?" William was on his feet. He burst out, "By whom?"

"By King Charles. For your part in the death of King James."

411

"No one laid a hand on him. Myself least of all."

"It is not the general view. But few will dare to oppose our anointed King. If he approves of your views, they may be accepted by some."

He stated angrily, "I do not desire a pardon, for I did no wrong."

"You will refuse the King's pardon?" Elizabeth was shocked.

"I don't know. How can I be certain that what you say is true?"

"Matthew told me. Sit down, William, you haven't finished your coffee, and if you don't you will blame me and be irritable the rest of the day."

Rachel was a few feet away, her head bent to hide her feelings, and he sat down, seeking to regain his self-control. He objected on principle to accepting a pardon, for that signified guilt, and yet it could serve a useful purpose. This could be the support he needed to publish.

"William, with your promotion to Censor at the College, you do have the power to reconsider Galen's application to practise in London. His Latin has improved. I have been tutoring him. You will help him, please?"

"I will arrange for another examination, but it will take another year."

"Does he have to wait until 1628?"

"Yes." He was quite firm. "No candidates are to be considered until then, for the Fellows believe London is overcrowded with physicians."

"Do you think so?"

He gulped down his coffee, eager to confirm her news with Matthew. The more he thought of how it could aid his book and even make publication possible, the less he objected to the pardon. He said, "Have Galen reapply, and he will be questioned as soon as there are new examinations."

Matthew was amused by William's mixture of annoyance and excitement about a pardon. He said, "It is true, a pardon is on the way. Charles wants to demonstrate that you, as a royal servant, must not be blamed for his father's death. It is also his way of defying Parliament."

"Then I am still Physician Extraordinary?"

"This has not changed. Charles respects your skill with physic."

"So the dogs have been called off."

"That depends on what you do with your views of the blood."

William had no intention of discussing them with Matthew. He returned hurriedly and avidly to his laboratory without another word.

A month later the King granted him a general pardon. By now he was willing to accept it, for it encouraged him to push on with his work on *De motu cordis*. And Mendoza's faith gave him the final energy he needed.

Yet when the justification for the last link came to him, it struck him as so simple and obvious, he wondered why he hadn't seen it sooner.

Rachel was complaining with outstretched hands that they were always icy these days, and he embraced her and she cried out, "What did I do?"

He caressed her cold hands and replied, "Your blood moves poorly."

She sighed wearily, but he was stimulated with an excess of energy. He lit the large candles which he preferred, which meant he intended to labour all night. He threw more wood on the fire, opened the window so the fresh air would revive him, and then he paced the length of the laboratory to construct his ideas while she sat down at the desk to write them in English; later he could translate these words into the necessary Latin.

"*The following conclusions prove that the blood circulates.*"

He was very excited. The pieces were fitting into place. "*The heart is a pump, which is the reason for its various movements.*"

413

She wrote this out with a special emphasis and flourish.

"The quantity of the blood is measurable, and of such magnitude that it proves it circulates through the body continuously."

His impetus is great now, she noticed as she put this down.

"There are three essential parts to the circulation."

She paused in her writing as if to ask, "What are they?"

"The pulmonary circulation, the arterial route from the heart to the periphery, and the venous route for the return."

She sensed that after many years he was convinced that he was right.

"Even though I cannot see them, there must be vessels which contain blood that communicate with one another and that run into one another."

Now she hesitated, not sure that had the right ring about it.

"Rachel, it must be so. It is logical. *A reasoned necessity."*

She was pleased he made an effort to reason with her, and she nodded.

"I came to the conclusion that this must be correct when I found that the blood passes from the arterial vein into the venous artery. It also explains the passage of the blood at the periphery from arteries to veins."

Deeply involved, she wrote easily and quickly now. She felt that the blood was stimulating William's mind, responding to his every wish.

"So it seems to me . . ." He halted, troubled suddenly.

"You are going to stop now? You are not certain after all?"

"No, no! These premises fit all my observations. It is you."

She was surprised, and she cried out, "What have I done wrong?"

He didn't answer.

"You want to get someone else to help you?" she asked apprehensively.

He stared at her, then blurted out, "You look so pale, so tired."

"Is that all?"

"It worries me. I don't want you to collapse from fatigue."

"I'm fine." She felt that her blood was circulating as fast as his, and she longed to write down whatever he said, however late it was. "Save your strength for *De motu cordis*. I have enough energy to finish your work."

"This late?" He heard the bells of St. Paul's tolling midnight.

"You were saying, William?" She felt as single-minded as he was.

"Of course." Nothing matters but the circulation, he thought, and she is as fascinated by it as I am. "What follows must be precise."

"Speak slowly and I will write it clearly." Her handwriting was a great source of comfort, much better than his. She knew now that it was dangerous for him to halt. He could lose his conception, energy and continuity.

"Since calculations and visual demonstrations have confirmed all my suppositions, to wit, that the blood is passed through the lungs and the heart by the pulsation of the ventricles, is forcibly ejected to all parts of the body, therein steals into the veins and the porosities of the flesh, flows back everywhere through those very veins from the circumference to the centre, from small veins into larger ones, and thence comes at last into the vena cava and to the auricle of the heart."

It is as if something wonderful has happened to him, she thought joyfully.

"Rachel, we must have a cup of coffee. It will refresh us."

"Are you finished? Does this fully explain the return of the blood?"

"The blood is expressed by the movements of the limbs and the compression exerted by the muscles, from capillary veins into venules and thence into comparatively large

415

*veins, and is thus more disposed and prone to move more
centrally than the opposite (even supposing the valves offered
no obstacles) and so reflects the normal passage from
extremities to heart.*"

Her hand ached from writing, and she was chilled to the
bone, but she couldn't complain. She couldn't diminish this
golden opportunity. She smiled, and he smiled back.

He examined her notes. She had put them down without a
single error. He gazed at Rachel with a new devotion. She had
helped him capture what he desired most of all. Even without his introduction, which he could finish easily now, this
was the real conclusion. *De motu cordis* did matter, did stand
for something, did exist for something. Its facts proved that
the blood did circulate. With Rachel's help and love, his
work was completely fashioned. He embraced her with an
affection that exceeded any emotion that he had ever
expressed to her.

"It is finished?" she asked, feeling on the verge of collapse.
Dawn approached, and now that they had halted she was
overwhelmed with fatigue.

"It is finished. And it is right. My suppositions are correct."

"You are certain?"

"Certain, Rachel, dear." Finally, after many years, he was
sure.

The next day he wrote the title page. "*Exercitatio anatom-
ica de motu cordis et sanguinis in animalibus. By William
Harvey, Englishman, Physician to the King and Professor of
Anatomy in the College of Physicians London.*"

Then he sent the book to William Fitzer in Frankfurt for
him to consider for publication. He was upset to discover that
a long time had passed since Mendoza had recommended the
printer, and he hoped that he wasn't too late or hadn't
waited too long. Unable to wait anxiously for this verdict, he
started work on further investigations of the circulatory
system. He had not allowed anyone to see his completed

book; he felt, in a way, that he was smuggling his book out of England.

He was pleased when Donne asked for his medical services, and he was relieved to find that the Dean was suffering only from a mild chill and was willing to accept his advice. Yet Donne wasn't reassured.

The Dean stated, almost as if he were preaching, although they sat in his spacious and comfortable Chapter House near the cathedral, "Harvey, I am never in a good temper, nor have a good pulse, nor good appetite, nor good sleep. Although I rest much. As you recommended."

William thought, Donne is preparing for death. His face, which had been attractive and dashing when he had met him, now had become sunken and cadaverous, and unusually grim, as if the Dean must use death to make the dramatic gesture. But William didn't love it, as his patient did, and he replied, "Sir, you are not grievously ill."

Donne looked disappointed and said, "Perhaps. Yet I have many strange feelings, Doctor."

"You have a vivid imagination, and it dominates you."

"I am also afflicted with many vehement coughs. But possibly it pleases God to pass me through many infirmities before He summons me. Have you found a publisher for your doctrines?"

"I am not sure."

"I pray that if you publish, you will not be attacked with ferocity. There is merit in your views. Why don't you address your work to the King?"

"Sir, you believe that he will not be offended?"

"He may be honoured. Charles fancies himself a patron of learning. Consider it." He dismissed William so that he could pursue his oratorical flights from the pulpit while there was still time.

A troubled Silas greeted William on his return home. His servant didn't even wait for him to sit down at the dining-room table, but met him at the door, looking haggard and anxious. And as soon as Silas saw him, he blurted out, "Rachel is ill. Master, I'm worried about her."

"What is wrong?" William hurriedly discarded his cloak.

"I don't know. She coughs and has many chills, but she won't let me see her, which makes me think it could be a female complaint."

William wondered if she was pregnant, although he had been careful. Outwardly calm, inwardly troubled, he said, "I will examine her."

Silas followed him belowstairs to her room in the cellar, muttering, "Sir, I hope she will allow you. She wouldn't let me into her room."

"I must examine her. If you are worried, she must be quite sick."

He knocked on her door and there was no reply. He asked himself, Is it possible that she isn't in her room but has fled, like Ruth? That thought left him stricken, and he was relieved to hear a muffled cough. Then it was so racking he was shocked, and he realised that she was ill indeed; it was no female complaint, but a severe lung affliction.

This time he put his fist to her door so loudly he felt it would awaken the dead, and the wooden frame vibrated from his intensity.

He heard a stirring in the room, then her voice whispering between coughs, "You mustn't come in. It would be wrong. Please go away."

"You must be examined by a physician. Before it is too late."

"No! Heaven will take care of me. I am content."

William shouted through her door, "If you don't admit me, I will force my way in." He hammered on it, and suddenly she opened it, facing him in her shift, blushing as if she had sinned.

He ordered her to go back to bed, which she did, frightened by the sternness of his voice. He told Silas to put the light by her side so that he could examine her and ordered him to wait outside, and as Silas obeyed he sat by her side. He tried not to notice her room, for she was embarrassed by his presence, yet he had to observe it, it was so much a part of her life. He was relieved to see that she wasn't sleeping on straw, as most servants did, but had a bed with a good mattress. Instead of the usual stools, she had chairs and a desk, on which there were books, which was unusual. But the room was chilly, the walls a thin mixture of wood, brick, and plaster, and he felt fierce draughts seeping in.

She cringed as he asked, "Rachel, what hurts?"

"I have pains in my chest. My mother died before she was forty. I inherited weak lungs from her, and I lived so poorly as a child."

"You will be in grave danger if you remain here."

"What do you mean? This room is spotlessly clean."

"Yes, but unsuitable for your condition. It is also cold and damp."

"It doesn't matter," she said suddenly, "I'm being punished."

"Nonsense. Helping me, you overworked, and that and the damp and the cold have attacked you. It is no wonder you are ill. You must move."

"Where?"

"I will decide after I examine you. But you can't stay here."

Breathing was so difficult, she felt she was suffocating. Certain she had consumption, she thought that nothing he could do would cure her. She lay back, feeling a vast load on her chest.

William noted her white, set face, her icy hands and feet, her frequent chills, her racking cough. His concern grew as he saw the severity of her condition. He decided that Rachel was suffering from the way she lived: strain, bad weather, and indifferent care. He summoned Silas and ordered him to prepare his laboratory as a bedroom and added, "Make it as comfortable as you can. I'm putting your sister into it."

She cried out, "That is out of the question!"

419

"There is no other solution. If you stay in this room you will die. Hurry, Silas. I will wait here until the laboratory is ready."

He stifled her protests and tucked her in so that she was warm.

Gradually, reassured by his presence and his authority, she fell asleep. When she awoke it was from a strange dream. She had been in a vast crowd and she had seen his face, yet she couldn't find him. Then she heard him speak.

"It's time to go upstairs." He picked her up to carry her there.

Silas said, "Master, I can do that. You mustn't strain yourself."

He had to reiterate that he was strong enough even if he was approaching fifty, and he replied, "Silas, I need you to light our way."

"As you wish, sir." The doctor's tone was not to be questioned.

Rachel was happy as she felt the comfort of William's arms. Then she thought of Elizabeth, and she reminded him, as he carried her up the stairs, that his wife would become suspicious, it would be safer to remain below, but he refused to heed her and held her tighter. She was too sick to argue, and she sank back into the bed that her brother had prepared.

He sat by her side all that night, and he was concerned only that she sleep soundly. This time when she awoke she had not lost him. He stood by the window, gazing at the rising sun, and turned to greet her. She was almost glad she was ill, if William could always greet the morning with her.

From then on he allowed nothing to distract him from his treatment of her. When her cough ended and she was no longer afflicted with chills and she began to feel better, he was glad that he had had the good sense to move her upstairs. She was starting to smile, there was some colour in her cheeks, he felt that her cure was truly progressing. And now she wanted to know if he had heard from the Frankfurt printer, William Fitzer.

"Not yet."

"Not a word?" she asked anxiously.

"It is too soon. You mustn't worry. You must get better first."

But what then? she wondered. The idea of returning belowstairs was even harder to bear now. He had moved back to the table to write again. Then, as his wife stood in the doorway and refused to go until he had spoken with her, Rachel felt poor and young again in Cambridge. Worse, she heard his wife speaking in the hall, although he was trying to quiet her.

"William, what you must do is to put her in St. Bartholomew's Hospital."

"Elizabeth, that is impossible."

"Why not! It is for the poor, the servants."

And it could kill her, he thought bitterly, and at the best leave her with a permanent cough and chest condition. He didn't reply.

"You surely don't owe her that much loyalty."

"Please, we will discuss it some other time."

"No! This is the time and place!"

Rachel realised that his wife had no intention of moving out of earshot, that Elizabeth was determined that she hear her.

His wife's voice rose. "I've often wondered about the two of you."

"I will not discuss it."

"Now I realise what I thought was just a tendency to favour her was much more than that to you. No wonder you moved her up here."

"I moved her into the laboratory to cure her. As a physician."

Elizabeth laughed hysterically and declared, "It is one thing to be a Good Samaritan and give a servant medical attention. But to put her in your own room, with me sleeping below—you expect too much. If she stays up here, I will go. And I mean every word. She must know her place."

William stared at his wife. Her eyes were bloodshot, and she looked so old, her face almost fleshless and her hair completely gray. Even her carriage, in which she had taken such pride, was bent and aging. Her declaration had a frantic ring to it, and he was determined not to give in to her threat, yet he was afraid that Rachel could hear them. He said softly, although he was furious, "No one will tell me how to treat a patient. But after that, I will think of something." That silenced her, as he had hoped, and he took her by the arm and led her downstairs.

"But what did you expect?" Rachel said, when he returned to her. He didn't know who was more embarrassed, but she was more upset. "Will you stand still!" He had moved back to his desk. "Something terrible has happened. She knows about us now."

"Nothing has changed," he cried out. "We are the same people."

"Your wife isn't. William, what does she mean to you?"

"Please, you must trust me."

"I'm leaving here."

"You can't, Rachel. You're not fully recovered yet."

She thought bitterly, He behaves as if his wife acts only out of bad temper, but this affair goes far deeper. She said, "Your wife wants me out. I'm in the way. She has made that very plain."

"I run this house. We've had many happy years, and we'll have more."

"We'll have no more privacy. I can't stay in such a situation."

Rachel was as pale as death, yet he knew she was almost cured. One more week of his treatment and she should be healed. He said, "This will only make you worse, give you a relapse."

"Consult your wife. She knows what is wrong with me. And she has not given it her blessing." She tried to get out of bed, but he wouldn't allow it. Then she had to ask what she had wanted to know for a long time: "William, would you ever leave her? I must know."

"Don't push me, Rachel!" he felt like shouting back, but she looked so miserable he tried to be kind, and he said, "That is not the issue."

"I'm just a servant. Even when I help you with your notes."

"We will discuss this later. Your illness has made you feverish."

He kissed her to express his love, but she felt confused. The thought of his wife's knowing about their intimacy was unbearable, yet to leave him would hurt just as much. She decided that she must regain her strength.

During her convalescence he was grateful that neither she nor his wife mentioned the other. They are obedient after all, he thought with relief, as women should be. He felt he had been right to handle the matter as he had. Elizabeth wanted to know when her brother would be reexamined by the College, and he assumed she would overlook Rachel's presence if Galen got a license to practise in London, and was using that as her weapon. At the same time, Rachel was concerned that he hadn't heard from Frankfurt. "Does this indicate Fitzer has rejected your book?"

He said with an assurance he didn't feel, "Your anxiety is unnecessary. The longer we wait, the more hopeful we should be." He was glad she was calm and her health was almost normal. "You can get out of bed tomorrow."

"When do you want me to return belowstairs?"

"We will discuss that later."

"William, we must look ahead. Some things have changed."

"First you must get completely well. Then we can talk."

* * *

423

Rachel was grateful she could walk without weakness, and William celebrated this by having Silas serve her a fine dinner, which he insisted on sharing with her. He resolved not to worry about what others felt, but her brother's presence made her uneasy. She was not accustomed to Silas's waiting on her, and she couldn't accept it the way William did. She wondered how much they would miss her if she left.

When she did so a few days later, without a word of warning, neither of them could believe it. William heard footsteps at the front door, and he couldn't wait for Silas to open it, but hurried to do so himself, hoping it was Rachel, thinking how desirable she was, how much a part of his life. When it wasn't she, he was miserable and lonely. After a week without any trace of her, he had to ask Silas, "Do you know where your sister went?"

"Probably to Cambridge, sir. I never expected her to go without me."

"If you want to join her . . . ?" He paused, for the idea of losing Silas also was too much to contemplate, especially with Rachel gone.

"I can't, sir!" Silas cried out despairingly. "I owe so much to you!"

"Did she ever tell you that she would leave my service?"

"No sir," Silas didn't add, But he had dreaded for a long time this might happen, ever since he had sensed their feelings for each other. "I do think she will communicate with me. We have never been apart from each other, except when . . . I thought I would never see her again."

Silas had to halt to restrain his tears, while all William could say was "If she communicates with you, tell her that I would like to see her too." He strode away grimly to control his own emotion.

Fitzer's reply to his submission came a month after her departure.

Twenty-eight days to be exact, he thought sadly; he had

counted each one of them. He opened the letter, and expecting a rejection, read:

Dear Harvey,

I have had difficulty in deciphering your hand, which is almost illegible, but your treatise is short, which is good in these frugal times. I read it with interest, for that esteemed physician, Baruch van Mendoza, recommended you as a distinguished anatomist who has confirmed and declared with ocular demonstrations that blood moves in a circuit.

I am not certain I share your views, but they will cause a stir.

Thanks to your brevity, I will be able to print your pages to sell for 6 schilling, 2 pfennig, but I will have to economise on the printing.

Most of all, I desire to publish your book in time to appear at our Frankfurt Book Fair in the autumn of 1628. This great Book Fair will make a strong impression in Frankfurt itself and all the surrounding country, and we must not let slip this grand opportunity of getting your book known throughout all of Europe.

William's joy was tinged with sorrow. He yearned to tell Rachel the good news—she who had contributed so much to it—but Silas said there still hadn't been any word from her. So he read Silas the letter from Fitzer, as he would have read it to her, and that made him feel better.

At the news of the publication Silas smiled, for the first time since Rachel had left. Then William told Elizabeth about the acceptance.

She asked, "Are you pleased?"

"Very much. I've worked towards this end for many years."

"Then I'm pleased too."

He was surprised. He had expected a caustic rejoinder.

"William, you got rid of that girl, and I am appreciative."

"Aren't you afraid of what the world will say about my views?"

"I will pray for you."

After Elizabeth was gone he sat in the dining room, thinking of Rachel. He heard someone at the front door, and he felt it could be her, for Silas, who answered the knock, was speaking excitedly. But he mustn't act too eager, and he stayed in his chair and waited hopefully.

A minute later Silas informed him, "Master, it is an invitation from Doctor Donne. He wants you to attend him at St. Paul's tomorrow afternoon."

Disappointed, he observed that Silas, who until recently had appeared indestructible, had aged perceptibly since his sister's departure. He asked, "Do you think Rachel has enough money to live properly?"

"I think so, sir. She saved most of what she earned."

Where could she have gone? By saving her life, he had lost her.

He started for his laboratory to begin work on a supplement to *De motu cordis*. For, now more than ever, with her absence, it was his work that sustained him. Whatever reception it received.

f you tell them what is unknown
to them
they will throw the stone
you threw at them . . .

William's request for a personal audience with the King was granted.

It was the following year, and as he waited impatiently in

the Presence Chamber of Whitehall Palace for Charles to receive him, he was assailed by misgivings. He was alone except for stern Yeomen of the Guard, who stood with sharp pikes before the entrance to the royal rooms, and while the red velvet chair on which he sat was upholstered, he squirmed uncomfortably and his uneasiness grew. Although he had been prompt, he had waited an hour, and there appeared to be no relief in sight.

He had looked forward to 1628 and this occasion. He had celebrated his fiftieth birthday, and he had just received copies of *De motu cordis*. But now that he was about to present the book to the King—he had dedicated it to him, the President of the College of Physicians, and the Fellows —his trepidation increased. Buckingham had been assassinated, and he had heard that Charles had taken the news as an attack on himself. He hadn't treated the King for many months, and he felt out of favour.

It must be my book, he reflected, and he found no reassurance in it. Now that it was published, he was concerned about its reception. He stared at it, seeking to calculate its chances. It was brief, 68 pages of type, and he thought, His introduction and seventeen chapters were soundly argued and complete, but otherwise insignificant. Despite Fitzer's pride that it would be appearing at the Frankfurt Book Fair in a few days, he felt that it would crawl into the world unseen and die for lack of interest. Or arouse such a storm he would be unable to withstand the attack. While Fitzer had printed a few copies on a thick paper of good quality, which he had sent to him as presentation copies, the edition for the public appalled him. Fitzer had done it on such thin, mean, cheap paper, he feared it would crumble. The type was small, faint, and difficult to read. Worst of all, while Fitzer had included a leaf of 126 errata, he had found twice as many mistakes. There were so many, he wondered if the printer had dropped the type while setting it. But the King's copy was beautifully bound and contained a splendid title page.

When he saw Moore and Bedwin leaving Charles's quarters with Mayerne and Matthew, he felt he should retreat, for they had testified against him at the Buckingham trial. But Mayerne halted him and said, "Charles waits for you to attend him."

"Is he ill?" So many physicians at Court indicated that he was.

"Just an attack of melancholy caused by the murder of Buckingham."

Matthew asked, "Are you going to present your book to him?"

"I had planned to. Would you like to read it?"

Matthew said that he wasn't sure—actually, he was reluctant, for his mind was made up. Mayerne was eager to look at it, whilst Moore and Bedwin regarded him contemptuously and strode out to express their hostility.

"Never mind," said Mayerne, "you will survive their ignorance."

Matthew said, "I don't agree. Your book will cause controversy and be regarded with distaste by Charles. He is grief-stricken and embittered."

His impulse was still to retire, but it was too late, for the steward had entered, and informed him, "Harvey, the King is waiting for you."

Again there was no one in the audience chamber but two stern Yeomen of the Guard, heavily armed. The steward presented him to Charles and bowed out. William saw that Charles, who was orderly and austere where James had been disorderly and sentimental, looked especially remote.

Charles asked with a slight stammer, "Harvey, what do you desire?"

"Nothing, Your Majesty."

The King regarded him sceptically, but he didn't comment. "Except . . ." He coughed to compose himself, then halted awkwardly.

"Never fear. Your support of the Duke was appreciated."

"Sir, I simply told the truth."

"I wish more had. This dreadful murder is an attack on me."

"I'm sorry, Your Majesty. Is there anything I can do?"

"It has been done. Felton, the Puritan bigot who did it because he was rejected for a promotion in the army, who slew my devoted friend with a mere threepenny knife, has been punished by the ax. Why are you here?"

"Sir, a work of mine is about to appear at the great International Book Fair in Frankfurt, and I wish to give you the first copy."

"And it is dedicated to me."

William was surprised that Charles knew; he had kept that a secret.

"It is a matter of right. You are still a Physician Extraordinary."

"Always at your service, Your Majesty."

"What is the subject of your work? What does it propose?"

"Sir, it concerns the heart and the blood and how it circulates."

"Such doctrines are not accepted by others."

"Sir, I have worked many years on my explorations."

"If you are wrong, you will be greatly embarrassed and hurt."

"It is true, sir. The heart is made up of two muscular pumps. One side pushes the blood into the lungs, then it is returned to the second side, which delivers it into the arteries and the rest of the body, and finally the blood travels back to the heart through the veins."

"Do any other physicians share your views?"

"Some must, Your Majesty. For this is so."

The King shrugged, then asked, "What else have you decided?"

William felt tested, but he was curious how Charles would respond. And if the King was sympathetic, it could lessen the objections. *"Sir, when I began, I thought the heart's movement was understood by God alone."*

"And now?"

"*Sir, now I believe I have as much right to call the movement of the blood circular as Aristotle had to say that the air and rain emulate the circular movement of the heavenly bodies.*"

"Then you think that you are absolutely right?"

"*Sir, since calculations and visual demonstrations have confirmed all my suppositions, I am obliged to conclude that in animals the blood is driven around a circuit with an unceasing circular kind of movement; that is an activity of the heart which it carries out by pulsation, and it is the sole reason for the heart's pulsatile movements. And in man.*"

William stopped. The King wasn't listening.

There was an awkward pause, and then Charles cried out, "What were you saying?" and as William replied, "Sir, I was speaking about the movement of the blood," the King interrupted him abruptly and coldly: "Give me your book and it will be considered. Harvey, you are dismissed."

When he returned home he went directly to the new laboratory he had put in on the ground floor. Ever since Rachel had left, he had been unable to work upstairs; it reminded him painfully of her. He ignored the animals and the instruments he kept there for his experiments and turned to his book.

He examined the copies even more carefully, and he was unhappy when several broke at the binding as he opened them. The title page was the only attractive part, and he wondered if anyone would read it.

Yet Fitzer had sent him ten finely bound copies for presentation, with a note that they were his gift to the author. He hadn't told anybody of the receiving of *De motu cordis*, and now he sat down to mail it to those he wanted to read it. As he posted copies to Mendoza, Galileo, Riolan, Hofmann, Ross, Mayerne, Argent, and Hall, he felt that nothing he said mattered—the book must speak for itself—so he added only his good wishes.

This left him with one good copy for himself. If he could only give it to Rachel! He called Silas and asked, "Have you heard from your sister?"

"No, sir." But he could recall every word she had written him:

"Dear Brother, I communicate with you so that you will not worry, but I cannot give you my address, I do not want the Master to know where I am. And so you will stay with Doctor Harvey. I am aware how much your service means to him, and how much his person means to you. Your loving sister."

Silas was so pale that William asked, "Are you telling the truth?"

He gulped, but he managed to say, "Of course, sir."

"Do you think that she has enough money?"

"Sir, she saved whatever she earned, and she is a fine housekeeper."

The need to tell her was irresistible, and William added, "If you should hear from her, inform her that my book has been published."

"She would be pleased, Master. She talked about it often to me."

"Did she tell you how much she helped me with my notes?"

"We quarrelled because of them. I wanted to aid you too, but she wouldn't allow it, sir. I wish I hadn't differed with her. Maybe that drove her out." Rachel had promised to write him again, but he wasn't certain that she would. "Master, would you like some coffee?"

"Yes. Bring me two cups, please."

When Silas did, he wanted to ask his servant to join him, but he knew this would embarrass Silas, and so he said only, "Thank you."

The coffee didn't distract him, even the aroma which he loved.

Suddenly he entered his wife's bedroom. It was the first time he had done so in years, and Elizabeth was shocked and frightened. Although she was swathed in two thick wool nightgowns that covered her from head to foot, she drew up her bedspread to her chin and cringed from him. And now the idea of making love to her was ludicrous and impossible.

He said, "I want to give you a copy of my book, which I just received."

"Now? It is improper. I will look at it tomorrow. Good night."

Neither of them mentioned the book the next day. Elizabeth was deeply preoccupied: When would Galen be reexamined by the College?

He assured her that this would happen within a few months.

None of those he had sent his book to for their opinion responded in the next few weeks, and he avoided the subject whenever he saw any of them. He assumed that they disagreed with him or disliked the book. There was no word from the King, and while he knew that *De motu cordis* had appeared at the Frankfurt Book Fair, he heard nothing about it. There was such a vacuum that sometimes he wondered why he had striven so hard to publish.

Some copies appeared in London for sale early in 1629. He hoped this would give emphasis to his views, but again there was only silence.

Fitzer sent him ten pounds in gold and acted as if it were a noble gift, given to him out of the goodness of his heart, but didn't say a word about *De motu cordis*. William's concern seemed unfounded. He felt alone, that no one was interested in the circulation of the blood. That was so discouraging he was unable to enter his laboratory and work on any experiments. He was thinking that it was better to stress his practice when Silas handed him a letter from Hofmann. He read:

"It was kind of you to request my views, but you undermine our faith in God, you accuse Nature of folly in that she went astray in a work of prime importance, the making and the distribution of blood, and you must be careful or you will become a circulator, a quack."

Soon after he received a response from Riolan, who wrote:

"You give the heart too much prominence and show too little respect for the liver. Your assumption there is a circuit to the blood is wrong, contradictory, useless to physic, and harmful to the life of man."

Their views distressed him. Riolan was Professor of Medicine at the University of Paris, while Hofmann held the same post at the University of Altdorf, and each had great influence in his country and school. Despite their polite tone, he realized that both physicians were harsh and implacable enemies of *De motu cordis* and that they would continue to teach the ancient Galenic errors to thousands of aspiring medical students.

This left him shaken. He couldn't surrender his convictions, and he decided to find out whether anybody supported him.

He invited Eliab to his house and offered his brother, who was the one in the family he felt closest to, a copy of his book and asked him to read it. He was startled when Eliab looked upset and replied, "William, I'm not qualified, and I'm very busy. All of us except John, who is running the properties at Newington and Arpinge that Father left him, are investing as merchant adventurers in the Persian trade of the East India Company, and I trust this will not injure the family name."

"I cannot predict what will happen to my findings."

"It is not an attractive book."

"And the pages are smelly and could rot."

"William, you mustn't be angry. What do your colleagues say?"

433

"Several have opposed my views. From abroad."

"What do your colleagues in England say?"

"So far they have said nothing."

"Why don't you ask them?" Eliab returned *De motu cordis* to William. "Whatever strange and new views you advocate, you know that we all will support you. The Harveys are a tightly knit family."

"Aren't you going to read my book?"

"My Latin is poor, and I will misunderstand it. Ask your colleagues."

This struck William as a good idea, and he announced he was going to use his next Lumleian Lecture to show that the blood circulated, and he asked all doctors who were interested to attend his anatomy. He was pleased that the room was filled when the cadaver was brought in, a newly hanged criminal in his thirties and in perfect health, and that Mayerne, Matthew, Scrope, Hall, Wilkins, and Argent joined him at the table. This was unusual, but he didn't object; he wanted them to follow his account as closely as possible. None of them had said a word about his book, not even Argent, President of the College, who had become a good friend.

He pointed with his silver wand to the heart and resolved, No unseemly haste, I must carefully light the inner circle of the blood, without compromise. Outlining its circuit, he grew excited again, still fascinated by the order and symmetry of the circulation. When he ended, he felt that most of them must agree with the logic of his views.

Wilkins shouted, "I have written my refutation of this in ten days!"

Which took me twenty years to find, thought William, but he turned to the others and asked, "Have any of you read *De motu cordis?*"

Mayerne nodded, Matthew did so reluctantly, then Argent and Hall said so openly, but no one else appeared to have read his book.

434

William asked those who had, "What did you think of it?"

Mayerne said strongly, "I must be sure to make myself master of your piece. I prefer your discovery to that of Christopher Columbus."

"No!" Wilkins stated more strongly. "He subverts accepted authority!"

Chambers said, "He commits heresy. He attacks the liver."

William felt, Maybe I will have to mould anew the brains of men, but he said, "The circulation establishes the heart in the primary place."

Wilkins said, "You are convicting Nature of folly and error."

Chambers added, "You speak against all we have been taught and know. The ebb and flow of the blood acquires natural spirit from the liver, vital spirit from the brain, and these are distributed through the body by the nerves, which are hollow. This must be true. Galen said so."

Moore joined in. "You profess to know better than Hippocrates, Galen, and Aristotle. This is farfetched, and a sharp and dangerous practice."

Chambers insisted, "He attacks God's work. We must charge Harvey with heresy. There is authority for this action. John Caius, when he was President of the College, caused a young Oxford doctor, who publicly questioned the teachings of Galen, to be imprisoned until he recanted."

William replied, "God is to be found in the study of nature."

"And Bruno went to the stake for professing that," sneered Chambers.

"And because of the Inquisition," John Hall retorted angrily. "But there is much in Harvey's views that is worthy and Godly."

Others joined in the argument, and there was so much yelling that no one could be heard and the dignified Argent, who had been chosen President because of his skill at reconciling opposite opinions, rapped for order. Then he stated, "As Harvey's guests, we must allow him to finish."

William resumed. "I suggest that those who differ with me read *De motu cordis,* then conduct experiments on cadavers and animals, as I have."

Wilkins cried, "To say we are the same as animals is heresy in itself."

"You will lose your whole practice for such views," declared Moore. "I wouldn't read your book now under any circumstances."

"Indeed!" Chambers snarled. "You are crack-brained, a circulator!"

Shouts of *"Circulator! Circulator!"* were repeated by the majority of the physicians, and it became a vicious chorus, and their intention was plain. Everyone knew that signified an itinerant quack.

Furious, William threw down his scalpel and strode out of the theatre.

Later that day Argent, Mayerne, and Matthew came to apologise for the bad behaviour of their colleagues and assured William that it would pass.

William, who sat at his dining-room table, replied, "I doubt it."

"It must," said Argent. "Whether or not your views are correct, they should be heard. I will see to that. And they could be true."

"Besides," Mayerne added, "you must realize that the more informed the medical opinion, the more difficult it is for them to accept new views, for to do so means to abandon much of what they have learned."

"What about you, Matthew? Do you think I am a quack?"

"There is much professional jealousy. You serve the King, St. Bart's, the College as Censor and Treasurer, you have a fine practice, and many physicians envy you. Your opinions are an excuse to attack you."

"You haven't answered my question. Do you believe them?"

436

Matthew sighed and said softly, "I would like to. There is reason in what you advocate. But so much of it is contrary to what we are taught."

No one spoke for a minute, and then William suggested coffee. All of them refused—they had stopped in just to express their friendship—and there was an uncomfortable pause before Argent, who disliked unpleasant feelings between colleagues, said, "Harvey, do not heed the howls."

William stood up, and while he was the shortest one, he seemed to tower over them as he stated with great care, "*It cannot be helped that dogs bark and vomit their foul stomachs, but care must be taken that they do not bite or inoculate us with their mad humours, or with their dogs' teeth gnaw the bones and foundation of truth.*"

When *De motu cordis* was read in London and the knowledge that this was Harvey's view circulated, his practice suffered; he heard that he was vulgar and crazy, and that medical opinion was against him. He wasn't upset by the last, he had expected such attacks, but he was irate when he heard Wilkins say, "*No one admires his therapeutic ways, there are many of his patients who wouldn't give threepence for one of his bills.*"

Many of the doctors in the College wouldn't talk to him, and he heard Moore whisper, "See, the *Circulator* can't even cure his own wife."

He was so angry at this slander that he wasn't able to concentrate on any new experiments. This troubled him deeply, and was so contrary to his nature that he felt a part of him was dead. Perhaps, he told himself, I wasn't wrong when I said *Man is but a great, mischievous baboon.* Yet when he reread *De motu cordis* with painstaking care to see if he could find any errors, he was more convinced than ever that the blood circulated as he had described it. But he was surprised when the King summoned him to Windsor. He hadn't

437

heard from Charles or seen him since he had presented a copy of *De motu cordis* to him many months ago.

He was ushered into Charles's presence as soon as he reached Windsor, at the entrance to the royal park where the King was preparing to hunt. Charles was escorted by many courtiers and Mayerne, Matthew, and Scrope.

William realised that the King was most at home in the saddle; then he was not self-conscious about his bowed legs, his shortness, for he knew that he rode better than anyone else in the Kingdom. When his hand was on the reins, there was no indecision in him and he ruled without hesitation.

Charles said, "Harvey, we will be hunting deer. The bucks are fat and in season, and you may dissect them. Mayerne and Ross informed me that you are a clever anatomist, and your findings may be of some interest."

"Thank you, sir, but if I may, I prefer to examine the does. I am most interested in how they conceive, and it is the rutting season."

"As you wish. You may wander at liberty in the woods, but if you are interested in dissection, follow me and you will have a doe for your scalpel."

But all he carried was his dagger, which could be used as a hunting knife but for little else. Yet he felt he was being tested by Charles, although that was difficult to know. Charles was secretive and inclined to keep his own counsel, and yet he sensed that the King wished to observe him, but for what purpose he couldn't tell.

Charles motioned for the hunt to start, and William rode in the rear. A few minutes later he came on Mayerne, Matthew, and Scrope examining a wounded deer on the King's orders. Charles watched them with amusement, for none of them seemed eager to touch the animal, which was trying to struggle to its feet. William dismounted, for he was curious about this deer; it looked like a lusty doe bearing young within it.

438

Then Scrope, vain about his ability as a hunter and annoyed at what he took to be derision on the King's face, went to pin down the leg of the wounded deer. He was so absorbed in what he was doing that he didn't see the snake nearby, and the venomous fangs drove deep into his wrist, puncturing his skin.

Scrope shrieked, "I'm done! It's a poisonous adder! I saw a man bitten on the hand by one and soon after he died!" Terrified, he collapsed.

No one moved but stood impotently. A courtier tried to get the King to ride away, but he refused; Charles wasn't afraid, but curious.

Thoughts raced through William's mind. If the blood circulates, it will carry the poison through its system, and so there is a possible remedy, but speed is essential. He took his dagger and cut a crosswise incision around the fang punctures. He cut as deep as the punctures, but he was careful not to touch an artery. Then he applied suction to the wound with his mouth. The others regarded him with amazement and fear, but he felt there was no danger in sucking out the venom—if his views about the blood were correct. He believed Scrope had fainted and not died, as the others assumed. He put the piece of flesh he had cut out on the ground so he could examine it later, noting that it was about the size of a shilling.

Then, grateful that he had worn a cravat today to look his best, he tore it off and ordered Matthew to use it to tie a ligature at once above the wound while he squeezed out the blood about it as an added precaution. Matthew wasn't sure what he wanted, and he shouted, "It must be tight enough to halt the passage of the poison through the blood!"

William was glad he had done these experiments himself, for his fingers were still strong, and they secured the ligature as he desired.

There was a brief pause as Scrope lay motionless. William adjusted the ligature to be sure it was tight enough to check the flow of the blood towards the heart. But as the victim

439

didn't move, he thought fearfully, Perhaps I am wrong, perhaps the blood doesn't circulate, yet I have seen poison spread in the body from the bite of a mad dog, and how else could it have been carried but by blood that circulated? He saw disbelief in the King, Matthew, even Mayerne. Yet even as he was assailed with doubts, he couldn't give up. He felt Scrope's body, and except for the part below the ligature, where the blood was cut off, it was warm. There is still life in him, he decided excitedly. William ordered the Yeomen who accompanied the King to build a stretcher out of the branches. And when Scrope was placed upon it, he examined the bite once more to be sure all the poison was gone, and the victim stirred.

"It is a miracle!" exclaimed the King.

"Begging your pardon, sir," William replied, "but it is because the blood circulates, and we were able to utilise that fact." He felt such a joy, he couldn't express it to anyone else. Even after he had published *De motu cordis*, he had had some doubts that the blood passed through the entire body, but now he had none. He put Scrope's head between his legs so that the blood would be encouraged to return to it, and as it did—for colour returned to his cheeks, and Scrope revived and regained consciousness—he felt this was further proof that the blood circulated.

Charles ordered Scrope carried to the castle. He was surprised that Harvey didn't follow the snakebite victim. He asked him why.

"Sir, he will recover. The essentials are done. This doe is still alive, and I would like to examine its heart. That is exposed, which is rare."

He pointed to the deer, which had fallen on its side, having lost the strength to struggle, and indicated what absorbed him.

"Sir, it was wounded on the left side, with a large hole there, but the heart is undamaged. I can put my hand on the ventricles, and if you put yours on them, you will observe the motion of the heart, that in the diastole it draws up and retracts, and in the systole it thrusts out, more proof that it is a pump and propels the blood to circulate."

William wasn't certain that Charles was convinced. The King couldn't bring himself to touch the beating, exposed heart, but resumed the hunt.

Yet when Scrope recovered fully from the poison, Charles summoned William for a private audience in his bedchamber in the castle. It was two days later, and Charles was putting on the royal blue robe that he wore as a dressing gown, and William realised this indicated that the usually reserved King was accessible. He ordered him to sit—another sign of royal favour—and then faced William across his marble table.

He was pleased that the King looked well—his advice had been good.

Charles said, noticing the doctor's gratification, "Ever since you recommended, for health's sake, that I spend time here and hunt, I have had few complaints, except when melancholy has afflicted me. And I liked that you supported my dear martyred Buckingham during his crisis."

Before William could express his appreciation, he was halted.

"On the other hand, a group of physicians have petitioned me asking for your removal from St. Bart's and the College of Physicians."

William cried out indignantly, "Why, sir?"

"You know that your views have provoked much criticism and hostility."

"Your Majesty, have you read them?"

"That is not the point," Charles said sharply. "I have decided that you will have to resign your posts at the hospital and the College."

"But, sir . . ." William had to halt to control his temper.

"I am quite determined on this course of action."

Meditation failed William. He felt as if his whole world

441

was collapsing. He blurted out, "Sir, I was afraid I would suffer from the ill will of some, but I didn't expect you to turn against me."

"Who said I have?"

"Your Majesty, I don't understand. If I'm to resign . . . ?"

"And if you are going to accompany my cousin, the seventeen-year-old Duke of Lennox, beyond the seas, it is reasonable to assume that you cannot continue your responsibilities to the College and the hospital."

William didn't reply. He knew this was considered an honour, but what about his work? Charles hadn't said a word about *De motu cordis.*

"Lennox needs the services of a doctor and scholar that I can trust."

"Thank you, sir. But I published my views so that you might pass judgement on me, and that you might see that I have not lived in vain."

Charles gazed out on the royal park, which he loved. He felt that if this doctor had his way, he must support him openly, and that would not be wise. If Harvey was wrong, although he doubted that, he would not be at fault. If the man was right, his use of him would be praised. He had summoned him here to examine him, and he was pleased. This physician would attend his young cousin excellently. Unless he didn't want to. Upset by that thought, he asked, "Don't you want to serve the Duke in Europe?"

"Very much, sir. If I may take a leave of absence from the College and the hospital, not resign." Then, he felt, it wouldn't be a retreat.

Charles deliberated, then smiled and said, "This can be arranged. But afterwards, when you return, that will be difficult." Amused by the puzzled expression on the doctor's face, he added, "For when you return, I have decided on the following and put it in writing. Read it."

"*Charles R: Whereas we have been graciously pleased to admit Doctor Harvey into the place of Physician in Ordinary to our Royal Person.*"

William exclaimed, "Your Majesty, I never expected this!"

"A good reason for appointing you. As my personal physician, a post I propose for you when you return, you will be tied to me by daily practice and service. Then you will have to resign your other duties. I must have the proper attention, and you are the physician best qualified to perform it."

"You are very kind, sir. I will serve you faithfully."

"I'm sure you will. That is why I appoint you." Then he saw a strange look on Harvey's face, as if the doctor was still in a dilemma, and, curious—he had never met a physician quite like this one—he asked, "What concerns you now? Is this appointment so difficult to accept?"

"Sir, I'm privileged. But I would like to continue my experiments."

"You are interested in dissecting the deer?"

"The does chiefly, sir. Examination of animals has always been my delight, for I believe we might not only obtain an insight into the mysteries of nature, but there perceive a kind of image or reflection of the Omnipotent Creator Himself. I could do this at Windsor."

"That is permitted. As long as you attend me when I need you. Remember, when you are abroad, you must remain an Englishman and never lose control of the situation. The Duke of Lennox must be properly educated."

Physician in Ordinary, what a nourishing sound, thought William.

There was a letter from Mendoza waiting for him when he arrived home, and he took it into his laboratory to read.

The sight of your words in print gives them even more conviction. It causes me to believe that there will be three stages to your medical discovery. When it is announced, people say it is not true. Then when the truth is borne in on them, and it can no longer be denied, they say it is not important. After that,

when its importance becomes obvious, they will say
that somehow it is not new.

But I find *De motu cordis* a remarkable work. It
is a profound source of enlightenment, stimulus, and
pleasure, with its revelation of clear premises, cogent
and wise, and its precise deductions and incontro-
vertible conclusions. You never sound afraid, but
always say what you think. Your views are more
than discovery, they are a medical revolution.

William was reflecting about Mendoza's reassuring words
when Silas handed him another letter. Silas said, "Sir, it was
given to me at the door by a boy, but before I could ask
him who it was from, he fled. The handwriting looks familiar.
Do you think it could be from my sister?"

He hoped that it was, but he couldn't reveal the prayer
he was uttering. He said, "I doubt it. It is probably from
another doctor about my book."

Silas realized that his master desired to be alone, whom-
ever the letter was from and whatever it contained, and so he
excused himself, saying, "Sir, I will make you some coffee.
That is always a comfort to you."

William hesitated before opening this letter, afraid it might
have bad news. Then the uncertainty was unbearable. He was
almost sure that the handwriting was Rachel's, he knew it so
well, and yet he had a premonition that if it was, it was a
farewell. But he couldn't remain in the dark.

He opened it with great care so not a word would be
marred, and he was glad he had, for, as he had suspected,
it was from her. He read emotionally:

Dear William:
I wrote to Silas and told him that I could not go
on living like a lily in a pond, where I could see all
the shores but never my own shore. That was the
reason I left. But whether he understood, I do not
know. You protected him from the world as you

protected me. He needs it and likes to live that way.
However, with you I can speak the truth.

When I was young and unhappy, if a person said,
"Today is the happiest day of your life," I would
think, How do they know, it could become the sad-
dest before it is over, since my days were often sad.
After I met you and learnt happiness, I believed
them when they said that.

When I left you, I needed to free myself from
myself and I needed to free you from me, even if
you didn't think so. I hope you will understand this
now. You couldn't understand it if I were standing
before you and telling you this. That is why I left the
way I did.

Yesterday I saw a copy of your book in Cambridge and yesterday was the happiest day of my life.
And it hasn't changed today.

Please, do not try to find my whereabouts or ask
Silas about me. It would burden him and make him
wonder about your interest, which would show more
feeling than you intend. Silas is not too curious and
sees what he believes, and he never saw us as we
were. Perhaps that is for the best.

I wish I could read every word of your book and
each night I pray for its success. But, as you know,
Latin is not a language for my sort of folk. I am
trying to learn some, and in the meantime I am
asking one of the learned professors at Cambridge to
translate your words for me, although I recall many
of those you told me while you were thinking and
writing them.

Since I must not depend on anyone else, I have
returned to what I knew in childhood. I work for a
squire who needs a housekeeper who can read and
write in order to keep his accounts. He is a lazy man,
so unlike you, but as long as I know my place, I am
allowed to run his household without interference.
Do not seek me out and please do not worry about
me.

My chest complaint is gone and I feel in a suitable condition to support myself. And whenever I feel alone, I pick up your book. There is much wonder about your words but I am convinced they will believe them in time. As I do. And always will. If I hide from you, it is because I love you.

Rachel

And please, William dear, do not tell Silas about this letter. It would only worry him and confuse him. For he loves you too.

Silas stood in the doorway. It was unusual for him to interrupt, and William wondered if he knew whom this letter was from after all.

"What do you want, Silas?"

"Master, is there any answer?"

William paused, sighed, and then said softly, "No." But as he put the letter in his doublet so that he could keep it by his side, it warmed him. He was grateful that Rachel had learned to read and write. Perhaps, as she suggested, they had come to a close shore from a great distance, and now the distance was greater than ever, but the book would link them forever. Silas hadn't moved, as if he wanted to know whom the letter was from, and William said, "It is about my book. It is from a friend. Where is my coffee?"

Silas blushed and cried out in his embarrassment and vexation, "I forgot, sir." He hurried out to get it.

William's mind was off on another subject. With all the excitement about the snakebite, he had never finished his experiment on the doe. But he was excited by the generation of animals. He repeated this concept in his mind, searching for a title for this new work. If he could find the right one, it would be a good start for this exploration.

When he came upon it he wrote it out to see if it read as accurately as it sounded: "*Exercitationes de generatione animalium.*"

He translated it into English so that Rachel could read it if she ever saw it. Then he said it aloud to see if he still liked the sound:

"*Exercises on the Generation of Animals.*"

He felt free of all the criticism and scorn now, and he wrote the title in his notes and added: "*The rest of my life will not suffice for all that I would like to learn about the blood and the generation of animals. W-I.*"

A few minutes later Silas brought him a cup of coffee. This devoted shadow of myself, he thought gratefully, who answers even my unspoken wants. He said softly, "Silas, I am to be Physician in Ordinary to King Charles." If he couldn't tell Rachel, he could tell her brother, and possibly, somehow, she would find out.

"How wonderful, sir!" Silas brightened. "I must tell your wife!"

"Yes, do. It will please her."

After Silas was gone, blushing from his unexpected embrace, he sat drinking his coffee. He said a silent prayer to his blood, thankful that he still had the time and energy to start another new exploration.

447

SOURCES

AKRIGG, G. P. V. *Jacobean Pageant.* 1962.

ALLBURT, T. C. *The Historical Relations of Medicine and Surgery at the end of the 16th Century.* 1905.

AUBREY, JOHN. *Aubrey's Brief Lives,* Edited by O. L. Dick. 1950.

AYDELOTTE, FRANK. *Elizabethan Rogues and Vagabonds.* 1967.

BAGROW, LEO. *History of Cartography.* 1964.

BALD, R. C. *John Donne, A Life.* 1970.

BARZINI, LUIGI. *The Italians.* 1965.

BEATTY, BADEN. *How To Live with Your Blood Pressure.* 1956.

BENESTEAD, C. R. *Portrait of Cambridge.* 1968.

BENNETT, RISDON. *The Diseases of the Bible.* 1887.

BERNAL, J. D. *Science in History.* 1965.

BEVAN, BRYAN. *The Real Francis Bacon.* 1960.

BLIGH, E. W., and S. G. B. STUBBS. *Sixty Centuries of Health and Physic.* 1931.

BLOOM, J. H., and R. R. JAMES. *Medical Practitioners in the Diocese of London.* 1935.

BOWEN, CATHERINE DRINKER. *Francis Bacon.* 1963.

———. *The Lion and the Throne.* 1956.

BRADFORD, E. *Drake.* 1965.

BRADFORD, G. *Elizabethan Women.* 1936.

BRESFORD, J. *Gossip of the Seventeenth and Eighteenth Centuries.* 1924.   ·

BRION, MARCEL. *Venice, The Masque of Italy.* 1962.

BRODERICK, JAMES, S.J. *Galileo, The Man, His Work, His Misfortunes.* 1964.

BROWN, IVOR. *How Shakespeare Spent the Day.* 1961.

———. *The Women in Shakespeare's Life.* 1968.

BROWNE, T. *Religio Medici.* 1682.

BRYANT, W. W. *Galileo.* 1925.

BURCKHARDT, JACOB. *The Civilization of the Renaissance in Italy.* 1961.

BURTON, ELIZABETH. *The Pageant of Stuart England.* 1962.

449

BYRNE, M. ST. CLARE. *Elizabethan Life in Town and Country*. 1970.

CALDER, RITCHIE. *Medicine and Man*. 1957.

CAMDEN, C. *The Elizabethan Woman*. 1962

CARLYLE, THOMAS. *Historical Sketches of Notable Persons and Events in the Reigns of James I and Charles I*, edited by Alexander Carlyle. 1898.

CECIL, ALGERNON. *A Life of Robert Cecil*. 1915.

CECIL, DAVID. *The Cecils of Hatfield House*. 1973.

CECIL, EVELYN. *A History of Gardening in England*. 1910.

CHAMBERS, E. K. *Sources of a Biography of Shakespeare*. 1970.

CHAUVOIS, LOUIS. *William Harvey, His Life and Times*. 1957.

CHUTE, MARCHETTE. *Ben Jonson of Westminster*. 1954.

CLARK, R. L., and R. W. CUMLEY. *The Book of Health*. 1973.

CLIVE, MARY. *Jack and the Doctor—The Story of John Donne*. 1966.

CONNOISSEUR, THE. *The Stuart Period (1603–1714)*. 1957.

COPEMAN, W. S. C. *Doctors and Disease in Tudor Times*. 1960.

CORNWALLIS, JANE LADY. *The Private Correspondence of Jane Lady Cornwallis, 1613–1644*. 1842. (Wife of Nathaniel Bacon.)

CROMBIE, A. C. *Augustine to Galileo*. 1952.

CROSS, CLAIRE. *The Puritan Earl*. 1966.

CROW, JOHN A. *Italy, A Journey Through Time*. 1965.

CUMSTON, C. G. *An Introduction to the History of Medicine*. 1926.

CUNNINGTON, C. W. and P. *Handbook of English Costume in the 16th Century*. 1970.

CUSHING, HARVEY. *A Bio-Bibliography of Andreas Vesalius*. 1943.

DA COSTA, J. M. *Harvey and his Discovery*. 1879.

DAVIES, J. C. *The Decline of the Venetian Nobility as a Ruling Class*. 1962.

DE KRUIF, P. *The Microbe Hunters*. 1926.

DUGDALE, GEORGE. *Whitehall Through the Centuries*. 1950.

DUGDALE, SIR WILLIAM. *The History of St. Paul's Cathedral*. 1818.

ECKSTEIN, GUSTAV. *The Body Has a Head*. 1971.

EDWARDS, D. I. *A History of King's School Canterbury*. 1957.

EDWARDS, FRANCIS. *Guy Fawkes, The Real Story of the Gunpowder Plot*. 1969.

EDWARDS, W. *Notes on British History*. 1959.

ELTON, G. R. *England under the Tudors.* 1969.

EMISON, M. *Tudor Food and Pastimes.* 1964.

ERLANGER, PHILIPPE. *George Villiers, Duke of Buckingham.* 1952.

FAHIE, J. J. *Galileo, His Life and Work.* 1903.

FAUSSET, H. P. *John Donne.* 1924.

FISHMAN, A. P., and D. W. RICHARDS. *Circulation of the Blood.* 1964.

FRANKLIN, K. J. *William Harvey, Englishman.* 1961.

FULLER, THOMAS. *The History of the Worthies of England.* 1840.

GEBLER, KARL VON. *Galileo Galilei.* 1879.

GIBB, M. S. *Buckingham, 1592–1628.* 1938.

GIBBS, PHILIP. *The Romance of George Villiers.* 1908.

GLOAG, JOHN. *English Furniture.* 1905.

GOTCH, J. A. *Architecture of the Renaissance in England.* 1894.

GRABAR, A., and M. MURARO. *Treasures of Venice.* 1963.

GRAEME, BRUCH. *The Story of Windsor Castle.* 1937.

GRAY'S ANATOMY. Edited by D. V. Davies. 34th Edition. 1967.

GREEN, J. R. *A Short History of the English People.* 1960.

GUTHRIE, DOUGLAS. *A History of Medicine.* 1945.

HAGGARD, H. W. *Devils, Drugs, and Doctors.* 1929.

———. *The Lame, the Halt, and the Blind.* 1932.

———. *Mystery, Magic, and Medicine.* 1933.

HALE, J. R. *The Renaissance.* 1965.

HALLIDAY, F. E. *An Illustrated Cultural History of England.* 1967.

———. *Shakespeare, a Pictoral Biography.* 1961.

HANDOVER, P. M. *The Second Cecil.* 1959.

HARVEY, WILLIAM. *Exercitatio anatomica de motu cordis et sanguinis in animalibus.* 1628. Translated by K. J. Franklin, 1957.

———. *De generatione animalium.* 1651. Translated by R. Willis, 1847.

HAYES, JOHN. *London, a Pictoral History.* 1969.

HIBBERT, CHRISTOPHER. *Charles I.* 1968.

———. *London, The Biography of a City.* 1969.

HOLMES, RONALD. *Witchcraft in British History.* 1974.

HORIZON BOOK OF THE RENAISSANCE, Edited by J. H. Plumb. 1961.

HOUSTIN, J. C., and C. L. JOINER. *A Short Textbook of Medicine.* 1968.

HUNTER, R., and I. MACALPINE. *Three Hundred Years of Psychiatry (1535–1860).* 1970.

HUTCHINSON, R. *Harvey, the Man, His Method, and His Message for us Today.* 1931.

IRWIN, KATHERINE. *Queen Elizabeth.* 1929.

JENKINS, ELIZABETH. *Elizabeth the Great.* 1959.

JENKINSON, W. *London Churches Before the Great Fire.* 1917.

JONES, JOHN. *Medical and Vulgar Errors.* 1791.

KEELE, K. D. *William Harvey.* 1965.

———. *Leonardo da Vinci on Movement of the Heart and Blood.* 1952.

KENYON, J. P. *The Stuarts.* 1971.

KEYNES, GEOFFREY. *Life of William Harvey.* 1966.

———. *The Personality of William Harvey.* 1949.

———. *Bibliography of Dr. Donne.* 1973.

KING, L. S. *The Road to Medical Enlightenment.* 1970.

LATHAM, P. M. *Diseases of the Heart.* 1946.

LAWRENCE, R. N. *Primitive Psycho-Therapy and Quackery.* 1910.

LILLYWHITE, BRYANT. *London Coffee-Houses.* 1963.

LOFTIE, W. J. *Westminster Abbey.* 1914.

MACAULAY, THOMAS B. *History of England.* 1861.

MACCURDY, E. *The Notebooks of Leonardo Da Vinci.* 1938.

MACFIE, R. C. *The Romance of Medicine.* 1917.

MACKINNEY, L. C. *Early Medieval Medicine.* 1937.

MATHEW, DAVID. *The Age of Charles I.* 1951.

MATTHEWS, C. M. *English Surnames.* 1967.

MATTHEWS, L. G. *Antiques of Pharmacy.* 1971.

———. *The Royal Apothecaries.* 1967.

MCKUSICK, V. A. *Cardiovascular Sound in Health and Disease.* 1958.

MEE, ARTHUR. *Cambridgeshire.* 1965.

———. *Kent.* 1969.

MEYER, A. W. *An Analysis of De Generatione Animalium of William Harvey.* 1936.

MILLINGEN, J. G. *Curiosities of Medical Experience.* 1837.

MITCHELL, H. J., and M. D. R. LEYS. *A History of the English People.* 1950.

———. *A History of London Life.* 1958.

MITCHELL, S. W. *Some Recently Discovered Letters of William Harvey.* 1912.

MOORE, N. *The History of the Study of Medicine in the British Isles*. 1908.

MORESHEAD, SIR OWEN. *Windsor Castle*. 1951.

MORRIS, JAMES. *The World of Venice*. 1960.

MULLINGER, J. B. *The University of Cambridge*. 1884.

MUMFORD, LEWIS. *The City in History*. 1961.

NEALE, J. E. *Queen Elizabeth I*. 1958.

NICHOLS, JOHN. *Progresses of Queen Elizabeth and James I*. 1928.

NOPPEN, J. G. *Royal Westminster*. 1957.

O'MALLEY, C. D. *Andreas Vesalius of Brussels (1514–1564)*. 1964.

ORDISH, T. F. *Shakespeare's London*. 1897.

OSLER, W. *The Growth of Truth as illustrated in the Discovery of the Circulation of the Blood*. 1957.

OSMAN, CHARLES. *Castles*. 1926.

PARE, AMBROSE. *Of Poisons*. 1840.

———. *His Works*. 1950.

PAUL, HENRY R. *The Royal Play of Macbeth*. 1950.

PEVSNER, NIKOLAUS. *The Buildings of England*. 1962.

PLATTS, BERYL. *A History of Greenwich*. 1973.

PLOWDER, ALISON. *Elizabeth I (As They Saw Her)*. 1971.

POWERS, D'ARCY. *William Harvey*. 1897.

———. *Selected Writings (1877–1930)*. 1931.

POYNTER, F. N. L. *The Evolution of Medical Practice in Britain*. 1961.

PRESCOTT, ORVILLE. *Lords of Italy*. 1972.

QUENNELL, M. and C. H. B. *A History of Everyday Things in England*. 1960.

RAPPORT, S., and H. WRIGHT. *Great Adventures in Medicine*. 1952.

RASMUSSEN, S. E. *Experiencing Architecture*. 1960.

———. *London: The Unique City*. 1961.

REEVES, DAVID. *Furniture*. 1959.

ROBINSON, E. F. *The Early History of the Coffee-House in England*. 1893.

ROSS, LYSBETH. *Coronary Wife*. 1972.

ROTH, MORITZ. *Andreas Vesalius*. 1892.

ROUGHTON, F. J. W. *Harvey at Cambridge*. 1958.

ROWDON, MAURICE. *The Silver Age of Venice*. 1970.

ROWSE, A. L. *The Elizabethan Renaissance*. 1972.

———. *The English Spirit*. 1945.

————. *Sir Walter Raleigh.* 1962.

————. *The Tower of London.* 1972.

————. *William Shakespeare.* 1963.

————. *Shakespeare the Man.* 1973.

ROYSTON, O. M., and M. HARRISON. *How They Lived (1485–1700).* 1963.

RUBENSTEIN, STANLEY. *Historians of London.* 1968.

RUKEYSER, MURIEL. *The Traces of Thomas Harriot.* 1971.

RUSSELL, J. R. *The History and Heroes of the Art of Medicine.* 1861.

RYE, W. B. *England as seen by Foreigners in the days of Elizabeth and James I.* 1863.

SAUNDERS, HILARY ST. GEORGE. *Westminster Hall.* 1951.

SCHOENBAUM, S. *Shakespeare's Lives.* 1970.

SIMPSON, R. R. *Shakespeare and Medicine.* 1959.

SINGER, CHARLES. *The Discovery of the Circulation of the Blood.* 1958.

————. *A Short History of Scientific Ideas.* 1959.

————, and H. E. SIGERIST. *Essays on the History of Medicine.* 1924.

SINGER, CHARLES, and W. A. UNDERWOOD. *A Short History of Medicine.* 1962.

SITWELL, SACHEVERELL. *British Architects and Craftsmen.* 1948.

SMOUT, C. F. E. *The Story of the Progress of Medicine.* 1964.

SPENCER, H. R. *William Harvey, Obstetric Physician and Gynaecologist.* 1921.

————. *The History of British Midwifery (1650–1800).* 1927.

SPRIGGE, S. S. *Physic and Fiction.* 1921.

STEARNS, F. P. *Four Great Venetians.* 1901.

STEEGMAN, JOHN. *Cambridge.* 1945.

STOKES, M. V. *William Harvey at Bart's, St. Bart's Hospital.* 1957.

STORIC, ANTHONY. *An Essay on the Medicinal Nature of Herblock.* 1762.

STOW, JOHN. *A Survey of London, reprinted from Text of 1603.*

STOW, W. *Remarks on London and Westminster.* 1722.

STUDIES IN LONDON HISTORY. Edited by E. J. Hollander and W. Kellaway. 1969.

SUMMERSON, JOHN. *Architecture in Britain (1530–1830).* 1953.

SUTHERLAND, C. H. V. *English Coinage (600–1900).* 1973.

TANNER, I. E. *History and Treasures of Westminster Abbey.* 1953.

TAYLOR, F. S. *Galileo and the Freedom of Thought.* 1933.

TAYLOR, R. A. *Leonardo the Florentine.* 1928.

TERRY, BENJAMIN. *A History of England.* 1901.

THOMPSON, C. J. S. *The Quacks of Old London.* 1910.

———. *Magic and Healing.* 1949.

———. *The Mystery and Art of the Apothecary.* 1929.

THOMSON, G. M. *Sir Francis Drake.* 1972.

THORNBURY, WALTER. *London Old and New.* 1897.

TREVELYAN, G. M. *A History of England.* 1952.

———. *Illustrated English Social History.* 1966.

TREVOR-ROPER, H. R. *Essays in British History.* 1964.

UNDERWOOD, E. A. *The Healers, The Doctor, Then and Now.* 1968.

VESALIUS, ANDREAS. *De humani corporis fabrica.* 1543.

WAITE, S. O. *The Doctor Writes.* 1934.

WALCOTT, M. *Memorials of Westminster.* 1851.

WALL, C. H. J. *Four Thousand Years of Pharmacy.* 1927.

WALLACE, W. M. *Sir Walter Raleigh.* 1959.

WALSH, J. J. *Medieval Medicine.* 1920.

WICKHAM, GLYNNE. *Early English Stages (1300–1660).* 1972.

WILLIAM, PENRY. *Life In Tudor England.* 1964.

WILLIAMS, CHARLES. *Bacon.* 1936.

———. *James I.* 1936.

WILLIAMS, J. A. *Building and Builders.* 1968.

WILLIS, R. *William Harvey.* 1878.

———. *The Works of William Harvey.* 1877.

WILLS, GEOFFREY. *English Furniture (1550–1760).* 1971.

WRIGHTMAN, W. P. D. *The Emergence of Scientific Medicine.* 1971.

WYATT, R. B. H. *William Harvey.* 1924.